JIHADI BRIDE

ALASTAIR LUFT

Black Rose Writing | Texas

ISBN: 978-1-68433-339-4
PUBLISHED BY BLACK ROSE WRITING
www.blackrosewriting.com

Printed in the United States of America
Suggested Retail Price (SRP) $19.95

Jihadi Bride is printed in Calluna

For Anna,

Your hand in mine.

JIHADI BRIDE

PROLOGUE
THE OPENING

RAQQA, SYRIA
11 APR 2015 – 1733 LOCAL

Abu Noor al Kanadi stood near the center of Raqqa's crowded main square, hands clenched at his sides. At least two thousand people stood with him in a circle that surged forward and back, anchored by gruff commands from men in black hoods with assault rifles. Two such men stood at al Kanadi's side to protect a space of several feet around him. A perk of rank, although he would earn it today.

He always did.

Across the plaza, the crowd parted to let through a small procession. Two hooded men in tan camouflage half-led, half-dragged a third man dressed in orange coveralls, his emaciated limbs held together by chains. Behind these three strode a rotund, hooded man in the same desert camouflage, combat shirt stretched taut across his distended gut, the flip-flop sound of his cheap leather sandals echoing in the square. He might have been comical except for the wicked three-foot curved blade slung over his shoulder. Together, the group marched toward a plain metal chair in the center of the square.

Al Kanadi's lips pressed together in a thin line. He thought of his former brothers-in-arms from 5th Special Forces Group, how they'd laugh to see how he'd fallen. If they only knew. He had no idea why the ragged-looking man was to be executed, perhaps spying or maybe for being an infidel. There were countless roads to the executioner's blade, many of them unpredictable which, after all, was partly the point. It was far easier to reap terror where confusion had been sown.

The guards shoved the prisoner onto the chair and grabbed his hair to force his head down over his chest, the rest of his body slumped. With a shove, they indicated the prisoner should remain seated with his head down, then both men withdrew several feet. In turn, the fat man with the sword sauntered into the vacated spotlight at the center of the square.

Such savagery, but Ibn Tamiyya's writings were explicit as to the need for these acts. A French philosopher, Guy Debord, had said that the masses could be distracted and pacified through entertainment, but Ibn Tamiyya understood that fear was as effective. The symbol was the important thing, in this case of a new power ascendant, and it was the reason that though his stomach revolted at the sight of the executions, al Kanadi would watch and be seen to watch. To look away would incur doubt in his faith, reinforce the belief that Westerners were inferior fighters, cannon-fodder. He would not have it. There was too much to accomplish and Protean-like, he would take any form to ensure success.

Beside him, one of his bodyguards stiffened and then stepped aside. Al Kanadi frowned – he'd made it clear he was to be left alone – and turned to see who presumed to disturb him. He found himself face-to-face with Mamdouh al Qassam, his second-in-command.

Mamdouh leaned close, his hand coming to al Kanadi's back. "Another two girls are on their way," he said in his gravelly voice.

He shrugged off Mamdouh's hand. "It can wait."

Mamdouh's eyes narrowed. "They're from Canada."

Al Kanadi's frown deepened. "When?"

"They've already begun to travel." Mamdouh's gaze flickered to the scene in the square, where the fat man was reading the prisoner's sins from a piece of paper. "I thought you might want to oversee the preparations yourself. I can represent you here."

"I'm sure you would." Al Kanadi gestured for Mamdouh to stand beside him. The offer was attractive – he'd been awaiting this development for almost a year now. "My place is here."

"My apologies," Mamdouh said, almost licking his lips as he assumed his place beside al Kanadi. "I know how these...sights...bother you."

"They have their place." He made a mental note to reprimand his subordinate. Mamdouh's ambition served him well, but it would get him into trouble sooner or later. "I prefer more subtle methods of instilling fear."

"I would never have guessed."

The corners of Abu Noor's mouth spread up as he focused on the executioner, who stood with his blade extended above the prisoner's neck. He willed himself to be silent, an image of stoic resolve, yet couldn't resist another question. "When will they arrive?" He could feel Mamdouh's smile grow wider. He didn't care, he needed to know.

"Within a few days."

His heart quickened. *Insha'Allah*, these recruits would be more suitable than the last ones. What was it the British said, fortune favors the bold? He smiled. His plan was nothing if not bold.

The executioner's sword began its descent, and for the first time in ages, Abu Noor al Kanadi did not flinch as it fell.

CHAPTER ONE
THE HOUSE OF THE SPIDER

Ottawa, Ontario
11 Apr 2015 – 1210 Local

For the second time in his life, Erik Petersson was at war.

Perched on the pedals of his yellow hardtail bike, his butt inches above the saddle, he pushed the thought from his head. A rock garden was up ahead, and he needed to concentrate. Knees and elbows bent, he coasted past towering pine trees and scanned for the safest line through the obstacle, trying to ignore what would happen if he fell. As in war, it was easy to become paralyzed by analysis.

This war was different. There were no uniforms, nobody shooting at him. There was no dirt or sweat or blood or hours hunkered in a concrete bunker to escape wayward rockets and mortars. But the biggest difference was that although he was still a soldier, still bent on capturing or killing the enemy while starving them of resources, he wasn't in the Army anymore.

Mud sprayed his legs as he splashed through a puddle and sideswiped a partially submerged rock. The handlebars wrenched in his grip and he tightened his hold. He should've missed that one, but it had been awhile. With his riding partner opening up distance, Erik might need the excuse for falling behind. He could still keep up with men half his age, but all the same, he could do with less time hunting people and more time in the saddle, yet another thing different about this war.

Indeed, this war made up for his first experience with a host of other features.

This war had Twitter, Facebook and YouTube, not to mention overtime, Starbucks, and trail riding, however rare that might be. In this war he never left home, never deployed to combat zones despite being on duty twenty-four hours a day, seven days a week. At times, this second war was so different he almost forgot he was even at war, as so many people did, more concerned with the inconvenience of clearing airport security than why those measures were necessary.

But war it was.

The crowded bush gave way to a field of bulrushes under a clear, spring sky. He rode onto a narrow wooden boardwalk, blinked to clear the sweat stinging his eyes and pedaled faster in pursuit. Competition, at least, was one thing that would always be the same.

This war remained a struggle between opposing forces. There were still people trying to kill each other, even if they used medieval methods like beheadings and crucifixion. Tactics and strategies adapted and evolved and because of that, combatants still needed to protect their vulnerabilities. It was a full-time job with this enemy, who were so innovative in their callous disregard for life. If the public knew what didn't make the news, they'd be too scared to leave their homes. The plot to detonate pressure-cooker bombs during Ottawa's Winterlude Festival, the plan to explode a train carrying crude oil in Winnipeg, and others, all prevented with help from Erik's team.

Times like that made him feel like a neurosurgeon must feel after removing a brain tumor, it didn't get much better. Sure, much of his work involved sifting through piles of reports, contradictory reports, false reports, reports overcome by events, and his personal favorite, circular reports. Yet it wouldn't be war if the hours of boredom weren't broken by bursts of intensity, and when he uncovered links that led to the neutralization of a threat, the sacrifice was worth it. He was a good soldier. He served his country and protected his loved ones.

Like Arielle.

The bike's front wheel jerked and he pitched from side to side, put out his foot to steady himself and then his handlebar clipped a tree and he fell. A mix of mud and water sprayed where he hit, the muck ice-cold from the spring melt. He gasped and pushed into a squat, then looked up as his riding companion approached.

Jordan skidded to a stop. "You hurt?" he asked around swigs of water.

"Just my pride," Erik said and stood up his bike.

"Maybe if you got out of the office a bit more..."

"About that..." Erik looked at his watch. "Mind if we head back?"

"Seriously? It's Saturday. Tell me you're not going to work."

"Well, now that you mention it..."

"Give it a rest, man. You're like a dog with a bone."

"Then you'll be happy to know I'm not going to work," Erik said. He stood tall, although he still had to look up at the younger man. "I've got a date."

"I don't believe you." Jordan flashed a smile that never failed to catch the attention of many women and some men. "I have dates because I have a life outside work. You don't." Jordan squinted in pretend suspicion. "Who's this date with?"

Erik cleared his throat. "Arielle. We're playing World of Warcraft."

"I knew it. Your daughter doesn't count," Jordan said. "And you're like fifty years old. That's too old to play video games, you know that, right?"

"It's something I do with Arielle," he said and shrugged. "We've missed the last few weeks, so I want to make this one."

"Why not go for coffee, like normal fathers and daughters?"

"She lives in Montreal," he said and frowned. "Remember? And I'm forty-five, that's a long way from fifty."

"All right, all right," Jordan said with a smirk. "Is your character at least cool?"

Erik grimaced. "No, not really. If I wasn't in Arielle's guild, I'd get my ass kicked by twelve-year-old kids every time I played."

"Or fat dudes pretending to be chicks." Jordan sighed. "At least you're honest. Okay, old man, let's go. You take the lead."

Erik faced the bike in the opposite direction, leaned into the pedals and pushed back onto the boardwalk. His thoughts turned to Arielle. For all Jordan's kidding, he had a point; Erik needed to get to Montreal more often. Hell, it was less than two hours door to door to Arielle's university.

"You think Stephanie would play Warcraft?" Jordan called over the rattling of the wooden planks.

"Fuck you," he said over his shoulder, his cheeks warm and not from the exertion.

"Think about it," Jordan said. "You have lots in common, like being workaholics."

"It's unprofessional to date a colleague."

"Plus, you'll have to fight her off once you catch that asshole radicalizing people in Montreal. That shit's like Spanish fly to the ladies."

Laughter spurted from Erik's mouth, and he wobbled on the bike. He dragged a foot on the ground and skidded to a stop, then smiled back at Jordan. "What's wrong with you?" he said as Jordan stopped beside him.

"What? Why are we stopping?" Jordan said in mock exasperation. "I thought you had to nerd out?"

"I'm not asking Stephanie out," he said. "And al Kanadi isn't from Montreal, he went to school there. All I need –" Ringing came from the black bag on his handlebars. "You'll see," he said and dug for his phone. The number was familiar, although Arielle shouldn't have been calling already. They weren't supposed to be online for another ninety minutes.

He glanced at Jordan. "Gotta take this. I won't be long."

Jordan nodded up the trail. "I'll go slow so you can catch up."

"Right behind you," he said and brought the phone to his ear.

"Stephanie. Warcraft. Genius," Jordan called out as he rode off. "Start a blog."

"Asshole."

"Dad?" Arielle sounded confused.

"Not you, sweetie, sorry. I'm talking to Jordan."

Silence, filled by the throaty rasp of crows in the trees overhead.

"Arielle?"

"I'm here."

"Thought I lost you for a second," he said. "What's going on? Are we still on for two o'clock? I know how –"

"Dad…"

He stopped. "What is it?"

"I can't make it."

"What do you mean? We had a date." More silence. The dense canopy of trees pressed in upon him, the air at once thick and dark. "Is everything okay? Talk to me."

"I love you."

"I love you, too," he said. "What's wrong?"

"I'm not going to be able to see you for a while."

"What are you talking about? Did something happen at school?"

"I'm not at school."

"You're not…" He switched the phone to his other ear. "Where are you?"

"Frankfurt."

"Frankfurt, Germany?" Mud squelched underfoot as he shifted weight.

"I don't have much time. My flight's in a couple of minutes."

"Wait, what? Flight to where? Why are you in Frankfurt?"

"I don't disown you." Her voice had a slight waver. "We're supposed to – that's part of it – supposed to erase our previous lives. But I still love you and I pray for you."

She prayed for him? She may as well have said he'd sprouted horns from his forehead. He realized she'd kept talking and he forced himself to focus.

"– to Turkey," she said.

"What? What about Turkey?"

"We're going to Turkey," she said. "We're meeting someone there who'll take us into Syria."

His mouth opened and closed and no sound came out.

"Dad?"

"I'm here." He rubbed the bridge of his nose, had to remind himself he was on the phone with his daughter and not for one of his investigations. "Listen, there's a civil war in Syria right now. It's dangerous. Don't do this. Whatever you –"

"I have to," she said in the same hardheaded tone she'd used since she was three years old. "I have to go," she continued. "Now that there's a Caliphate, *hijrah* is an obligation."

"What are you talking about?" He shivered, chilled at the resonance to his work. The *hijrah,* or duty to migrate to the Caliphate, was what the most radicalized high-risk travelers said these days, the ones he tracked on a day-to-day basis. "There's no obligation and even if there was, what does it have to do with you?"

"I converted six months ago," she said, her words barely audible.

"Say that again?" He realized he needed to fight for time. *Keep her talking.* "Did something happen at school?"

"No...yes..."

"Arielle –"

"It's not just school, it's everything," she said, louder. "I can't live like this anymore. Naomi says it's better there."

"Who's Naomi?" he said. "Is she with you?"

"I met her at school," she said. "She introduced me."

"To who?" He ran a hand through his short brown hair. "No, no, no. Do you know how dangerous this is?"

"I have to go. My flight's boarding."

His heart pounded in his ears. *Think.* He was almost out of options. "Okay, stay put in Turkey. I'll get in touch with my team, we'll call ahead and have the police pick you up there."

"You're not listening, Dad. I don't want to be picked up," she said. "Besides, there's not enough time. You know that."

He checked his watch. How long could her flight be, two hours? Three, max? *Shit.* "Stop. Come home," he said. His free hand found its way to a plain metal ring that hung from a leather cord on his neck.

"Dad..."

"I'll find you," he said. "I'll bring you home."

Another voice sounded through the line, a girl.

He needed to change course. "Be careful, sweetie," he said. "Text me when you get to Turkey. Texting should be safe."

Silence.

What else? "Don't go with anybody you don't trust," he said and shook his head. *Stupid advice.* Well, what did he expect – his job was to stop would-be extremists from going to the Middle East, not coach them through the process. "Be careful."

"I will. I promise," she said. "Bye."

"Arielle –" The line went dead. "I love you." He lowered the phone and stared at it.

His daughter was going to Syria.

Images of black flags, masked men, and blindfolded prisoners with saw tooth knives at their throats flashed through his mind. The woods closed in on him and he fought for breath, blinked up at the dense canopy where the muffled croaks of crows rose in discord as they took flight to the northeast. His grip tightened on the ring. Damnit, he couldn't lose Arielle, too.

He tucked the ring back into his shirt, then speed-dialed the duty officer for the High-Risk Traveler Task Force.

* * *

FRANKFURT, GERMANY
11 APR 2015 – 1820 LOCAL

Arielle Petersson stared at the phone, the echoes of her dad's voice in her ears.

"Come on." Naomi tugged at her sleeve. "They called final boarding."

It was hard to believe she was really doing this. It was rash, Arielle knew, but for the first time in eight months, she felt alive. She trailed Naomi into the dwindling line, her gaze fixed on two police officers on the far side of the concourse. A male and a female officer stood beneath a departures screen, the woman with a blond ponytail and an assault rifle, the man with a tightly groomed beard and a walkie-talkie. Their white, peaked forage caps contrasted with the deep black of their Kevlar vests and the dark gleam of the woman's rifle.

She thought again of her father, of the faded pictures and mementos in his home office, what he jokingly called his I-love-me room. There was a photo of her father seated, maroon beret on his head and parachute strapped to his back, the olive-drab reserve chute a bundle in his lap. He'd looked confident, like the police officers, ready to drop from the sky. She wished there'd been another way to say good-bye, and then hurried after Naomi before the officers turned in her direction.

Her heart beat faster, and she suppressed a smile. All that security and it was on the lookout for her, and those like her. They no doubt thought they would keep her safe. Where had they been last September?

Loud voices came from across the departure lounge, where several boys her age laughed and pushed each other. Arielle stiffened. The harsh voices, with their mocking, masculine tones, evoked half-buried memories, even with the German accents. The police officers left their post and meandered toward the boys. As the officers drew near, the boys quietened, but it did little to quell the goose-bumps that stood out on Arielle's arms. Her dad's voice came to mind, his familiar refrain that someone's freedom to do something always butted up against someone else's freedom from something. His job was to protect the border between the two, even if he sometimes disagreed with where the boundary was set.

"Arielle," Naomi called from the entrance to the boarding passageway. Between them, the airline agent held out an outstretched hand, polite smile on her face as she waited for Arielle's boarding pass. The process was still business as usual, but if Arielle delayed any longer, it might not be.

Arielle spared another glance behind, to where the police stood with their backs to the group of boys who had now pushed farther down the concourse. Two of the boys turned and leered after the female police officer, and one of them drew an hourglass shape in the air until his hands finished at his waist. He mimed clenching something with his hands and thrust his hips forward. The rest of the boys laughed, and their jeers carried across the departure lounge.

These were the freedoms her dad would defend, to treat women as objects. Her whole life he'd tried to protect her. But when it had mattered most, he hadn't been there. What she needed wasn't more protection, or more freedom, but more respect. More community. And she'd found it. Naomi's boyfriend had been right, it was never too late to start over.

Arielle took a deep breath, then offered her boarding pass and passport to the ticket agent. Then she smiled and waited to be cleared through the gate.

* * *

OTTAWA, ONTARIO
11 APR 2015 – 1355 LOCAL

Erik flung open the door to the operations center of the High-Risk Traveler Task Force and stormed into a room the size of a small movie theatre. The task force nerve center had three rows of desks arranged in auditorium style tiers that faced the front of the room, where several oversize, digital screens hung from the wall, maps of Europe and the Middle East on one, flight information on another. There were workstations for thirty people with standing room for at least fifty more, although today, a Saturday, only a handful were present. Erik sought out one in particular.

"Stephanie?" he said as he sprang up a short set of stairs to the second tier of desks and headed for his work station. "How are we doing?"

A tall, brunette woman with her hair in a shoulder-length bob looked up from a raised dais near the back of the tiered desks. "We've narrowed down the flights," she said. "Marty? Can you walk us through the options?"

In the front row of desks, a man with a goatee, slicked-back hair, and clothes too nice for government work straightened in his chair. "The top-left screen shows today's direct flights between Frankfurt and Istanbul. A Pegasus Airlines flight that should have left Frankfurt an hour and forty-five minutes ago, a Turkish Air flight that should have left an hour and fifteen minutes ago, and last, a Lufthansa flight leaving around the same time as the Turkish Air flight. There's also an Aegean Air flight leaving right now, and keep in mind, these are just the direct flights."

Erik furrowed his brow. "She didn't say she was flying to Istanbul."

"Good point," Marty said, and a blow-up map of Turkey with several red airplane icons appeared on a screen. "There are a number of other possible destinations, but most of those flights depart Frankfurt in the morning or mid-afternoon."

"Most?" Stephanie asked.

"A Sun Express departed Frankfurt an hour and fifteen minutes ago, headed for Antalya. That's the only direct, non-Istanbul flight I've been able to find so far, which is why we're focusing on Istanbul." Marty's gaze flickered to Erik, then to Stephanie. "For now."

Erik's lips tightened, but he ignored Marty's comment. "Flight time?"

"Roughly three hours."

"What about indirect flights?"

"Too many to mention," Marty said. "The good thing is that given the time in Europe, most of the indirect flights have lengthy stop-overs and won't arrive in Istanbul until tomorrow. The bad thing is that all of Turkey's other international airports then come into play."

"You said most?"

"There's one, a KLM flight connecting through Amsterdam with the same departure time as the Lufthansa flight. But I don't think that one's very likely. It's too long."

"So where does that leave us?" Stephanie asked.

Marty referred to a notepad. "Best case scenario, we've got almost five hours for the KLM flight through Amsterdam. Worst case, we've got less than –"

"An hour," Erik said.

"Maybe ninety minutes," Marty said.

Erik frowned at the time zone clocks near the monitors while he processed what Marty had said. The clocks, the monitors, the ten different classified and unclassified computer networks, they all fed data to this room, the spider at the center of a virtual web. All that information, yet it wasn't useful until it had been analyzed. "So based on when she called, and the fact that she was boarding, the Turkish or Lufthansa flights are the most likely options, right?"

"Maybe not." Stephanie moved to stand beside him. "The Pegasus flight was delayed, so she could be on that one as well."

"They," Erik said.

"Excuse me?" Stephanie asked.

"There was somebody with her," he said. "Sorry, when I called, I was only thinking of Arielle."

Stephanie put a hand on his shoulder. "It's all right," she said. "Do you have a name?"

"Naomi."

"Last name?"

He shook his head and his frown deepened. Flight details, travelling companion, so many things he should have asked instead of telling Arielle not to use her phone.

"It's a start," Stephanie said, her voice quiet. "Team," she called out, "there's a second traveler, also a female. First name is Naomi, last name unknown." She leaned closer to Erik. "Why don't you sit down?"

"What else do we have on the go?" Erik asked. "Have we put out an advisory?"

"We're in touch with airport authorities in Frankfurt, but haven't established communication with Istanbul yet," Stephanie said, repeatedly clicking the plunger of her ballpoint pen. "Depending on the flight, it could land at either Ataturk or Sabiha Gokcen."

"What about the airlines?"

Stephanie nodded at a portly, bald man at the workstation beside Marty, his shirt crumpled as if he'd slept in it. "Joe's following up on that. No luck reaching Lufthansa, but he did get ahold of Turkish Air."

"Didn't accomplish much," Joe said over his shoulder. "All they said was they were only responsible for checking visas and boarding passes, pre-flight security was a responsibility of the airport authorities. Then they hung up on me."

Erik picked up a picture of Arielle from his desk and stared into her eyes, tried to get into her head. "What about police? Border agents?"

"Erik –" Stephanie said.

"Are we in touch with police?" Erik sought out the desk for the analyst from the RCMP. Empty. Likewise the desk for the Border Security Agency, Camille. "Where the hell are they?"

"It's the weekend, they're not here," Stephanie said, a slight furrow appearing between her eyebrows. "You know they're not staffed to operate 24/7."

He clenched the picture frame tighter. "So call them in."

"We are –"

"Call them in faster."

"We're doing everything we can."

"Besides, what will we tell the Turks anyways?" said a man in the same row as Erik's desk. "That two girls are showing up in Istanbul? They'll laugh at us."

"Not helping, Stu," Stephanie said.

"But true," Stu said. "They haven't done anything wrong."

Erik massaged a throbbing vein at his temple. "Cancel her passport. Maybe that'll trigger a secondary search when she clears customs."

"We can't just cancel a passport," Stu said. "There has to be reasonable suspicion of an offense –"

"She's going to Syria," Erik said, louder than he'd intended. He lowered his voice. "What more do you need?"

"Did she say she was going to fight?" Stu asked. "Because traveling there isn't illegal. Highly inadvisable, but not illegal."

Erik glared at his computer screen, the tendons in his forearms taut as his hands balled into fists.

Stu sighed. "Even if we wanted to cancel the passports, nobody here has that authority. It has to go through Wiggins." He looked at Stephanie. "And I'm not even sure it would do any good. If she's on a direct flight, there are no other steps to have her yanked. Maybe at Turkish customs, if we're lucky, as in win-the-lottery lucky. This is why we do prevention, not catching people at their destination."

"Have a seat, Erik." Stephanie tucked a wayward bang of hair behind her ear. "Let us work this."

The prospect of being trapped, helpless at his desk was the last thing Erik wanted. There had to be some tactic, some tool they hadn't used.

Stephanie moved toward Stu.

"What about a no-fly list?" Erik said to her back. "Hell, even a terrorist watch list, at least they'd get detained."

Stephanie hesitated. "You know it's not that easy."

"Fuck." He slammed a hand on his desk. Activity in the operations center stopped as heads swiveled to look at him. He ignored them, focused on Stephanie. "Do something."

Stephanie's face hardened. "Why don't you wait outside for a bit."

"I'm sorry," he said and held up his hands.

"I know this is difficult, but you're not helping," she said. "Let us do what we need to do."

"I need to be here, trying to stop her," he said and met Stephanie's gaze. She was always so composed – some might say cold – so adept at orchestrating this diverse group of individuals pulled from the alphabet soup of three and four-letter government agencies. He might be a better analyst, but she was without a doubt their best operator and her reproach stung. "We have to stop her," he said. "We can't let her get past Turkey."

Stephanie sighed. "We will, but you're not helping right now. You need to let us do our jobs. We'll do everything we can, I promise."

He leaned on his desk and scanned the room. The screens on the front wall were connected through fiber optic cabling to the computers, which in turn connected to intelligence partners across the world, none of which was bringing his daughter any closer to home. A sudden urge to take a sledgehammer to the whole place gripped him.

"Go, Erik. Please," Stephanie said. Her tone left little room for disagreement.

"Find her," he said and then headed for the exit.

***

ISTANBUL, TURKEY
11 APR 2015 – 2252 LOCAL

Arielle had a hard time remembering the last time her heart had beat so fast, at least from excitement as opposed to fear.

She was proud of herself, her hands hardly shook as she busied herself in front of the restroom mirror, tucking her long bangs austerely behind one ear and tying the remainder of her brown hair into a braid. Her cleansing wipes were on the counter to strip off the little makeup she wore, and then her transformation would be almost complete.

"Hurry," Naomi hissed. Her friend stood at the next sink, her *hijab* already wrapped around her head and hair. "We're wasting time."

"Calm down." Arielle's fingertips tingled with the feel of her own *hijab*, a gold-colored headscarf fringed in brown. "This is time well spent. Are you sure you don't want some of these wipes?"

"What I want is to get moving." Naomi used a professionally manicured nail to remove a tiny speck from the corner of her eye while Arielle secured her headscarf. "Changes will make us stand out."

Arielle's gaze flickered to Naomi, then back to the mirror. For all Naomi's confidence at the start of the trip, she'd grown more agitated the longer they traveled, criticizing every little thing, even the size of Arielle's carry-on bag. Arielle had explained her bag was big enough to be prepared; she had something to eat, something to drink, something to stay dry, and something to stay warm. Naomi had rolled her eyes. "We aren't the only ones wearing them. They'll help us blend in."

Naomi glared at her. "We're the only ones whose dad can have us arrested," she said and stomped toward the exit.

Arielle's cheeks grew hot. Naomi's boyfriend, Hamza, had told them not to call, but Arielle hadn't seen a way around it. The obligation was clear, she needed to say farewell to be true to her *fitrah*, her instinct to seek God. Of course, it could be argued this obligation was limited to mothers, after all, the hadith said that paradise was at the feet of the mother, not the father. But with her mother dead, the duty was clear and had to be done. She fixed her *hijab* in place, then followed after Naomi.

Outside the bathroom, Arielle caught up to her friend and they walked down a wide corridor in the direction of other travelers. Arielle picked out several people who'd been on their flight from Frankfurt, so they hadn't spent too long in the bathroom. After a few minutes, they spied large blue signs with white and yellow letters that marked the way to passport control, while the sign for Turkish citizens displayed a white star and crescent on a red background. Arielle followed Naomi into the line for non-Turkish nationals, where ten or so other people waited.

"We should have been ahead of all these people." Naomi crossed her arms, and her foot tapped on the floor.

"We have lots of time," Arielle said while she took in the airport. The lofty ceilings and spacious concourse gave off a feeling of lightness that matched her eagerness to move on. "Our flight to Urfa isn't until tomorrow morning."

"Be quiet," Naomi said as she eyed the surrounding travelers. "Nobody needs to know our travel details."

"You draw more attention by the way you're talking," she said. "Act natural." Her dad had taught her that the first part of fitting in was to act as if she belonged. And with her *hijab* on, fitting in didn't seem like an act. She smiled at Naomi. "Doesn't it feel good to show off our faith?"

"Sometimes I don't think you appreciate what we're doing," Naomi said and glanced at the person in front of them in line.

Arielle's smile broadened. She understood the risks all right, her dad talked about them all the time since he'd joined the High-Risk Traveler Task Force. What mattered more, what sang to her soul, was that she was coming home. She'd found sisterhood and a sense of purpose in a community where she wouldn't be victimized, either because of her faith or her sex.

The customs agent waved them to the desk, and Arielle's heart began to race. This was the moment of truth. Her dad shouldn't have had enough time to alert the authorities, but it wasn't impossible. Maybe the taciturn-looking agent in the light blue shirt was about to separate them for a secondary screening, or maybe he was just annoyed at having to work so late. She forced the smile from her face.

The agent took both their passports, and his gaze darted between the pictures on the inside covers and their faces. Then, he flipped the passports and stared at the outside covers. Looking up, he returned the passports and pointed back to the entrance to passport control. "Visas," he said in a heavy accent.

Arielle felt Naomi tense, and she glanced at her friend, then back to the agent. "Excuse me?"

"Visas," the man repeated.

"Sir -" Naomi said and leaned closer to the desk.

Arielle looked in the direction the agent had pointed and spotted a small office at the opposite side of the hall. Above the office, VISA was written in bold white letters. She tugged Naomi's shoulder before her friend got them in trouble. "We need to get visas."

Naomi allowed herself to be dragged away from the agent. "Hamza didn't say anything about visas."

"I should have thought of it," Arielle said. She pulled out the pay-and-go phone she'd purchased in Frankfurt. "I'll find out what we have to do."

"What are we going to put on the paperwork?" Naomi said. "Why didn't Hamza mention this?"

"It's okay," Arielle said. "Shoot, I'm already out of minutes." She thrust the phone into her pocket and pulled out her other phone, the one she'd brought from home.

"What if it's closed and we miss our flight?" Naomi's voice rose.

"Then we'll catch the next one," Arielle said. "All we need is a valid passport and a payment. And a visa is only twenty dollars, which is nothing."

"I thought you said you were out of minutes?"

"I am," she said. Closing out the browser, she saw a text message. Automatically, she clicked on the icon to see a note from her dad.

"Then how did you check?"

Arielle stopped in place as she read the text. *Be safe. I miss you.*

"What are you doing?" Naomi spoke right into her ear.

Arielle frowned. "I'm figuring out what we need to do." She waved Naomi off and began to type a response to her dad.

"Are you texting somebody?"

"My dad." She gasped as Naomi snatched the phone from her hands. "Give that back."

"You were supposed to throw this out."

"Well, I didn't," she said and took Naomi by the shoulders, "and it's a good thing since we have no other way to contact Hamza."

"But -"

"Get ahold of yourself," Arielle said. "See the agent at the visa desk? You're drawing his attention by the way you're acting."

Naomi's face went pale.

"Now give me back my phone and let's finish this up."

"Promise you won't text your dad."

Arielle bit her lip, then nodded.

Her hand trembling, Naomi offered up the phone.

Arielle smiled. "Don't worry, we're almost there." And it was true. "Now, let's take a deep breath and get through this. We're strong. We're lionesses, right?"

Naomi nodded.

Arielle took her by the arm and supported her until they reached the visa office. Behind the glass, the agent's face was unreadable. Like the passport agent, he might have already alerted security. Or maybe he was simply annoyed at having to look up from the magazine he'd been reading. In either event, five minutes and forty dollars later, Arielle and Naomi both had tiny stickers on the back of their passports and had rejoined the passport control line.

"See, no need to worry," Arielle said. The lightness she'd felt the first time she'd been in the passport line returned, stronger than ever. She'd believed and Allah, the Most Gracious, had delivered.

"We didn't even fill out any paperwork," Naomi said, an incredulous look on her face. "We're going to make it."

Fifteen minutes later, the same agent who'd declined their passports waved them through after a cursory glance at the stickers.

"We're through," Naomi said. "We did it."

Arielle smiled. Her friend had been struggling, but she'd passed her trial. She took Naomi's hand. "Do you feel better?"

Naomi nodded and gripped Arielle's hand tighter. "Thank you. I don't know what I would have done without you."

"That's what sisters do, right? I wouldn't even be here if not for you." Arielle squeezed Naomi's hand in return. "Now we just need to get our tickets to Urfa."

Naomi checked her watch. "The ticket office isn't open until 6:45."

"Let's find somewhere out-of-the-way to wait," Arielle said and nodded at the airport concourse. "Maybe we'll even get some sleep."

But as she led Naomi in search of a passenger waiting area, Arielle knew there'd be time enough for sleep later. For now, she didn't want to miss a second of this adventure.

*　*　*

OTTAWA, ONTARIO
11 APR 2015 – 1735 LOCAL

Erik paced the length of the breakout room, his gaze split between his watch and the view of the woods that surrounded the building in this area. He'd never paid attention to this part of the campus before, not even the paved trail that would have made for a nice, easy ride. Still, as the shadows lengthened beneath the trees, they reminded him that time marched on.

It was long past midnight in Turkey, which meant all the direct flights would have arrived. If Arielle and her friend had been on one of those flights, the small opportunity for airport security to pick them up might have already passed. He swore under his breath and wondered if Stephanie would let him back into operations center, the one place he felt comfortable in this building, and then turned as one of the room's double doors opened.

Stephanie's head appeared in the gap. "How are you doing?" she asked.

"What do you have?"

"Some photos." She entered, a folder held to her chest. "We need you to take a look." She pulled out several grainy prints and laid them on the conference room table.

Erik bent over the nearest picture, a blow-up of a dark-haired girl in a bright yellow blouse walking through the thin, gray pillars of a metal detector.

"That's from Trudeau Airport in Montreal," Stephanie said.

He stared at the girl in the photo. "Never seen her before," he said.

Stephanie spread out a series of other photos. "Try these."

He studied the second picture, an identical shot of the metal detector except for the girl between the pipes. She was frozen in mid-stride, chin held high. "That's Arielle."

"You're sure?"

"Absolutely." He pointed to her muted brown clothes. "She's trying to blend in, but her posture's a bit wrong. It's too strong, she's inviting eye contact."

"She seems confident."

"Is the other girl Naomi?" he asked.

Stephanie nodded. "We think so. The passenger manifest lists her as Naomi Lohrenz."

"Doesn't sound familiar." His gaze shifted to the other photos. "What else?"

"These were taken from a security camera in Frankfurt Airport."

Stephanie selected a different picture and pointed with a pen to a group of people in the center. "This is the transfer zone. You can make out what we believe are the same two girls here." Naomi's bright yellow shirt stood out beside the edge of the pen's nib, right beside the more muted colors of what appeared to be Arielle. "Then there's these ones."

In the last set of photos, the girls were again passing through a metal detector. "That's definitely her." Erik glanced up at Stephanie with a smile. "Good work. Did these help narrow down their flight?"

She nodded. "The Lufthansa flight that left at 1840, or twelve-forty PM our time."

"So they're there."

"Yes."

"And since you didn't mention anything, I take it they haven't been picked up yet."

Stephanie cleared her throat. "Communication with Turkish officials has been slow."

He straightened. "What do you mean? This should be easy."

"We're in touch with the national police, but reaching the airport authorities has been...problematic." She gave a small smile. "We're working it."

"Can I come back to the ops center?" He asked and then gestured around the sterile room. "Waiting here is killing me."

"I understand," she said as she gathered up the photos, "but we've got it covered. I know it's difficult, but this could take a while." She nodded at the trail shirt and mountain bike shorts he still wore. "Why don't you go home? Take a shower, get something to eat. I'll call you if something happens."

"What? No way," he said, frowning. "I'm coming with you."

"I don't think that's a good idea," Stephanie said and headed to the door. Erik tagged along beside her. "Why not?"

"Wiggins doesn't want you in the ops center. He says it's protocol."

"We don't have a protocol for this. It hasn't happened before."

Stephanie glanced down. "He's adapting policy from kidnappings, and he's adamant. You know how he gets. He made a point of saying it was a direct order."

Erik threw up his hands. "He just likes to use that phrase because it makes him think he's in a movie."

"I'm sorry, Erik." Stephanie met his gaze, resolve in her blue eyes. "You can't come."

"I'm being compartmentalized out?" He struggled to close his mouth.

"Wiggins says it's standard procedure."

"It's bureaucratic hand wringing," he said and slammed his hand on the door. "This isn't a kidnapping. Is there something you're not telling me?"

"I have to get back," she said. "Go home and get some rest."

"Let me talk to Wiggins."

"It won't help, Erik," she said and then looked over her shoulder. "Please. We all need to do our part."

As much as he hated it, Wiggins was the chief. "All right, Stephanie, I'll play along. But I don't like it."

"I'll call you as soon as we know more." She gave him a small smile, and then walked out.

"Now what?" he asked, and his words echoed in the empty room.

* * *

SANLIURFA, TURKEY
12 APR 2015 – 0854 LOCAL

Arielle's ears popped and she turned from the window to get Naomi's attention. "Can you feel it? We're landing." Before Naomi could reply, Arielle pressed her face back to the glass, squeezed to a corner to get a better view of her first glimpse of the Turkish landscape in daytime. Seconds later, an announcement came through the plane's cabin, followed by the stewardesses prompting passengers to straighten their chairs and raise their trays. Arielle mentally rehearsed their actions upon landing.

First, she and Naomi would exit the arrival section, an easy task since there would be no security checkpoint. The man Naomi had called before they'd left Ataturk had been clear about that. Next, they'd make a call to confirm they'd arrived in Sanliurfa and who they were to meet and then they'd be on their way to Syria. It was like a story from one of her dad's cases mixed with a fairy tale, except in this story she was the heroine, about to complete her escape from a world where she was little more than a possession.

The plane touched down with a shudder and taxied to a stop. Arielle ignored the seatbelt sign, unbuckled herself, and grabbed Naomi's shoulder. "Come on, get your phone."

"In the airport." Naomi's tone matched the sour expression on her face.

Arielle took a deep breath. Neither of them had been able to sleep in Ataturk Airport, and fatigue was likely catching up to her friend. She'd be better once they made it into Syria.

A stewardess opened the front exit, and the other passengers stood and began to fill the aisle. Arielle nudged Naomi out of her seat, almost pushing her friend toward the exit, and when she stepped through the door onto the metal stairs, a wall of hot air greeted her.

Arielle paused and looked around with wide eyes, already sweating beneath her *hijab*. The brown landscape shimmered with heat waves as it disappeared into the distance. Across the tarmac was the Sanliurfa terminal, a squat rectangular building covered in windows that reflected the bright sun. She shielded her eyes and a smile came to her face. Another obstacle overcome.

Arielle floated down the stairs after Naomi and into the terminal. "Your cousin will be impressed," she said to Naomi as they neared the exit to the arrivals section. "Maybe it will convince him to come."

Naomi grunted and fished for the phone she'd purchased in Istanbul. "He'll never come." Arielle had met Naomi's cousin, Reyad, one night after attending study group together. Reyad had converted to Islam several years ago, then introduced both Naomi and her boyfriend, Hamza, to Islam. After Hamza had traveled to Syria the previous year, Naomi had pressured Reyad to travel as well, but he always had a reason to stay in Montreal.

"One day," he'd said. "Right now, I'm of more service here."

"To the almighty dollar, perhaps," Naomi had said, half-joking, but Reyad never laughed.

While Naomi spoke in French on the phone, Arielle studied the other people in the airport. Many travelers wore Western jeans and t-shirts, but unlike Ataturk, there were many others in more traditional Islamic garb, especially the women. Most wore *hijabs*, with the occasional *niqab* paired with a black, all-enveloping *chador* visible as well. Arielle felt on the verge of a new world. Her body trembled with excitement even as her thoughts strayed to what she'd left behind, her dad, her studies, people she'd met at school –

A cloud passed over her face. Some memories were better left in the past. She closed her eyes and repeated the *shahada* under her breath. *La ilaha ill Allah*. By the time Naomi got off the phone, Arielle's pulse had almost returned to normal.

"The plan changed again." Naomi tucked away her phone. "We're supposed to meet a woman at the main entrance. She'll escort us to a driver who will bring us across the border."

"There's the main entrance over there," Arielle said and pointed across the concourse. They began to walk. "Weren't we supposed to meet a man?"

"There was a problem."

"So who are we meeting?"

"Her name is Umm Fatima."

"How will we recognize her?"

"She's dressed all in black?"

Arielle and Naomi took in the multiple women in black *niqabs,* then giggled.

"*Gunaydin,*" a man said from behind them.

Arielle jumped and turned to find two tall men clad in light blue shirts, black Kevlar vests, and black pants. Both men wore ball-caps emblazoned with an eight-figured star and the word *Polis,* and the one on the left carried an assault rifle. She stiffened as the policeman on the right, older and wearing sunglasses, continued speaking, his words an indecipherable, staccato. She glanced at Naomi, who'd frozen, then turned back to the policemen.

"Do you speak English?" she asked. Her heart beat so loud she thought the men might hear it.

The policemen shared a glance, then the older policeman lowered his sunglasses. "*Merhaba.*" He scanned her from head to toe. "Visa."

Arielle fumbled in her bag while Naomi did the same.

"Visa," the policeman said, louder this time, more insistent.

"Give me a minute," Naomi said, irritation in her tone.

The policeman said something else, more urgent now, then reached for Naomi's bag.

"Hey," Naomi said. "That's my bag."

The policeman with the rifle stepped back a couple of paces, and his grip tightened on his rifle while his companion wrestled Naomi's bag away from her.

Arielle watched Naomi struggle with the police officer and then a sharp command from the policeman with the rifle drew her attention to him. He gestured to her bag with the muzzle of his rifle. The meaning was clear, and once more she fumbled through her bag, with more urgency now. It was hard to concentrate. The men reminded her of the police she'd spoken to in Montreal, in September. She hadn't wanted to talk to them, but the police were supposed to help. When she'd realized they didn't believe her, it was like the earth had opened up and swallowed her.

"Give that back," Naomi said to the older policeman.

Then a woman in a *niqab* was beside them, speaking to the men. The officers waved her off, but she continued to talk and as she went on, their faces relaxed. The younger policeman lowered his rifle, and after a minute, the older policeman dropped Naomi's bag and stepped closer to the woman, who extended her hand. Arielle glimpsed a wad of rolled up bills in the woman's hand, which the policeman took and shoved into his pocket. With a nod to his younger partner, the two moved off to stand beside a nearby post where they continued to watch.

The woman in the *niqab* addressed them. "I am Umm Fatima," she said, her English accented in French. "We must go."

"Finally." Naomi snatched up her bag. "Thanks for getting those thugs off our back."

"Stupid girl," Umm Fatima said. "Those thugs will arrest us if we're not gone in five minutes. You should never have drawn their attention. Follow me."

Naomi's mouth dropped, but she did as Umm Fatima commanded.

Arielle trailed a few steps back as Umm Fatima led them outside, down a walkway toward a white sedan. This wasn't the reception she'd expected, but she felt pulled, compelled by the glaring eyes of Umm Fatima, as if in the presence of a *djinn*. They paused outside the car.

Umm Fatima gestured to the car's rear door. "Get in."

Arielle hesitated, swallowed. A stale, dusty smell came from the car and it occurred to her that getting into the back seat was the last thing in the world she wanted to do.

"Get in," Umm Fatima repeated. She stepped closer, raised a hand as if to strike.

Naomi flinched, then obeyed. While her friend struggled into the rear of the car, Arielle peered behind her. The two policemen had moved to the entrance of the airport and continued to observe, their faces impassive. Maybe all of this was one big mistake.

"This is your last chance. Then you can let those beasts throw you in jail and do what they want with you," Umm Fatima said.

Arielle thought of Montreal again, of another time she'd been browbeaten into a car, and a night she couldn't quite remember. She shuddered. She would never allow herself to be humiliated again and if what Umm Fatima said was true – and Arielle had no doubt it was – then she had no other choices. She summoned her courage, stooped and let herself be pushed into the back seat. When the car door shut, she prayed it would also shut on her old life.

* * *

OTTAWA, ONTARIO
14 APR 2015 – 0925 LOCAL

Erik stared into his locker, barely aware of the change of clothes inside. *Almost time to see Wiggins.* He shook his head, hung up his towel and began to get dressed.

In the three days since Arielle had slipped through their fingers, he'd talked to the team twice. Once when Stephanie told him not to come in until they called him, and once more when Wiggins's secretary had told him about today's meeting. For all he knew, Arielle might have been found and on her way back to Canada.

Except he hadn't heard anything, which meant there was no good news to be shared.

He rubbed his eyes, strained from the caffeine-fueled internet searching that had consumed his past 48 hours. More likely, the team had been chasing every possible lead to make sure they didn't give him false expectations. Still, bad news never got better with time, and he'd worked enough kidnappings to know that missing Arielle in the first days meant there was a good chance this would become a multi-month to yearlong episode.

Dressed, he made his way to the locker room's exit, past several colleagues. Nobody talked to him, perhaps they didn't know what to say. Not that he blamed them. Most wouldn't understand how it felt to lose someone in war. Unlike himself.

And now he was in danger of losing two people.

He paused at the mirror and reefed on the half-tied Windsor knot at his throat. He hadn't lost Arielle yet. With a final tug on the tie, he headed into the hallway.

The way to Wiggins's office took him through the central atrium of the new headquarters. Modern in every sense, the best feature was the glass-encased walls that let in natural sunlight. It was a welcome respite from the walled-off security rooms where he spent most of his time. The building even had private sector perks, such as the Starbucks on the ground floor.

Too bad the organization's culture hadn't kept pace with the new building. Or maybe it had, since underneath the veneer of openness the building was like a spider's web, with corridors that led to compartmented spaces and isolated individual operations. The task force's unofficial motto was that it took a network to defeat a network, but in reality, the building and its occupants continued to operate in the shadows, no matter how much light came in through the windows.

By this time, Erik stood outside the reception area for Wiggins's office. He entered and waved to Wiggins's secretary, who nodded.

"How are you doing?" a woman said from behind him.

He turned to find Stephanie in a corner of the waiting room, a manila folder on the table beside her.

"Fine," he said, too fast. "Are you sitting in on this?"

"Listen, I'm –"

"I asked Stephanie to join us," Wiggins said from the doorway of his office. He waved them in. "Come on, we'll bring you up to speed."

Erik followed Stephanie into the office and sat in one of the two chairs across from Wiggins. With his commanding jawline and Herculean frame, Wiggins was the poster-boy for law-enforcement agents. He even wore his suit well, as if born in it. Too bad the man's brain was also made of muscle. But in a few years, Wiggins would have moved on, dragged upward by the inexorable tug of his career. In fact, the working theory was that Stephanie was next in line.

Wiggins leaned on the desk, fingers clasped together. "The past few days must have been tough, but we wanted to get as complete a picture as possible before briefing you." He paused and gave a small smile. "How are you doing? Hanging in there, I hope."

"What do we know?" Erik asked.

Wiggins studied him for a second, then nodded to Stephanie.

"We think they made it to Syria," she said and removed several papers and photos from the folder and spread them onto Wiggins's desk.

Erik clenched his jaw. Not a surprise, but like a kick in the groin, knowing it was coming didn't make it any easier.

Stephanie pointed to a blow-up map of Turkey, Syria, and Iraq. "After arriving in Istanbul, we believe they took a connecting flight to Sanliurfa, near the Syrian border –"

"You think she's going to Raqqa?"

"We don't know that," Stephanie said, "but it's the closest major city."

"What happened in Istanbul?"

"We think they had about an eight-hour stopover in Ataturk airport." Stephanie's voice grew in confidence. "We eventually reached the Turkish airport authorities, but given the time difference and the fact that it was the middle of the night there, I suspect it took some time for the message to reach their officers. In the interim, we believe the girls purchased connecting tickets under different names and likely paid in cash."

"Then how do you know they went to Sanliurfa?"

She pointed to a series of photos. "These are from GAP airport in Sanliurfa," she said. "They match the ones from Montreal and Frankfurt, all showing the same two girls. Or, technically, two girls wearing very similar clothes, except for the *hijabs*."

His chest tightened as he spied the girl in the yellow blouse. Beside her was the girl in the muted dark brown clothes from earlier pictures.

Wiggins pointed to another photo. "If this was them, they met a woman in Urfa airport."

Erik picked up the photo, took in the two girls in a group with a woman in black *niqab*.

"The girls were stopped by a pair of policemen. This woman intervened, and the policemen let them go," Stephanie said. "After that, the woman escorted them to a waiting car."

"Say that again?" Erik said. "The policemen let them go?"

"We think there was a bribe." Stephanie pointed to another picture. "This shows what looks like an exchange between the woman in the *niqab* and one of the policemen. It's not all that surprising. Many people in Urfa are sympathetic to the Caliphate, including in the police. Whatever happened, after that contact the cops let the girls depart with the woman."

Erik stared at the supposed transaction, but the policeman's body obscured the woman's hand. He dropped the photo on the desk. "That's great work."

"I'm sorry we couldn't do more," Stephanie said as she returned the documents to the file folder.

Erik looked at Wiggins. "What now?"

Stephanie exchanged a glance with Wiggins, then stood. "I'll leave you two to talk."

"You should be here to talk about where we're taking the investigation," Erik said. "I have some ideas. Naomi's friends and family for starters. We need to know –"

"Why don't we get a coffee?" Wiggins asked and rose from his desk. "I'll talk to you later, Steph."

Stephanie glanced at Erik, then dipped her eyes and left.

"Come on, my treat," Wiggins said and held out his arm to Erik.

"I don't need a coffee," he said. "What I need is to figure out how we get Arielle back."

"I insist." Wiggins dropped his hand on Erik's shoulder and guided him out of the office and into the corridor. "I know this must be tough on you."

"I'm fine," Erik said. The thought of spilling his guts to Wiggins was about as appealing as shaving with sandpaper. "I just want to get to work."

"That's what I want to talk about." Wiggins walked a step behind Erik, herded him into the main atrium.

Erik's skin prickled. "What's there to talk about?"

"How long have you been with the Task Force?"

"I don't see how that's relevant."

"Humor me."

Erik shook his head. "Since 2012."

"Almost the start." The High-Risk Traveler Task Force had stood up in 2011 and evolved from a nascent intergovernmental Task Force created during the Afghanistan conflict to address a global terrorist threat. "And you've been in operations the whole time."

"I'm good at it."

"No argument here," Wiggins said as they got in line at the café. Wiggins leaned closer and spoke in a conspiratorial tone. "Stressful though, right? I understand you got pretty worked up in the ops center."

"My daughter just –"

"Two large coffees," Wiggins said and held up two fingers to the cashier. "Keep the change."

Erik bit the inside of his lip while he waited for the coffees, then followed Wiggins to the creamer bar. "Of course I got upset, who wouldn't have?"

"I get it, trust me," Wiggins said while he stirred sugar into his coffee. "But I'm worried about this cumulative stress on you. We all are."

"I can handle it," Erik said, and then his eyes narrowed. "I hope you're not thinking about taking me off this case."

Wiggins sighed. "You have a conflict of interest that compromises your ability to work objectively."

"Besides Stephanie, I'm the best analyst you've got," Erik said. "And she's the team lead so there's only so much analysis she can do."

"Which is why I need her focused on the task at hand," Wiggins said. "She's got a good head, but a soft heart. You'll distract her."

The woman who'd done her Master's thesis on the role of savagery in contemporary terrorism had a soft heart? "That's not going to happen. Stephanie's –"

"It's like this, Erik." Wiggins straightened and put a hand in the pocket of his pants. "You either take another assignment, or I send you on indefinite leave."

Erik's index finger pistoned out at Wiggins. "You put me on leave –"

"Lower your voice."

Erik grimaced, forced himself to lower both his hand and his voice. "You put me on leave, and I'm liable to go to Syria and sort this out myself."

Wiggins snorted. "This isn't something to joke about. That would be reckless. It would endanger yourself, and in all likelihood it would end up making things harder for us. The last thing we need is more cowboys in the battlespace, like your old friend, MDK. You know better than that."

"Arielle is my daughter."

"You think I don't know that?" Wiggins said. "For Christ's sake, what the hell am I supposed to do? The superintendent would have my ass if I let you stay on the case. And how do you think it would look if it came out in the news?"

"Since when does the Globe and Mail test determine what we do?"

"Since forever."

"So you want me to just, what, pretend I don't care?"

"Of course not," Wiggins said. "You'll be kept informed, and in the interim, you'll be reassigned to Danny's task force."

"The counter-radicalization team?" He wanted to throw his coffee in Wiggins's face.

Wiggins stuck out his chin. "Here's the deal. You either work with Danny, or you go on forced leave. You're right, you're one of our best, but I can't leave you with Steph." He placed a hand on Erik's shoulder. "You've always put the team ahead of yourself, I need you to do that again. Can you soldier through this?"

The bastard always knew what buttons to push. Erik nodded.

"Good man," Wiggins said and squeezed Erik's shoulder. "I wish we had more people like you, able to put the needs of the country ahead of their own." He dropped his hand and started to walk away. "Take the rest of the day off. You can start with counter-rad tomorrow."

He opened his mouth to respond, but Wiggins had already turned his back. "I can't wait," he said under his breath, then shook his head. Counter-radicalization, great. It did more harm than good, sipping chai tea with community leaders as a pretense for surveillance when the real problem lay not there, not with hard-working people trying to succeed in their new country, but with holes in immigration policy that terrorists exploited. This assignment would get him no closer to getting Arielle back.

He sipped his coffee and grimaced at the bitter taste.

CHAPTER TWO
MIXED TIDINGS

RAQQA, SYRIA
14 APR 2015 – 1736 LOCAL

The reception center in Raqqa had a Ferris wheel.

Arielle exited the car, unable to look away from the amusement park set up amid copses of pale trees, their leaves and branches entombed in layers of brown dust. In the still air of early evening, the yells and laughs of kids blended with the mechanical clanks of the rides to create a surreal harmony.

"Can you believe it?" she said to Naomi, who stood beside her.

"There's no music," Naomi said, her tone sullen. In the day and a half it had taken to cover the hundred-mile trip from Sanliurfa to al-Raqqa, Naomi's mood had worsened. "And the rides all look like they're about to break."

"But it's like Hamza promised," Arielle said. "Life is improving."

"There will be time for festivities later." Umm Fatima gestured for the girls to follow her. "You can get a better look on the way to the registration center." Umm Fatima left the park behind and walked toward the remnants of a bombed-out building.

Arielle followed, her head on a swivel. Hamza had said the Caliphate placed as much emphasis on improving the lives of its citizens as it did on defeating its enemies, and here was the proof. Yes, this amusement park was poor compared to a western equivalent, but the smiles on the kids' faces were not for show. They were happy. During the ride from Sanliurfa, she'd had her doubts about what she might find in Raqqa.

Much of the trip had been as expected, tucked in the back of the car as it alternated between furious dashes from safe house to safe house and lengthy stops when the driver waited for a phone call before proceeding. Arielle had imagined she was in one of her dad's Army stories when he'd run counter-surveillance routes on his way to meet informants. As vivid as her imagination was, the signs of war always dragged her back to reality.

The road had been cratered in several spots, forcing the driver to pick his way through or even clear rubble. Along the side of the road, burned out wreckages of pick-up trucks and other vehicles had littered the landscape. On the outskirts of al-Raqqa, normality attempted to reassert itself. They passed several busy markets where the stalls were laden with piles of cucumbers, tomatoes, and other vegetables, although about half the stands were huddled at the bases of hollowed out buildings. There had been no air attacks on the drive, but Umm Fatima had explained what to do if aircraft appeared, which for the women, amounted to making themselves visible from the air. The enemy was so concerned about civilian casualties that women and children were almost always safe. Almost.

"The *kafir* don't have the heart for what must be done in war," Umm Fatima had said.

Arielle smiled. To hear Umm Fatima speak, one would think it was the West that was the underdog. Spoken amid the carnage from the bombing runs, it was an example to emulate. She held her chin up as her smile faded. She'd soon have her chance to tend to the injured and do her part to ease the suffering of her new community, like Hamza had said.

A child's yell drew her attention to a large chair swing ride, where children dangled at the end of chains that splayed out as the ride spun. Smiles decorated the children's faces, including a young, blond girl with a ponytail. Arielle paused to watch. At a tug on her sleeve from Naomi, she resumed her trek, followed Umm Fatima across a street.

She nudged Naomi. "Do you think this is when we'll find out about our assignments?"

"Will you stop talking about being a nurse?" Naomi asked. "I just want to see Hamza. He said he would be here."

They passed into a small courtyard that had been obscured from the street. "He's probably just –"

Two single, black poles had been erected in the courtyard, both with crossbeams mounted near the top. From each pole hung a body dressed in orange coveralls, the wrists nailed to the crossbeam, the legs lashed firmly to the upstretched pole with barb wire.

Arielle froze, unable to avert her gaze from the lolling heads, bloated tongues protruding from the mouths. "Who are they?" she asked.

"Spies," Umm Fatima said. "Informers for the apostate Syrian regime." She spat. "Their punishment was too lenient."

"Crucifixion?"

"Bah. They were executed before being raised up," Umm Fatima said.

"Far more effective to hear their moans while they atoned for their actions."

Arielle's feet wouldn't move, her vision consumed by the men on the crosses. Tucked between the feet of one of the bodies was a single, dust-covered flower. An urge to brush the dirt off the petals came over her, to restore the flower to its natural beauty. She shivered. Did the children walk past this horror to get to the amusement fair? She could still hear the rides – for all she knew, the kids could see this sight even now, and she wondered which was the true face of her adopted society, the fairground or the crucifixes.

"Come on," Naomi said. "They got what they deserved."

Arielle focused on Umm Fatima's back. Placed one foot in front of the other while her mind trotted out all the lines Naomi and Reyad had repeated over the past six months. This was a war for survival, and they could not be faint-hearted. Brutality was a part of war, and this was no more savage than killing women and children in air raids. This was the only way the West would listen.

By the time she made it to the entrance of the reception area, the crucifixes out of sight if not out of mind, Arielle had almost convinced herself.

* * *

OTTAWA, ONTARIO
17 APR 2015 – 1025 LOCAL

Erik studied the mug-shot of a young Somali from Alberta, one Farah Roble Xarbi. At age twenty-three, Xarbi had left his studies at the University of Calgary, as well as a moderately successful software venture, to fight in Syria. He'd dragged along his younger brother, Aaden. The men were pictured in another photo, both clean-cut, shit-eating grins on their faces as they sat at a table covered in beer bottles and empty pint glasses. Nothing in the picture to suggest that less than a year later, both men would be dead jihadis, Aaden martyred in a suicide attack, Farah presumed killed in a coalition bomb strike after a stint as a Caliphate executioner.

He let the photos fall onto the wooden conference table where he sat. Rubbed his temples to ease the ache that had settled behind his eyes and gazed about the austere room. There were uniform work stations along the walls, a single workplace motivational poster in both French and English, and aside from that, it could have been purgatory. Given his failed promise to look after Arielle, perhaps he'd earned it.

Stop feeling sorry for yourself. He was a good analyst, he'd figure out why these men – why Arielle – had left their lives behind. Radicalization didn't happen in a vacuum, there was always a reason people sought meaning and purpose elsewhere, even in the extremism of Islamist terrorism. He felt the answer narrowly out of reach, knew it would keep him up at night. Again.

He picked up a third photo, a close-up of Farah Xarbi in army fatigues, his head covered with a tan *shemagh*. He compared it to another, a still from a Caliphate execution video. The killer, dressed in black with a balaclava pulled over his face, pointed a hunting knife at the camera, the body of a former hostage at his feet. The eyes that peered out from the balaclava were the same as in the other photo, although harder, lifeless.

"How's it going?"

Erik glanced up at Jordan. "Okay," he said and held up a picture. "Just getting to know a couple of prairie boys."

"Find anything?" Jordan came into the room.

"Farah and Aaden Xarbi. Parents are non-practicing Muslims from Somalia. The boys converted while in University." Erik frowned. "I take it we're targeting the Somali community?"

"The counter-radicalization task force engages the Somali community, it doesn't target them," Jordan said in an artificially deep voice. "We target criminal activity and national security adversaries, not citizens. That would be wrong." His voice resumed its normal tone and he pointed to yet another photo, this one of a pale, thin man with long hair and a scraggly blonde beard. He wore a hockey jersey in the picture. "What's this guy's story? He looks like he should be on a midget hockey team, not on your table here."

"Nathan Martel," Erik said. "He's 23. Hails from Montreal and was in communication with the Xarbis, at least until they died."

"Sounds like a candidate for the high-risk traveler program."

Erik snorted. "Yeah, the one positive thing I've found in two days, and it's not even in my lane. I should be helping find Arielle, not stuck in here."

"I take it you haven't heard anything."

"No." He leaned back in his chair. "Look, I get Wiggins's reasoning for taking me off Arielle's case, and as much as I don't like it, I'll do what I'm told. But counter-radicalization and community outreach? That's a police responsibility. Intelligence analysts shouldn't be tasked with engagement, we should be targeting extremists. They're the ones we should be worried about."

"Technically speaking, I'm not an intelligence analyst. I'm a mechanical designer."

"I meant the royal we."

"I know, but I couldn't pass up the chance to bust your balls." Jordan sat at the table. "Look, you know as well as I do that link analyses are needed for community engagement. They give start points for key-leader meetings, and what's more, they generate leads for investigations. That's why the counter-rad team needs intel analysts."

"Most of the leads are on common criminals."

"And we all know that crime, radicalization, and terrorism often go hand-in-hand."

"Thanks, Captain Obvious. I know terrorism is a crime."

Erik stared at Xarbi's picture, but it wasn't the image in his mind. Instead of some Somali refugee cum entrepreneur cum jihadi, he saw a young girl in a yellow *niqab*. Arielle. What had he missed? Something at school, or had it been earlier than that? He'd tried his best to protect her, and sure, he'd spent a lot of time at work these last few years, but she was always first in his thoughts. It had been that way since they'd lost Audray. He swallowed, and his knuckles went white where he held the photo.

"You in there?" Jordan asked.

"Yeah," he said and glanced at Jordan and then back at the photos. "I know the analysis isn't different, but it's redundant. We already know the Somali community needs to be engaged."

"That's one part. Radicalization –"

"There's no way to predict self-radicalization. Some people do, and some don't. Let the police build relations with these communities while the intel resources bust out the networks."

"Are you sure you're ready to come back to work?"

He closed his eyes and took a deep breath. "I'm sorry. I'm good," he said and ran a hand over his head. "You know she told me she had to stay at school over Easter to study for exams? I could've driven out to see her, and I didn't, and now I keep looking for a reason why she left, for what I'm missing." He held up one of the photos of Xarbi, then flung it onto the table. "I'm banging my head against the wall. It's like it's random."

"That's not Erik talking, that's Erik's frustration."

"So now it's Doctor Obvious?"

Jordan smiled. "This isn't random because that doesn't explain why places like Calgary and Montreal have higher incidences of radicalization."

"That's easy. Because of their large, unintegrated, immigrant communities."

"Which is a precondition," Jordan said. "That's the engine, not the spark that tips people into action."

"Then it's the Imams, guys like Abu Qatada in the UK." Erik snapped his fingers. "Or our own version, what's-his-name. Sahraoui."

"Those guys are the closers, what makes people seek them out in the first place? What if extremists could manipulate people to make them more susceptible to reach out to an Imam?"

"How? Through social media?"

"I don't know," Jordan said. "I'm an engineer, man. This isn't my specialty."

"Could have fooled me." Erik smiled. "Don't you have a project that could sort this out?"

"My funding didn't come through," Jordan said and returned the smile. "But you should see the mini-GPS trackers I'm working on. Awesome." His face grew serious. "Really, they're pretty cool."

"I believe it," Erik said. What he would've given for a small device when he'd been running sources in Afghanistan, instead of having to give out a GPS the size of a small brick, which practically guaranteed the source would get busted and in turn, killed. "You really believe there's something more going on behind the scenes?"

"I know it," Jordan said. "Somehow the extremists are setting conditions that drive people to consider radicalizing. Maybe it's random who bites, but the process itself is deliberate. They're not just throwing shit against the wall hoping some of it will stick."

"How can you be sure?"

"Because if I was them, I'd be looking to manipulate pre-conditions as well." Jordan placed a hand on Erik's shoulder. "That's why intel geeks are working counter-radicalization – so a big brain can figure out what they're up to. Can you dig it?"

Erik nodded. "Yeah, I dig it." He sighed and went back to the photos. "You're wasted at a desk, you know that? You've got a great mind for the field."

"For a minute I was starting to think you were wasted at a desk, too."

"Seriously, you'd be good at it."

"I'm good at designing equipment," Jordan said. "You miss it?"

"Miss what?" Erik didn't look up from the photo.

"The field."

"I don't think about it. I made that choice long ago."

Jordan glanced at his watch, then stood. "I should get going."

"Thanks," Erik said. "I needed the talk."

Jordan paused. "Figure this out, man, break it open. The most important action of the Second World War wasn't D-Day, it was cracking the Enigma code. You're the code breaker."

"I guess," he said. "Good speech by the way. Short, but effective, so not much like you."

"Appealing to a sense of duty generally works on ex-soldiers. You're very rules-based, you know that?" Jordan chuckled as he walked to the door. "Give it a shot, what's there to lose?"

* * *

RAQQA, SYRIA
18 APR 2015 – 1120 LOCAL

Arielle sweltered beneath her *chador*. The run-down room where she waited had an air conditioner, but like everything else she'd seen so far in Raqqa, it was a victim of intermittent electricity and did little to cool things down. Seated with nine other women, one of whom was Naomi, Arielle studied the woman at the desk in the center of the room. "Could she go any slower?" she whispered to Naomi and got silence in return.

Arielle slipped her hand onto Naomi's knee and Naomi glanced over, her eyes bloodshot through the narrow slit of her *niqab*. Beneath Arielle's hand, Naomi's leg bobbed as her foot tapped a fast rhythm on the floor. Hamza hadn't come, and despite Naomi's protestations that she had a boyfriend she'd come to marry, she was being placed along with the other women who'd arrived over the past week. Arielle squeezed Naomi's knee, wished she could tell her it would be all right. Naomi had done so much for her, had introduced her to Islam when school went so bad. Arielle could never pay back that debt.

The woman at the desk, whose name was Deeba, spoke to a man beside her, then nodded in Arielle's direction. The man, a hairy, olive-skinned gorilla in a blue Adidas tracksuit, pointed at the woman seated to Arielle's left. The woman rose and under the man's direction, stood before Deeba. After a short minute, the woman nodded at Deeba, then returned to her seat.

The man pointed at Arielle next. "You."

Arielle stood, her stomach in knots. Soon she'd be assigned to a hospital, able to help. The past two nights, airstrikes had terrorized the city. Most of the attacks had been distant, checkpoints at the entrance to the city, but one bomb had struck close to the sisters' *maqar* – a quarters for single women – and knocked out the electricity. The bombardment had continued long into the night, accompanied by the screams of the wounded, and Arielle had lain awake while tears burned down her cheeks and she yearned to help.

The man grunted as she neared and pointed to a spot in front of Deeba. Arielle obeyed.

"Name?" Deeba did not look up from the paper on the desk.

"Arielle Petersson."

Deeba's finger traced along a column of Arabic script. "You have been given the name, Hafsa. You will –"

"Hafsa?"

Deeba glanced up. "It is a good name, it means lioness." Deeba returned to her list. "You will marry Mus'ab Saleh."

Arielle frowned. "Mus'ab Saleh?"

"A proud mujahideen, one of Qassim al Shishani's. A British brother. You must make him a good wife. Return to your seat."

Arielle did not move. There must be a mistake. Hamza had said she didn't have to marry and she'd even written it on her in-clearance form. Her mouth opened of its own accord. "I'm here to work in the hospital."

"There are enough faithful for the hospital," Deeba said. "Your first duty is to make cubs for the Caliphate. Your wedding will occur when Mus'ab Saleh returns from the front. Now go." She nodded at the man, whose hand settled on Arielle's shoulder and shoved her along.

The pronouncement raced through Arielle's mind as she returned to her seat. *I told them I wanted to embrace surrender to Allah by healing others*, she thought, *not be a servant to a brother.* She sat down without a word to Naomi, said nothing to her friend, even when Naomi's name was called. Marriage meant a wedding night. She shivered and crossed her arms over her chest. Tears gathered at her eyes, and she did her best to blink back the moistness. She didn't want to show weakness, Umm Fatima had said women needed to be strong. Perhaps she could talk with this Mus'ab person, or maybe she'd be assigned to the hospital later. And kids, how could she –

"Excuse me?" Naomi's voice rang out from the middle of room in an out of place Valley girl pitch. From the way she stood, one hand on a hip, the other in Deeba's face, Naomi must have received a similarly unpleasant assignment. Deeba's mouth moved, the words too quiet to be heard across the room and then Naomi interrupted. Deeba nodded to the man and pointed at Naomi. Her attention on Deeba, Naomi did not react as the man drew back his left arm, the fingers of his meat-hook hand extended like a knife.

Arielle half stood. "Naomi –"

The man slapped Naomi across the face, and she fell into a heap onto the floor. She struggled to her hands and knees, and the man stood over her and blood dripped from her nose and onto the man's boot. Under his large, simian brow, the man's wide spaced-eyes were expressionless, and he reached down to take Naomi by the neck and dragged her to her feet. Held her like a rag doll with his right hand while he rained blows on her face with his left.

Arielle's mouth went dry, and she was almost to her feet when a tug drew her up short. She turned to the woman beside her, who'd taken ahold of Arielle's *chador*. Arielle shrugged, tried to dislodge the woman's grasp.

"Sit down," the woman said in a hiss. "You can't help her."

"Let go," Arielle said, then froze as she caught a glimpse of her friend. Naomi's arms hung limp at her sides and the man continued to hit her, his face as impassive as if he was chopping wood. He struck her one last time and a spray of blood flew through the air, and then he let go. She crumpled to the floor and her head thunked against the dirty ceramic tiles.

The woman beside Arielle released her grip and Arielle stumbled against her chair. The clatter drew the man's attention, and he looked at her and then stepped over Naomi's body. Icy sweat broke out over Arielle's body as the man stormed closer and then he stood before her. She had time to see the flecks of red on his knuckles and then he grabbed her by the throat and dragged her to her tiptoes.

"Who told you to stand?"

"Let me help her," she said. "Please."

She stared into his eyes, and the man's dead gaze was worse than his hand around her throat. He leaned closer and breathed in through his nose. "You will make a good wife."

She grimaced at the garlicky stench of his breath and twisted in his grip.

"Tariq." Deeba's voice cut through the room.

The man's heavy brow lowered over his eyes.

"That is enough, Tariq."

Tariq chuckled and released Arielle. Stepped aside to allow an unbroken sight path to Naomi's body.

Arielle clutched her throat, her gaze torn between Tariq and Deeba, unable to move.

"Go!" Spittle flew from Tariq's mouth.

Arielle crawled on hands and knees to Naomi's side and cradled her friend's head in her lap. Naomi's *niqab* had come loose, and blood from a deep cut over her right eye flowed down her face to mix with snot from her smashed nose. Tears welled in Arielle's eyes, and she rocked back and forth.

"Oh, Naomi," Arielle whispered. Her throat burned and she swallowed back the tears and wiped her friend's forehead with the back of her hand.

"She is Abdia now," Deeba said and then raised her voice, spoke to the women still seated at the edge of the room. "Let this be a lesson. You are here to serve, not make demands."

Then the tears came and Arielle no longer cared if anyone thought she was weak. She put her mouth to Naomi's ear and whispered, "Ssh, you'll be all right."

She wished she believed those words herself.

CHAPTER THREE
SENT FORTH

Erik circled his opponent. Sweat trickled down his cheeks and he wanted to wipe it away and instead threw a jab. Except his hand didn't connect, and he was upside down in the air and then slammed onto the blue mats that covered the wooden floor of the dance studio. A knee jabbed into his solar plexus, forced out what air he'd been able to hold onto, and then his opponent had twisted Erik's arm like a chicken wing. Erik tapped a furious rhythm on the floor with his free hand until the knee lifted and the pressure on his wrist eased.

"You okay?" Jordan's hand appeared in front of his face.

Erik nodded, tried not to wheeze too much as he fought to regain his breath.

"All right," Jordan said. "Can we try the other side now?"

Erik wiped his brow with the sleeve of his *keikogi*, then readopted a fighting stance and threw a left punch. Moments later, he was back on the mats.

"Your turn," Jordan said.

Erik nodded and took up a relaxed stance, inches out of Jordan's reach. He willed himself to ignore the other students, to empty his mind, but his thoughts strayed. To Arielle, to work, the lone thing that had quieted his mind these past days. He should be at headquarters now, not this jujitsu class –

Erik blinked, realized Jordan's punch was on its way and stumbled out of the way. "My fault," he said, thankful he'd missed getting smashed in the face, never mind practicing the throw the instructor had shown.

"It's okay," Jordan said. "Let's go at your speed."

"That might be pretty slow."

"Hey man, you've got other things on your mind."

"I think it's the drugs."

"That, also, would explain your slowness," Jordan said. "Though I'm kind of surprised you'd take something."

"What?" Erik frowned. "Not me, I mean the connection you were talking about between extremists, radicalization, and crime. I think drugs could be the connection."

"I dragged you here so you'd leave work behind."

"Think about it," Erik said, "the Taliban has raised money through heroin for years, so why not other groups?"

"The Taliban aren't exactly hard-core God freaks," Jordan said. "They have convenient ideals."

"So do many other extreme groups, including the Caliphate or whatever we're calling them these days."

"So what? It's a money-raising thing, their version of getting seed capital. How does it tie to radicalization?"

"I wish I knew," he said. "But there are lots of reports of terrorist groups linked to cartels, and it goes beyond money. Their methods are merging, even their goals. It's not just about financing, it's about recruitment, propaganda, everything."

"You're saying they're learning from each other. Makes sense, they're operating in similar spaces."

"But I think it's more than that," Erik said. "People turn to drugs when they're stressed or unstable, and one of the biggest stressors these days is terrorism. What if there's some sort of strategy or link behind that? What if they're creating new users?"

"More users, more money, I like it," Jordan said.

"All right," the *sensei* called out, "we'll finish with limb destruction. Remember, put your knuckles into the back of your opponent's hands, like knocking on a door."

Shit. This was a brutal exercise, one that had no value when the gloves were on but worked on unprotected hands. Soon enough, Erik's hands stung and every other thought had been driven from his head except the drill, and at that point, the instructor spoke again.

"That's it, everybody, let's bow out."

Erik straightened and dipped his head to Jordan, then joined a line of students and bowed out with the instructor. The ritual done, he shrugged out of his heavy cotton uniform in silence, then helped stack the mats and return the dance studio to how they'd found it. His hands ached, but not enough to stop his thoughts drifting once more to Arielle. The cleanup went by in a blur, and then he'd collected his gym bag and said his good-byes and moved outside to wait for Jordan in the parking lot. The cool, night air cleared his head, and he breathed deep, stared up at the stars and savored the stillness. Arielle was under those same stars, wherever she was.

The dance studio door squeaked open. "Did that help?" Jordan asked.

"It always does," Erik said. "Thanks."

"Anytime," Jordan said. "Got time for a beer?"

"I don't think so," he said. "I'm up at five."

"Boo. You know, you're not a soldier anymore. You don't need to get up at dawn."

Erik smiled. "Hah-hah. I thought my army experience was a good thing."

"It's good because you were basically a ninja."

"Hardly. You would definitely not say that if you'd seen the other HUMINT operators."

"Like MDK?"

"Really? Did you really just go there?"

Jordan's laughter filled the parking lot as they walked. "Easy fella, settle down."

"It's been almost ten years since I worked with Matt de Kalb. It's not like I'm in business with him."

"Partnered with a mercenary, that's what I'm talking about. What would Wiggins say then?"

"Shit." Erik shook his head in disgust. "You know Wiggins brings up de Kalb at least once a week? 'MDK's mercenaries are not helping. MDK makes us all look bad.'"

Jordan stifled his laughter. "Who, Mr. I-Get-Upset-When-People-Color-Outside-The-Lines? Why am I not surprised? But I'm not talking about MDK, I'm talking about you. A spy and a martial artist? Yup, your military occupation was ninja."

He chuckled. "I wasn't even training then. I picked it back up after I got out, after..." His face grew hot.

Jordan cleared his throat. "So, tell me more about this terrorism link to drugs."

He blinked. "You think there's something there?"

"Maybe. I've been working with JIATF-South for years now. Most of the action is routine drug runs, but every now and then there's an indicator of bigger things beneath the surface. It's not outside the realm of the possible that terrorists are taking a more active role in the drug trade. So yeah, you should look into it."

"I'll think about it."

He was almost at his car. He fished out his key fob, pressed a button, and the car's lights blinked.

"You heard anything from the team?" Jordan asked.

He shook his head.

"Have you asked?"

"A few times. The official answer is I'm off the case, and they'll let me know when there's something significant."

"Sorry, brother." Jordan shook his head. "Want me to poke around for you?"

Erik smiled at the gesture. "Thanks, but no. I don't want to put you in an awkward spot."

"Well, the offer stands. Let me know if you change your mind." He held out his hand. "You should just use your ninja skills to find out what's going on."

"Did you forget? I'm off the case."

"No shit," Jordan said, "but it's not like they changed the codes to the team room. This is why Wiggins likes that you were a soldier, you'd never consider going against the rules."

"Rules are there so we all know what each other are doing."

"Boring." Jordan moved away. "Study your Koran a little more. 'The deed is sound if the intention is sound.' There's no harm trying to find out what's going on."

"I think that might be crossing a line of some sort."

"No way. Your security clearance hasn't changed. Besides, you're a ninja, remember?" Jordan smiled as he walked backward. "'Night."

Erik raised a hand and then got into his car. It was stupid, but Jordan's suggestion stuck with him. There was no question he had the skill to make it happen, which meant that all he had to worry about was whether it was the right thing to do. He stuck the key in the ignition and turned on the car, and as he drove, he began to nod. The right thing was to get Arielle back and to do that, he needed information. If the task force wouldn't share, he'd have to be proactive.

CHAPTER FOUR
THE MOON IS SPLIT

RAQQA, SYRIA
22 APR 2015 – 1923 LOCAL

The wedding was held in the shadow of a building used for executions, a ten-story office tower where gay men and spies were pitched to their deaths. The day before, a crowd had been forced to watch a man thrown from the top and the image of him in mid-air, hands bound while his legs kicked in silence, seemed etched inside Arielle's eyelids. Led by her new husband, she walked past where the body had landed, dark-red stains still visible on the pavement. The memory gripped her, how the crowd had been ordered to stone the body, how it had twitched with every rock, not a person anymore, but a thing. She reflexively gripped her husband's elbow tighter, then remembered she was being taken to consummate her marriage. She shivered.

Her husband's name was Mus'ab Saleh. He had a light tan and a hardness around his eyes, offset by a soft downturn at the corners of his mouth. Unlike many of the other men, his hair was short and spiky. Had she met him a year ago, she might have thought he was good looking, maybe a model. As it was, her skin crawled at his touch.

The apartment building was a block or so ahead, and every step closer made her stomach churn. She hadn't been with a man since – no, what happened in Montreal was not being with a man. A lump formed in her throat and she called to mind a prayer and repeated it over and over in silence. This was part of her duty.

Too soon, they reached the dust-covered glass doors that led into the six-story building. Mus'ab Saleh held open the door and gestured for her to enter. He placed a hand on the small of her back as she passed and she tensed, then forced herself to let his hand guide her to the elevator. Was it her imagination or did his hand tremble? *Ridiculous*, she thought. He was a killer. A savage who'd been at the front a few days before.

The elevator ride was short, and before she knew it, he'd led her into a tiled hallway, tiny rivulets of dust along the base of the walls. Electric lights flickered on and off from periodic sconces, a good sign compared to the other buildings she'd been in.

"Here we are." He stopped to open a door. "After you."

His spoke with a soft, British accent, not what she'd expected. Then again, nothing in this country was what it seemed. She willed her gaze to the front and walked past him, through the door. Her personal feelings didn't matter. This was a test and but one price for her service to God. If this is what it took to lead a meaningful life helping people, then it was a price she'd pay.

The apartment was small, but tidy, the main room dominated by a large, embroidered red carpet. A small kitchen and dining room table took up one side of the room, while on the other side was a short hallway that led to a bedroom. A clatter caused her to jump, and she whirled to find Mus'ab Saleh standing beside a small table.

"Just the keys," he said. "I didn't mean to startle you."

"I'm sorry," she said and dipped her gaze. "I'm nervous."

He exhaled as he scanned the room. "I think we both are."

"Please excuse me," she said and backed toward the bathroom. "I need to –"

"Wait," he said and stepped forward. "May I see you?"

She froze and then nodded, and he began to raise her veil, his body so close his heat penetrated her robes. Shoulders rigid, she clenched her eyes shut, cringed at blurred images of other men who'd reached for her face, pulled her hair, pinned her down. The veil lifted, delicately, as if she was a stack of bricks that might tumble at the slightest disturbance. When she sensed his hands leave her face, Arielle opened her eyes, her heart fit to burst from her chest.

Mus'ab stood before her, head cocked, his serious features expressionless.

Heat flushed her cheeks, and she looked down. "I'm sorry. I shouldn't have –"

"You're very beautiful," he said. He raised an arm, paused when she flinched, then caressed her cheek with the back of his hand. "How have you come to such a place?"

"By Allah's will."

He smiled, a small tightening of the lips that did not reach his eyes. "Of course." He dropped his arm and took her hand, drew her into the hallway.

"Come."

She prayed for courage and followed. *Be strong.*

He led her into the bedroom and to a small, simple bed. A blend of cardamom and chai tickled her senses as he held her shoulders and pushed her onto the mattress.

She reached for his hands and slowly pulled them off. "Let me change," she said and stood. The weight of his gaze followed her into the bathroom until she closed the door, leaned back against the flimsy wood frame with her hands clasped to her chest. She had to make it through this, she had no other choice. To fight her fate would lead to far worse things, as had happened with Naomi, who had disappeared. She took a breath and then her body seemed to move on its own as she stepped out of the protective embrace of her *niqab* and robes. Beneath the clothes, the flimsy silk negligee Umm Fatima had given her was damp with sweat. Arielle shivered, her skin like gooseflesh at the memory of the woman's knobby hands as she'd helped Arielle get ready, the clothing passed along with words of advice.

"This will set you free," she'd said. "It is your permission to enjoy your wedding night."

Even now, the words were pathetic, an excuse of the worst kind. Umm Fatima's words were filled not with joy, but resignation, submission, a perversion of Arielle's childhood fantasy to have her mother help her prepare to be wed. Arielle pinched the bare ring finger of her left hand, where her wedding ring should be, her mother's ring that she'd carried halfway around the world. She'd longed to wear it, but it was *haram*, a Western tradition forbidden in the Caliphate. She wanted to put the *niqab* back on, to pretend its enveloping grip was her mother's comforting arms, but instead closed her eyes. *Mother, help me be strong.* She hadn't talked to her mother since she was a teenager and now, like then, she received no response. With a last, hard look in the mirror, she exited the bathroom.

Mus'ab Saleh, barefoot and shirtless, looked up from where he sat. He stood and gestured for her to take his place.

She walked to the bed and sat gingerly in the indentation made by his weight. He moved in front of her and placed his hands on her knees, then lowered himself to the floor, ran his fingertips along her calves to her ankles. When he cupped the heel of one foot, she closed her eyes and inhaled, tried to picture her tension easing under his touch, but the electricity of his skin on hers instead caused her body to stiffen, her hands to clench the bedsheets.

Moistness dripped onto her foot, and she gasped, opened her eyes and pulled back her foot. "What are you doing?"

"It's all right." He raised his free hand to calm her. "I'm washing your feet."

"Why?"

He held her foot over a small bowl filled with water, then scooped a handful of cool liquid and trickled it over the bridge of her foot so that drops ran down to drip back into the bowl. He scooped more water and massaged her toes, then her ankles.

Her body warred against the tingles of pleasure in her leg, and it took conscious effort to relax her hands, release the bed cover she'd grasped tight in her fists.

When both feet were washed, Mus'ab Saleh stood and picked up the bowl and moved to a corner of the room. He dipped his fingers into the water and then flicked his fingers to send a sprinkle of fine mist onto the walls where they met.

"I don't understand," she said. "What are you doing?"

"You didn't study your wedding night traditions," he said and moved to the second corner, where he repeated the motion. "I'm consecrating our wedding room."

Her face grew hot. "I don't remember that one."

"I'm not surprised." He moved to the next corner.

"What do you mean?"

"Nothing. I shouldn't have said that." He finished and set the bowl on the bedside table. Then he took one of her hands and sat beside her.

"I –" she said.

"Don't be frightened." He reached up and tucked a loose strand of hair behind her ear.

"I can't help it," she said. "I'm not ready for this."

"It's all right. I understand."

She breathed easier. "None of this is happening how I thought it would."

He lowered his gaze to stare at her hand in his own, his thumb stroking hers. "I know," he said, his voice soft. "Like so much that happens here."

"Won't the other mujahideen harass you?"

"What happens on our wedding night is none of their business."

"But Umm Fatima said the duty of a lioness –"

"I can imagine what she said," he said. "But when the time comes to consecrate our marriage, I hope it's because we love each other, not because we're forced to. I refuse to believe our faith would force people to do things against their wills, including in this, the sanctity of marriage." He stood and turned down the sheets. "You must be tired. Why don't you get into bed?"

She slid between the sheets, stopped halfway into the bed. "Shouldn't we pray?"

"We should," he said, without enthusiasm. "But I think we can do it quietly ourselves." He turned out the lights and then lay beside her, his hands folded across his chest.

In the darkness, her thoughts kept her awake. Such a strange place, so many contradictions. Amid all the horrors since she'd arrived, when she'd resigned herself to marriage with a beast, she'd met this man. Maybe that had been her test.

She reached over and grasped Mus'ab Saleh's hand, thankful when he returned the squeeze. But long after he'd begun to snore, she remained awake beside him.

* * *

OTTAWA, ONTARIO
22 APR 2015 – 2120 LOCAL

Erik had every reason to be outside his old team room, even if it was in a separate wing of the building from his new office. He rehearsed his line, what his tradecraft called cover for status, his reason to be somewhere he had no business being. He hadn't paid attention, and out of habit, he'd taken the route he'd used for the past three years. Maybe not plausible, but at least possible. It was better than his cover for action, which explained what he was doing. *I left some things here when I cleaned out my desk.* Sure, and those things necessitated a private search of the room late at night. It was weak all right, but chances were slim he'd have to put it into action.

The team room's door was about ten meters down a glass walled corridor, one of many rooms locked behind frosted windows that obscured their contents yet maintained the illusion of openness. Unlike the ops center, which ran around the clock, these rooms were mainly used in the daytime. If his door code still worked – which it should since his tasking was temporary – he'd be able to scan the planning materials on Arielle's case and get out with no one the wiser. Unless someone was at work late.

He pushed the thought from his head and headed down the hall. His shoes squeaked on the floor and his heartbeat thumped in his ears, like on his first meet with an informer in Afghanistan. Which was silly considering the differences and that the team room would no doubt be empty.

The problem with the frosted glass was that it made it impossible to tell if anyone was inside the room. The lights were on, but they were on all the time. Ironic that a world-class modern building hadn't incorporated basic energy-saving principles, but this was the government after all. He knocked on the door, waited almost a minute, then held his swipe card to the security reader on the wall and punched in his access code. A green light came on.

He grabbed the door knob, then paused. Wiggins had removed him from the team and yet here he was, about to disobey that order. He could lose his job, even be criminally charged for breaking multiple security agreements. More than that, he'd never disobeyed an order, either in uniform or since joining the Task Force. Then he thought of Arielle. If he found one thing that helped get her out of Syria, it would be worth it. He entered the room and closed the door.

The rectangular room looked like it always had, a large conference table in the center, work stations on the outside walls, and several big whiteboards on the walls. His gaze drifted to his old workspace, where he'd kept his picture of Arielle, then he walked to the conference table and spread out the poster size papers that had been left out.

Most of the papers were link analysis charts covered in tiny icons and pictures of people connected to other tiny icons in a spider's web of associations. He was familiar with the first chart, which showed links between significant worldwide attacks that had been inspired by the caliphate. His fingers lingered on the tiny Canadian flag, which had two spokes that branched out to represent the two incidents in Canada.

They'd been lucky so far.

Another chart showed the organizational diagram for the Caliphate as a whole, a black flag in the center with a myriad of protruding dark lines, like a mini-black hole. A red circle drawn over one of the first-level branches drew his attention. Abu Noor al Kanadi. The circle hadn't been there the last time he'd seen this chart. He shuffled through the remaining charts, strewed them about the table to get a better look. There was a chart depicting affiliates of the Caliphate, and several more for other terrorist organizations, including Boko Haram, al-Shabab, and Ansar al-Sharia. Al Kanadi's icon had been circled on all of them. Why?

Al Kanadi's connections to other terrorist groups wasn't new. The intelligence community believed he led planning for Caliphate attacks outside Syria and Iraq, concentrating on Europe with a secondary focus on North America, and networking with peer organizations would be what an effective planner would do. So far, al Kanadi had proven to be one of the best. Erik left the charts and moved to the whiteboards.

The scribblings on the whiteboard seemed to be derivative of the link analysis charts, except Arielle's name was front and center in one, along with Naomi's name and one other, Dominique Boudreau. Erik pored over the lines and nodes.

From Arielle's name in the center, he traced a short line to an icon for Montreal, where two additional names were listed. He didn't recognize the first, Sayyid el-Kateb, but the second name was well known.

Omar Sahraoui.

After 9/11, Sahraoui had been detained by the RCMP under a security certificate, an expedited process to detain and deport foreigners deemed to be threats to national security. But he'd been released in 2004. Although police surveillance had continued, in 2008 Sahraoui challenged his status as a terrorist sympathizer through a human rights tribunal and won. He now worked as a professor, although given the payout he'd received from the government, he worked because he wanted to, not because he ever had to work again.

From Montreal, a long line led across the board to connect with an icon for Ansar al-Sharia, a terrorist group based in Tunisia. Erik's thoughts raced as his gaze skipped to the next line, one that linked Ansar al-Sharia with the Caliphate, where al Kanadi's name was written. Goosebumps rose on his arms. Al Kanadi was three degrees of separations from –

The muffled beep of the security reader outside the room grabbed his attention, and he whirled to face the door. There was nowhere for him to go and as the door opened, he moved toward his desk.

"Hi Stephanie," he said.

"Erik?" Stephanie frowned. "What are you doing here?"

"I forgot some of my things."

"You should have come by during the day."

"I guess I lost track of time." He tried to smile. "And you? Burning the midnight oil?"

"We're working on a briefing for the deputy minister. Wiggins needs it by tomorrow." She shook her head. "You can't be in here." She glanced at the uncovered whiteboards. "Did you look at anything?"

"I did." No point pretending. "I see there's a connection between al Kanadi and Arielle. What is it?"

"I can't tell you," she said, and redness colored her cheeks. "You should leave, Wiggins could come in."

"Stephanie, please," he said. "Where she is? Who she's linked to?" He pointed to the whiteboard. "What does this show?"

"It's not clear," she said and moved to her desk where she flipped through some papers. "There's a report al Kanadi is specifically recruiting girls from North America, but we don't know how or why."

"How is that connected to Ansar al-Sharia?"

"Counterfeit travel documents. It's a single source, uncorroborated." She held a hand to her temple. "I shouldn't be telling you this."

"Then how is –"

"You need to go." She pointed at the door.

"Do you know where she is?"

"If I tell you, will you leave?"

"Yes."

"Raqqa, we think."

"You're sure?"

"You said you would go."

"I did," he said and fought the thirst, the thirst for more knowledge that had replaced the thirst for the bottle, the one that had ruled his life before he'd met Audray. He glanced once more at the whiteboard and then headed for the door.

As he walked past Stephanie, she took his arm. "I know this is tough for you –"

"You do, eh?" he said, unable to hide his frustration. "I wasn't sure the team even remembered I existed, so at least there's that."

"You think it's my choice to keep you in the dark? We could use your help." Her voice softened, and the citron notes of her perfume filled his nose. "I'm sorry."

"She's all I have," he said. "I told her I'd be there for her."

All those months after Audray had died and it was just the two of them, the mornings it took everything he had to beat his hangover and get out of bed. Arielle had been eleven, and she'd been his rock instead of the other way around. "Daddy," she'd said one morning. "I need you to come back." Her hand had gripped his. "Please come back."

He'd squeezed her hand in return, so hard his wedding band had dug into his fingers. "I'm sorry, Sweetie. It won't happen again. I promise." Now she was in a place where women were sold as sex slaves and prisoners were burned alive, and he was powerless to help.

"Look," Stephanie said, "our best guess is that the connection to Ansar al-Sharia is a recruitment chain."

"Through Africa?" He frowned. "I thought the most common route was through Europe and Turkey."

"That doesn't mean there aren't others."

"And Sahraoui?"

"On the surface, he's clean, but his name keeps coming up. It's not clear why, or even if there's any connection to Ansar al-Sharia." She put a hand on his chest. "Now you have to go."

"Who's Dominque?" The name was familiar.

"Her roommate, now go."

"No, it's not," he said. "It's Mary-Beth."

Stephanie raised her eyebrows. "She also goes by Dominique."

"I don't understand." He opened the door and stepped into the hallway, followed by Stephanie. "She has an –"

"Petersson, what are you doing here?"

Erik looked down the hallway to where Wiggins stood. "Boss," he said. "I was just –"

"Erik forgot some things here," Stephanie said.

"It's okay, Stephanie," Erik said. "I came by to check up on Arielle's case. Stephanie caught me and was kicking me out."

Wiggins looked at Stephanie, who nodded, her cheeks flushed.

"Go home," Wiggins said to Erik. "See me tomorrow. Stephanie, my office. Now."

"Yes, sir," he said. He paused long enough to mouth an apology at Stephanie, then swallowed and walked in the other direction. He'd seen the look on Wiggins' face before, and he knew the man wouldn't back down. The main effort now would be to keep this mess from getting on Stephanie. Still, as he walked, his stride grew stronger.

Now he had a start point.

* * *

RAQQA, SYRIA
23 APR 2015 – 0440 LOCAL

Arielle bolted upright in bed, frantic to find whatever had woken her. Out of the corner of her eye she caught sight of the bearded face beside her. *Not again.* She threw off the covers and leapt from the bed. Her breath came in ragged pulls as she cast about for a way out and then shivered in her black, lace negligee. Halfway out the door she paused, frowned down at the clingy garment as if unsure how it got there, then crossed her arms over her chest.

She changed direction and tiptoed into the bathroom, and then closed the door behind her. Stood on the soft, black fabric of her *abaya* and then the memories flooded back like water into an empty hollow, the wedding, the apartment, Mus'ab Saleh's hands on her feet. Heat rose in her cheeks, and she snatched the *abaya* from the floor, wrapped it around herself and returned to the bedroom.

Mus'ab Saleh had rolled over and lay facing her. She studied him, his aquiline nose and proud jaw. Asleep, his face was more peaceful, and the thought returned that he might have been a model in a different life. But this was Raqqa. She clutched her robes tighter and backed out of the room.

It wasn't supposed to be like this. She was friendless, wary of every word, every action. For the fighters she'd met, or even women like Deeba, the name of God wasn't compassion or mercy, it was an excuse to kill and inflict pain, on their enemies as much as on their brothers and sisters. What had Naomi done to deserve the beating she'd received? At most, she was guilty of being silly, naïve.

Like Arielle had been.

A bitter lump formed in Arielle's stomach. She had no idea what had happened to Naomi. She'd asked Umm Fatima and received no answer. She would have searched for her had she been able to leave the *maqar*, but it was impossible to even step foot outside without an escort. In truth, for the last week Arielle had been little more than a prisoner. She'd been so stupid.

She passed through the living room, her face clouded. She'd come to begin anew, to escape how she'd been treated, like a piece of meat. Naomi and her cousin, Reyad, had talked about the cherished role women had in a true Islamic society. Yes, they wore veils, a prudent tradeoff to enable them to be the directors, the protectors of society through behind-the-scenes organizing. Some, like Umm Fatima, did exactly that. And yet, Arielle had been married off with no more consideration than she'd been targeted that night in September. All she'd done was trade one hell for another.

An assault rifle propped in the corner of the living room drew her gaze. She recognized it as the vaunted AK-47, worshipped in the streets. It drew her near, the real bedrock on which her new society stood, faith from the edge of a saw-toothed knife. She knelt beside the weapon and brushed a finger along the metal. Her touch slow and gentle, as if it might bite her. It was cold, greasy and she drew her hand back. Sniffed her fingers and recoiled at the mechanical stench of gun oil. It smelled of the violence she'd seen on every corner in al-Raqqa, the sawed-off heads and screams of people burned alive.

The room pressed in on her until, like a caged animal, she clawed open the door and tumbled headlong into the hallway. Into the stairwell and up to the top of the building where, in the chill dark, she moved onto the roof and stared out over the city. The city was almost pitch black, a city of thousands of people who'd stayed to eke out an existence under the Caliphate's thumb, unable to use electricity lest they be bombed into the Stone Age. They were the true heroes, the ones who'd been under attack for years and still had the will to survive. She'd seen them, the merchants, the mothers, they'd crash into each other in the market with their eyes fixed on the sky for coalition aircraft. No jets flew overhead now, only stars, the sky an ocean of glittering white lights. She stared at them until the stairwell door pushed open.

Mus'ab Saleh stepped onto the roof. "You shouldn't be out here." He moved to her side, careful not to touch. "It's dangerous without your *niqab*."

He was right, she would be lashed if found outside without a veil. And yet, for some of the women she'd talked to, the imprisoning robes were not much better than the whip. Arielle wasn't sure, the veil was not everything the propaganda said, but it had the potential to liberate as much as imprison. Under her *niqab,* she was whoever she wanted to be.

She stared at the vast sky, millions of pin-prick lights like holes in its dark veneer. "They're amazing," she said. "I haven't seen them like this since camping as a kid."

He stepped closer. "Beauty sometimes comes in unexpected places."

"When my mom died, my dad told me she was still with us, that she'd received her own star and would always be looking down on us."

"How old were you?"

"Eleven." She paused and let the vastness of the sky wash over her. "He pointed out which star was hers, but I kept forgetting which one it was. I would lie awake at night and stare out the window, wondering why she'd left a second time and apologizing for not being good enough." *Crying myself to sleep.* Even now, nine years later, the thought caused her eyes to burn.

Mus'ab placed a hand at the small of her back. "It wasn't your fault."

She tensed under his touch. "You don't know that. You know nothing about me."

"I know that you love your family," he said.

She took a deep breath. "I miss them," she said. "Even though we're not supposed to."

"I miss my family as well," he said. "They didn't want me to come here."

She released her breath, unaware she'd kept it pent up. "It doesn't seem fair we can't contact them." It was *haram*, forbidden. Her dad was a *kafir*, a non-believer who at best she could never associate with and at worst, should be killed if he wouldn't convert. A harsh edict, not the guidance of a loving god, but of cold surrogates. Her father was the same person he'd been five years ago when he'd sat with her for half an hour each night to talk. "There's Orion, the hunter." She pointed low on the horizon to the three stars in the mythical hunter's belt. "It's barely visible this time of year."

"He is called al Jabbar here, but he's still a hunter."

Arielle sighed. "My dad used to say Orion was hunting the morning, looking for the light." She felt Mus'ab's gaze on her. "His punishment was that he'd never catch it."

"And you?" he said in a whisper. "What are you hunting?"

She met his gaze, surprised at her directness. "Myself," she said. She remembered who she'd once been, not so long ago, before her confidence had been destroyed amid alcohol-stained memories. She'd been naïve in the aftermath, she knew that now, but she could be that person again, more than that. Each mistake was an opportunity to grow if she had the strength.

"May I join you in your hunt?"

"You would join me?"

"Of course."

"I don't know where it will take me."

He held out a hand. "Wherever that is, I'll be by your side," he said. "Marriage is a holy covenant, most sacred before God. I will be measured by my loyalty to you."

Tingles pulsed through her skin as their fingers brushed together. "This place is nothing like what I expected," she said.

"I know." A faint smile appeared on his face. "For me, too."

"How do I know what's real and what to believe?"

"Trust your senses. They are like the five pillars and will not steer you wrong." He held out his arms.

She hesitated. "I don't want to get hurt." She'd come for community, maybe a community of two was enough. At a certain point, she had to trust in something.

He pulled her close. "Whoever tries to hurt you shall first have to go through me."

For an instant, she stiffened, his arms more confining than the black cloth of her *abaya*. All the old memories pressed in on her, the cameras, the laughter. The pain. Throughout, Mus'ab held her, rubbed her shoulder as if he felt her turmoil.

She took a deep breath, then exhaled and rested her head on Mus'ab's chest. So be it. From now on, she would trust in herself.

CHAPTER FIVE
CAST OUT

Erik wondered how much more trouble he'd get in if he reached across the desk and punched Wiggins. It wasn't that he didn't deserve to be chewed out – he did – it was how Wiggins laid it on.

"What did you think you were doing?" Wiggins asked for what must have been the fifth time. He leaned back in his chair, hands steepled in front of his chest and glared out from beneath his lowered brow. "Did you not understand what being assigned to another team meant? Stephanie has enough resources. She doesn't need you nosing around."

"Maybe if you'd been an analyst, you'd know how much work goes into these cases."

"Don't start," Wiggins said. "And in case you forgot, the primary role of the task force is to identify and stop high-risk travelers from leaving the country. Not getting back those who've already left. Maybe if you'd kept better tabs on your daughter, this wouldn't have happened."

Erik's hands tightened into fists.

Wiggins held up a hand. "All right, that was over the line. I'm sorry." He rose from the desk and walked over to a window, braced himself on the frame and stared outside. "We're all a little tense right now, but I wish you'd left things alone."

Erik stared straight ahead.

"It's not like you're not helping. The counter-radicalization team is doing important work, and Danny's told me you've got a knack for it. I understand you have a theory about drugs as a radicalizing agent, that's an interesting lead. If the Islamists are linked up with the cartels, that's a problem for everybody."

"That's why it's important to check out Montreal," he said. "This whole thing with Sahraoui and the university –"

"You're not supposed to know about Sahraoui's involvement or his link to drugs," Wiggins said and then returned to his chair. "Oh, but wait, you do know since you broke into an off-limits room and snuck the information."

"Look, there are too many coincidences. Put me back on the team."

"Listen, even if I wanted to do that – and I'm not saying I do – it's out of my hands." The edge in Wiggins's voice grew softer. "This is difficult, but it's policy. The least you could do is recognize that."

"Would you? If it was your daughter?"

Wiggins sighed. "Here's the deal. You need to do what you're told. We all do, that's how this national security thing works. Each of us puts the greater good ahead of ourselves."

"I don't need a lecture on serving my country."

Wiggins leaned forward and rested his elbows on the desk. "I need to know this stunt won't be repeated."

"You think this was a stunt?"

"Call it what you like, it was against the rules. You said you were a good analyst and you're right, you are, and we have a job for good analysts. It's not what you want to be working on, but I have no room for maneuver on this. If you want to be with the program, this doesn't happen again."

Erik pushed back his chair and stood. Over a lifetime of service, he'd always accepted the needs of the country as more important than his own. But what did it say if his loyalty to his job was greater than to his own daughter? "I'm going to find Arielle," he said. "And I'll use every available resource to do so."

"You might not have any."

"I'm a resourceful guy," he said. "I'll figure something out."

"So be it," Wiggins said. "You're suspended, indefinitely." He nodded at the door. "Pack your shit and get out of here."

* * *

RAQQA, SYRIA
23 APR 2015 – 1749 LOCAL

The crowd ebbed and flowed around Abu Noor al Kanadi, Raqqa's citizens going about their daily business in the bazaar. The closeness made his skin crawl, but he made sure at least two or three people were within a couple of steps at all times. This was not as easy as it sounded since the presence of Mamdouh at his side parted the crowd before him.

"No matter how much publicity we give it, this market is depressing," al Kanadi said.

"There are many good perfumes," Mamdouh said.

"I'll never get used to the Middle Eastern fascination with scents and colognes," he said.

"Then you will always miss out." Mamdouh paused to stare at a vendor's cart.

"I'll take your word for it," Al Kanadi said. He reached out to sample some dates from a stall. "Where do we stand with our most recent additions?"

Mamdouh sneered. "A waste of time. Neither girl has potential."

"Tell me."

"The main girl –"

"The main effort," al Kanadi said. "It's called the main effort, the action that's most critical to achieving success."

"As you say," Mamdouh said. "That girl had to be disciplined. Tariq went too far."

"What does that mean?"

"Her face is broken. She will need time to recover."

"We spent almost a year grooming her." Al Kanadi forced himself to draw a steadying breath. Good help was hard to find. "What happened?"

"The *sharmuta* drew attention to herself and then disrespected Tariq." Mamdouh shrugged. "She needed to be disciplined."

"She'll heal." There was always a way to salvage a situation.

"Not for months. Her spirit is broken as well."

"That's not necessarily a bad thing," al Kanadi said.

"True," Mamdouh said, "but the operation requires someone with a certain profile, someone with spirit, yet who can blend in. She did not fit that profile, both Deeba and Tariq swear to it."

Al Kanadi sighed. "Tariq should take her as his wife. It would be a suitable punishment."

"We should just kill her," Mamdouh said as he contemplated a bottle of cologne. "It would be the same result."

"Tariq's bloodlust is getting worse," al Kanadi said. "Discipline him. The pool of recruits isn't so big that we can abuse them, even if they're not suitable."

"I understand," Mamdouh said. "If the plan was simpler –"

"Then it wouldn't achieve the desired effect," al Kanadi said in a sharp tone. "The plan itself is simple. It's the preparation that is complicated."

"Using the ratlines would remove the need to recruit a carrier."

"Neither us or our Mexican partners want unnecessary attention drawn to those routes. They're too important."

"As you say." Mamdouh's face could have been carved from stone. "Maybe you'd like to supervise recruitment yourself?"

Al Kanadi considered the idea. "No. I trust you to handle this," he said Tempting as it was, getting involved might raise his electronic signature, never a good thing for a person sought by Western security forces.

"And what of the girl? She can still make babies."

Al Kanadi pondered the problem. There might be a way to salvage the girl's potential, but she would need to be pushed to the point where death seemed attractive. "Send her to the front lines," he said. "The fighters can put her to use."

"I'm sure," Mamdouh smiled, a grim sight that cleared several bystanders away.

"What about the other girl?" al Kanadi asked. "What's her name?"

"Hafsa," Mamdouh said. "She's a university student, computer engineering. Wanted to help in the hospitals. More of a believer than the first girl. She married one of the European fighters." He scoffed. "Next to useless, like most of them. Yourself excluded."

"I'm not European." Al Kanadi stopped to rifle through some fruit.

"She'll break, like the other, and then we'll lose her."

"The broken ones still make good wives," Al Kanadi said and held an apple to Mamdouh. "In the meantime, let's put her to work. Maybe something with the al-Khansaa Brigade."

Mamdouh stared at the apple as if it was from Mars. "They will never accept her as police."

"They would in the Ghost Section."

"The Cyber Caliphate Army? *Muhajirat* are not permitted."

"Then figure something out," al Kanadi said. "It's not every day we get a woman with a computer engineering degree, and it makes no difference if it's a man or a woman sitting behind a monitor."

"This will not work."

"Maybe, but we have nothing to lose and everything to gain." Al Kanadi bit into the apple. "And send that husband of hers away, too. We don't need him getting in the way because his wife has a job."

Mamdouh grunted, but bowed his head.

Al Kanadi clapped Mamdouh's shoulder. "Have faith, my friend. Rome wasn't built in a day."

"But it did burn in one."

"Don't worry," al Kanadi said. "*Insha'Allah*, it will burn again."

* * *

OTTAWA, ONTARIO
23 APR 2015 – 1140 LOCAL

Erik walked through the open atrium toward the main entrance, an office box of pictures and books in his arms. The conversation with Wiggins replayed in his head, and each time it made him angrier.

"Erik, wait up," a woman said from behind.

He looked back and saw Stephanie and felt the anger subside a bit. He'd dragged her into this too and no doubt she'd also gotten ragged out.

"I just heard, I'm sorry," she said when she reached him.

"I'm the one who should apologize," he said. "I'm sorry for putting you in that situation, it was selfish of me."

"We all make mistakes," she said. "I'm sure Arielle would have appreciated what you did."

He snorted. "Maybe."

"Need some help?"

He glanced up and was glad to see her smiling. She had a beautiful smile, the kind that made everyone else smile too, although she guarded it with care. "I can manage," he said, "but if you wanted to walk me out, I wouldn't say no."

"Deal." She walked with him to the exit, and they swiped out of the building and then headed down the stairs to the parking lot.

Outside, the sunshine felt good on Erik's face, and he found more spring in his step. He glanced at Stephanie. "I thought you'd be mad at me."

"I was."

"Was?"

Her hand came to his back, her touch light, but firm. "You did it because you love her. How can I be mad at you for that?"

"You know this is the first time I've ever been suspended?"

She smiled. "Seems hard to believe."

"Twenty years in the military, eight years with the RCMP, but this is a first for me."

"How does it feel?"

"Embarrassing," he said. "But kind of liberating, too."

"What will you do?"

"I don't know." It was the truth, but it wasn't enough, so he said the first thing that popped into his head. "Maybe I'll go to Syria after her."

"I hope you're joking."

"Others have done it," he said. "There was the Belgian father last year."

"He was beaten and tortured."

"But he got his son out."

"Who's now in jail in Belgium." On their return, the boy and several others had received sentences for being part of a domestic terrorist organization. "Please, put that thought from your head right now. It's ludicrous."

He stopped and faced her. "I understand, Stephanie, believe me, I do. But what do you expect me to do, sit on the couch and play video games?"

"That's not what I'm saying."

"Then what?" He stared at her until she looked away.

"I don't know," she said. "I don't know what to tell you."

"And I don't know what I'm going to do. But I promise I'll figure something out."

"And when you do?"

"You'll be the first to know."

"Thank you," she said. They walked in silence, then she chuckled. "It's hard to picture you as the video game type."

He grinned. "I'm not. Arielle was into some online fantasy game for a bit, so I played with her as something to do together. She humored me."

"Not World of Warcraft?" Stephanie's face was a picture of incredulity.

"I think that was it. You've heard about it?"

"I have. I would never have guessed."

"I know, pretty embarrassing." They'd reached his car. "This is me." He shifted the box to one arm. "Listen, I'm glad it's you running the investigation. If anyone can find Arielle, it's you."

"Thank-you."

"I'd tell you not to work too hard, but in this case, I don't mean it."

"It would also be the pan mocking the cauldron."

"What?"

"You know, *la poêle qui se moque du chaudron.* Something that you do also."

"Oh, the pot calling the kettle black," he said. He smiled once more as he dug for his car keys. "There's not much you need to work on, but English expressions are definitely one of them."

Stephanie's cheeks flushed and she took a deep breath. "You're right about the link to Sahraoui. There's something there."

"Like what?"

"I'm not sure. Maybe drugs, maybe recruitment. Sahraoui's name comes up in both contexts."

"Why don't we run him in?"

"The intel's too weak," she said. "After the shambles with his security certificate, we need something ironclad. Wiggins won't even put surveillance on him."

"Speaking of Wiggins, he was pretty clear I should stay out. Why tell me this?"

She sighed. "I remember the look on your face when I caught you in the team room. It's the same one you have now. You're going to keep looking for her no matter what you're told, so you might as well be pointed in the right direction."

He snorted, then recalled the team room, a connection on the whiteboard that hadn't made sense. "What about Arielle's room-mate? What's the link there?"

"Mostly suspicion. She was evasive during her police interview."

"Are we following up?"

"There are other priorities right now," she said, and her face grew serious. "We don't have enough resources to look into every lead."

"Wiggins decided that?"

Stephanie didn't react, but nor did she need to. He shook his head. "Do you think she knows something?"

"I think we should investigate every lead," she said. "I'm just surprised nobody wanted to get in touch with her." She held out what looked like a playing card.

"What's this?" He took the card and almost dropped it when he spied a curvy blond woman in a one-piece bathing suit that left little to the imagination. "Who's that?"

"That's Dominique," Stephanie said. "Or as you know her, Mary-Beth."

"Islamic girls don't normally parade around in their birthday suits. How is she linked to a professor of Islam?"

"She may not be, but something doesn't add up," Stephanie said, then placed a hand on his chest. "It might be nothing, but those leads are there, waiting to be followed up."

He had an urge to reach up and place his own hand on hers but now was hardly the time. "I'd need someone to bounce ideas off."

"I'm sure Jordan would help."

He laughed, in spite of himself. "Jordan's a techie, he'd tell you that himself," he said. "What about you?"

"We'll see," she said. "There are risks. If Wiggins catches you –"

"I know," he said. "I want so much to listen to him, believe me, but I'm not sure I can. Arielle's out there, in danger."

"Take some time and think about it." She gazed into his eyes. "I think what you're doing is very noble. I admire you, I wish…" She paused, took a short breath. "I wish all fathers thought as much of their daughters."

"Thank you," he said, conscious of the warmth of her body near his.

Stephanie patted his chest, seemed about to say more, then reached into a pocket and pulled out a small parcel wrapped in tissue paper. "Here. I got this for you."

"What is it?" he asked as he took the parcel.

"Just a little something." She backed away. "Whatever you decide, be careful. And call me before you do something stupid." With a final smile, she turned.

"How will I know it's stupid?"

"You'll know," she called over her shoulder, then carried on toward the building.

He watched her disappear up the stairs and thought about what she'd said. There were leads all right, slim ones and there was every chance he'd find no more than what the police investigators had found. Plus, he had to admit that as much as he hated his current suspension, it was lenient. If he blew this, Wiggins would have no choice but to hang him out to dry, and Stephanie might go down as well.

The safe bet would be to not rock the boat, although it would be the hardest to get through the days. He might have to play the loyal soldier for years, and after all that time, there was no guarantee he'd be any closer to finding Arielle. A difficult choice.

He exhaled and peered at the parcel Stephanie had given him. Peeled off the tissue paper to reveal a black, silicon bracelet with engraved words on both sides. He'd seen these Missing-in-Action bracelets before, symbols that represented the hope that lost or captured soldiers would one day come home. Had never expected to get one himself and he held the bracelet up, traced the words with his fingers.

Arielle Rose Petersson. 01-May-2015. You Are Not Forgotten.

It was no choice at all.

CHAPTER SIX
CLEFT APART

RAQQA, SYRIA
01 MAY 15 – 1329

Arielle followed Mus'ab Saleh through the market, her hand in the crook of his elbow. It was Friday, the first day of the weekend, and the handful of people in the square scurried among the distressed buildings that hunkered like mausoleums around the open space.

Mus'ab offered a tight-lipped smile and gestured to an empty stall. "I'm sorry," he said. "I thought at least something would be open."

"We can come back," Arielle said in a hushed tone.

"When I first arrived, Fridays were the highlight of the week. People were everywhere, talking, enjoying each other's company. Now..." he nodded around the deserted square. "Friday's are only busy if there's an execution."

"I need to rest, anyways." It was true. She had blisters on both feet, and her shoulders ached.

They'd walked all over the city, Mus'ab the ever-attentive guide for what attractions remained. They'd walked along the Euphrates and trekked to the Baghdad Gate, always conscious of the threat of bombardment, although the biggest obstacle proved to be the *Hisbah*, or religious police. Mus'ab had been stopped twice because his beard was not long enough. He'd trimmed it for the wedding, but the excuse did not save him from being fined. So far, the best sightseeing had been during a daytime airstrike, when fighters and police had fled for cover. The newlyweds had crept onto their apartment's balcony and savored the fresh air and the chance to view the city free from the judging eyes of Caliphate enforcers.

"My parents visited sometimes, drove up from Beirut before they had enough of that war and left for the UK. My father spoke fondly of the *Crac des Chevaliers* in Homs, of Palmyra," Mus'ab had said as they'd gazed over the haze-covered city. "I would like to see those things with them."

"Maybe one day," she'd said.

"In my worst dreams," he'd said, a far-off look in his eyes. "Besides, at the rate everything's being destroyed, there won't be anything left."

Now, as Mus'ab led them through the twisting streets, potholes, and collapsed buildings, his words seemed prophetic. He nodded to a pile of rubble that had once been an office building. "This is Assad's work."

"How do you know?"

"Western planes strike targets on the edge of the city, outposts, and checkpoints," he said, his face a mask. "Assad attacks the people instead."

Ahead, a man and two boys struggled to push a car off the street, a woman to one side. As Arielle and Mus'ab approached, the man gathered the others on the far side of the vehicle, the kids tucked to his sides, his body a shield to hide the woman from view. A frown creased the man's face and although he was careful not to look at them, distaste radiated from him, more palpable the closer they got. Arielle stepped closer to Mus'ab, who steered her past the car. They hurried along in silence.

Outside their apartment building, Mus'ab caught sight of a man and stiffened. "Ahmed," he said under his breath. It seemed like Mus'ab would turn around, but then the man saw them and waved them over. When they neared, Mus'ab placed a hand over his heart and bent his head. "*Salaam Alaikum.*"

"*Walaikum Salaam,*" Ahmed said and bent his own head. His eyelids covered half of his eyes as if he was half asleep, but Arielle got the sense there was more going on behind those eyes than could be seen. She was glad he didn't talk to her.

"I hope things are well," Mus'ab said, then held a hand out to Arielle. "This is my –"

"Tomorrow we leave for the front," Ahmed said.

A tremor passed across Mus'ab face. "It's barely been a week," he said. "It's supposed to be two weeks for a honeymoon."

"Ten days," Ahmed's gaze lingered on Arielle.

"Then we have three days left."

"We leave tomorrow," Ahmed said. "Make sure you're with us." He hitched his rifle on his shoulder and shoved between them, breaking Arielle's hold on Mus'ab's arm.

Arielle watched Mus'ab stare after Ahmed. Every few seconds his face twitched, and he would dip his head as if struggling to swallow something. When Ahmed was out of sight, Mus'ab faced her, his face ashen. "I must get ready." He led her into the building.

They did not talk. Arielle was surprised to find she didn't want her time with Mus'ab to end. In their short week together, threatened with physical and moral harm, it seemed they'd lived a lifetime. They'd both followed their hearts to find higher meaning in a shallow world and instead, they'd found each other, and while God had brought them together, it had been Mus'ab Saleh who'd whispered poetry to her at night. It had been Mus'ab Saleh who'd let her lean on him when she'd needed to rest, and given her water when she was thirsty.

They entered the apartment, and she shut the door, then loosened her *niqab* as Mus'ab collected his rifle. "I could come with you."

"The front lines are no place for a woman."

An image of Naomi's face appeared, ghostly in her mind, already faded. She shoved the image aside. "Our place is together."

"Not at the front," he said and clutched the rifle to his chest as if it were a shield.

She stepped closer. "Can you talk to Ahmed's commander? Get a few more days?"

"To not obey is to die," he said as he stared at the gun. "The only way out is to flee."

She reached out and raised his chin, got him to look away from the rifle. He returned her gaze with hollow eyes. "I would come with you." The words did not seem like hers, the thought unimaginable even a few days ago. But they were true nonetheless. She'd found her polestar and would not give it up without a fight.

"I can't ask that," he said. "I have no plan, and there's no time." He turned his head and a frown creased his face. "It was a mistake to come here."

She placed a hand on the rifle, forced the weapon down until it hung by his side. With her other hand, she cupped his chin, brought his face back to her.

His eye twitched as his gaze darted between her and the rifle. His face seemed thin, his body gaunt beneath his loose t-shirt. "I'm scared."

She took his face in her hands. "So am I. And I was mistaken as well, foolish. But I don't feel that way with you."

"I'd given up hope," he said, "but now I want to live." He looked away. "I don't think I'll come back."

"You must," she said. In the maelstrom of politics, violence, and religion, he was a kindred spirit. He had to be strong, and so must she. She put her hands on his shoulders, pulled him close and rose on her tiptoes to press her lips against his.

He tensed, pulled his face away. "You don't have to –"

She put a finger over his lips. "I want to. This is my choice." She guided his free arm to the small of her back. Kissed him again, harder, pressed into him until at last, he pushed back. He took her in his arms, and the rifle clattered to the floor. She jumped and her heart raced and her breath caught in her throat and then he pulled her closer, his arms around her, the touch of his lips electric against her own, against her neck. She pushed him toward the bedroom and he followed, wordless, his gaze locked on her.

"You must be strong," she said, her steps resolute. Her breath quickened as they entered the bedroom and goosebumps rose along her arms at the sight of the bed, but she exerted her will, chased the sights and smells that had lurked beneath the surface of her consciousness for so long. *No more.* She was the strong one now. She was in control.

She tilted her head upward and kissed her husband, then pulled him down onto the bed.

* * *

MONTREAL, QUEBEC
02 MAY 15 – 2005 LOCAL

Erik glanced at the wallet-sized glossy Stephanie had given him. In the picture, Mary-Beth, or Dominique as the name on the card read, was spread-eagled against a graffiti-covered wall. Two strips of thin fabric straddled her shoulders and struggled to cover the nipples of her large breasts and then came together at her crotch to form an electric-green 'V' shape on the front of her body. On the back of the card was the address for Le Cabaret, where he now stood.

A passerby tsked, and he jammed the photo into a pocket, his cheeks warm, and studied the club. The entrance was dominated by a blinking, neon sign, twenty feet high and decorated with flying women in bikinis and capes. He hesitated on the sidewalk and realized he didn't want to go in, didn't want to face what had once been familiar territory. In another life, he'd been no stranger to night clubs and strip joints. Or to bar-clearing brawls and nights lost in an alcohol-fueled black-out. The Army had been 'work hard, play hard,' and he'd taken that philosophy to heart.

Until Audray.

He didn't know what she'd seen in him. He'd been rough around the edges, a new intelligence officer who hadn't left behind the hard-partying ways of being an infantry sergeant. She'd been a government translator, and they'd met at work when he'd needed to get a set of documents translated. The rest was happily ever after, at least for a while. He left the bottle behind, they got married and created perfection, Arielle.

Then the war had come, Afghanistan, a new kind of war, but with the same lure of glory that had drawn him to the army in the first place. There was always one more mission, one more task. Too late, he realized it would never be enough and by that time, Audray was dead. Even then, after he'd quit the army for the stability of a desk job with the police, his biggest mistake had been to think he'd beaten the odds. Old dogs, as everyone knew, didn't learn new tricks.

Except this time he would, for Arielle's sake. He set his jaw and entered the club.

A bouncer in a black polo-shirt stood inside the entrance. Erik walked past him and went into a large, dim room with two oversized island stages surrounded by chairs. A bar lined the near wall and on the far wall were booths and doorways to other areas. Another polo-shirt clad bouncer stood by one of the doors and Erik crossed the half-filled room toward him, tried not to stare at a naked woman perched frog-like midway up a pole to his left. When he neared the door, the bouncer held up a hand.

"This area's off limits," the bouncer said.

"I'm here to see Dominique." She'd said to use her stage name. "She's expecting me."

"Sure, bud, same as half the guys here," the bouncer said. "She's not on for another hour, so you'll have to wait."

"I'm not here to watch," he said. "I just want to talk to her about my daughter. They were roommates."

The bouncer stuck out his chest. "Are you deaf? I don't care if you're her sugar daddy, take a seat."

"Listen, can you just let her know that I'm here?"

The bouncer stalked nearer. "What part of no don't you –"

Erik side-stepped and gave the bouncer a tiny shove, enough so he could get past, then darted through the door. "Mary-Beth?" He strode down a short hallway lit in red neon. Along the hallway were several changing rooms and he poked his head into the first one. "Mary-Beth?"

A brunette girl seated inside shook her head. "*Non.*"

"Excuse me." Erik hurried to the next room, one eye tuned to the angry bouncer behind him. "Mary-Beth? It's Erik Petersson."

"All right, cockjaws, I've had enough of you." A large hand fell on Erik's shoulder.

"It's okay, Mo. Let him in," a woman said from farther down the hall.

The bouncer paused. "Dom? You expecting this creep?"

"Yes." Mary-Beth appeared in the hallway, her body covered by a white terry cloth robe. "Send him back. We won't be long."

Mo shoved Erik down the hallway, pointed at him. "You got ten minutes, bud."

Erik followed Mary-Beth into her change room, where she sat in front of a mirror and pulled out a makeup case. "Thanks," he said. "I appreciate –"

"Mr. Petersson, I don't mean to be rude, but my time is valuable," she said in a clipped tone. She pulled out an eyeliner pencil. "What did you want to ask me?"

"It's about Arielle." He sat in a small velour chair near the door.

Mary-Beth's gaze dropped from the mirror. "I'm sorry for your loss."

"She's not dead."

"That's not what I –"

"I know. It's all right." He held up a hand. "Everybody kind of reacts that way."

"I'm sorry. She seemed nice. Even after she…"

"Converted?"

Mary-Beth nodded.

"That's what I wanted to ask you about."

"I talked to the police already."

"I read the transcript."

"And? What else do you need to know?" she said and preened in the mirror.

"The details not in the interview, for starters. Whether she'd been seeing anyone new, what you knew about her friend Naomi, any changes around the time she converted. Did you spend much time with her?"

"Not really." She changed the eyeliner pen for a makeup brush and swept it under her eyebrows. "We did a few things together at the start of first semester, but then school and work got busy. Besides, I don't think she enjoyed herself."

"Why's that? Did you come here?" He cringed inside, told himself to relax.

Mary-Beth laid the brush on the table, her gaze cold as she contemplated him in the mirror. "Mr. Petersson, do you know how much I make in an average night?"

"I'm sorry, I didn't mean anything by that. I'm a little on edge."

"Guess."

Erik sighed. "Four or five hundred dollars?"

"Fridays and Saturdays, I earn between a thousand to twelve hundred – each – for approximately five hours work. That puts me through law school. Any idea how much I'd earn articling at a firm?"

"I'm guessing not that much."

"Good guess," she said. "Try half, at best. Dancing is also instructive. It's taught me to read people very well, which helps me be persuasive. Good qualities in a lawyer, don't you think?" She smiled at him in the mirror, an open smile that should have been warm, but did not reach her eyes.

"I'm sorry. I didn't mean to judge," he said. "Arielle didn't mention anything, and I wasn't expecting it."

She sighed. "It's not your fault. My anti-stripper hater rant is always beneath the surface." Her smile faded, the coldness did not. "I'm not surprised Arielle didn't mention it."

"Is it dangerous?"

"If you're stupid." She swiveled in her chair to face him. "About a month into the fall semester, I invited Arielle to come out with me," she said. "She was into the books a lot and seemed shy, and I thought going out would relax her. At first, everything went okay..." Small dimples appeared over her eyebrows as she frowned.

"But then?"

She blinked as if her thoughts had wandered. "We were at a local bar, La Distillerie. We met some guys from one of the frat houses who recognized me. They bought us some drinks, and I thought Arielle was having a good time. Then one of them started to get mouthy."

"Occupational hazard?"

"Kind of, but I'm usually either by myself or a guy like Mo is close by. If I don't like the situation, I walk."

"So what happened?"

"Arielle was farther down the bar with another guy from the frat house. When the asshole near me got louder, she came over to see what was happening. The guy she'd been talking to came over and told the drunk one to leave. Arielle asked if I wanted to go, but I said I just needed to freshen up. Like I said, I thought she was having a good time."

"Was she?"

Mary-Beth's eyes widened, and for a moment gave a glimpse of the young woman she was, instead of the one she portrayed in her photo. "I've asked myself that question a number of times, but I don't know anymore," she said. "On my way back from the bathroom, some more guys from the frat house stopped me."

"What did they want?"

"What all college boys want." A small, twisted smile came over her face. "We talked for a while, and one of them offered me a drink. I said no, and they got upset. When I tried to leave, they kept blocking me. They were being stupid, like it was one of their Frosh Week rituals. I got past eventually, but when I got to the bar, Arielle wasn't there."

"Where was she?"

"I don't know," she said.

"You don't know? When did you see her again?"

"I thought she'd gotten sick of waiting for me and left. I would've done the same."

"Was she in the room when you got back?" He wanted to shake her. Arielle would never have left somebody behind.

She shook her head.

"What did you do?"

"I went to a…friend's…house."

"Did you call her?"

"I texted her."

"Did she reply?"

She shook her head.

"Did you call anyone else? Campus security?"

She shook her head again.

He ran a hand over his face. "When was the next time you saw her?"

"A couple of days after –"

"A couple of days?" His voice rose.

"It's not what you think." Her shoulders slumped. "I had class the whole next day and was working that night. When I came back, I could see that she'd been there, but I didn't get a chance to talk to her. I was working the next night as well. One day turned into the next."

"Did you ask her what happened?"

She nodded.

"And? What did she say?"

"Nothing."

"She disappeared and said nothing?"

Mary-Beth worried the edge of her robe. "I asked if she'd hooked up with the guy she'd met. It didn't seem like she wanted to talk about it, so I dropped it. I invited her –"

The bouncer's body filled the frame of the door. "All right, bud. Time to leave."

"A few more minutes," Erik said over his shoulder.

"I said, you're done." The bouncer's hand dropped on Erik's shoulder.

"Mo –" Mary-Beth said.

Mo leaned over, his balance already sacrificed, although he didn't know it. Erik pictured how it would happen. He'd feint at Mo's head. Mo would flinch back and his outstretched arm would be vulnerable. Erik would seize Mo's wrist and it would be his. By reflex, Mo would pull his hand back and Erik would stand, move into the bouncer's space and capture Mo's elbow as well. Then he'd wrench on a wrist lock and Mo would be on the ground.

Instead, Erik remained in the chair, gaze leveled at Mary-Beth. "What happened next?"

"Mo, please, give me a minute." Her eyes made an appeal to the bouncer, then she turned back to Erik. She spoke fast, her words like gunfire. "I didn't see her much after that. She changed, even changed the way she dressed. Midway through first semester, that Naomi girl started to come by, but I didn't see much else, not until she disappeared."

Mo's fingers dug into Erik's shoulder, and he forced himself to concentrate on Mary-Beth. "Where did she meet Naomi?"

"Professor Sahraoui's study club," she said. "He runs a bible group. Naomi started bringing Arielle."

Erik frowned. "I see."

"Sometimes other people from that club would come by, but we never talked," Mary-Beth said. "They made me uncomfortable."

"Who were they? What were their names?"

"I don't know."

"Then how did you know they were in the study group?"

The twisted smile reappeared on her face. "This is Quebec, Mr. Petersson. Muslims stand out."

"I see," he said. "Which frat house was this boy from?"

"I don't know."

"Think."

"I really can't remember."

"Then take a guess."

She met his gaze, pulled the robe tighter to her body. "There are a lot. Delta Upsilon, maybe. Alpha Delta Phi. I think it had an Alpha in the name."

"Anything else that might help?"

Mary-Beth shook her head.

"Well, that's it, then. I'll let you get back to work." Erik stood. "Thank you."

Mary-Beth nodded, her eyes averted.

Erik glanced at Mo. "Happy?"

Mo grunted and pushed Erik toward the door.

"I hope you find her," Mary-Beth said.

Erik met her gaze. Underneath the eye shadow and the mascara and the lipstick, a young woman peered out, someone's daughter, maybe someone's sister. "Stay safe, Mary-Beth. I know a thing or two about places like this." He gestured over his shoulder at the bar. "It's not a courtroom. You play long enough, you always lose. The question is how much."

Erik nodded to Mary-Beth, then let Mo push him into the hallway, his mind already on to next steps. He had some more visiting to do.

* * *

RAQQA, SYRIA
03 MAY 15 – 1038 LOCAL

Arielle followed Umm Fatima out of the bright sun and into a dimly lit shop and waited for her eyes to adjust to the dark. A long, rectangular room took shape, computers on rickety desks, walls covered in chipped white paint, a ceramic-tiled floor decorated with elaborate cross patterns. The light in the room came from the computer monitors, a sign of how important this café must be to have a reliable power source, unlike most of the neighborhood.

"You're late." A man emerged from a smaller office deep in the room, his thick, unkempt beard halfway down his plump stomach. He sauntered up to Umm Fatima and then gazed up and down Arielle's body. "So, this is my new recruiter."

"Excuse me?" Arielle asked and glanced at Umm Fatima.

"That's right, part of the al-Khansaa Brigade." The man sat at a small, faux-wooden desk and nodded at Umm Fatima. "Like your mentor here."

"Careful, brother," Umm Fatima said. "One day your ego will overcome your value."

"What a dreadful thing to say." The man leaned back and patted his stomach. "And also ridiculous. As long as our glorious movement is in the internet age, I'll continue to be more valuable than front-line fighters." He leered at Arielle. "Although there'll always be a need for cannon-fodder, eh?"

Arielle's chest tightened. Mus'ab Saleh had left for the front lines three days ago, and she'd heard nothing from him. He'd told her it would be difficult to get in touch, but even still, with Naomi gone she hadn't realized how alone she was, or how much Mus'ab had filled that void. She'd carried the stress until the muscles in her neck and shoulders had grown stiff as if a load of bricks had been stacked on her back. "Who are you?" she asked.

"Abu Mustapha," the man said. "You'll be working for me."

"As a recruiter? I didn't think that was appropriate for a woman."

"Oh yes, we wouldn't want to interfere with the divinely appointed right of women to lead a sedentary lifestyle," Mustapha said in mock seriousness. He shook his head, then picked up a package of gum and popped one into his mouth. He grimaced. "If there's one thing I wish the Caliphate would change, it would be the smoking ban. Nicorette is truly horrible."

"It is *haram*," Umm Fatima said.

"Yes, yes, but chewing gum is perfectly fine." Abu Mustapha waved a hand as if to swat a fly. "And things are *haram* until we need them. That's the power of having the Imams on our side." He turned back to Arielle. "Luckily for you, it is written that women are permitted to serve outside the house, as long as the work is suitable for her abilities. And since women gossip, using social media is appropriate."

She frowned. "I don't even use social media."

"I'm sure you'll pick it up." He rested his meaty forearms on the desk. "I'm surprised you're not more excited. Most people here would sell out their neighbor for a chance to use the internet."

"I want to serve in the hospital."

"There are many who can work in the hospital," he said. "You're needed to recruit."

"I don't know how."

"I will teach you."

She bottled up a scream. Little more than a month ago, she'd extolled the virtues of an Islamic society in discussions at school, pointed out that the Prophet Muhammad, peace be upon him, had said, 'none of you will truly believe until you love for your brother what you love for yourself.' Yet any love in this place survived in spite of the Caliphate's violence and hypocrisy. The friendly smiles at prayers, the market vendors who gave food to the homeless – food she knew they couldn't spare – these wells of kindness existed in constant danger of being snuffed out by those who claimed to defend the faith. There was no way she would dupe others into making the same mistake she'd made. She wracked her brain for a way out of this situation.

"What does the al-Khansaa Brigade have to do with recruiting?" she asked.

"Like most of us, it does whatever it's told," Abu Mustapha said, his mouth open as he worked his gum. "They were created to enforce female morality, but have expanded into propaganda, social media, and now recruiting, which is what you'll be doing."

She turned to Umm Fatima. "I'm not –"

"Hey, look at me." Abu Mustapha smacked the desk. "You seem to think you have a choice in this. You don't. I will not be disrespected by a woman, least of all a western one." He pointed at Umm Fatima. "Tell her."

Umm Fatima stared at him with her expressionless eyes.

"Tell her!" Spittle flew from Abu Mustapha's mouth.

"There is no choice." Umm Fatima's monotone voice gave no comfort. "You will do it."

"Or else what?" A smirk twisted Abu Mustapha's face.

"Or else?" Arielle asked.

Umm Fatima paused, then looked at Arielle. "Or you will join your friend."

"Naomi?" Arielle asked and glanced at Umm Fatima. "Where is she?"

"Satisfying the lions at the front." Abu Mustapha leered across the desk. "And she's lucky at that. The life of a whore is too good for you western bitches."

Arielle's mouth dropped. "You're lying. She's in hospital recovering from her injuries. That's what you told me." She put a hand on Umm Fatima's leg. "I've asked every day, and that's what you've told me."

Abu Mustapha chuckled. "Of course she did. She's the one who got rid of her."

Arielle's eyes watered. "Why?" she asked. It couldn't be, and yet Umm Fatima's dead, black gaze offered all the confirmation she needed. "I hate you," she said. "I will never work here."

Umm Fatima slapped Arielle across the face. Slapped her again from the other direction and knocked her from her chair.

"That's your choice," Abu Mustapha said, "but defy me and the best possible outcome will be to end up like your friend. As for the worst..." his eyes flickered to Umm Fatima. "I'm sure you get the idea."

Arielle's cheeks stung. She wanted to curl up in a ball, but she knew they wouldn't stop, they would continue to treat her like chattel. She could not work for this greasy, arrogant man, could not fool more people to this sham of Islam. But nor could she refuse. She would open the veins in her arm before she ended up like Naomi.

In silence, Arielle struggled back into her chair, blinked back tears and dipped her head to Abu Mustapha. "By Allah, the most wise, I look forward to serving."

Abu Mustapha smiled. "Good. Tomorrow, your training begins."

Arielle dipped her eyes. "As you say, brother." *And if God has any justness in his heart, he will help me find a way to escape.*

CHAPTER SEVEN
ASCENSION'S DAWN

MONTREAL, QUEBEC
05 MAY 15 – 1040 LOCAL

Erik leaned against a short stone wall that bordered a downtown park and stared at the University of Montreal's Islamic Library. The converted Catholic church held the office of Dr. Omar Sahraoui, adjunct professor of Islamic studies, an outspoken critic of Islamophobia, and one-time – in truth, ongoing – terrorism suspect. Part of Erik wanted to stalk into the building, yank Sahraoui into the nearest office and force-feed him questions until the man caved. An attractive idea, but foolhardy and so he leaned on the wall and did his best to act as if sipping his latte was his most pressing care in the world.

He needed to know if Sahraoui was under surveillance. The man had been detained for two years after the 9/11 terrorist attacks and had then fought the security certificate process and won against a government appeal at the Supreme Court to have him deported back to his native Algeria. Since his release, he'd continued to polarize, and every few years an accusation would arise that he used his university post to proselytize, or as his detractors would say, radicalize. No, best not to rush in.

Erik pulled out his phone and called Jordan.

"Hello?"

"What's the current situation with Omar Sahraoui?"

"I love you too, buddy. No small talk?"

Erik smiled. "Sorry. How are you? Is the family okay? And the girlfriend? Theresa, right? How's she? Or is it Tara?"

"It's Trista."

"Ah, shit. I can never remember from week to week. They all seem to start with T."

"Theresa was a month ago."

"There was a Tiffany as well, wasn't there?"

"She was the one – you know what? Forget it, you already ruined the moment," Jordan said. "And I've never heard of Omar Sahraoui."

"No? Teaches at Montreal University?"

"Nope."

"Won a multi-million-dollar payout for wrongful detainment?"

"Still no."

"I think he dated your mom."

A snort of laughter came through the line. "Oh, you mean that Omar Sahraoui. Yeah, that guy's a dick."

"My mistake, I should have been more clear." Erik scanned a walkway through the park, studied a young man who looked like someone he'd seen in Le Cabaret. "Anything to suggest he might be involved in recruitment?"

"Let me check, but I don't think so."

While he waited, Erik tracked the young man. They made eye contact and then the man glanced away and continued heading for the cluster of buildings around the Islamic Library.

"Aside from the security certificate stuff, there's not much recent," Jordan said. "A couple of students in the mosque he attends tried to go to the Middle East, but no links shown. He's on record saying he disapproved of their actions and tried to convince them otherwise."

"I'm sure."

"Last thing is a note about the unusual frequency of students in the Islamic studies program who both attend his mosque and also have links to the drug trade. And that's all I can access."

"What constitutes unusual?"

"Looks like...two or three."

"Think that could be linked to what we talked about earlier?"

"Where there's smoke, there's fire, I guess. But in this case, I don't think it means much. A good number of young people in Montreal get involved in drugs, then stop their downward spiral by converting to Islam. Some of the youth detention centers even have programs."

"I thought that was only in prisons," Erik said.

"One of the teams would have access to more info." The other side of the line went quiet. "Should I be wondering why you're asking these questions?"

"I'm going to interrogate him."

"That would be something I didn't want to know."

"Relax, I just have a couple of questions for him."

"This is why I shouldn't joke around with you because you're no good at it." Jordan's voice sounded strained. "You should talk to Stephanie before you do that."

"You think so?"

"She specifically told me to tell her if I talked to you, so yeah, I'm about as sure as it gets."

"Then I'd better be proactive." Erik smiled. "Thanks." He hung up and thought about what Jordan had said and then dialed Stephanie. The line was busy, so he gave it a couple of minutes then redialed.

"Please tell me you're not planning on talking to Sahraoui," Stephanie was saying seconds later.

"Why?" Erik asked. "Is he under surveillance?"

"Not yet," she said and her voice had a note of hesitation. "But he'll file a complaint. He does that every time we talk to him."

"How many times has he been questioned?"

"Enough to know how he'll react. His position with the university is very tentative, so he fights hard if he feels threatened."

"Good to know," he said. "I got a tip that Naomi and Arielle went to his study group. I've got some questions for him and wanted to make sure I wouldn't interfere with one of our teams."

"Talking to him is a bad idea."

"Aren't you the one who suggested I dig around?" He paced in front of the stone wall.

"That didn't include talking to Sahraoui," she said.

"It's not like I'm not going to rough him up," he said. "I'm just a father asking about his missing daughter."

Stephanie sighed. "Can you wait?"

"For what?"

"I'll talk to Wiggins and see about getting him to support questioning Sahraoui."

"I can handle myself."

"It would be better if the interview was official."

He ran a hand over his head and stared at the Islamic Library. Stephanie's approach made sense, but it would take time, and it might not even be possible to convince Wiggins.

"Still there?" Stephanie asked.

"I don't like it, even though you're right. We're wasting time."

"I'll put together a briefing for Wiggins right after this."

"While you do that, I'll see if I can find out more about his pattern of life. If it's been awhile since he's been under surveillance, he might have changed things up a bit."

She sighed. "Whatever you do, do not make contact. Understood?"

"Absolutely."

"I'll call you later," she said and hung up.

Erik tucked away his phone. Stephanie was a great boss, but her experience in field work was limited. Time spent on reconnaissance was seldom wasted, and while she worked on Wiggins, he'd find out what he could about Sahraoui. And if he happened to run into the good professor, well a few questions from a concerned dad wouldn't hurt, right?

He smiled and headed in the direction of the library.

* * *

KOBANE, SYRIA
05 MAY 15 – 1803 LOCAL

Crack!

Mus'ab Saleh ducked as a bullet split the air nearby. Fractions of a second later, the thump of the rifle blast followed. Laughter erupted from behind.

"Getting closer, eh brother?" Ahmed's face was marred by a sneer.

Mus'ab crawled deeper into the ruins of the abandoned building his section had been tasked to defend.

"You heard the delay between the crack and the thump? That means he's far, maybe 500 meters," Ahmed said from a makeshift table he'd erected from bricks. A sheen of sweat glistened on his dark, olive skin and a black bandanna on his head kept his dark, scraggly mane in check. "But don't worry, there haven't been any ricochets yet, so they have room for improvement."

Mus'ab held his rifle and leaned against a wall. On his left was the remains of a window. He shuffled to the side of the window frame, got ready to take a shooting position.

"I wouldn't do that," Ahmed said between sips from an energy drink. "Those dogs may be terrible shots, but even they can't miss someone who's sky-lined. But go ahead if you want. I'll keep that bride of yours satisfied when I get back to Raqqa."

Mus'ab paused, then peeked through the window to get a glimpse of their surroundings. When he'd come to the Caliphate, it had been at the height of its military prowess. They'd pushed north to the Turkish border and east into Iraq, came within a hundred miles of Baghdad. Their success seemed divine. When Tikrit and Mosul had fallen, the Caliphate captured tanks, artillery, thousands of the American's HMMVWs, enough to conquer the entire Levant.

Then the glorious advance had bogged down.

His section had been tasked to regain the momentum. They'd been assigned to a bunch of rubble near the Syrian / Turkish border, in what had been a vibrant village three short years ago. Here, they fought the Kurds, so they thought, although it was possible they were fighting one of the other rebel groups – al-Nusra, Ahrar al-Sham – since they all fought for control of the same ground. All Mus'ab wanted was to get out alive.

Mus'ab ducked beneath the window and searched for another, safer position. This situation was stupid. He was a student, not a soldier. He should have listened to his parents when they'd said the Caliphate was a sham, but his religious conviction had been so resolute. His beliefs, unassailable in the safety of London, had lasted until his first battle, when he'd pissed himself during a mortar barrage. Nothing had worked out as he'd hoped. Until Arielle. "You'll never touch my wife."

Ahmed snorted and took another sip of his energy drink. Ex-military, Ahmed Sallum had struggled between petty crime and half-hearted efforts to succeed as a rapper before he'd embraced the Caliphate. In Syria he had flourished, reveling in the lack of rules and savagery to become a rising commander.

Mus'ab wasn't sure who he feared more, the Kurds or Ahmed. If there was one good thing, it was that the violence that made Ahmed a mockery of how Mus'ab understood Islam, also let the section flourish in battle. During Mus'ab's first time on the front lines, he'd frozen in the face of three Kurdish fighters. He'd rounded a corner and stumbled across the men in an alleyway. They'd reacted first, brought their guns to bear, and then Ahmed had appeared on a flank and mowed down two of the three before they even knew he was there. As the third man oriented to the new threat, Ahmed had taken his fighting knife and stabbed it deep into the man's neck, his face blank as dark blood spurted over his arm. No, in many ways Ahmed was the true embodiment of the Caliphate.

Another crack split the air. Bricks shattered on the wall opposite from where Mus'ab crouched and the shooting from outside increased. He cringed and hunched his shoulders, tried to make himself as small as possible.

"They'll come soon." Ahmed stood and shouldered his rifle. "Get ready."

"Where are the others?" Mus'ab asked.

"On our flanks, where they've been for the last hour," Ahmed said. "We'll chew those dogs up if they ever come."

From behind them came the sound of footsteps along ground-up bricks and they both turned. Ahmed raised the butt of his rifle to his shoulder and drifted to a corner where he could observe whoever approached. Mus'ab gripped his own rifle tighter, concerned that Ahmed seemed to think their lines of communication might have been breached.

The footsteps grew louder and then Bilal al Noury slunk into the room. Al Noury worked as a runner for the sector commander, and if he was here, it wouldn't be good news.

Mus'ab caught al Noury's attention and nodded at the open window. "Stay away from it."

Al Noury contemplated the window, then crouched beside Ahmed, who'd dropped his rifle from his shoulder and held it by the pistol grip, the barrel almost dragging on the ground.

"What news?" Ahmed glowered at al Noury. Up until a few months ago, their force had communicated with hand-held radios. In the last few weeks, however, a no-radio policy had been implemented on suspicion that the enemy was intercepting their transmissions. Ahmed had argued to let them – all the better to feed them lies – but he'd been overruled. "Are we attacking?"

"Pull back," al Noury said. "We'll regroup at the previous line of defense."

Mus'ab frowned. Things must be very bad indeed.

"Retreat?" Ahmed said. "Has Qassim lost his nerve?"

"Just pull back," al Noury said. "Qassim wants to figure out another way to come at this. Move now." Without waiting for a reply, al Noury spun and returned the way he'd come.

"Qassim al Shishani is a coward." Ahmed stomped to the center of the room and smashed a fist into the makeshift table. "If I spit in his face, he'd say it was raining. We should attack."

Mus'ab glanced up. "Isn't it a good thing we'll live to fight another day?" He wanted nothing more than to flee this room, this hateful existence. If it was up to him, he wouldn't even stop at the next line of defense. He'd go all the way back to Raqqa, or across the border into Turkey or his native Lebanon. He shoved the thought away. He couldn't abandon Arielle.

Ahmed stalked closer, his face red. "Our strength is our savagery," he said. "If we pull back, the enemy gains hope. An attack where we all died would still be better than a retreat."

The enemy fire intensified. Mus'ab crouched lower, stared up at Ahmed. "How is it better if we're all dead?"

"We'd inspire countless others to take our places," Ahmed said. "We've never retreated. Our reputation is worth more than a thousand tanks. I spit on Qassim and al Noury and the cowards." With a yell, Ahmed thrust his rifle through the window frame and began to shoot.

"Watch –"

Ahmed's head exploded.

Unable to look away, Mus'ab watched as Ahmed's limp body crumpled to the ground. The enemy gunfire built up even more. Bullets smacked into the building in a rising crescendo and drove Mus'ab to cower on the ground.

"Merciful God, protect me." Mus'ab crawled to the exit, in the direction al Noury had gone. Bullets filled the air, struck the walls and showered him with fragments of plaster and dust. It was hard to see, and he repeated his prayer as he groped along the floor. He sensed a wall to his front and by touch, he hand-railed along until he tumbled into the hallway.

This was madness.

He rolled onto his back amid the rubble, eyes clenched shut, hands over his ears. Ahmed the Indestructible was dead. He'd barely finished the thought when the air seemed to split, the explosion so close he felt the shock wave more than he heard it. The walls shook, and the blast wind tore his breath from him. He opened his mouth to scream and was flung against the far wall of the hallway and his open mouth filled with dust and dirt. Parts of the ceiling tumbled to the floor and covered him, and sunlight streamed through newly formed holes and cut laser-like beams through the dust-filled air.

Mus'ab groaned, the sound loud inside his head. A coalition jet must have scored a hit. It occurred to him that Ahmed would have said an attack would soon follow and sure enough, the gunfire escalated even more, this time mixed with the shouts of men.

Get out, get out, get out. He went to stand and felt himself trapped. Panic blasted through his brain. He flailed, freed himself from a pile of rubble that covered his legs. He regained his feet, careened headlong into the ruined building and into the street beyond.

He reached an intersection and leaned against a wall to catch his breath. The other section members had been to his right. He raced down the alleyway until he came to a corner where he was confronted by a rubbled wall of bricks and mortar. *Shit.* The entire section must be dead. He stumbled back to the intersection, slowed to a stop. Yells and shouts came from behind him. Or was it to his front? It was difficult to tell, difficult to keep his bearings.

He was alone. Al Noury and Qassim would assume that they had all died. Nobody would come for him. He had to move, had to escape.

He peered over his shoulder, back to the building where Ahmed's body lay. The sun had begun to set, and it occurred to him that Ahmed's body would not be buried before the end of the day, maybe not at all. Ahmed's spirit would be left to suffer until the end of days, and this would be what waited if Mus'ab continued this fight.

Coughs racked his body, and he bit his hand to muffle the sound. When the fit subsided, scarlet flecks had intermingled with the dirt on his hand. Wild thoughts raced through his head. He could flee, head back to London. No, he would surrender to the Kurds. They'd give him medical treatment at the very least.

He shook his head, willed himself to think. The Kurds might kill him as easily as accept his surrender. Even if he lived, he'd be imprisoned, tortured. Worse, if he was wrong, if the enemy was a competing rebel group, beheading would be the most likely reward.

An explosion came from behind, and he cringed, clutched his ears as smoke and dust poured into the alleyway. Whoever the enemy was, they'd blown into the building he'd just fled. If he was going to surrender, he needed to decide now, or he'd get shot as he retreated. And then he knew. Above all else, he had to live, for one reason.

Arielle.

Ears ringing, he pictured her face, their few nights together. Like him, she had learned the truth of the Caliphate, and he knew that truth would be hard for her. She would need him, and he'd taken a vow. If he surrendered, he would have abandoned his family not once, but twice. Men's voices rose in sharp commands from inside the building, and Mus'ab took one last look and then ran.

* * *

MONTREAL, QUEBEC
05 MAY 15 – 1420 LOCAL

Erik walked through what had been the nave of a Catholic church, now part of the main library of the Center for Islamic Studies. On the far side, in an old tower that housed the journal section, Dr. Sahraoui would be in a tutorial session, at least according to the schedule outside his office. Erik's gaze roamed the rows of books, the multitude of Islamic decorations on the walls. He wondered if he'd find a copy of Salman Rushdie's *Satanic Verses* tucked away on a shelf.

Unlikely.

These days freedom of speech issues seemed to be limited to freedom from being offended, like the Dutch cartoons of the prophet Muhammad. It was okay to call for the cartoonist's head, but God forbid the cartoons had been printed in the first place. Erik shook his head and headed for the journal section. Dr. Sahraoui no doubt knew a lot about the exploitation of western freedoms, but right now that wasn't Erik's concern. Finding Arielle was, even if he had to ignore what Stephanie had said.

Still, the thought drew a pang of guilt. Stephanie was right, a meeting with Sahraoui was risky. If he complained to the police, it could set off a chain of events that might cost Erik his job. But the risk would be worth it if Sahraoui knew who'd helped Arielle plan her trip to Syria. Plus, he hadn't talked to Sahraoui yet. He could always back out, although he was confident he could steer any conversation to a harmless spot.

Erik passed into the tower, a squat, two-story building that had been converted into an open atrium. In the mid-day sun, the space was well-lit. A large circular table took up the center of the room, surrounded by several students and presided over by a familiar face with a trimmed beard. Sahraoui. Erik tucked himself into an alcove near the entrance and studied Sahraoui as he moved from student to student, here and there stopping to offer a few words. One of the students was the boy Erik had seen outside, the one he'd thought had been in the strip club.

After fifteen minutes or so, Sahraoui gave a small speech in a voice too quiet for Erik to make out. When he was done, the students began to file out. The strip club boy was one of the last to leave, and before he did, he paused to exchange a few words with another man who had an athlete's body, a shaved head, and a thick, dark beard. The boy handed a package to the man, and then they left together, passing Erik without any recognition. Soon, Sahraoui was the only one who remained, occupied with several journals that had been left on the table. As Erik stepped into the room, Sahraoui looked at him.

"May I help you?" Sahraoui spoke softly, much softer than Erik had expected.

"I hope so." Erik extended his hand. "Dr. Sahraoui?"

"Please, I'm no doctor. Omar is fine." Sahraoui made no move to take

Erik's hand. "And you are?"

"My name is Erik Petersson. I was hoping to talk, if you had time."

Sahraoui gathered several journals from the table. "My secretary will be happy to make an appointment during office hours."

"I just need a few minutes." Erik gestured to some chairs in an anteroom. "Can we sit?"

"What is this about?"

"Arielle Petersson."

"Are you with the police?" Sahraoui clutched the journals to his chest.

Erik held up his hands. "No, no, I'm not representing the police."

"I don't believe I can help you, sir," Sahraoui said. He stepped past Erik toward the exit. "Good day to you."

"I'm Arielle's father."

Sahraoui paused, halfway out the door.

Erik cleared his throat. "Dr. Sahraoui, just over a month ago Arielle called me from Frankfurt to say she was on her way to the Middle East. That's the last I've heard from her." He held his hands out low, as if trying to calm a wild animal. "Arielle's roommate told me she'd come to your study group and I was hoping you might have heard her say something."

"I've already spoken to the police," Sahraoui said over his shoulder.

"Please. My daughter left with no explanation, and I'm trying to understand why." Erik stepped closer. "Can you help me?"

Sahraoui turned. "All right, Mr. Petersson. Although I'm not sure you'll learn much more than what I've already said." He sat at one of the chairs in the anteroom.

"I didn't realize you'd been interviewed." Erik took a seat across from Sahraoui. "The police gave me some information, but they didn't mention that."

Sahraoui snorted. "It's standard procedure whenever someone from Montreal radicalizes," he said. "It would appear as if my being cleared on a security certificate was more for appearances than anything else."

"Then you knew Arielle?"

"She first came to my study group in November," Sahraoui said. "I was opposed to it at first, but she seemed...troubled. She seemed to find solace in the sessions, so I let her continue."

"Why did it bother you?"

"As much as it's depicted otherwise, I don't run prayer groups." He peered over the top of his glasses. "I run study groups. There's a difference. Attendees should be registered in the Islamic studies program, which your daughter was not. From time to time, I invite non-students to discuss issues in the forum, but there aren't many exceptions."

"I see. You said she seemed troubled?"

Sahraoui nodded. "She was very quiet, at first, and wouldn't leave her friend's side."

"Naomi."

"Yes."

"And was Naomi in the Islamic studies program?"

"Of course. Naomi made a personal appeal to let your daughter attend, and it seemed to work. Your daughter grew more confident, even more so after she took the *shahada*, but even then, it was rare for her to talk to the men in the study group."

"Did Arielle convert with Naomi?"

"Reverted, actually," Sahraoui said and nodded. "I witnessed her *shahada* myself."

"But you said this was just a study group." Erik struggled to keep the heat from his voice. It annoyed him that Sahraoui had known of Arielle's conversion before he did, doubly so to have the man lecture him on semantics like the belief that people are born with a natural faith in God and thus revert to Islam instead of convert.

Sahraoui frowned. "If you're assuming there was something duplicitous, there was no such thing. She asked me a number of times before I agreed."

"Why?"

"Revert or convert, people should be rational when they accept Allah as the one, true god. Not grasping for him out of desperation as if for a short-term pain-killer."

"I thought –"

"Very many people think, and yet very few get beyond considering Islam as anything but a source of problems instead of a salve for the troubles of our worldly life."

"Pardon?"

Sahraoui drummed his fingers on the arm rest of the chair. "Your daughter lived on campus, correct?"

Erik nodded.

"And have you spent much time on campus? Enough to get a feel for campus culture?"

"I'm not sure how that's relevant."

"No?" Sahraoui asked. "Not even some of the finer aspects?

"Like what?"

"Materialism for starters, and glorification of celebrity. Next, I would mention the over-sexualization and objectification of women, or perhaps the abandonment of morals."

Unbidden, Mary-Beth's calling card popped into Erik's mind, and his face grew hot. "Arielle didn't talk much about school." Except that wasn't the complete truth. She had, at first. But around the end of September, once classes had gotten underway in earnest and her workload had built up, she'd mentioned less and less.

"A shame, because all of those things exist here," Sahraoui said, "and I can tell you they're the proverbial tip of the iceberg, because what's interesting and tragic at the same time is that this institution of learning is simply a microcosm of broader society. Some aspects are magnified or lessened as the case may be, but in general, it reflects society writ large."

Erik shifted in his chair. "It might not be perfect, but it's better than the alternatives."

"Spoken from a position of privilege."

"Right." Erik dropped his gaze and bit back a retort. "Listen, Dr. Sahraoui –"

"Omar."

"Of course. Omar." Erik seemed to recall an old report that had said Sahraoui was difficult to question. He'd disregarded it at the time, but he was beginning to appreciate the sentiment. "What I'm trying to figure out is who convinced Arielle that going to Syria was a good idea and then helped her go."

Sahraoui sighed. "I find your assumption that your daughter did all of this against her will fascinating. Do you find it hard to accept she might have voluntarily decided to accept God and fulfill her obligations?"

"I find it surprising, yes," Erik said. "Arielle and I were always open with each other. If she was considering something like this, I would have expected her to tell me."

"Maybe she suspected you wouldn't have supported her decision."

"This isn't about me." Erik blurted out the words and then ran a hand over his mouth. "I have my faults as a father. We all do, but right now my concern is getting Arielle out of Syria. To do that, I need to know who put the idea in her head and helped her get there so I can see if they can tell me where she is and how to get in touch with her. I'm not here to have a philosophical argument with you about Islam and western society."

"Can't you see those issues are linked?" Sahraoui asked. "Is it so hard to believe your daughter might have come to this university with certain expectations, and when those expectations were not met and were instead shattered, that she decided to open herself to a new experience?"

Erik rubbed the bridge of his nose. "You'll have to explain yourself."

Sahraoui frowned. "How about the treatment of women? Western thought would have us believe that women are equal and yet, beneath the surface, this is manifestly a lie. Women are treated as possessions, no matter how much they're allowed to earn, or what they can wear. And even in those examples, we cannot forget irregularities such as the inconvenient and largely undiscussed wage gap that continues to persist between genders. In Islam, women are treated as equals."

Erik shook his head. "Equals who are forced to cover their bodies and not allowed to vote. Some equality."

"Women choose for themselves to follow *hijab*. They are not compelled."

"Except in places like Syria. Or places with honor-killings, like Afghanistan."

"Of course, there are variances in practice across the *ummah*, but I can tell you that in general, Islam strives for equality while also recognizing the differences between men and women." Sahraoui held up a finger. "We should not create artificial equality. This is not what Allah Almighty intended, it is what man intended. In Islam, women are treated with respect, that is why they cover themselves and conduct prayers separately, to protect themselves from men's sexual desires. In this, Allah the Most Wise knows best about the fallibility and weaknesses of people."

"Is that what you told Arielle?"

A polite smile came over Sahraoui's face. "Mr. Petersson, earlier you admitted to having spent little time on campus. Tell me then, are you aware of the number of rapes and sexual assaults that have occurred on campus grounds over the past year? Over the past five years?"

"No."

"Are you willing to guess?" Sahraoui asked. "No? It's a lot. Would you say that this is reflective of a culture that respects women? Where each day, the best and brightest fear for their safety at a so-called institute of higher learning?"

Erik's eyes narrowed. "Her roommate mentioned an incident with one of the fraternities."

Sahraoui removed his glasses and held them in his lap. "I know from her friend that something happened with a boy. As for your daughter, she would say nothing, and yet it is no wonder she was looking for an alternative view of the relationship between men and women than what is espoused here on campus."

"Do you know this guy's name?"

Sahraoui shook his head.

"What he looks like? What frat house he's in?"

Sahraoui sighed and began to clean his glasses with a cloth pulled from his pocket. "I believe it was Alpha Kappa Omega."

Erik made a quick note. "Did you tell anybody about this?"

"Mr. Petersson, it's possible your daughter's roommate was mistaken. Although there have been many complaints about boys in that fraternity, there are others that are no different."

"You're a professor. You have a duty to report."

"Why would I? For it to be dismissed as baseless?" Sahraoui's eyes flashed. "And to what end, so Arielle could suffer the indignity of a sham investigation? Do you have any idea how difficult it is to prove sexual assault when the case is 'he-said, she-said' and alcohol is involved? Who do you think the police side with in those cases?" Sahraoui drew a breath, replaced his glasses. "What's important is that Arielle was in pain when I met her. Islam provided her solace, so for that reason, I assisted her." His gaze darted to the entrance of the anteroom, where the athletic, bald man who'd been in the study group now stood. "And now if you'll excuse me, I have another commitment."

"Do you know who could have helped her get to Syria?"

"I'm sorry, Mr. Petersson." Sahraoui stood. "I wish you the best of luck, but I fear you will need to confront some hard truths before you'll be able to accept your daughter's decision."

Erik rose to his feet as well. "Wait. I have more questions."

Sahraoui smiled. "Some other time, perhaps. With lawyers present?"

"I told you, I'm not an investigator. I'm just trying to –"

"Find your daughter, of course. Perhaps you should direct any further questions to the police. Good day to you." Sahraoui nodded and took a few steps toward the exit, then stopped to peer over his shoulder. "I do hope you find what you're looking for with Arielle." He studied Erik's face for several seconds more – seemed about to say something else – then continued on his way. The athletic man glared at Erik, then followed the professor.

A maelstrom of thoughts and emotions whirled inside. What had Sahraoui been talking about? He had more questions than answers, but he knew he'd already pushed his luck. He'd need to find another way.

* * *

MOSUL, IRAQ
06 MAY 15 – 0912 LOCAL

The smoldering pile of ashes cast off enough heat to make Abu Noor al Kanadi shield his face. To his front, the pock-marked windows and bullet-riddled walls of the Mosul Central Library paid silent testament to the travesty. The building remained standing, but to no purpose. All the books had been removed, dumped in burn heaps that dotted the streets outside the building.

Al Kanadi poked at the edge of one pile and unearthed a smoldering manuscript, which he bent to pick up. The pages were covered in Arabic script and the sheets fluttered to the ground one by one as he flipped through what remained. Hundreds of years of history and knowledge, lost.

Footsteps crunched on the gravel behind him, stopped at a respectful distance. Mamdouh.

"This is barbaric," al Kanadi said. "All this knowledge, gone for all time."

Mamdouh shrugged. "These books promote infidelity and call for disobeying Allah, the All-Knowing. They must be destroyed."

Al Kanadi tossed the remains of the charred book back into the ashes. "There are times I wonder how a movement with such disregard for knowledge can ever prevail."

"Not all knowledge," Mamdouh said. "Only knowledge of the infidels. It is un-Islamic and must be cleansed."

"And the artifacts? They're un-Islamic too?"

"This is why you'll never be accepted into the inner circle," Mamdouh said. "With respect, of course."

Al Kanadi snorted and stared up at the library's imposing bulk. Rumor had it the building sat atop miles of underground caves, which if true, would prove useful. He needed a location to work from in Mosul and Western forces would hesitate to bomb a heritage site such as this library. But that didn't excuse destroying the books. "With respect, the inner circle accepts me because I get results. Do you have something for me?"

"A brother in Montreal is concerned about operations there. Someone was asking questions."

"So? Why bring this to me?"

"I asked that question." Mamdouh's tone suggested he was insulted. "It's the father of one of our recent travelers."

"Which one?"

"Petersson. He questioned the professor."

"Interesting, but not unusual. Again, why bring this to me? The cell should be able to handle it. Breaking silence needlessly exposes us to risk." He might have added it also wasted valuable time.

"Sayyid feels the man is a threat."

"Let the professor run interference like he always does. That's what we use him for." Al Kanadi headed for the library's entrance.

"In this case, it would appear the professor knew more than was good for him. Sayyid fears he gave this man information that might lead him to our other operations."

"I see." Indeed, that would be annoying. The fool. Things in Montreal were just getting off the ground. The smuggling routes would survive any sort of investigation – his partners had been running them for years – but the recruiting efforts had barely begun to bear fruit. He crouched and rummaged through some loose pages in the library's doorway. There had to be a way to both remove a potential threat and perhaps also bring the battle to foreign shores.

"Can we give the police something else to think about?" he wondered aloud. "Maybe cut away some low-hanging fruit?"

"What did you have in mind?"

Al Kanadi closed his eyes. As much as he delegated, tried to promote initiative, their default was to turn to him for the answers. Perhaps if Mamdouh had read a book or two, he'd have more creativity. "Create some noise, give them something else to look at." He glanced up. "Ideally it would get this father to back off and give the police something else to investigate. I'm not doing our brother's work for him. Sayyid knows the intent, tell him to sort out the details."

"As you wish." Mamdouh placed a hand over his heart and then walked away.

Al Kanadi's fingers traced a path through the dirt and ashes until they came to rest on a yellowed piece of parchment. It was a risk to let Sayyid and Mamdouh handle things, but micro-managing wasn't the answer. Trust was the foundation that let many become one, let them seize opportunities in line with one plan, Allah's plan.

And his own, of course. Whatever Sayyid planned, if it failed, it would be easy to shift blame to the cell. If, on the other hand, it succeeded, well, in that case, al Kanadi would be the first to take the credit.

CHAPTER EIGHT
THE DARK OF THE NIGHT

Once, in a different life as an airborne trooper, long before he'd met Audray, hard-partying had been a way of life for Erik. In the shacks he'd called home on Base Petawawa, testosterone-fueled drinking had led to many crazy nights, nights that seemed tame if they didn't end in a fight or in parts of the barracks being destroyed. They'd shot rifles and thrown pilfered Army pyrotechnics inside the buildings, even dodged crossbow bolts, but they'd always fixed what they broke. A lot of those memories were gone now – he'd been in black-out mode half the time anyway – but in all his partying, he couldn't remember the slimy feeling that covered his skin as he stood outside the Alpha Kappa Omega frat house.

From outside, the three-story, brick-faced building appeared stately, the fraternity's Greek letters carved into red blocks beneath the second-floor windows. Inside, though, was a different story from what he could see from the doorway. He stepped to one side as a young woman with short blonde hair and long, dangling earrings staggered out the door, the reek of stale beer and smoke close behind. She clutched a sweater around her shoulders and stumbled down the stairs, righted herself on the path that led to the sidewalk.

"Are you all right?" Erik asked and reached out to help steady the woman.

The woman flinched, held a hand to her forehead and shuffled off.

Erik exchanged a glance with Stephanie. "Maybe you should wait outside."

Her lips were pressed together in a thin line. "I didn't come here to stand around."

"In that case, I'm glad you're here." He'd tracked down the frat house in hours, but in that time, Sahraoui's comments about campus culture had festered and what had been a spark of anger inside Erik had grown. He'd bided his time, observed the house and done his research while he waited for the tightness to leave his chest. When it hadn't, when he realized his first impulse was to break in the door and shake down every person he saw, he'd asked Stephanie to come along. She'd make sure things didn't get out of hand.

"I'm a little surprised you didn't call Jordan."

"I thought about it, but figured we'd just get each other worked up."

"Good decision." A slight smile touched her lips. "Besides, I'm pretty good at getting people to talk."

"Why are you doing this, Stephanie?"

"I asked you to call me before you did anything stupid, remember?"

"I know that, but you didn't have to come out here. Especially after I talked to Sahraoui."

"Which was incredibly dumb," she said. "But this isn't just about terrorism anymore. If I were a parent, I'd want answers too. And if I were a daughter..." Her gaze dropped. "I guess I'd want to know that my dad cared enough to do what you're doing." She shook her head. "Besides, as you've already shown, if I'd said no, you would go in anyways and who knows what would happen then."

"Thank-you," he said and drew a deep breath. "Well, no time like the present." He opened the door and entered. Just inside was a large whiteboard with rules drawn in multi-color marker, edicts like, "Don't be a cockblock," "Don't hog the shisha," and the underlined phrase that, "Violators will be bitch slapped!!!" He stepped past, boots sticking to the wooden floor. "Hello?" He poked his head into a living room. "Anyone here?"

A young man's head rose from a tired couch to peek over a coffee table covered with red plastic cups, and empty booze and pop bottles. "What do you want?" The man reached for the hose of a shisha pipe.

"I'm Erik Petersson," he said and walked into the room. "About a month ago my daughter ran off. Her roommate said someone from this fraternity might know what happened, and I wanted to ask a few questions."

The man settled back into the couch. "Maybe tomorrow," he said, staring at the television. "I'm busy right now."

"*Ayoye*," Stephanie said from behind him.

Erik turned. "What is it?"

Stephanie nodded in the direction of the television. On the screen, a small woman with short, blond hair lay on a threadbare mattress. Her body rocked back and forth as a muscular, naked man thrust away between her legs. Several other men stood in a circle, visible from the chest down, most with drinks in hand. The view bobbled as the camera panned the crowd and then a second naked man came into view near the woman's head, his cock in hand which he used to slap the woman in the face. Erik studied the woman, her eyes closed, so much like the woman who'd passed them on the stairway, even down to the long, dangling earrings.

Heat rose in his cheeks. He caught Stephanie's attention and nodded at the door, a questioning look on his face. When she shook her head, he clenched his jaw and squared off to the young man. "This won't take long," he said.

The shisha pipe bubbled as the man took a long drag.

Erik reached across the coffee table and plucked the hose from the man's hand. "Arielle Petersson. You heard of her?"

The man flinched, and a semblance of clarity crossed his foggy eyes. "Arielle..."

"Try to remember," Erik said, "I'd appreciate it."

"What would you appreciate?" a man asked from across the room. "More importantly, who the fuck are you?"

Erik glanced at what appeared to be a doorway to the kitchen and took in the newcomer, a tall, muscled young man whose lip curled in a contemptuous sneer. "I'm Erik Petersson," he said. "My daughter –"

"Well, Erik fucking Petersson, I'm Johnny, and this is my fraternity." Johnny reached inside his bathrobe and scratched an armpit. "And you're trespassing. Get out."

"We're with the police," Stephanie said, "and we're following up on a missing person."

Johnny's eyes narrowed, and he crossed the floor to the couch. "You know what this is about?"

The young man on the couch looked back at the television.

"Hey, Shit-pump." Johnny kicked the man's leg. "I asked you a question."

"I don't know what they're talking about." Shit-pump sprang into a sitting position. "They're asking questions about a girl. I haven't said shit."

"Well, there you have it." Johnny spread his arms wide. "There's nothing to say. You can both be on your merry way."

"Hold on." Erik straightened and squared off with Johnny. "I'm trying to track down my daughter, and I was told somebody in this fraternity might have some information. I have a few questions, and then we'll leave."

"Ask your questions on the way out." Johnny waved at the door in dismissal.

"Can I use the washroom first?" Stephanie asked.

Johnny sighed, took in Stephanie for what seemed like the first time. "Well, hello. How you doing?" He nodded up the corridor. "Of course you can use the facilities. There's one past the kitchen." His gaze roamed over Stephanie as she disappeared into the hallway.

Erik cleared his throat and Johnny looked at him. "I'd like to know more about some events that happened at La Distillerie, around the end of September."

A frown creased Johnny's forehead. "You said La Distillerie?"

"That's right," Erik said. "My daughter was there with her roommate, a girl named Mary-Beth –"

"I don't know any Mary-Beths." Johnny folded his arms across his chest.

"She also goes by Dominique. She's a dancer."

"Oh, Dirty Dominique," Johnny smirked. "Dancer's being generous. Why didn't you say she was your daughter's roommate? Sounds like she was a lot of fun."

Erik's pulse quickened. "On this particular night –"

"Back in September?"

"Yes –"

"Like eight months ago?"

"That's right, September. Comes after August and before October. There –"

"Do you know how many clubs I've been in since September? You know this is a frat house, right?"

"Can you stop interrupting?"

Johnny stepped closer. "Or what?"

"Or it's going to take us longer to get through these questions." Erik held his ground.

"Well, I don't know anything about your daughter hanging with a stripper, so I guess we're done." He glanced toward the hallway, where Stephanie had reappeared. "Right on time. Looks like visiting hours are over." He leered. "Although you're welcome to stay a little longer, Trix. I'll make it worth your while."

Stephanie ignored Johnny, held out a small white bottle to Erik. "This is interesting."

Erik squinted at the lettering on the label. "Rohypnol. Roofies."

Stephanie nodded. "Right on the edge of the sink, if you can believe it."

"The fuck are you doing?" Johnny snatched for the bottle. "That's private property."

Erik held the bottle out of reach. "Tell me, Johnny, why do you have date rape drugs?"

"It's for insomnia," Johnny said, "and you can't go snooping through our shit."

"I wonder what else would we find if we did."

"A big, fucking goose egg." A sneer contorted Johnny's face as he straightened to loom over Erik.

Erik slammed the bottle into Johnny's chest. "I'll bet a month's salary this is how you get girls to be in your little homemade movies. Is it?"

"I don't have to answer your fucking questions, if you're even cops," Johnny said. "In fact, I don't remember seeing any badges."

"You scared to answer? Are you hiding something?" Erik asked. "Then we'll talk to the university."

"Erik..." Stephanie stepped closer.

"You mean the university my family donates millions of dollars to?" Johnny's smirk grew. "The one with a building named after my father? I'd like to hear what they have to say, that'd be interesting. In fact," he spoke to Shit-pump, "why don't you get off your ass and go call campus security?"

Shit-pump stumbled off the couch.

Erik ground the box of pills against Johnny's chest, drove the larger man back. "I asked you a question. Do you use these to drug girls? Did you use this on my daughter? Is she in one of your..." He didn't want to finish the thought.

"Steady, old timer," Johnny said, his lip curled in a sneer. "That's assault."

"Erik, that's enough," Stephanie said.

"Listen to your partner, Erik," Johnny said, "her mothering instinct must be kicking in." He folded his arms across his chest and looked down at Erik.

Erik glared into Johnny's face. The smart thing to do would be to leave, he knew that. This wasn't the playground, and he wasn't an eight-year-old kid, taunted by a schoolyard bully. And Johnny was wrong. The Task Force had lots of tools. Given time, they'd unearth any link this frat house had to drugs, regardless of well-connected fathers. So again, the responsible thing to do would be to back off, let the team do its work.

"Come on, calm down." Stephanie pulled on Erik's arm.

"This is kinda hot, actually," Johnny said. He nodded at Stephanie. "You sure you don't want to hang out after you ditch this loser?"

Erik tossed the pill bottle at Johnny's head. It tumbled, and Johnny shifted back, made a wild grab. Johnny's attention on the bottle, Erik lashed out with his foot, struck the inside of Johnny's right ankle. The leg buckled and Erik rebounded his foot and heel-kicked the inside of Johnny's left knee.

His base destroyed, Johnny fell. On his way down, Erik caught Johnny by the arm and shoulder and drove him to the floor, ground his face into the sticky wood while he locked up Johnny's elbow in an armbar.

"Now you're fucked," Johnny said through gasps of pain.

"Well, when campus security gets here, you can explain that, as well as why you have date rape drugs." He wrenched on Johnny's arm. "Do you use these drugs on women?"

"Fuck you."

Erik applied more pressure to Johnny's arm, was rewarded with a muffled groan. "You don't need this for anything, do you? After all, you have another one."

"All right, all right. We use the drugs," Johnny said. "Not much, it's an initiation thing."

Erik's lips peeled back. "Did you use those on my daughter?"

"I can't fucking remember," Johnny said. "Maybe, I don't know. It's not like we keep a fucking tally."

"Erik, that's enough," Stephanie said.

Erik leaned close to Johnny's ear, and as he did, he added more tension to the armbar and Johnny moaned. "Where do you get this stuff? Who supplies you?"

"Some rag-head piece of shit," Johnny said. "Mohammed something or other."

"A name."

"Reyad," Johnny said, "Reyad Slimani."

"Where can I find him? Is he a student?"

"Yes, fuck," Johnny said. "He's in the Islamic studies program."

"What?" Erik eased off the pressure.

"It's true, goddammit," Johnny said. "Religion's a front for half those rag-heads, a cover for drug dealing."

"Erik," Stephanie said, her voice urgent.

"Okay, that'll do," Erik said and then let go of Johnny's trapped arm and backed off. One eye on Johnny, who clutched his arm as he struggled to his feet, Erik joined Stephanie at the door.

"It's time to go." She grabbed his elbow.

"You heard it, right? The drugs. They're a direct link."

"We can talk about it outside." She tugged him toward the entrance.

"That's right, get the fuck out of here," Johnny called from the living room.

Erik froze on the doorstep, looked back.

Stephanie grabbed him by both shoulders and forced him to look at her. "Hey, what are you thinking? You thinking of going back in there? Would it make you feel any better?"

He dropped his gaze and she reached out and lifted his chin.

"What'll it get you?" she asked.

"You saw what they did to that woman."

"And is any of that going to bring Arielle back?"

He stiffened.

"We learned a lot here," she said. "Let's make sure we're able to put it to use."

He shuffled in place, held by Stephanie's royal blue eyes until the tension in his body began to ease, and he was left with an empty ache in the pit of his stomach. Stephanie took his hand, and he concentrated on her touch. The warmth felt good, an ounce of stability in a world that was spinning out of control. He nodded and focused on Stephanie's touch as she led him down the stairs.

* * *

SOMEWHERE BETWEEN KOBANE AND RAQQA, SYRIA
06 MAY 15 – 1814 LOCAL

The remains of what had been apartment buildings provided scant cover for Mus'ab Saleh, but it was what he had. He flitted from pile to pile, stopped long enough to catch his breath and listen. Then he'd move on, his sole companion the increasing fear that he was being watched.

He didn't know where the threat was anymore. His initial flight from the front lines had taken him through a spider-web of buildings mixed with fighting positions. He'd almost stumbled into an enemy position, had been about to call out and then he'd caught the sound of Kurdish voices around a corner and been able to slink away. Finally, he'd found a hole in the rubble and curled up for several hours of shivering half-sleep. When he'd woken, the sun was high, a hazy, orange disc visible through a perpetual cloud of dust and smoke that hung over the battlefield. Since then, he'd worked his way back to what he thought was his own position.

He poked his head out of his hiding spot and watched the street where minutes before he'd been walking. Plastic bags, cardboard boxes, all kinds of rubbish covered the landscape. Pencil-thin columns of smoke rose from a dozen different locations and the skeletal buildings that lined the road stared at him from hollowed windows. A bullet cracked overhead, and he ducked, instinctively counted until the thump of the rifle blast reached him. A second, maybe two. Ahmed had said that meant the sniper was close – or had he? The shot might not have even been at him. It didn't matter. It was time to move.

He crouched low and scuttled along a depression toward another building, one with an open wall that faced the street. Beyond that, more destruction, although the buildings seemed less damaged. A bullet kicked up dust in the street. He ducked lower, then dove into the building where he'd been going. He scrambled behind one of the walls, thankful for the chance to breathe. Still, he couldn't stay here long. He peered up through a hole in the roof, searched for the tiny fast-moving specks that indicated enemy aircraft. There hadn't been any bombing runs in this area for a few hours, which was a good sign he'd left the battlefield.

Unless he'd gone in the wrong direction and had infiltrated Kurdish lines.

He squinted and peered out over his direction of travel. Nothing moved, but nor did he have good observation beyond the first row of buildings. Not that it mattered. Returning the way he'd come was not an option, not with a sniper. He licked his parched lips, scanned for a bottle of water that might have been left behind. All he found was a muddy pool of water near the entrance to the building, bands of color reflected in the oily slick on its surface. He wasn't that thirsty. Yet.

He summoned his strength for his next bound. Counted to three then dashed from cover. By the time he reached the shelter of the next buildings, coughs racked his body. He forced himself to keep going, passed through the building into an alleyway where he sank to the ground, head rested against the wall, eyes closed.

He sat and rested for a few seconds and then opened his eyes and spied graffiti on a wall opposite him, a little girl hanging from a single red balloon adrift in the sky. Behind the girl, the outline of a collapsed building, part of a backdrop of a blasted city landscape. Black balloons drifted up from the city, like the towers of smoke caused by coalition bombs. It was upon this devastation that the girl gazed. Mus'ab Saleh worked his dry throat, unable to look away.

He recognized the inspiration. At home in London, he'd tried his hand at graffiti. The Tunnel on Leake Street had been a favorite haunt, also the skate park in South Bank, for a time. He'd moved to more isolated places, driven by his increasingly religious tastes but had never been able to create anything he enjoyed and he'd often gone over his work himself. His parents had been livid when they'd found out. To them, graffiti was artless, political propaganda synonymous with the militias who'd torn Beirut apart in the civil war. His father would rage at the paint cans, would throw them at Mus'ab Saleh when he found them. He'd stuck with it, though. He'd thought his pieces were serious, that they'd come from the heart and would incite change. How wrong he'd been. The Syrian street artists who risked their lives to adapt Banksy knew more about heart than he would know in a lifetime.

He picked himself up and worked along the alleyway, the fingers of one outstretched arm along the wall to keep his distance. If fired at the right angle, a stray bullet could ricochet and travel along the hard walls, and while he thought he'd passed through the worst, he had no wish to be caught in that zone of death. When the alley met a cross-street, he angled to get a better view before he exposed himself, what Ahmed had called piecing the pie. Then, hunched over, he bounded to the alley on the other side of the street and kept going.

A man yelled at him, and he stopped short, ducked down onto his hands and knees. At the other end of the alley, a fighter dressed head to toe in black appeared, rifle at the shoulder and pointed in his direction. The rifleman yelled again, and from the other side of the alley, the head and rifle of another fighter appeared.

Mus'ab Saleh held up his hands. The black clothes of the first rifleman, the de facto uniform of Caliphate soldiers, suggested he was an ally. Kurds would sooner die than wear all black, but there remained a slim chance the fighters were from another rebel group, maybe al-Nusra, although they weren't supposed to be in the area. Whoever it was, he was lucky they'd decided to talk before they shot.

"My name is Mus'ab Saleh." His voice cracked. "My commander is Ahmed Sallum. We were in Qassim al Shishani's battalion. We were overrun."

"Shut your mouth," the rifleman in the alley yelled. The other fighter said something Mus'ab didn't catch, and then the first rifleman waved his hand. "Come here. Move it."

Hands up, Mus'ab Saleh rose and walked. Near the end of the alley, the first rifleman backed up, maneuvered Mus'ab around the corner with the barrel of his rifle. Once clear of the corner, the second fighter grabbed him and flung him to the ground. A knee jammed into Mus'ab's back, and his face was forced into the dirt and rubble. Hands rummaged through Mus'ab's pockets.

"You say you're with al Shishani's battalion?" the second man said.

"Yes," he said. "Ahmed Sallum was my commander."

"Was?"

"He's dead."

The man took Mus'ab's wallet. "What are you doing back here? The front is two miles in the other direction."

"The front is all over the place." The knee dug further into Mus'ab's ribs. He winced. "Qassim ordered us to pull back and regroup. After that, we were bombed. I got separated."

"Retreat?" The man stood. "Qassim al Shishani ordered a retreat?"

Mus'ab shook his head from side to side. "Not retreat. Regroup."

"Where is the rest of your section?"

"Dead. Or like me, separated."

The man tossed Mus'ab's wallet to the ground. It landed beside his face, flopped open to the picture of his mother and father. "I don't believe you."

"It's true."

The man grabbed Mus'ab Saleh by the hair, dragged him to his feet and shoved him up against a wall. "I think you're a coward, fleeing the battlefield." The first man, the one dressed all in black, kept his rifle at the ready.

"No, that's not it." His mind raced. "We were –"

"We should take you to Raqqa to be executed as an example, but I don't have the people to guard you, or the time to waste." The man reached to his waist and pulled a pistol, placed the barrel against the side of Mus'ab Saleh's head.

With a scream, Mus'ab Saleh smashed his forehead into the bridge of the gunman's nose. The man dropped the pistol and clutched his face. Mus'ab dropped low into a lineman's stance, and while the other rifleman angled for a clear shot, Mus'ab shoved his would-be executioner into him. The two came together with a grunt and tumbled into a heap of arms and legs. Mus'ab stooped to grab the dropped pistol.

Gunfire filled the alley, and a wild spray of bullets screamed off the wall behind Mus'ab Saleh. Chips of brick and mortar dug into his back, but his world had shrunk to the pistol in his hands. He pointed it at the two men, one who clutched his destroyed nose while the other struggled to free his rifle from the weight of his partner. He aimed at the center of the tangled limbs and bodies and pulled the trigger. He pulled again. And again, and again until the hammer clicked on an empty chamber. Numb, he waited for them to move. They didn't.

From the body on top came a tinny voice. After a brief silence, the voice repeated.

Mus'ab Saleh rolled the top body over, tracked the noise to a radio handset in a breast pocket. The voice echoed from the speaker, insistent. It wanted a report, a report, it must have a report. Someone would come, they were on their way. They were on their way and would find the bullet-riddled bodies, bodies that he would not be able to explain. He turned and fled, and now he knew that he was a dead man who could only hope to see his wife before he died.

* * *

MONTREAL, QUEBEC
06 MAY 15 – 1120 LOCAL

On the street outside the frat house, Erik paused and looked up at the sun, let its heat warm his face, even if it did nothing to warm his body. "They raped Arielle."

Stephanie paused in mid-stride. "You don't know that."

"Do you have another explanation?"

She half-turned from him and folded her arms across her chest. She started to speak, then stopped and faced him. "I'm sorry."

"I thought it would be a good idea for her to come to school here. I thought it would be good for her to get away from home." He walked down the sidewalk, then looked back at Stephanie. "We need to find this Slimani kid."

"Let's think this through."

Rage rippled through him. "It's all linked, Stephanie. The drugs. The study group. Slimani. That's no coincidence. The link to Sahraoui –"

"Is tenuous at best, and what's there is criminal, not national security." Stephanie's eyes were moist, but her voice was strong. "That's outside our jurisdiction. We need a plan, so we head back to the office, review our information and go from there."

"We'll lose momentum." Erik threw up a hand. "Johnny's probably making calls right now. It won't be long before Sahraoui knows we're on to him."

"Stop for a minute. It's not even clear there's a connection. Being in the Islamic studies program – which we still need to confirm – is not a direct link to Sahraoui," Stephanie said. "And even if Sahraoui is involved, a couple of hours won't make a difference."

"It will if we're not the ones to break the news. We need to be the first to talk to him, or we'll miss his genuine reaction."

Stephanie shook her head. "No. It's one thing to rough up a frat member. Rushing into a criminal investigation is totally different."

"This is the break I need, I can feel it," he said. "I don't want Sahraoui to clam up."

"You might be right, but we have to do this properly. I'm sorry." She nodded up the street. "They must have called the police instead of campus security. Why don't you take a walk while I clear things up?"

Erik peeked over his shoulder. Several houses down from the frat house, a white Dodge Charger with roof lights pulled to a stop along the sidewalk. "You think Johnny'll push for charges?"

"No chance," Stephanie said. "He's not the kind of guy who'd admit to getting beat down. Let me take care of this."

Erik nodded and watched Stephanie head off to intercept the police officers near the steps of the frat house, then crossed the street to lose himself in the late morning crowd. A slight shiver passed through him when he entered the shade on the other side of the road, and then two people glued to their cellphones almost ran him over. He darted aside, a frown on his face. It was a wonder more people didn't walk into traffic and get killed.

A gap opened up, and he moved into the space, got a chance to breathe and took in the street, its cobblestone sidewalks, lush trees, and carved building-fronts. Montreal's sidewalk culture felt more European than Canadian, the women in an eclectic mix of bohemian, vintage, and modern clothes, their hair and makeup done as if they'd come from a fashionista's ball instead of a visit to the local café for a latte. It was Audray's crowd, Stephanie's as well for that matter.

He glanced over his shoulder. Stephanie had corralled the two police officers, and as they spoke, her hands waved in the air as if in front of an orchestra. He was too far to hear the conversation, but it wasn't difficult to imagine her *Quebecois* accent as they spoke. *Franchement, officers...frankly, officers.* She could almost pass for a university student herself, wild and carefree and talking the police down after a wild party.

For all that, it was impossible to forget that he'd encouraged Arielle to come here for school. In the process, all he'd done was shove her into a shark tank. He lowered his head and jammed his hands into his pockets and walked, forced his thoughts onto the case.

Slimani, the name was not a common one. If he was under Sahraoui's influence, it was possible he was also radicalized, although he might simply be a low-life drug dealer who preyed on college kids. The mention of the Islamic studies program was important, although he understood Stephanie's point. Johnny might have said Reyad was in the program, but that didn't mean it was true, nor did it create a link to Sahraoui. He swore under his breath. Rushing in was a bad idea, but sitting around felt worse.

She'd been raped. His daughter had been raped. He balled his hands into fists. Sahraoui knew something, he had to –

A scream from up ahead broke his thoughts. He rose on his tiptoes to look over the crowd, but all he saw was the approaching windshield and cab of a 5-ton delivery truck. He squinted, and did a double-take.

The truck was on the sidewalk.

More sounds reached him, panicked shouts of "*Attention!*" or "Look out!" The truck advanced, accompanied by intermittent thumps when the cab bounced up and down, as if on rough ground. He looked for Stephanie, saw her and the police officers several hundred yards down and on the opposite side of the street from the truck. She was as safe as possible, at least for now. He, however, was right in line with where the truck was headed.

He backed up, scanned his surroundings. About a hundred feet down on his side of the street was a set of elevated stairs that entered an apartment building, but his gut warned him it would be difficult to reach, not at the truck's speed. Something closer. There – on the opposite sidewalk was a large maple. He lunged across the road toward the tree and the entrance of a building just beyond. The screams were louder now, and so was the roar of the truck's engine.

Halfway across the street, he risked a glance behind and saw that the truck had veered in his direction. Sunlight flashed off the truck's windshield and he shielded his eyes from the glare and then ran faster. He had time to wonder if the tree would be big enough to stop the truck and then he was across the street. He dove behind a concrete stairwell and huddled in the space where the stairs met the building and covered himself with his arms. A second later there was a deafening roar and fragments of glass rained down on him. Then there was silence, less the groans and hisses of the truck.

He poked his head up and saw that the truck had clipped the tree and careened into the stairwell. In the cab of the truck, he recognized the man from the strip club, the same man he'd followed into Sahraoui's study group. This man now sat at the truck's steering wheel, and as Erik struggled to process what he was seeing, the man pulled a pistol and pointed it at him through the space where the windshield had been. Erik ducked back into the cover of the stairwell to the cracks of gunfire. Bullets ricocheted off the bricks near his head, and he cowered lower, tried to become part of the concrete itself.

The gunshots echoed in the street and then Erik heard the truck's door open, followed by the clatter of a pistol magazine as it dropped to the ground. He scanned for better cover, but there was nothing close, nothing that wouldn't leave him exposed. He braced himself, scuttled to the edge of the stairwell and hunched near the ruined front hood of the truck. The gunman fired, this time in a different direction from the sound of the shots. Maybe he'd gone for the police.

Glass and debris crunched underneath the gunman's feet as the man moved, taking him around the stairwell. Erik tensed and when the barrel of the gun appeared, he lunged, pushed the muzzle up and away. The gun went off in his hands, and the slide rocked back and pinched one of Erik's fingers, and for a second he lost his grip. He grabbed for the gun again, but the lull had been all the assailant had needed to wrest back control.

The gun swung toward him. It would be impossible for the gunman to miss at this distance, and so Erik crouched and readied himself to lunge at the man. He met the other man's gaze, felt the hate, and then Indian music began to play from the gunman's jacket pocket. Both he and the gunman froze, and then shots rang out, and the gunman's body rocked to the side as if punched by an invisible assailant. First in the shoulder, then the gut. The gunman's head rocked up and back with a wet thud and then, like a puppet whose strings had been cut, the man crumpled to the ground.

Hands near his face, Erik stared at the body. Tiny ink spots of red on the man's chest grew larger, stained through the man's clothes. Shouts came from the direction of the frat house, commands he didn't understand. He sank to his knees beside the body, aware that two police officers had moved up along the opposite side of the street, guns trained on where the gunman lay. The music sounded again from the gunman's pocket.

"He's dead," Erik called out. He looked up and made eye contact with the police officers. "He's dead." They nodded, and he lowered his hands. Music split the air again, and Erik leaned over the body and pulled a phone from the back pocket of the man's jeans. One of the police officers yelled at him in French, but Erik ignored him. Instead, he answered the phone.

"Reyad?" The man asked and he sounded familiar. "Listen, man, forget my last message. Don't come around here, there's some shit going on outside."

"Who is this?" Erik asked.

"It's Johnny, who the fuck do you think it is?" Then a pause. Erik could almost hear the gears in Johnny's head turning. "Who's this?" Then the call ended.

Erik stared at the phone and when the police officers arrived and muscled him onto the ground, he barely noticed.

* * *

MONTREAL, QUEBEC
06 MAY 15 – 1540 LOCAL

Erik shivered on the examination table as the doctor bandaged his back and shoulder.

"We're almost done," the doctor said from behind him. "I apologize for how long it's taking, but there were a number of small wounds to your back. Lucky for you, most of them were shallow."

Erik glanced at the door, where Stephanie stood. "I think the jury may still be out on how lucky I am."

"*Lui donne une claque si il arrête pas de brailler*," Stephanie said.

The doctor chuckled.

"What'd she say?" Erik asked.

The doctor pressed a cold, wet swab against Erik's back. It stung, and a wince slipped out.

"Not to go easy on you," Stephanie said.

"We're done here, Mr. Petersson, you can get dressed." The doctor stepped out from behind the table and tore off her Latex gloves. "Check the bandages once a day and keep the wounds clean."

"Thanks," he said and hopped off the table. He reached for his shirt and the patchwork pattern of bandages on his back shifted and pulled and he had to contort his body to get an arm into a shirt-sleeve.

Stephanie made room for the doctor to leave and then walked to Erik's side. "There are other ways to shave your back, you know." She reached out to help.

"What?" He twisted to look at her, his brow wrinkled in confusion.

"The bandages, they look like little shaving cuts." Her face reddened. "Forget it."

"Was that a joke?"

"I said forget it."

"I don't think I've ever heard you tell a joke," he said. "It was terrible. Is that why?"

Stephanie let go and stepped around him. "You almost died."

"I'm sorry." He finished struggling into his shirt. "The doctor's right. I got lucky."

Stephanie's lips pressed together. "Maybe not."

"What do you mean?"

"Wiggins will be here any second."

"I didn't think he'd find out so soon."

"I called him." She had the decency to look sheepish. "He needed to know. Two of his people almost got killed, and a Montreal neighborhood is in lockdown."

He took a deep breath. "Did you mention the frat house?"

"It came up. I told him I'd explain later."

"Well, that's something, anyways." He straightened and stretched. "The gunman was Reyad Slimani."

She started. "How did you know?"

"The call that I answered was from Johnny." He leveled his gaze at Stephanie. "But I don't think it was Johnny who tipped him off."

"Maybe there was no tip-off," she said. "Maybe he'd been planning this attack for a while, and you were just a target of opportunity."

"He veered after me with the truck," he said. "Think about it, the same guy who supplies Johnny's frat house with drugs tried to kill me as I start digging into my daughter's disappearance. There's a common connection here, and you know what it is."

"It's too early to jump to conclusions."

"No, it's not, Stephanie," he said. "It has to be Sahraoui."

The door to the examination room burst open, and Wiggins appeared in the gap, his designer suit rumpled. He glared at Erik, then turned to Stephanie, and his face softened. "Are you all right?"

Stephanie nodded.

"I'm fine, too," Erik said and leaned against the examination table.

"Good. I won't have to hold back." Wiggins stepped into the room and closed the door. "You want to tell me what you were thinking?"

"I'm finding out what happened to my daughter," he said, more heat in his voice than intended.

"By harassing a bunch of college kids?"

Erik glanced at the floor and bit his lip.

Wiggins moved in front of Erik, hands on his hips. "I asked you a question."

"One of those college kids raped Arielle," he said.

Wiggins drew back and then looked to Stephanie. "Is that true?"

"It looks that way," she said. "We found rohypnol in the bathroom, and the head of the frat admitted they use them."

"And where do you think they get the drugs from?" Erik glared at Wiggins. "Sahraoui."

"We don't know that," Stephanie said.

"Then why did the guy who supplies the drugs – a guy in Sahraoui's study group – try to kill me?"

Wiggins rubbed his chin. "Sahraoui is sticking to the line that Slimani was a troubled youth. He said he'd been involved in drugs and gangs since he was thirteen."

"You already questioned him?"

"Not questioned, no," Wiggins said. "We called him under the pretense of looking for information to notify Slimani's family. I wanted to get his reaction."

"And?"

"And nothing. He was appropriately dismayed, but didn't seem all that surprised the boy had done something like this. Not after his cousin recently fled to Syria."

Stephanie's eyes narrowed. "Who was he talking about?"

Wiggins met Erik's gaze, then looked back at Stephanie. "Naomi Lohrenz."

"What?" Erik said and then turned to Stephanie. "Did you know this?"

She shook her head. "Of course not. We questioned her immediate family, but that never came out."

"Then how much more do we need?" Erik asked. "I'm telling you, Sahraoui is the key."

"Maybe," Wiggins said, "but it's also possible the kid just gravitated to Sahraoui's class. Either way, we'll question him once Montreal settles down. Right now, every cop in the city is tied up making sure there aren't any more attacks."

"I want to be there when it happens," Erik said.

Wiggins snorted. "Like hell. You've done more than enough."

"I uncovered a network. I deserve to be there."

Wiggins threw up a hand. "You created a goddamn firestorm here when you were supposed to be at home, drinking scotch or whatever you do when you're not at work. Not sticking your nose into national security investigations involving politically sensitive suspects."

Erik shook his head. "You're spineless."

"For God's sake," Wiggins said and rubbed his temple. "Sahraoui was held for four years on secret evidence that a judge ruled was inadmissible. He sued the government for millions of dollars in damages, and now you're suggesting we investigate him again not just for terrorism, but for drugs as well." Wiggins pointed at Erik. "We. Must. Proceed. With. Caution."

"He's involved."

"Your head is not in the game," Wiggins said. "This is why I took you off the case in the first place. Doing things without a plan is not a recipe for success."

"We're farther ahead now," Erik said.

"If," Wiggins said and held up a finger, "and this is a big if here, if you haven't jeopardized the investigation. So no, there's no way you're involved any further."

He was so close. "I can help."

Wiggins turned to Stephanie. "Say something to him."

"It's his daughter. He –"

"We've been over this," Wiggins said. "There's nothing we can do about that. We deal with the world as it is, not as we want it to be."

Erik looked at Stephanie. "What's he talking about?"

Stephanie sighed. "Erik, we all want to help find Arielle," she said and her lips tightened. "But even if we find that Sahraoui helped her get to Syria, she's there now. If that's where she wants to be, I'm not sure what we can do."

"Then why did you come to Montreal? Why did you help me?"

Her gaze flickered to Wiggins, then back. "We knew you wouldn't let it go."

"You knew?" he said to Wiggins, who nodded.

"Erik, we never thought we'd uncover something like this. We're going to be tied up in this investigation for months." She stepped closer. "But if you think about it, nothing has changed. Even if we find out Arielle's exact location and how she got there, we have no way to get her, not while the Caliphate is in control of half of Syria and Iraq."

"We can follow the leads, work the contacts –"

"And what then?" Stephanie asked. "What will you do then?"

He stuttered a response. "I'll reach out to her, get her to change her mind, come back –"

"How?"

"I'll find a way," he said. "I have to find a way."

Stephanie put a hand on his shoulder. "Erik –"

He put one of his hands on hers and met her gaze. "I promised I'd be there for her," he said, "and I wasn't. Not now, and not when she was...when they..."

"I know, Erik," she said, her voice almost a whisper. "But you're not going to get her back like this."

CHAPTER NINE
SONG OF THE SIREN

Arielle sat in front of her work station and rehearsed her routine. First, she'd check for new friend requests. Abu Mustapha had said the majority of these would be people already interested in travelling to Syria, but who needed an extra boost. Next, she'd cruise several chat forums to provide comments and find users whom she'd follow up with on Facebook. After that, she'd respond to direct messages. By then it would be close to the late afternoon prayer, so she'd close out with some posts on Hafsa's profile. *My profile*, she thought. And maybe, if she was brave, she'd resurrect her avatar for a minute or two.

She glanced around as the login process continued. Abu Mustapha was ensconced in his office at the rear of the café, hidden, but not far. For a large man, he moved with incredible quiet. Several times over the past four days he'd materialized behind her, his breath on her neck while he watched over her shoulder. At the thought of him, she pulled her *abaya* tight.

Focus. She closed her eyes and counted to ten in her head, then opened Hafsa's Facebook account. *My account.*

Hafsa had eleven new friend requests, more than triple the day before. Most came from usernames that started with Umm, the preferred jihadist *kunya* for women. There were also several messages from 'friends,' to which she had to reply. She was thankful that most responses didn't require much thought, which almost made up for the ones that did. She pulled out her manuals, propaganda on the role of women and life in the Caliphate, then opened the first message.

Umm Salim wrote, "What is life like? Is it difficult for women?"

An easy one she'd received multiple times. No need to refer to manuals for this one. "Do not worry, life is wonderful here!" she typed. "Women are treated like princesses, not disrespected like in the West."

"Is it dangerous?" Another easy one, this one from Umm Ahmad.

"It is not dangerous at all in the cities," Arielle wrote. "Our brave men keep the infidels occupied, leaving us free to raise children and conduct humanitarian work. Women have a truly great role, nurturing and raising the next generation of lions!"

Arielle hovered the mouse over the send button but did not click. Yesterday, as she walked with Umm Fatima to the market, she'd spied two young boys in tan camouflage, white Arabic writing emblazoned into black headbands on their foreheads. They'd looked no older than ten. With pride, Umm Fatima had said they were members of the Cubs of the Caliphate, the next generation. They'd scared her, with their unflinching eyes. The next generation indeed.

She swallowed and sent the message, then opened the next one.

"What should I bring?"

Arielle knew this one by heart. "Bring your *hijab* and a veil, my sister, but beyond that, travel light. Most designer clothes are available here! You could, however, bring lingerie if you wish. It is okay for us sisters to talk about it and you should know that it is not *haram* to wear whatever you like underneath your *abaya*. Your future husband will appreciate it!"

Abu Mustapha had insisted on the last point, hunger in his eyes even as he'd assured her his advice was pure. Lingerie had done nothing for Naomi, who hadn't even had – Arielle shook her head, took a sip of water. Thinking of Naomi would do no good. She opened the last message, from a girl named Umm Aminah whom she'd befriended yesterday.

"My family is very pious and have supported me in my religion since I was little," Umm Aminah wrote. "I don't think they would be ashamed of me for traveling to the Caliphate, but they are afraid of the killing in the name of religion, and I'm afraid as well. I know I should be happy to embrace death when my time comes, but I fear I won't be able to, at least not in a way that will make them proud. I don't know what to do. My religion tells me I need to travel to be loyal and I recognize the injustices done to us here in the West. Still, I find myself paralyzed with fear and indecision. How did you find the strength? How do you deal with the things you miss? Please help me be brave like you."

Arielle closed her eyes, her rigid self-discipline forgotten as the images flooded her attempts to forget. Grocery stores flush with every food imaginable, days spent in the mall, uninterrupted power. She wanted to walk down the street by herself, wanted to remember a time when her back and shoulders didn't ache from the stress of being caught by religious police in some untoward act or being forced to witness another execution. Her breath came faster.

Her strength had come from ignorance. Naomi had found her at the exact right time and if she'd had half the foresight of Umm Aminah, she wouldn't be here now. She imagined her father's face, the sound of his laughter. A flash of anger surged through her. In a normal world, she'd pick up the phone and call him, not be forced to dupe a confused teenager into putting her head into the lion's mouth.

A hand fell on her shoulder, and her eyes jerked open.

"You're not working," Abu Mustapha said.

"I am thinking of a response, brother." She kept her voice even. "This question requires a deft touch."

"I, too, have something that requires a deft touch," he said in a husky growl.

She could feel her heartbeat in her ears and she forced herself to focus on the computer screen to her front. "I'd best answer this question, brother."

Abu Mustapha grunted and Arielle's hands clenched into fists. *I will not give him the excuse to touch me*, she thought and then he grunted again and moved back to his office. She sat for a moment and then opened her hands and felt a tingling sensation spread through her fingers and toes. This was too much. If Abu Mustapha held to his normal pattern, she might have half an hour before he returned. More than enough time to activate her avatar.

She minimized the browser and double-clicked on a circular icon that contained a letter W in gold. Her heart raced, and she scolded herself, but she'd needed the trace of familiarity, the closest she could come to her old life. Even more, it was her tiny rebellion. They had not taken everything from her. Within a minute, she'd assumed the mantle of Galembor, the Night Elf. She donned a headset she'd been given for Skype recruiting sessions and roamed the world, her travel guided by the need to avoid people who might know her.

She longed to seek out her dad. Instead, she made for a dark online cave where she found two other characters. It wasn't an official recruiting spot, but more like a hidden virtual space that had been taken over by gamers to talk about Islam, spots that hid in plain sight if one knew where to look. Sure enough, the conversation appeared to be about the Caliphate. She didn't recognize the other two characters, but they sounded young and eager for information.

"Are you in the Caliphate?" an Orc named Pralo asked her, the alto pitched voice in her headset at odds with the hideousness of his avatar.

"I am," she said.

Keilath, a human character, jumped in. "Are you married?"

"I am." *I think.*

"Did you have a hard time adapting?" Keilath asked.

What could she say to that? "Yes," she said after several seconds of silence.

"But it must have been worth it to live in a land where laws are guided by our religion," Keilath continued. "We both want to come. Even if you say it was hard, both of us want to prove we can't be oppressed and disrespected."

"There's more to being a good Muslim than leaving your families." She found herself glaring at the screen. "This isn't a game. The most important thing is to treat people with goodness, regardless of where you live."

A hand fell on her shoulder, and she yelped, twisted in her chair. The headset tangled on her head and she yanked it off, turned and found Abu Mustapha behind her.

"What are you doing?" His glare darted between her face and the monitor.

"I am recruiting," she said, her voice quiet.

"You are playing a game," he said. "It is *haram.*" He began to walk away, stopped at her touch on his arm.

"It is an online platform that enables social networking," she said, a tremble in her voice. "Let me show you." She let go of him and replaced the headset over her ears.

"– still there?" Pralo asked. "You cut out for a second."

"I'm here," she said. "Just a minor glitch."

"Keilath had to go, but I said I'd wait," Pralo said. "I still had some questions."

Arielle was once again struck by how youthful Pralo sounded, but she had to ignore that now. "What did you want to know?"

"Do you really believe that the important thing is to be good to people?"

"Of course," she said and closed her eyes. *Forgive me.* "But you didn't let me finish. While it is important to treat people well, the need for the Caliphate supersedes that obligation. When the Caliphate is more established, then we can be more concerned about how people are treated."

"But you said it didn't matter where you lived."

"In normal circumstances," she said. "But these circumstances are anything but normal. We must all be prepared to do our duty."

"What about the killing?" Pralo said. "My dad says it's against religion."

She took a deep breath. "The need for the Caliphate comes above all else," she said. "Have you thought about making your *hijrah* to do your part for your religion?"

"I have."

Her heart sank. "I can help."

"I'd need to think about it."

"You'll be strong, I can tell. Give me a moment." She flicked the microphone to mute and glanced at Abu Mustapha. "You see, brother?"

He grunted. "I must consider this. Keep working," he said, and left her alone.

She returned to the monitor and stared at the screen.

"Hello?" Pralo said. "Are you there?"

Her shoulders slumped. "Yes, I am." She'd been wrong. The Caliphate could indeed take everything from her.

CHAPTER TEN
THE LIGHT OF THE MORNING

Arielle trudged in silence beside Umm Fatima, down empty alleyways festooned with black banners on the way back to her apartment. There were no men to escort them, and so Umm Fatima walked with her, and when stopped by the religious police, Umm Fatima would leverage her status in the al-Khansaa Brigade to talk their way through.

Arielle wondered how long she could keep this up.

It was impossible to know all the rules or evade detection. Umm Fatima cleared most things up, like the time Arielle had been accosted by the *Hisbah* for forgetting her black gloves, but to Arielle, it felt like a question of time until she felt the lash of the whip. Even worse was her job, how fast the Caliphate propaganda had become normal, and how fast she was able to forget the people she recruited. Soon, perks like the internet and Umm Fatima's privileged status would be enough of a reward to help her forget her actions.

Almost.

They entered the apartment building, and Arielle fell back. She dreaded the nights, cooped up in the apartment. It should have been welcome relief, but there had yet to be a night when the explosions of bombs hadn't descended on the city, the main difference being how close and how loud the screams were in the aftermath. She'd try to block them out, would think it impossible to ever close her eyes again, then fall into a fitful, exhausted sleep.

"Come." Umm Fatima beckoned.

Arielle glanced up and then caught movement out of the corner of her eye. From behind a pillar in the lobby, Mus'ab Saleh peeked out. Her heart leaped, and she stepped in his direction and then stopped when he held a dirty finger to his lips. He gestured at Umm Fatima, who had her back to him. Arielle nodded in return, a nod she hoped Umm Fatima would interpret as intended for her, then followed Umm Fatima into the stairwell.

Umm Fatima accompanied Arielle as far as her apartment, then departed the same way she'd come, her cargo delivered safe and sound. The woman was no sooner out of sight before Arielle tore off her veil. She tried to wait in patience, but the time dragged. The minutes seemed like hours before a quiet knock came at the door. She almost tripped over her feet as she rushed to the door and yanked it open.

Mus'ab Saleh fell into the apartment and slammed the door closed behind him. "Will she return?"

"No." She watched as he tugged down the blinds to the apartment's windows. "What's happened?"

He waited until the room was in near darkness and then came to her, a shadow visible by the hint of late-afternoon light around the edges of the blinds. "It's been a disaster."

"Are you all right?" She peered up at him, noticed a cut on his eye and reached for it.

He brushed her hand aside. "We have to go. Gather what you can fit in a bag."

"Go where?"

"Lebanon. We have to get across the border."

"Slow down." She placed a hand on his back and he tensed and flinched from her touch. "Tell me what happened," she said.

He stood for several seconds and then his shoulders slumped. "My unit was overrun."

"But you're okay."

"I'm the only one who survived," he said. "Two of our soldiers stopped me, accused me of desertion. They were going to execute me." He shifted his gaze to her. "I killed them."

"Did you have a choice?"

He shook his head. "Not that it matters. There will be questions, accusations. It's no longer safe here, for either of us."

Gooseflesh prickled on Arielle's arms and she thought of the Dutch fighters executed the day before, all beheaded in the public square for desertion. Even that had been a blessing of sorts given the rumors among the crowd that deserters would begin to be burned alive.

Mus'ab Saleh stripped off his shirt and headed for the bedroom. "We have to go. Now."

She followed. "Do you have a plan?"

"We head for Lebanon," he said. "I can contact my family from there."

"And if we're caught?"

Mus'ab Saleh paused, half dressed. The unspoken answer in his face was plain. "I never meant for this to happen."

"Of course not." She was ready to leave – wanted to leave – but faced with the choice, it occurred to her that while her life was miserable, she was at least alive. If caught, she would take her place in the public square. "Would it be better for you to go on your own?"

Mus'ab took her by the shoulders. "If you stay, you'll be killed."

"If I go, I'll be killed."

"I'm sorry."

"I could turn you in." Umm Fatima's words in her mouth. Shame colored her cheeks.

He stiffened. "You could."

She gazed into his eyes and wondered how it had come to this, how she was able to consider trading his life for hers. He wasn't some nameless person but her husband, however it had come to pass, a man she'd felt connected to, even if their time together had been short. This was the worst part about the Caliphate, how it turned people against each other and forced them into total subservience. She wrapped her arms across her chest and looked away. "That's what the Caliphate would want."

"It is," he said, his voice steady. "The Caliphate wants lots of things."

Like her. The Caliphate wanted her, body and soul. Abu Mustapha didn't value her as a sister or as a person, he wanted her ability to use social media to support the Caliphate. Likewise Umm Fatima, whose most important concern was that Arielle would submit, which was, after all, the meaning of the word 'Muslim' – one who submits. But if she submitted in this, it was more than Mus'ab Saleh's life at stake.

"Why didn't you flee when you had the chance?" she asked.

"You would have still been in danger," he said. "I came back for you."

"What?"

"I made a vow." He took her hands in his own. "I know our marriage was rash. And it was forced, but it's important in Islam, and it's important to me. As it is said, the most perfect in faith amongst men are those who are kindest to their wives." He caressed her cheek with the back of his hand. "I feel like we're on the same path and I believe you feel it too. That's more important to me than even my own life."

His words touched her in a place she'd done her best to wall off and she looked away, but he guided her face back.

"If I'd fled across the border, you would have been executed in my place. Now, you have choices. Turn me in, and you should be safe, and I'll have accomplished my goal. Or come with me and take a chance on a life together." He sighed and pulled his hand from her cheek. "Whatever you decide, it needs to happen soon." He released her and continued changing.

She watched him shed his pants and disappear into the bathroom, fought to control her breathing. As the sound of the shower filled the room, she struggled with her thoughts. In her short life, Mus'ab was the first man who didn't view her as an object to protect, a possession to order around. She could submit to his love, because in coming back for her, he had already submitted to hers. She knelt beside the bed and began to pack clothes into her bag.

* * *

OTTAWA, ONTARIO
09 MAY 15 – 1942 LOCAL

The punching bag swayed at the edge of Erik's reach. He shuffled about the dusty floor of his garage and then lashed out. His fist connected and the bag rocked back, and the chain from which it hung rattled. Twinges of pain bit into his back, and he grimaced and then threw another punch. This was stupid, but he didn't care. He had no other release.

Well, there was one other way. He glanced at the two bottles he'd placed on the stairwell that lead into the house. The one, plastic and filled with water. The other, glass and filled with whiskey, a friend he hadn't touched for eight years. He wasn't sure which one he'd pick.

He grunted and jabbed again and then stepped back to adjust the straps on his gloves while his thoughts drifted. *I promised I'd keep her safe.* He shook his head and kept punching and his knuckles whined through the thin gloves as the skin frayed, but he didn't stop. *Let it come*, he thought. *I promised.*

At the time he'd made that promise, Audray had been dead a few weeks. He'd been coming off a bender – how long had that one been? – and had left Arielle with Audray's sister yet again, the one who'd taken her in when he'd stormed out of the funeral. When he'd picked her up, Arielle had stared at him with the innocent eyes of an eleven-year-old. An eleven-year-old he'd deserted.

"Where did you go, Dad?" she'd asked.

"I had some things to do," he'd mumbled. He couldn't look at her. The reek of alcohol hung over him, he saw it on her aunt's face. "I'm sorry." Christ, he'd needed a drink.

"Don't leave me again, okay?" she'd said and fell into his arms. "I was scared."

"I won't," he'd whispered into her hair as he held her close. Eyes clenched shut, he'd mouthed a silent prayer. *I'll do better, Audray, I promise. I'll keep her safe.*

But he hadn't.

He'd been so stupid. He realized now what an ideal candidate Arielle had been for recruitment. He'd been too wrapped up to notice the signs, like with Audray, but they'd all been there. It had started early October, around the time Mary-Beth had described. The short phone calls. The increasingly rare visits, how hard it had been to get in touch. He'd thought she was adjusting to college and then it was late-October, the Parliament Hill shooting happened, and his every waking moment was spent either at work or thinking about it.

And what did he have to show for all his precious time at work? In the past three years, he'd stopped almost fifty people from heading to the Middle East. He'd helped prevent three attacks on Canadian soil, including a plan to explosively derail passenger trains in the Greater Toronto Area, an attack that would have killed hundreds of people. In return, he'd lost his daughter, who was in the one place he'd worked to keep people from going. He would trade everything he'd accomplished, everyone he'd saved to have Arielle back.

He yelled and launched a flurry of blows on the bag. His back throbbed and ached and he pictured the bag exploding under his fists and punched harder and then it was too much. The bag swung back and bumped into him, and he clung to it and held on, his legs weak, his lungs burning for air.

What now?

He didn't know. He clawed off the gloves, grimaced as they rubbed against the sores on his knuckles. He sat on the stairs and reached for the plastic bottle, then paused and picked up the glass bottle instead. The cap came off with an easy twist, and the bottle was halfway to his lips when his cell phone rang. He stared at it and then picked up the handset to cancel the call and saw that it was Stephanie. Checking up on him. Anger gripped him, and he answered in a voice hoarse from yelling. "You can tell Wiggins I'm at home."

"I'm more concerned with how you're doing," she said.

"I'm fine," he said and stared at the bottle of whiskey. "Nothing a little ice won't fix."

"Do you want to talk about it?"

"I don't know if I can."

"It's okay if you don't want to talk to me," she said. "There are others, though."

"That's not it." He set the bottle down and fingered the ring hanging from his neck. "I just...I don't know where to begin."

"I understand."

He swallowed. "All I've done is make things worse."

"That's not true."

"Isn't it?"

"If that's what you think, maybe you should try something new."

"Like what?"

"I don't know," she said, "talk to your family, read a book. Take up religion."

"I'm not the praying type." It was easier to talk about that then explain his rare talks with his parents or brother back on the family farm. He'd been gone for 26 years, been in the army, had a family of his own, yet his mother and older brother still treated him like he was a sixteen-year-old kid waiting to become a man.

"Sorry, I'm a lapsed Roman Catholic, so religion always comes up in heart-to-hearts," she said with a light laugh. "Priests can be good listeners if you find the right one. Maybe you should go see one. Or an Imam."

"Yeah, right."

"Erik," she said, "I know you're struggling with why Arielle did what she did. Maybe you need to stop looking at this through your lens and put yourself in her shoes."

His chest tightened. "I –"

"Just think about it," she said. "And whatever you do, try not to get run over."

"I promise," he said.

"Whatever happens, call if you need something."

"Thank you," he said, then hung up. Maybe Stephanie was right, maybe he'd been going about this the wrong way. He'd tried finding Arielle as if she was another case at work, with logic and analysis and everything he'd been trained to do. He needed a new approach. The Imam wasn't a bad idea, but it would have to be –

The phone buzzed with a text message, and he glanced at the screen.

```
Erik,
Seeking to establish comms. Heard about your
situation and thought we might have a mutually
beneficial solution.
Check out what we do, at www.1MEIB.com_ When you're
ready, talk to Chris Lewis clew@gmail.com.
Best Regards,
MDK
```

Erik snorted. Talk about timing. Like he told Wiggins whenever the subject of MDK came up, he hadn't heard from Matt de Kalb in almost ten years. They'd served in the same infantry battalion in the Nineties, lost touch when Erik switched to intelligence analyst. They'd deployed together to Afghanistan in 2004 but drifted apart after Audray's death. Erik knew de Kalb had retired from the military and formed a private security company based in the United States, one that helped Westerners fight the Caliphate with the Kurds, but that was it.

He shook his head. He wasn't sure what mutually beneficial solution meant, but if anyone knew about Syria and Iraq and how to get there, it would be MDK. He set the phone down, and his hand brushed the whiskey bottle. He hesitated, then took up the other bottle and squirted water into his mouth. His hands stung – more than his back – and they'd be painful for the next week or so as the scabs took hold. But when the scabs fell off, the new skin would be tougher than before, more durable.

This fight was far from over.

* * *

MANBIJ, SYRIA
10 MAY 15 – 0807 LOCAL

Arielle listened to the bus driver cry out the destinations.

"Al-Bab! Homs! Beirut!" the man called.

She tugged on Mus'ab Saleh's sleeve and glanced around the bus station.

"Do you really think this will work?"

He nodded, eyes sunken in his haggard face. They'd gone over the simple plan multiple times. Drive to Manbij, then get on a bus and ride to Lebanon.

"Wouldn't it be better to drive the whole way?" she asked. As hard as it was to believe that buses still operated, it was harder to believe they wouldn't attract more attention.

"We'd never make it through the checkpoints," he said. "In a group, we can blend in." The group meant the ten or so other passengers waiting to board the bus. He took her hand. "I have my Lebanese passport, which will get us through."

"And me?" she asked. "All I have is the temporary card I was issued in Raqqa and my Canadian passport."

"I know there's risk, but this is our best chance. We'll make it."

"How can you be sure?"

"Because I have to believe in something." He smiled and gazed into her eyes through the slit of her *niqab*.

The driver yelled again and moved to stand near the bus's front door.

Mus'ab Saleh's lips tightened. "It's boarding. Let's go."

Arielle and Mus'ab approached the bus, him in front as was proper, and they handed their tickets to the driver and then took their seats. Minutes later, the bus driver got on and stood in the aisle. He wiped his forehead, then spoke in Arabic.

Arielle leaned nearer to Mus'ab. "What's he saying?"

"He's welcoming us aboard, saying our final destination is Beirut, with stops in Al-Bab, Aleppo, and Homs. God willing, he hopes the trip should take a day and a half. We'll stop near Aleppo for the night as it's too dangerous to drive in the dark, then carry on tomorrow."

The driver advanced up the aisle as he talked and peered into the faces of the passengers.

Mus'ab continued to translate. "He's talking about checkpoints now. This side of Aleppo, they'll be Caliphate. We must show our identification when asked. Women fully covered. Men must ensure the bottoms of their pants are rolled up."

The driver paused to inspect Arielle and Mus'ab, then moved on.

"Near Aleppo, the checkpoints will transition, maybe rebels, maybe Caliphate. And on the far side of Aleppo, they'll be Syrian regime. But he says that if we make it through the Caliphate checkpoints, we'll make it all the way, *Insha'Allah.*"

"Won't the regime checkpoints be more dangerous?"

Mus'ab shook his head. "We can bribe our way through those ones, maybe even the rebel ones."

"But not Caliphate?"

Mus'ab smiled but did not reply.

His speech over, the driver returned to the front of the aisle, sat down and put the bus in gear. The bus lurched out of the station with a rumble, and as it picked up speed, a small breeze blew through several open windows. Arielle held Mus'ab Saleh's hand and stared out the window as the squat, brown and white buildings of Manbij slipped away. At the M4 highway, the driver negotiated the bus past the burned-out wreckage of a delivery truck, then merged. Farther down, a pickup truck lay abandoned by the side of the road and beyond, the horizon faded into haze, the sandy monotony broken by tiny bands of green.

"So far, so good," Mus'ab Saleh said, and Arielle nodded.

They encountered the first checkpoint thirty minutes later, outside the village of Arima. The checkpoint was a small one, made up of two pickups and four men. Two of the men trained their weapons on the bus until it stopped, then another boarded and said a few words to the driver, who handed over some papers. After the conversation, the man walked down a few rows and checked the IDs of two elderly men seated at the front. Done, the man scowled at the remainder of the passengers, then got off the bus and returned to one of the pickups. The riflemen lowered their weapons and the driver put the bus back in gear and carried on.

After another forty minutes, the bus slowed. They'd entered a built-up area with small apartment buildings, their shapes yellow and orange in the sun-tinted sandy haze that clouded the air. "Where are we?" Arielle asked.

"Al-Bab," Mus'ab Saleh said. "It's another checkpoint."

Like before, the bus driver stopped on the side of the road. A fighter clad in black climbed aboard and spoke to the driver, who again handed over his papers. After a quick look, the gunman handed the papers back, then faced the passengers. He spoke in Arabic, and when nobody moved, he pointed his rifle at the passengers seated in front. He repeated himself, louder.

"He wants us to get off." Mus'ab Saleh's face was pale.

The gunman dragged the bus driver from his seat and shoved him through the open door of the bus. He yelled again, and like a frozen herd stunned into movement, the passengers stood, heads bowed as they trudged to the front.

"Why are we getting off?" Arielle tried her best to sound calm.

"It could be nothing," Mus'ab said in a whisper. "Each commander runs his checkpoint how he sees fit."

Under the direction of several armed fighters, the passengers formed an extended line with their backs to the bus, their faces into the sun. Near the bus's rear, where the driver and the first passengers off the bus stood, several more gunmen moved up the line. Arielle struggled to get a glimpse of the fighters as they checked papers, spoke to the passengers.

A nearby gunman yelled, then stalked up to Arielle and jammed his rifle into her face.

Arielle tensed, and her eyes went wide.

The gunman yelled again and spit flecked the veil that covered Arielle's face. The other passengers and gunmen turned to watch, and Mus'ab Saleh raised his hand in front of Arielle's chest like a shield.

Without pause, the fighter smashed the butt of his rifle into Mus'ab's face. He collapsed to the ground, and Arielle dropped to her knees beside him. She grasped Mus'ab's shoulder and then the fighter grabbed her under the armpit and dragged her to her feet. She closed her eyes, tensed for the strike that was sure to come. Nothing.

When she dared to peek, the gunman who'd struck Mus'ab had backed off several steps to make room for another man, this one older, with deep lines on his face. He walked up with his hands clasped behind his back until he stood in front of her. The man nudged Mus'ab with the toe of his boot and barked a harsh command in Arabic. Mus'ab grunted a reply and struggled to his feet.

The man stuck out his hand, and Mus'ab handed over his ID.

"Give him your ID," Mus'ab said.

Arielle's hand trembled as she rifled through her bag. She felt the man's impatience, felt him reach for the bag himself, and then she'd found her temporary citizen card and held it out. The man took the card and stared at it, then flipped it over and studied the other side and then handed it to the fighter beside him. Then the man looked at Arielle and spoke in Arabic.

"He's sorry his man roughed you up," Mus'ab said. "He will be disciplined later."

The elder man studied Mus'ab Saleh and then dropped his gaze to pore over Mus'ab's ID card. With the yellowed nail of his index finger, he traced each word on the card. When he reached the bottom of the first side, he glanced up at Mus'ab's face and spoke. Mus'ab replied, and the man grunted, then headed for one of the pickup trucks.

Arielle leaned close. "What did he ask you?"

"Where we were going," Mus'ab said. "I said we were on our honeymoon."

"So where are we going?"

"Homs."

She glanced at him noticed the pallor that had come over his face. "Do you think he believed it?"

"No," he said.

The elder man turned from the pickup truck, barked several commands at the fighters closest to him, then pointed to Mus'ab Saleh.

Mus'ab took Arielle's hand and looked her full in the face. "I love you," he said. "Run."

She froze.

"Run!" Mus'ab yelled. He thrust her from him and then strode out to intercept the approaching gunmen, his fists brandished before him.

Arielle hitched up her *abaya*, but was unable to look away.

Mus'ab swung at one fighter, missed, and then the other fighter kicked out his legs. Mus'ab's head struck the ground and then one of the soldier's butt stroked him and the crack of the rifle hitting Mus'ab's head shocked Arielle into action.

She spun and ran toward the end of the bus. The other passengers shied from her as if she had the plague, but she ignored them. She made it to the end of the line, past the bus, and headed for a compound on the other side of the road, a mere fifty yards away. Halfway across the road, hands grabbed the fabric of her *abaya* and drew her up short. She screamed, and then arms wrapped around her body and dragged her back to the checkpoint.

* * *

KANATA, ONTARIO
11 MAY 15 – 1357 LOCAL

The sign read 'Ottawa Valley Muslim Society,' and it was the lone clue that Erik stood outside a mosque. He hadn't expected a towering domed building with minarets, but the corner lease of a small strip mall seemed more appropriate for an all-night convenience store than a religious center.

He wasn't sure Stephanie's suggestion was a good idea. He had a healthy skepticism of religious figures of any stripe. Too often their polished veneer hid something, a porn habit, gambling, worse. In his experience, this conversation had a good chance of turning into a political lecture, which he didn't know if he could handle. Still, nothing ventured, nothing gained. He crossed the parking lot and entered the makeshift prayer center.

"Hello?" he said. Inside the tiled foyer were several rubber mats for footwear and a coat rack. A little deeper into the room was a small office and beyond that, an open carpeted space.

A rakish young man wearing thick horn-rimmed glasses poked his head out of the office. "Yes?"

"I'm looking for Imam Vellani," Erik said.

"You must be Mr. Petersson, how nice to meet you." The man exited the office and extended a hand. "Welcome. I'm Ziad Vellani, thank you for coming by."

"Please, it's Erik." He shook Ziad's hand, wondered if he was Imam Vellani's son. "Is the Imam here?"

Ziad placed his right hand over his heart and bowed. "I am the Imam," he said. "And Ziad is fine."

Erik squinted and then realized he was staring at Ziad's gelled faux-hawk and stylish clothes. "I'm sorry," he said and his cheeks grew hot. "I think I was expecting someone older."

"I'll take that as a compliment." Ziad smiled. "If it makes you feel better, I'm older than I look."

"It doesn't." Erik forced a chuckle. "Now I feel like I'm aging poorly."

Ziad chuckled as well and gestured to the office. "Come, sit down. Can I get you something? Coffee?"

Erik nodded and then followed Ziad into the office and sat down in front of a simple desk. While Ziad busied himself with a coffee maker, Erik glanced around. Certificates dotted the office walls, a Master of Arts in Middle Eastern and Islamic Studies from the University of Toronto, along with a Master of Business Administration from the Ivey Business School.

"Here you go." Ziad set a mug in front of Erik then sat on the other side of the desk. "Now, how can I help?"

Erik sipped his coffee, then cleared his throat. "My daughter converted to Islam, and a month ago she went to Syria. I haven't heard from her since."

Ziad's smile disappeared. "I'm sorry. That –"

"Why would she do that?" He glared at Ziad as if the man knew and wouldn't share the answer and then he dropped his gaze to his lap. "I'm sorry, I should probably start at the beginning."

"It's all right." Ziad rested his chin on his folded hands. "First, let me say that I don't condone the philosophy of these groups," he said. "Their interpretation of Islam is self-serving, cherry-picked to reinforce their agenda and while it may be cold comfort, these groups are outliers." Ziad shook his head. "I can guess at your questions, but there are many reasons why people self-radicalize."

"Arielle didn't self-radicalize," Erik said. He met Ziad's gaze for a second and then blinked. "She was recruited."

Ziad resettled his glasses. "Were you close with her?"

"I thought so," Erik said. "I raised her myself the past ten years."

"You and your wife separated?"

"Her mother committed suicide when Arielle was ten."

"I'm so sorry."

Erik sighed. "I was in the military at the time. When Audray died, I got out and joined the RCMP so I could focus on raising Arielle. But work has always been how I've coped, and so I was still gone a lot, and a few years ago I transferred to a counter-terrorism unit and was gone even more." He left out that he'd requested the transfer. "I know what you're thinking, but she was always mature for her age and seemed to be handling it well." But had she? Looking back, how many school activities had he missed, how many meals had she eaten alone while he'd been saving the world? He clenched his jaw. "She was too smart to self-radicalize."

Ziad spread his hands. "Childhood tragedy does tend to be a predictor of higher risk individuals. A divorce, the loss –"

"I know that," he said. "This is what I do for a living. But Arielle is not an extremist."

"Then why are you here?"

"I don't know," he said and looked away. "I guess to learn more about Islam so I can show her how she was mistaken and convince her to come home."

"I see." Ziad paused, seemed to consider his words. "What if she won't change her mind?"

"She will." He didn't know how he'd live with himself if she didn't. "She has to. Her family is here."

"Of course." Ziad took a deep breath. "Mr. Petersson, did you know I used to be a banker?"

Erik held up a hand. "Listen, I know this must sound crazy."

"I was a banker, for several years. I'd finished my time in the trenches, had my own team, even a corner office." Ziad's gaze flickered to the MBA certificate on the wall, and he went on. "It was all meaningless. A cycle of working to make more money, then expanding my lifestyle, then working harder to make more money. In the end, I worked so much I had no time to spend my money."

"Sounds like a nice problem," Erik said with a half-hearted smile.

"Not as nice as you'd think," he said. "I had an epiphany one day that I was a slave, worshipping a god without even knowing it. Actually, worse than a slave, because I hadn't known I wasn't free." He paused and picked up a split picture frame from his desk, two different young girls on each side. "I left the bank and returned to school to study theocracy and then Islamic studies. After a few years, I was offered a position here, and accepted, and do you know what I've found out in that time?"

Erik shook his head.

"That people want to belong to something bigger than themselves. These days, that's difficult to attain." Ziad leaned back in his chair. "Big organizations, the banks, they try to fill that need, but to them, a sense of belonging is a means to an end, that's all. The profit motive. In religions, on the other hand, community is both the means and the end. That's why the word *ummah* has such significance in Islam."

"Community," Erik said.

"That's right." Ziad nodded. "The *ummah* transcends relationships based on kinship, to one based on shared beliefs and values. The community supports each other, and so I would ask you, Mr. Petersson, where was your daughter's community when she turned to this barbaric group for support?" He leaned forward. "More to the point, where were you?"

Erik recoiled. "This isn't about me."

"Isn't it?"

"I'm not the one who ran off."

"Then why do you think your daughter left?"

"I don't know," Erik said and looked down. "I don't know. Something bad happened to her, and she changed, and I missed all the signs."

"What was it?"

"She was raped."

Ziad held his hands together in front of his lips. "I'm so sorry, Mr. Petersson."

Erik nodded and did not trust himself to speak.

"How did you find out?" Ziad asked. "Did she tell you?"

Erik shook his head.

"Why do you think that was?"

"I was there for her, all she had to do was ask."

"Did she live with you?"

"No –"

"Did you spend much time together?"

"Not really –"

"Did you talk often?"

"We played Warcraft every couple of weeks –"

"I'm sorry?" Ziad's eyebrows rose. "Are you saying the extent of your contact was to play an online game?"

"It was our thing," Erik added in a soft voice.

"Mr. Petersson, do you want to know what I think?" Ziad asked.

Erik glanced up and saw his image reflected in Ziad's glasses and for a second, wasn't sure he was so eager to hear what Ziad thought. He hesitated and then nodded.

"I think you cannot learn what you think you already know." Ziad braced his elbows on the desk. "Mr. Petersson, with all due respect, you came here today to talk and yet it seems that your mind is already made up. You've said you were absent, and a workaholic, and since you know so much I wonder if you also know that we must all make time for the things that are important to us. And so I would ask you, how much time did you make for Arielle?"

Erik held up a hand. "Now wait –"

"Mr. Petersson, where were you when your family needed you?"

Erik opened his mouth and nothing came out.

Several months after Audray had killed herself, long after he'd redeployed from Afghanistan for her funeral, long after the nightly drinking sessions had begun, he'd received a letter from her. She'd written it weeks before she'd slit her wrists, but the mail had been slow to get to Afghanistan, and so it had arrived long after he'd already left and even longer to follow him back to Canada. For all that, he had no problems remembering her words.

"I can't do this on my own anymore," she'd written. "Where were you?"

"Where were you?" Ziad repeated.

"At work," Erik said, and struggled to keep his voice steady.

"Then you are also a slave. Like I was."

Erik clasped his hands together and rested his elbows on his legs. "What do I do?"

"Mr. Petersson, if you hope to bring your daughter home, I think your best chance lies less with showing her she's mistaken about Islam, and more with showing her that you're her community. At least as much as the group she decided to join."

"And how do I do that?" he asked. "I can't even get in touch with her."

Except he had at least one other option.

"Perhaps you should pray," Ziad said. "And trust that Allah does not give problems without also giving solutions."

Erik thought of Matt de Kalb and wondered if Allah had a sense of humor.

* * *

RAQQA, SYRIA
12 MAY 15 – 1134 LOCAL

It didn't take long – a minute, maybe two – until the man's screams stopped. Perhaps the man passed out, or perhaps the boiling water overwhelmed his pain receptors, either way, Abu Noor al Kanadi was glad when the shrieks ceased.

Across the crowded square, two hooded fighters stood beside a large, cast-iron cauldron. From within a cloud of steam that rose from the pot's surface, a pair of arms stuck up over the side, chained together at the wrists. One of the fighters used a stick to hook the chain and dunk what was left of Mus'ab Saleh back into the boiling water and his body sank out of sight.

Farther down, another two hooded men escorted a woman into the square. The wife of the coward Mus'ab Saleh, she wore a simple white robe instead of the black *abaya*, her head uncovered, hands bound behind her back. A blindfold covered her eyes, the black fabric in sharp contrast against the pale skin of her face. Half-led, half-dragged, she was marched to the center of the square where one of the men kicked her in the back of her legs, and she fell to her knees.

"I'm sorry it didn't work out," Mamdouh said.

"As am I," al Kanadi said.

"Why do we need a North American? There are others ready to go right now."

Al Kanadi shook his head. "It will be easier to negotiate border security when they're from there. This one, in particular, would have been perfect. She even has her passport, and would have just been going home." He glanced at his second-in-command. "Plus, there's the narrative. Using a native-born will have far greater impact than a Syrian, or Iraqi."

A hooded man in tan fatigues strode up to stand by the woman. He pulled out a sheet of paper and began to read. For the crime of aiding a coward who'd fled the battlefield, the woman would be put to death. When he'd finished reading the sentence, the man tucked the paper into a pocket and moved to a pile of melon-sized stones. He stooped to pick up a rock, hefted it a few times and then raised the stone over his head and brandished it to the crowd.

The girl remained on her knees, unmoving, her gaze vacant and fixed on the ground.

"She has given up," Mamdouh said. "She cannot even bring herself to be scared."

"Maybe she just has more courage than the man," al Kanadi said.

The executioner advanced on the woman. He dismissed the black-clad guards with a nod and then faced the crowd again. He yelled and rotated in a circle, the stone displayed overhead like he held a piece of heaven itself, and when the circle was complete, he lowered the stone and stood over the woman.

Silence fell over the square, so quiet al Kanadi was able to hear the man with the stone mumble to the woman, though not what the man said. She did not move. The man cocked his arm behind him, paused, then threw. The stone struck the woman in the chest, knocked her back. She put down a hand to steady herself, struggled to remain upright, and then looked up at the executioner and smiled.

The executioner stooped and snatched up the stone. Raised it and smashed it down on the side of the woman's head. Dislodged her blindfold and drove her to the dirt. The man raised both hands in the air and faced the crowd and then pointed to the pile of stones.

Al Kanadi studied the woman. When she'd looked up, he'd thought she might fight, and as the crowd advanced toward the pile of stones, he wondered what she would do.

The executioner stood with his back to the woman, oblivious that she'd pushed herself to her hands and knees. The hair over her left ear was matted red, and the blindfold had fallen down and uncovered one eye and through that eye the woman glared about the square. She pushed to her knees and stared at the brown-clad man and spat.

Mamdouh snorted.

"Stop this," al Kanadi said as the executioner grabbed the woman by the throat.

"Impossible," Mamdouh said.

"Do it."

"They'll tear us apart."

"Then shoot them before that happens." The bloodlust had not yet gripped the crowd, and it could be stopped if they acted now. The unexpectedness might even work in the Caliphate's favor. The people would wonder why the execution was stopped, would fear the uncertainty of not knowing. "She has fight in her. She's perfect. Save her."

"She will not obey." Mamdouh's voice was fierce. "Look at her."

The woman fought in the executioner's grasp, clawed at his arm and even as her face turned red, she tried to spit again. The man flung her to the ground and then picked up his stone, stained red on one side. Several other people appeared behind him, tentative even though they held stones of their own.

"She will obey. You will see to it."

"Me?"

Al Kanadi grasped Mamdouh's shoulder. "You will break her. Mold her into the weapon we need her to be. I can trust no other," he said. "Now save her. Before the crowd tastes blood."

At the executioner's feet, the woman struggled back to her knees. A stone lobbed from the crowd caught her in the leg, another struck the ground near her head, and against this backdrop, the executioner raised his stone over his head.

A concussion of gunfire erupted beside al Kanadi, and Mamdouh strode into the square. He fired his rifle into the air again, then trained it on the executioner and yelled at the crowd. The executioner paused, and the crowd pressed at his back, and Mamdouh fired another burst, this time into the front row of the crowd. Bodies fell to the dirt, and the executioner dropped his stone and held his hands in front of his face. The crowd surged once more and then began to melt away as the people panicked and ran.

Al Kanadi pushed through the people, into the space Mamdouh claimed around the woman. He stared at her, pinned under Mamdouh's knee. "Clean her up and bring her to me. We have a lot to do."

CHAPTER ELEVEN
DRAGGED FORTH

OUTSIDE OTTAWA, ONTARIO
12 MAY 15 – 1305 LOCAL

Erik plugged his ears to drown out the sound of bullets. The two men on the shooting range hadn't acknowledged him yet, so he waited, counted the minutes on his watch. After one staccato-like burst, the men straightened and let their rifles hang from single-point slings and then began to saunter the thirty yards toward the back of the range where Erik waited. When they got closer, the slighter of the two men pulled off his shooting gloves and made eye-contact. "You Petersson?"

"That's right," Erik said and extended a hand.

The man walked past Erik and laid his rifle on a picnic table.

"De Kalb asked me to speak with you," Erik said.

"He did, did he?" The man shed his shooting vest and placed it beside his rifle. "Well, I'm Chris. That Neanderthal over there is Mad Mark."

The other man stood over boxes of ammunition and held an empty magazine in his hands. He glanced at Erik and grunted and then grabbed a box of bullets and began to reload and the bullets made a steady, metallic rhythm as he slotted them into the magazine.

Chris sat at the table and pulled out a pack of cigarettes. "What did MDK say we should talk about?"

Erik looked downrange. It had been a long time since he'd had to do this type of ass-sniffing. He hadn't missed it. "About the 1st Middle East International Brigades. He said you needed people to help out in Syria."

"You want to go to Syria."

"That's right," Erik said and sat across from Chris.

Chris stroked his designer beard and studied Erik, then abruptly turned to the other man. "Hear that, Mark? He wants to go to Syria."

Mark grunted, did not look up from his magazine.

Erik suppressed an urge to leave. His every instinct told him these two were posers, former rent-a-cops or sheriff's deputies who got off on pretending to be ex-special forces. But de Kalb had vouched for them, said they knew their business. He forced himself to remain seated.

Chris looked back, teeth bared in a smile. "Why not join the army? Wouldn't that be safer?"

"Our army's not in Syria," he said. "De Kalb said your outfit could help."

"MDK talks a lot. Things in the field look different from the view in corporate headquarters."

Erik nodded and tried to recall Chris's biography from the website for the 1st Middle East International Brigade. It had said United States Special Forces, but that could mean a lot of things. Plus, he was pretty sure corporate headquarters consisted of Matt de Kalb and one other guy, not a huge team for an organization that claimed to help Westerners fight with the Kurds against the Caliphate in Syria and Iraq. *Private security*, he thought. *Never changes.*

Erik had considered private security after Audray died. Back then, some companies offered a thousand dollars a day, ninety days on, thirty days off. He and Arielle could've toughed it out for a year, maybe two, but he'd known it wouldn't work. Plus, he knew most contractors never left. They'd commit for a few years to make money and ten years later would still be at it, never confident about the backgrounds of the other contractors. But things were different now, and the important thing was that these men could get him into Syria.

Chris lit a cigarette. "What do you think, Mark? Think we should let him go to Syria?"

"He looks too old." Mark's gravelly voice matched his hulking body.

"Mark's right." Chris held up his hands as if he was helpless. "You're too old."

"I'm probably the same age as you guys."

"The fuck you know about us?" Mark glared at Erik with his too-far apart eyes.

"What I can see, like any good soldier." Erik pointed to his face, and the black bracelet on his right wrist slid down his forearm. "Isn't that what you're looking for? Soldiers to fight?"

"Easy, fella, Mark got his nickname in the United States Marine Corps," Chris said. "Oorah!"

Mark shifted his glare to Chris and then back to Erik.

"Don't let him fool you though, he wasn't a grunt, just a pretty flyboy," Chris said. "Tough as that is to believe."

"Fuck you," Mark said and went back to his magazine.

Chris's shit-eating grin widened. "Seriously, fella, what are you gonna do in Syria? You look like you're more used to sitting at a desk than in a bunker."

"Can we dispense with the monkey dance?" he asked. MDK would've told Chris everything he needed to know, that Erik had been an airborne trooper, fought in Somalia and Bosnia, and gathered on-the-ground intelligence as a HUMINT operator in Afghanistan, working on his own or with one or two others for support. He toyed with the bracelet on his wrist. "Can you help me or not?"

"Oh, we can do it, don't worry about that," Chris said.

"Then what's the problem?"

"Just trying to figure out your motivation." He blew a cloud of smoke in Erik's face. "You want to talk about your daughter? MDK mentioned something about that."

Erik tensed. "She's in Syria, with the Caliphate."

"Ouch," Chris scrunched up his face. "That explains a lot." His shit-eating grin returned, and he smacked the table. "You want to be like that Dutch guy, the Jihadi hunter who went and found his son."

"If it helps to think of it like that," Erik said.

"Can you believe this shit, Mark?" Chris said. "You couldn't make it up if you tried."

Mark grunted.

"So, you don't want to fight. You want to find your daughter," Chris said.

Erik nodded. "I'll fight, if I have to."

"What if we say no?"

"De Kalb said –"

"MDK's full of shit," Chris said. "He's not the one risking his ass down range."

Erik looked down and balled his hands into fists.

"What are you gonna do?" Chris chuckled. "Hit me? Mark'll be using your face for a boot brush before you ever touch me."

Erik glanced at Mark, who kept on jamming bullets into magazines. The man was huge, perhaps twice Erik's size, and looked capable enough to follow through on the threat. "I'll go with or without you."

"Not if I report you to your cop buddies."

He realized De Kalb and Chris had talked more than Chris was letting on. "Why would you do that?"

Chris's smile reappeared. "It never hurts to develop good relations with the police. I doubt they'd be too pleased at you heading to Syria."

Erik snorted and shook his head.

"So now you have your excuse." Chris's lip curled in a sneer. "You made the effort, tried your best. Your daughter would be proud. Now, why don't you get the fuck out of here?"

The words stung, so close to what Audray had said before his last deployment. He'd been home from Afghanistan for maybe two months when he'd been asked to go back – intelligence officers were in short supply, and he was needed. Audray had not seen things the same way.

"What about Arielle?" she'd said. "Every time the news mentions a soldier killed, she hides in her room."

"I won't even be leaving the base," he'd said. "This is important."

"She's eight years old, she doesn't know that." Tears welled in her eyes. "I can't do this again, not so soon."

"You can," he'd said and taken her by the shoulders. "It's not that long, and we could use the extra money."

"We don't need the money," she'd said. "We need you."

But a month later he was on a flight back to the sandbox. At the airport, he'd tried to apologize.

"I'm sorry." He'd been awkward in his uniform, an added layer of distance between him and Audray. "Arielle will understand when she's older."

Audray held her head high and blinked back tears. Anyone watching would have thought they were tears of sorrow at the departure of her husband. "I'm sure she will."

He'd moved to hug her, but she'd brushed him away. "Just leave."

Not knowing what else to do, he'd left. Three months later, she'd slit her wrists in a warm bath while Arielle was at her grandparents.

No, he wouldn't walk away again.

He stood. "I'm going, no matter what you do. Tell my colleagues, I don't care. I'll find a way." He spun and strode toward his car. The sooner he put this place behind him, the better.

"Wait," Chris said.

He froze. Footsteps approached and then Chris was beside him.

"I'm just fucking with you," Chris said, his toothy smile back in place. "Testing you to see how bad you want this."

"A test?"

Chris nodded. "Don't get all bent out of shape," he said. "If we're going to be working together, I want to know where you're coming from."

"Then we're good."

"Yeah, we're good," Chris said. "And if things work out, you'll be helping us at least as much as we're going to help you."

Part of him told him to keep walking, to avoid putting his life in the hands of this man, but it would be undeniably easier to go with their help than without it. He glanced again at the bracelet on his wrist.

You Are Not Forgotten.

He took a deep breath and let Chris lead him back to the picnic table.

***

RAQQA, SYRIA
14 MAY 15 – 1212 LOCAL

Abu-Noor al Kanadi was impressed.

The woman sat a few feet in front of him, on a stiff, metal chair under the beam of a flood light. There was a hood over her head and in the fifteen minutes since she'd been brought into the bunker, she hadn't moved once. If he remembered right, she'd taken the name Hafsa, which meant lioness. Whoever had picked that name had chosen well.

He nodded at Mamdouh, who yanked the hood off the woman. She blinked and scrunched her face against the light. A long, gouge ran up the left side of her face, and her hair was kinked and greasy, but under the cuts and dirt, perhaps some strength.

"Do you know who I am?" al Kanadi asked.

The woman stiffened and turned her face in his direction.

"I said, do you know who I am?"

The woman was silent and Mamdouh grabbed a handful of her hair and wrenched her head back. "Answer when he asks a question."

"Stop," al Kanadi said. "Let her go."

Mamdouh shoved her back into the chair and then merged into the shadows along the concrete walls of the bunker.

The woman's chest rose and fell, and she stared at him through the harsh light.

"Are you hungry? Thirsty?" al Kanadi asked.

She swallowed and then grimaced and then shook her head.

"Suit yourself," he said. "Do you know why you're here?"

She waited and then shook her head again.

"I saved you. I stopped your execution."

The muscles along her jaw tightened, and her gaze dropped to the floor.

"I'm sorry about your husband," he said.

If he'd looked away, he'd have missed her shoulders slump, the effort on her face as she fought to straighten her back and regain her posture. His instincts had been right, she had plenty of fight left. "I forgive you for helping him. Fear makes people do strange things."

"He was a good man." Her voice was hoarse. "He didn't deserve to die like that."

Mamdouh darted forward and raised his hand.

Al Kanadi stood and caught Mamdouh's arm in mid-swing. He met Mamdouh's glare, shook his head. Willed Mamdouh to understand that physical pain would have no effect on this woman.

Mamdouh struggled for a few seconds and then relaxed and when al Kanadi let him go, he returned to his place near the wall.

Al Kanadi looked at the woman. "He put you in an impossible situation," he said. "In fact, what you did took courage." He sat back down. "Since you won't guess who I am, I'll tell you. I am Abu Noor al Kanadi."

Her face twitched, and he knew that she'd heard of him. That would make things easier. "Do you know what I'm in charge of in the Caliphate?"

"No."

"Deep operations, if that means anything," al Kanadi said. "It is not enough to focus on our enemies in the Middle East, we must also engage our enemies around the world, and I have the honor of carrying out those operations."

A frown passed over her face, and her gaze dipped.

"Do you have a question?" he asked.

She glanced up at him and cleared her throat. "Why should I care what you do?"

He laughed, unable to contain himself. Raised a hand when Mamdouh moved off the wall and shook his head. "So you can understand who I am and what I'm trying to accomplish," he said, although he would keep the finer details to himself.

"Why?"

"Because I would like you to help me."

"That will never happen."

"Mamdouh would agree with you." Al Kanadi nodded at his second-in-command. "He thinks I should have left you to die and he may be right. He's a good judge of character." Which was an understatement. Mamdouh had cherry-picked dozens of men from the old Iraqi regime, intelligence officers, scientists, doctors. Helped them see how their interests aligned with the

Caliphate. But this woman was different and required a different touch.

"Then why are you wasting your time?" she asked.

"Because I believe I can help you find your purpose."

Her eyebrows knit together.

"Sister," he said, "we have both come from the West. We know the rot that is in Western society. It will collapse, we both know that."

Her gaze flickered away.

"The West cannot defeat us. We can only be defeated by ourselves, because this war is a test of our faith. By Allah's mercy, we will win, but to do so, we must be vigilant, which is why your husband had to die."

She looked up, met his gaze. "You boiled him alive," she said, and for a moment, he was glad Mamdouh was in the room. "You're a monster."

"It may seem savage, but I can assure you, it is strategy." He rose and began to pace, his right hand rested on the pistol at his side. "Our actions, precisely because they're savage, recruit more fighters to our cause, while at the same time demoralizing our enemies. So it is written in the *Idarat al Tawakhush*." He paused and stared at her. "And we're not alone in using harsh punishments. You think the electric chair is somehow more humane? Or lethal injections?" He resumed his walk around the bunker.

"It's not the same." Her gaze followed him. "And they'll never stop fighting you."

"Maybe so," he said and knelt before her. "But they'll never win and do you know why?"

She looked away, and he reached out and cupped her chin, forced her to meet his gaze.

"They're not in it, to win it," he said. "They prefer their material comforts and celebrity worship to real sacrifice, which is what it would take to defeat us." It was a weakness he would exploit. "But you're not like that, are you? You know all about sacrifice, the will to succeed."

Al Kanadi remembered Army Staff College well. Long hours crammed in hot rooms to discuss decisive points and centers of gravity, sources of power from which a country drew strength. If the source of that power was destroyed, the country would collapse. In the case of the West, their source of power was the will of the people. It was also their greatest vulnerability. Western countries had no stomach for casualties, no skin-in-the-game, and so his strategy was simple. Take the attack directly to their people and tough out the difficult years until they realized how much it would cost to succeed and gave up.

"They think their wealth and technology protects them, keeps them from getting their hands dirty. It lets them inflict all manner of violence on the world without feeling the consequences of their actions. But they're wrong."

Her gaze dropped. "It's not –"

"I've seen it." Heat flared in his voice. "I served in Afghanistan. Iraq. I fought their wars. They made things worse, not better."

He wanted to roll up his right sleeve, show her the tattoo of a dagger in front of crossed swords, the emblem of 5th Special Forces Group. He'd seen Afghanistan become a forgotten war, aid money funneled to warlords who worked to prolong the conflict. He'd seen the idiocy of Iraq, where every action gave birth to the next threat, the dismissal of Baathist officials that led to the Sunni uprising, and then to the Caliphate. So stupid, so predictable. He'd lost faith, retired in disgust, and like many veterans, smothered his idealism with alcohol, then drugs, then prison. It was behind bars that he'd accepted there was no God other than God and that Mohammed was His messenger. And then he'd followed the call back to the Middle East.

"The West is corrupt," he said. "This war is good for business, and the corporations don't want change. No, they want the money to keep flowing so they can make their annual bonuses."

She shook her head, and her eyes grew moist. "More violence is not the answer."

He nodded and then stood. "I used to think so, too," he said. "But sometimes it's easier to burn everything down and start from scratch. The West will not leave us alone because we challenge the status quo and so they have to taste defeat. After that, perhaps they can be saved."

"I won't participate in an attack."

"I never asked you to," he said. "All I'd like is for you to take a trip."

"Where?"

"Canada."

She shook her head. "I would be arrested."

"You haven't done anything illegal."

"I helped recruit, I –"

"And showed unique talent, but it can't be tied to you." He leaned close. "What I'm asking is important. I need to deliver a message. It must be carried by a person, and I'd like you to accompany the messenger."

She closed her eyes. "I don't understand."

"Look at us," he said and gestured to himself and Mamdouh. "A woman's presence will soften our edges so that the messenger can pass through security," he said, his voice quiet. "And you have the perfect narrative. Ran away to the Caliphate, found love, then lost it all. Heart-broken, you return home. Not so far from the truth, is it?"

She turned her face from him.

He felt her defenses weaken and he leaned in, moved to brush her cheek with the back of his hand. Too late, he saw her hand dart out for the pistol on his belt. He had time to curse and then he found the barrel of his pistol pointed in his face. Mamdouh left the wall, and al Kanadi shook his head and kept his gaze on the woman. "Well done," he said.

"I hate you." Her eyes were moist, but she did not blink. "I will not help you."

"All I ask is for you to deliver a message." He wondered if he should take the pistol. Kill her now and end this. But he sensed an opportunity, if he could appeal on a different level.

"I should kill you," she said and drilled the pistol's muzzle into his chest.

"Did you know my wife recently arrived in Raqqa?"

She blinked.

"I've been trying to get her and my sons here for years. We spent so much time apart."

"So what?" The pressure of the pistol against his chest lessened ever so little.

"If I'm to die, my last wish would be to see my family again." He peered at her. "Do you have anyone like that?"

She said nothing except a tiny gap of space opened between the pistol and his chest.

"Your father, perhaps?" he asked, and when a spasm crossed her face, he knew that his words had found their target. "I can make that happen. All you have to do is agree to travel."

Her eyes dipped, and the pistol began to drop, and now the greatest risk was that Mamdouh would step in and ruin everything when he was so close.

"What happens when I'm done?" she asked.

"That's up to you," he said. He had her, he knew it. "It will be difficult to start your life again, but not impossible."

"What happens if I say no?" she said and raised the pistol back up to his chest.

"You die," he said. "But we'll make it quick. It's the least we can do for your courage."

Her breaths were quick, ragged. She glanced at Mamdouh, then back to him. Remained silent and then nodded and lowered the pistol.

He bent and took the gun from her hands. "Thank-you."

Mamdouh held up the hood and the woman recoiled.

Al Kanadi raised a hand. "A precaution, nothing else. You will, after all, eventually speak to authorities in the West." His gaze was intense as he watched the hood descend over her head. "You will be a great carrier of our message. Go with God."

She submitted, and Mamdouh brought her to her feet, marched her to the door and handed her over to two men who waited outside. Before he walked out, he looked at al Kanadi over his shoulder. "She has too much spirit left."

Al Kanadi smiled. "Then break her."

* * *

OTTAWA, ONTARIO
15 MAY 15 – 1445 LOCAL

Erik checked several bullets off his to-do list and then bit the end of the pen while he considered the remaining items. Not many more. He looked up and scanned the food court of the World Exchange Plaza yet again, went back to his list and the next time he looked up, he caught a glimpse of Stephanie across the other tables, red leather tote bag over her shoulder. He waved to catch her attention. "Thanks for coming," he said as she neared his table.

"No problem." She moved to sit down.

"Don't get comfortable," he said and got up. "Let's walk and talk."

Her brow crinkled. "And where are we going?"

He waited until she was beside him, then started walking. "To a notary."

"A what?"

"A notary." He ignored her frown. "It's like a quasi-lawyer, they –"

"I know what a notary is," she said, and her tone suggested she wasn't impressed he'd been about to explain it to her. "Does this have anything to do with the package Jordan asked me to give to you?" She patted her handbag.

"It might." He sighed. "And by might, I mean yes. I need you to witness a power-of-attorney."

"Isn't that what a notary does? And where's your attorney?"

"I was hoping you'd be my attorney." He led them to an escalator.

"Slow down. For what?"

"Property and personal care." He held up a hand. "Don't worry, I doubt you'll have to do anything."

She cocked her head to one side. "Erik, what are you talking about?"

He took a deep breath and met her gaze. "I'm going after Arielle."

"And what does that mean?"

"I'm going to Syria."

Her eyebrows rose.

"While I'm gone, I need someone to act on my behalf –"

"Is this some joke you and Jordan dreamed up?"

"It's not as crazy as it sounds."

"What a relief," she said. "Because it sounds very crazy. You can't go to Syria."

"I leave in two days."

Stephanie closed her eyes and rubber her temples. "You're an intelligence analyst on a team that tracks and prevents high-risk travelers from going to places like Syria. You can't go there."

"Technically, I'm not on the team."

"Technically," annoyance crept into her voice, "you're suspended. And don't change the subject. Why are we even talking about this?" She dug for her phone.

He placed a hand on her arm. "Please, listen to me," he said. "I'm going to find her."

She hesitated and met his gaze. "Erik, this isn't the solution."

"It is." Now that he'd got to it, his calmness surprised him. A part of him understood her argument, would have said the same thing in her position, but the farther he went, the more he knew this was the right decision. "I can do this."

She folded her arms. "How are you getting there?"

"The First Middle Eastern International Brigades."

"Mercenaries?" Her face scrunched as if the word caused her pain.

"They've been helpful," he said. "They have a Canadian unit, the Pearson Battalion."

"And what do they get out of this?" she asked. "They don't care about you."

"Stephanie, I know all that, and it doesn't matter," he said. "They're in contact with rebel units on the ground. They can get me closer to Arielle, and I'm taking that chance."

She blinked and looked away. "And what's your plan when you get there?"

"I'll fly into Northern Syria and link up with some rebels near Kobane.

That's near where she crossed at Akçakale. From there, I'll start asking around. Something will turn up."

"If that's even where she crossed the border." The words came out in force and she glanced around the plaza, glared at the few people who'd turned to look at them. "You'll be looking for a...a...*mais tu chercherais une aguille dans une botte de foin*," she said.

"If you have a better plan, I'd love to hear it."

She held her hands in front of her lips, her eyes closed. "You could get killed. Or captured."

He nodded. "You're right."

"But that's not going to stop you."

"Again, what's the alternative?"

"*Mon criss de câlice,* to not be so stupid for starters." Her voice caught, and her hand flew up. "Why didn't you ask Jordan to go along with your *maudit* plan? Or your family? Why did you pick me?"

"Because I trust you the most."

She blinked several times. "What do I tell Wiggins? Did you think about the position that puts me in?"

"I did, and I'm sorry," he said and reached for her hand. "Stephanie, my whole life I've thought things through, balanced risks against rewards. None of that prevented this."

"It could stop it from getting worse."

"She's my daughter," he said. "What am I fighting for if not for her?"

A single tear traced a line down Stephanie's high cheekbone. A second tear formed and she wiped it off, squeezed his hand. "I'm scared for you," she said. "What if she's not who you remember?"

He rubbed her hand. "You know, we used to do this thing with her at bedtime. We'd ask her what her low and her high was for the day, and then Audray would tell her she was our favorite person in the whole world."

"Not favorite daughter?" Stephanie's voice was soft.

"Too small a sample size," he said and smiled. "When it was my turn, all I'd say was, 'and in space.' Because who knows, right? Maybe there'd be some kid in outer space somewhere, and then she might not be our favorite anymore. So Audray would say, 'you're our favorite person in the whole world,' and then I'd always say, 'and in space.'"

She squeezed his hand again.

"When Audray died, so much changed, but not that. I said it to her every day, even when it embarrassed her. And I never got a chance to tell her that before she left." He glanced away, blinked his eyes dry, then met Stephanie's gaze. "In the end, it doesn't matter if she's different. I want her to know she'll always be my favorite person in the world."

"And in space."

He chuckled. "Yeah. And in space."

Stephanie inhaled and wiped her eyes and then hugged him. "Be safe."

"I will." He held her tight, savored the warmth of her body. "I promise."

They stood in silence, and then she loosened her grip and backed off. She patted her tote bag and attempted a smile. "Don't forget to bring back Jordan's kit. He'll want to know how it worked."

"I will." He smiled back. "Tell him thanks."

"Tell him yourself." She stared up into his eyes. "You're a good man, Erik Petersson." She took a deep breath. "Are you ready?"

He nodded and took her hand. "As I'll ever be."

* * *

SOMEWHERE IN THE MEDITERRANEAN SEA
17 MAY 15 – 1155 LOCAL

The boat lurched, and Arielle's stomach followed. She covered her mouth and reached for a bucket at her feet and retched. All that came out was a trickle of green bile. She stayed like that for a minute and then let the bucket clatter to the floor and leaned back against the bulkhead and closed her eyes.

She'd been sick from the minute the boat had slipped its moorings. There were no windows in her postage-stamp-sized cabin, which must have been beside the engine compartment from the constant grumble and stifling heat. She'd opened the door several times to get fresh air, and each time a man in the hallway had shoved her back into the cabin.

She chided herself for her weakness. Mus'ab Saleh was dead, she'd heard his screams, and she hadn't even mourned him. She couldn't. Since al Kanadi had stopped her execution, she'd felt nothing but numbness, like a walking corpse. Perhaps she should be thankful for the seasickness. At least it made her feel something.

Or not. Her stomach rocked again, lower, down in her bowels. The bucket wouldn't be enough this time. She stumbled to the door and flung it open. A man wearing a grey pub cap pulled low over his eyes stood guard. When he saw her, he readied himself to shove her back into the cabin.

"I have to use the bathroom," she said.

The man's face blanched. "Use the pail."

"It's not clean. It will smell." She clutched her stomach. "Please, I can't hold it."

The man tugged his cap lower over his eyes and scanned the passageway in both directions. With a slight nod, he steered Arielle down and around a bend in the corridor. They stopped outside a door. "Here. Quickly."

"Thank-you, brother," she said and brushed past.

Before the door closed, he tugged on her elbow and peered into her eyes. "You must be brave." He resettled his pub cap again, then thrust her into the head and pulled the door shut.

For a moment, she forgot her stomach, forgot Mus'ab Saleh's screams. Why had the man said that? Then the cramps returned, and all that mattered was how quick she could shed her robes. She made it – only just – her embarrassment at the noise overcome by the relief of emptying her bowels. While she redressed, the man's words came back to her. What had he meant?

The man was not in the passageway when she exited the head. She walked in the direction from where she'd come and then paused. She wanted answers, and there might not be a chance like this again. As quiet as possible, she tiptoed in the other direction.

Ahead, the passageway split. The main corridor bent off to the right while straight-ahead was a small entryway that led to another part of the ship. She crept to the junction and poked her head into the entryway, craned her head to hear better. Voices came from inside, through another doorway. She crept farther into the alcove.

The voices grew louder, two men speaking Arabic. She strained and was able to pick out a few words: *Libi,* Libya. *Marad,* disease. Maybe they were discussing routes through Africa. It made sense. In the aftermath of the Libyan Civil War, she'd heard the country was lawless, as if diseased. Or if they were headed to the African continent, it might be a reference to the Ebola outbreak in Western Africa. Or maybe it was just talk. Another male entered the conversation, and her skin crawled in recognition. Mamdouh. She crept backward.

A hand fell on her shoulder and tugged her into the passageway. She raised her hands to claw whoever had grabbed her and found herself face-to-face with the man in the pub cap. His eyes were wide, and he cast glances at the entryway where she'd been listening.

"I'm sorry," she said. "I went the wrong way."

He put a finger to his lip and cast a glance at the entryway, then nodded back down the corridor. In silence, he took her by her elbow and steered her back to her cabin. At the room, he held the door open and gestured for her to enter.

She met his gaze. "I'm sorry," she said. "I needed some fresh air."

His face became grave. "You cannot do that again," he said. "The others would not be so forgiving."

"Thank-you, brother." She bowed her head. She entered the cabin, turned before the door closed. "What is your name?"

"Reza."

"Where are we going, Reza? Through Libya?"

"Do not worry about this," he said. He took a deep breath. "Our journey is dangerous enough, don't trouble yourself with details you can't control." He closed the door.

Arielle returned to the cot and sat down. Mamdouh and al Kanadi had told her almost nothing, how would she find out more? Then the ship heaved, and she forgot everything except keeping hold of the bucket.

CHAPTER TWELVE
SPLIT OPEN

Erik stood in the door of the small, double-prop airplane and looked out over Menagh Airfield. He had expected it to be smaller from the satellite photos. The Kurds had reclaimed it from the Caliphate a few short months ago, and already the tarmac was full of planes, civilian and military. All sorts of vehicles careened pell-mell across runways and service roads, their sound drowned out by the buzz-saw hum of the airplane's propellers. Erik slung his backpack over his shoulder and descended the air-stairs.

He heard the angry whup-whup-whup of a helicopter and spied two MH-60 Blackhawks droning down the taxiway and then the unmistakable roar of jet engines caused him to look behind him to see a lumbering grey monster screech down the runway and claw its way into the air, the words, 'U.S. Air Force,' stenciled near the cockpit windows.

"This is not Menagh," he said. Menagh was not big enough to handle a C-17.

"This way, over here," a man said, a light accent to his English.

Erik turned to the man, Middle Eastern and clad in green fatigues. "Where is this?"

The man scowled. "What do I look like, a tour guide?" When Erik failed to respond, the man's scowl grew deeper. "Where do you think? Erbil. Now come on." The man grabbed Erik's shoulder and pulled him in the direction of the other passengers.

"I'm supposed to be in Menagh." Erik's pace slowed.

The man barked laughter. "Are you stupid? Nobody flies into Menagh except Russians." He herded Erik toward what appeared to be a marshaling area for debarking passengers.

Erik wracked his brain. Chris had said he'd fly into Menagh in northern Syria, a mere hundred miles from Kurdish forces in Kobane. From Kobane, it would have been a short trip to Akçakale, which was where Arielle had supposedly crossed the Turkish border. Erbil wasn't the end of the world, but it would nonetheless take longer to get to Akçakale. More importantly, the Kurdish units he'd be working with were different. The Kurds in Syria were the People's Protection Units, the YPG, while the Kurds in Erbil were the Peshmerga, a hodge-podge of units split between the Ministry of Peshmerga Affairs, the Politburo of the Kurdistan Democratic Party, and Patriotic Union of Kurdistan.

"– are you?" the man beside him said.

"What?" Erik shouted in the man's ear as they entered a large hangar.

The man cringed. "Who are you?"

"Erik Petersson. And you?"

"Birwa Ahmadzadeh," he said. "What are you doing here?"

"That's a good question," he said.

"Birwa," a man called out from across the hangar. A Caucasian man with a dark tan and shaggy beard strode toward them. "I think he's one of mine."

Birwa scowled at Erik. "Are you with him?"

Erik took in the third man, who was dressed in khaki cargo pants and a baseball hat. "I don't even know who he is."

"Ray Parker. A mercenary."

"Easy, Birwa. We prefer conscientious volunteers," the man said as he neared. He thrust a hand at Erik. "Ray Parker. How's it goin'?"

Erik took Ray's hand as if the man was a genie who'd materialized out of the desert. "Erik Petersson."

Ray stripped off his wrap-around sunglasses. "Chris said you'd be here last night."

"That's funny, Chris told me I was going to Menagh," Erik said.

"What can I tell you? It's the goddamn Middle East, what do you fuckin' expect?" Ray pulled out a tin of chewing tobacco, offered it to both Birwa and Erik, then jammed a large pinch into his lip. "No offence, Birwa."

Birwa's face was impassive. "I assume you have paperwork?"

"Good to go," Ray said. He stowed the tin of tobacco in his pocket, then nodded to Erik. "Let's get your stuff."

"What happened to going to Menagh?"

Ray snorted. "Couldn't get clearance to land. Like I said, it's the Middle East. Consider yourself lucky you made it to Erbil." He headed for a small tractor pulling several luggage carts into the hangar. "That's where your bags'll be."

"Check him in through customs –" Birwa said.

"I got it, man." Ray gave Birwa an enthusiastic thumbs-up and a shit-eating grin. "And I'll make sure to tell Rafiq how helpful you were."

Birwa shook his head, then threw up his hands and walked off.

Erik found his two duffel bags on one of the carts. Ray grabbed one and headed for the hangar's exit, leaving Erik to toss the other bag over his shoulder and catch up. "So, you're with the International Brigades?"

"Shit," Ray said, "I'm one of the founding brothers."

"What do you do?"

"Operations officer." He stopped and pushed open the door. "Which includes meeting new guys. Not very glamourous, but someone's got to do it. Glad to have you aboard."

"What did you do before this?"

"Sergeant. 10th Mountain Div. First Battalion, 87th Infantry Regiment."

"And now you run operations?" Erik asked, glad Ray was several steps ahead and unable to see the surprised look on his face. Running brigade operations wasn't in the job description of any infantry sergeant he'd ever met. They stopped by a black SUV with tinted windows.

"Hell, yeah," Ray said. He raised the back hatch of the SUV and tossed the duffel bag inside. "You want to stop for some food? Pizza?"

"I'm not that hungry."

"You sure? It's not American, but it's fast, and it beats the local cuisine. Still might tear your guts apart though, no promises."

"I'd rather link up with Chris and figure out what's going on."

"I'm sure you would," Ray said lowered his sunglasses down his nose. "But first, I gotta take you to meet the battalion commander. Don't worry, it's a formality. He ain't in charge of nothing. Once that's done, I'll get you to the FLOT to see Chris and Mark. Better they brief you since I have no fucking idea what they have planned." Ray chuckled and reseated his sunglasses. "Shit, the FLOT – who'd have thought we'd be talking about Forward Line of Own Troops in this day and age? What's new is old, I guess. Get in." Ray jumped in the SUV, closed the door and revved the engine.

Erik paused and looked around the airfield. He'd never thought things would go smooth, but less than a day in was a little early for things to be falling apart.

The passenger side window rolled down, and Ray leaned across from the driver's seat. "What are you waitin' for? A goddamned twenty-page op order? Time to make like horse shit and hit the trail."

A tiny smile cracked Erik's face. Well said. He got into the SUV and held on as Ray sped away from the airport.

* * *

SIRTE, LIBYA
18 MAY 15 – 1058 LOCAL

Mamdouh stood in a small tower and supervised the shipyard. His men loitered in small groups within the tiny yard, some marshalled near the vehicles that had been waiting for them, some unloading supplies from the ship, a few even dozing. So much to do.

"Let's go, you sons of dogs," he yelled across the yard. Movement picked up as the men scurried about their tasks. If he'd been a man who was easy to please, he might have smiled. Instead, his attention was drawn to one area where movement had not changed.

Two people stood by a white Toyota Landcruiser, one in a black *niqab*, the other a pub cap. Hafsa and Reza, in the midst of a conversation from the way their heads moved back and forth. Any thought of smiling disappeared. He would not let the plan fail because of some Western *sharmuta*. Mamdouh strode down the stairway, where he met Faisal, his brother, and second-in-command.

"The supplies are almost loaded," Faisal said. "And the vehicles will do, although Abdel let us down with the weapons."

"How so?"

"They're rusty." Faisal grimaced. "Some might not even fire. Not much ammo either."

Mamdouh spat. He'd warned al Kanadi that their contact in Sirte would be more concerned about bootlegging alcohol and pornography than following through with mission-related demands. Mamdouh had known Abdel Fattah for a year, and the man had always been a convenient soldier of God. "I should be put in charge of Libya," he'd told al Kanadi.

"Sirte wouldn't know what to do with you," al Kanadi had said. "And Abdel is the right person to run things there while we establish a foothold. He's good with people. Have patience. When we're ready, the emir will send someone more suited to the task."

True, until Abdel was needed to outfit their trip across Africa. "Where is Abdel?"

Faisal nodded at the ship. "Onboard. Talking with the captain. No doubt getting drunk."

Mamdouh stared at the boat that had brought them across the

Mediterranean. Another loose end to tie up. "When will the convoy be ready?"

"Soon." Faisal shrugged. "We just need to load the fuel and water."

Mamdouh turned back to the vehicles, his gaze again drawn to the white Landcruiser. Reza's hands waved animatedly in the air, watched by the woman. Mamdouh ground his teeth and stalked in the direction of the Landcruiser. "Get her in the vehicle," he yelled.

Reza jumped, bowed to Mamdouh and stumbled over himself to open the rear door of the SUV, then ushered Hafsa inside.

"With all due respect, brother, Reza is a poor choice to escort the woman," Faisal said. "He is a good fighter, but soft-hearted."

"Keep them paired up for now. She listens to him."

"And if there's no change?"

"Then make an example of him."

"I understand."

At least the group had one good man. "Do you have any questions about what is expected?"

Faisal shook his head. "You can't come with us?"

"I have to go through Tunis for the passports and visas," he said. "The paperwork is complete?"

Faisal nodded. "Abdel came through with that, at least. Birth certificates, ID cards, photos. All in the glove compartment of your vehicle."

"I'll need documents for myself as well."

"That wasn't part of the plan." Faisal said and weathered Mamdouh's resultant glare. "But if you insist, you can do that in person in Tunis."

"It's good to have options," Mamdouh said.

Faisal snorted. "Except when those options needlessly increase the risk."

"Leave that to me," Mamdouh said. "Once I've arranged the passports and visas, I'll swing through Dakar. When I've finished checking on things there, I'll join you at the camp."

"Be sure to bring coffee. The Mexicans always throw some in."

Mamdouh nodded. Unlike al Kanadi, it took all his control to tolerate the cartel drug lords, although he recognized how much they were needed. The *kafir* were able to get almost anything through the cover of a legitimate import-export business in Dakar, and without them, al Kanadi's operation would be hamstrung, especially the camp with its specialist equipment. It was true that several of them had accepted the oneness of Allah, but Mamdouh preferred the simplicity of Hadith 9:4. "Wherever you find infidels, kill them." It left no room for doubt.

"Leave me three men and the vehicles I've picked out. Once the supplies are loaded, you can leave. I will rejoin you in a couple of days, *Insha'Allah*." Mamdouh looked at the ship. "I'll need rifles as well. And ammo."

"Is there no other way?" Faisal followed Mamdouh's gaze. "It's bad for business."

"Loose ends must be tied up."

"I understand," Faisal said and touched a fist to his heart. "*Fi Amanillah*."

"*Fi Amanillah*," Mamdouh said. While Faisal walked off, Mamdouh made his way to the black Landcruiser he'd claimed for himself. Three men made their way to this vehicle, and from one of them, he took a rifle. The gun's barrel was rusty, but when he cycled the action, the working parts ran smooth. It would do. "Grab your weapons and meet me at the gangway," he told the men.

Mamdouh watched as Faisal ordered the rest of the men into vehicles and then made his way to the ship. At the base of the gangway, he turned and raised his rifle in salute as Faisal drove off, and his gaze lingered on the white Landcruiser in the middle of Faisal's convoy. When the convoy was out of sight, Mamdouh lowered his rifle and watched as the other men returned.

"What now, emir?" a man called Ibrahim asked.

"Now we give payment." Mamdouh seated a magazine on his rifle and pulled the cocking handle to cycle a bullet into the chamber. So much to do, but soon there would be one less loose end, and he would be that much closer to the day when it would be him in charge and al Kanadi who took the orders. He was Mamdouh Qassam, the Butcher, and there nothing was beyond him while he remained the blessed of Allah.

He strode up the gangway, and the men followed.

* * *

ERBIL, IRAQ
18 MAY 15 – 1310 LOCAL

Erik followed Ray through an open office on the ground floor of a three-story building. What Ray had called the command post for the brigade headquarters turned out to be a small conference room set up with radios, computers, and a few projector screens.

"Not a bad setup," Erik said.

"I know what you're thinking," Ray said as he flopped into a rolling chair at a desk, "but this place is for show. We don't command anything from here."

"Is there another headquarters where that happens?"

Ray snorted. "Look, man, all we do is plus up Kurd units with ones and twos. Sometimes we run first-aid or shooting courses, but even those are mostly excuses for Chris and Mark to go to the FLOT and try to bag kills. That's where they are right now."

"What about the others?"

"What others?"

"The others in the Pearson battalion? How many are there?"

"In Pearson?" Ray's eyes rolled up. "Eight, maybe ten?"

"What?" Erik asked. He hadn't expected a western infantry battalion with numbers close to a thousand, but he'd thought there'd be more than eight. "Do they at least work together?"

Ray thumped his boots up on the desk. "Man, between all three 'battalions,'" he made rabbit ears with his fingers, "we might be able to field twenty-five guys on a good day, and most of them are hard-core mercs like the dynamic duo of Chris and Mark. These guys work with us because nobody else will hire them, so trust me, it's not necessarily a bad thing if they're not in your section."

The door creaked behind them, and Erik turned. A thin man with an olive complexion and dark hair entered, clad in a tight-fitting t-shirt and camouflage pants.

"Hey, boss," Ray said.

Erik stared at the new man, whom he took to be the battalion commander.

"You must be Mr. Petersson. *Salaam Alaikum.*" The man placed his right hand over his heart, and then extended it to Erik. "I'm Rafiq Talibani. Welcome to Kurdistan."

Erik took Rafiq's hand, returned what he hoped was the same light pressure the other man used. "Nice to meet you."

Rafiq dropped his hand. "All ready to join the fight?"

Ray chuckled. "He thought he was going to Menagh."

Rafiq's eyebrows rose.

"That's what Chris told me," Erik said. "It's closer –"

"Do you draw much?" Rafiq asked.

He paused. "Excuse me?"

"Do you draw?" Rafiq's right hand moved to the butt of a pistol in a drop holster on his leg. "I've been practicing. Some Special Forces soldiers trained me."

"Shit," Ray said. He dropped his feet and faced Rafiq. "Don't be doing stupid shit in the command post. You goddamn near put a round in one of the computers last time."

Rafiq moved to an open area between desks and spread his legs shoulder width apart, hands close to his thighs. "Call it," he said to Erik. The tips of his fingers wiggled.

"Hold on a second," Erik said and backed up, looked to Ray for support. "Boss –"

Rafiq's hand darted to the butt of the pistol. "Go!" he yelled. He fumbled with the catch and a second or two passed, and then he brought the pistol, up, up, up until the barrel stared Erik in the face. He smiled. "I'm getting better."

Erik stood frozen and stared at the pistol's muzzle.

"What the fuck did I tell you?" Ray walked up and grabbed the pistol from Rafiq. "Stop doing stupid shit."

Rafiq's face clouded. "You can't talk to me that way. I'm the battalion commander."

"You're a stupid fuck whose uncle's a general," Ray said as he unloaded the pistol's magazine. "Sir." He ejected the round from the pistol and snatched it out of the air and then slammed the pistol, magazine, and bullet onto the table. "For the last time, stop fucking around in the ops room." Lecture done, Ray sat back down.

Erik gripped the back of a chair to steady his hands. "Can we all just take a breath?" he asked. "I'm supposed to be in Syria."

"Man, do you know how much better it is here than in Syria?" Ray said over his shoulder. "They don't even have defensive lines there."

Rafiq scowled. "For once, he makes sense."

"I'm not worried about defensive lines. I'm here to find my daughter," Erik said. "Syria was the start point."

"Yeah, well, the plan's changed," Ray said.

"And what is the plan? Chris said he could help."

Ray snorted. "You'll have to ask him."

"Then I guess I'm ready to go," Erik said and moved to join Rafiq at the door.

"Listen, before you pop smoke, have you thought about how the fuck you're going to find her?" Ray asked. "It ain't like taking a stroll to your local Wal Mart out there."

"I agree," Rafiq said and shared a look with Ray. "I'd hoped to talk you out of this on the way to the front. I admire your courage, but you'd be better off staying here."

"I can't," Erik said.

"Hear us out," Ray said. "We get access to intelligence reports coming from the front lines in Iraq, and some from Syria, and we're also connected to the overall coalition intelligence effort. I know your background. Stay here and help while you figure out your plan. No need to go rushin' off half-cocked."

"There is a threat here as well," Rafiq said. "The Caliphate has sleeper cells throughout Erbil, and someone who could analyze the information would be useful."

Erik held up a hand. "I appreciate the offer, but I made a deal with Chris."

"And did he tell you what he gets out of this?" Ray tugged on his ball cap. "Listen, you seem like you're squared away, so I'll just say it. We might all work for the same company, but them two guys? I wouldn't follow them out of a wet paper bag, never mind into Syria."

Erik let his gaze wander the operations room, stared at a blown-up map of the Middle East with the borders of Iraq and Syria highlighted in bold black ink. Ray had a point, but Raqqa was a long way off, and the tightness in his chest told him he'd be too far away to learn anything in Erbil. Intelligence was always better the closer one got to the problem.

"I appreciate the offer," he said, "but I need to go."

Rafiq drew himself up to his full height. "Do you think God wills this?"

"I don't get paid enough for this shit," Ray said and shook his head.

"I'm not sure," Erik said. "All I know is that I need to keep every option open. My daughter deserves as much." He glanced at Ray. "If that means going with Chris, so be it."

Rafiq nodded. "It is said that if God closes one door, He opens a thousand others, so perhaps your sojourn here is within his will. I'll have the vehicle brought up."

"Well, that's just fuckin' great." Ray pulled out his chewing tobacco and put a pinch into his lower lip. "I hope you know what you're doing. These fuckers don't mess around."

"I know," Erik said, and his mouth felt dry. "Believe me, I know."

***

RAQQA, SYRIA
18 MAY 15 – 1540 LOCAL

Abu Noor al Kanadi stood outside a plain compound in Raqqa's Nazla Shahada neighborhood. Nestled among a warren of adjoining compounds, a sunbaked brick wall staked out a small courtyard with a simple two-story building. Seared brush threatened to overtake the yard, but aside from one corner of the building that had collapsed, the place seemed as well maintained as the other properties in the neighborhood, most of which were three and four-story apartment buildings. He, himself, would have preferred an apartment, all the better to blend in.

Too bad Tania did not feel the same. She stood inside the courtyard, one son clutched to her chest, the other attached to her leg. Her foot tapped a quick beat on the ground. "What is this?"

Al Kanadi waved around the courtyard with an open hand. "The emir was generous enough to give this to us," he said.

"It is an insult," Tania said and spat. "That Chechen commander was given a mansion."

"Which was bombed a month ago," al Kanadi said. "The emir offered a compound very similar, but this is much safer. It's in the middle of a residential neighborhood –"

"We deserve better than this." She dragged the older son toward the building. "I hope you don't expect me to live here for long."

Al Kanadi cleared his throat and ignored the shuffling feet of the two men behind him. At least they'd spared him the indignity of coming to his defense. When Tania had taken the kids inside, he put his hand on his heart and addressed the taller of the two men. "This is fine, Yahya, thank you."

Yahya glanced up. "There are others more befitting your station."

Al Kanadi shook his head. "No, this is safer." This compound would lower his profile and provide a measure of security if he was targeted. The neighborhood was relatively untouched, proof that the risk of collateral damage to civilians was too high to attack him here. If he was careful, if he kept the boys or Tania close at hand, he had a security blanket. The Chechen had been an idiot to take such a high profile. "We must all make sacrifices, even my wife," he said and smiled. "And if it gets too cold inside, I can sleep on the roof."

The men laughed, and then Yahya gestured to the other man to bring the bags inside. While he worked, Yahya stepped closer to al Kanadi. "Any word from Mamdouh?"

Al Kanadi shook his head. "He'll send word from Tunis, then not again until the date is set for travel."

"I wish he were here. I need his advice."

"For what?" He faced his junior lieutenant. Yahya was a capable man with potential, but that potential required careful grooming if it would bear fruit.

"It is nothing." Yahya lowered his eyes. "I do not wish to trouble you with minor business."

"I insist," al Kanadi said.

Yahya cleared his throat. "I have received word of two men who claim to be trying to contact one of our recent recruits. They say the father is trying to get in touch with her and will pay money to get her back."

"I see," al Kanadi said. "It would be unusual to consider that request."

Yahya nodded. "I understand. A Muslim who does not desire to be in the Caliphate is no Muslim at all."

"Although I would be curious to hear the offer. Sometimes the parents are able to string together surprising amounts of money." Al Kanadi scratched his temple. "Who is the recruit?"

Yahya shuffled his feet. "The girl who is with Mamdouh."

Al Kanadi's eyes narrowed. "Who are these men?"

"Americans," Yahya said. "They also claim to know you. My contact said they told him they served with you in the American military." Yahya spread his hands. "Of course, they're lying, but I thought Mamdouh would know how to handle the situation. These ones seem different. It's possible they're a threat and should be eliminated."

"Do you have names?"

"Roberts. Chris Roberts."

Al Kanadi stared out into the street.

"Evidently this Chris thinks you owe him a favor," Yahya said. "Again, a lie, an attempt to make us react to see what we would do –"

Al Kanadi stared out over the shimmering horizon of the city, eyes narrowed against the bright sun. "I owe my life to Chris."

It had been beneath another sun, a cold Afghani sun over Mazar-i-Sharif in late 2001. Chris and al Kanadi had both been in Special Forces detachments, al Kanadi working alongside General Mohammed Atta Nur from the Northern Alliance, while Chris had been partnered with the Uzbek warlord, General Abdul Rashid Dostum. They'd linked up in the Dari-e-Souf Valley and fought toward Mazar-i-Sharif, where thousands of Taliban fighters waited for them, along with more than a thousand Pakistani extremists. After a short battle for the town, the remnants of the Taliban and Pakistani fighters sought refuge in a local school, the Sultan Razia Girls' School.

Over the next days, the Northern Alliance attempted to negotiate the fighters' surrender. Multiple peace envoys had been sent and al Kanadi – he'd been known as Captain Luther Siegel then – had volunteered to escort one of these on the second day. He and two Afghans had accompanied a town mullah to within a couple hundred feet of the school's entrance when bullets kicked up dust at their feet. The mullah proceeded alone from that point and entered the building to talk.

Five minutes later, the front door opened and the mullah's head was tossed out. Machine gun barrels poked through the windows of the school and bullets zinged past al Kanadi and the Afghans beside him. They'd raised their rifles, then one of the Afghans had gone down, then the other. Al Kanadi had stood over their bodies and returned fire, and then a volley of explosions and dust levelled the front of the building. Al Kanadi fell to his knees, risked a glance over his shoulder through the haze. Chris stood on a ridge, radio handset to his ear as he directed fire at the building. He'd lowered the handset to cup his hands to his mouth.

"Get your ass back here!" Chris yelled.

Al Kanadi hadn't waited for another invitation.

"Emir?" Yahya said. "What do you think I should do?"

Al Kanadi blinked and gave Yahya a tight smile. "Let me think," he said. He didn't like his past coming back to haunt him, especially someone like Chris. And yet perhaps this unexpected engagement presented an opportunity to repay a debt. He set his jaw. "You were right to bring this to me. Find out more details."

"As you will it." Yahya bowed.

He nodded and raised a hand in dismissal. "Go now. Let me tend to my wife."

Yahya bowed again, then corralled the other man and returned to the vehicle.

Al Kanadi watched them depart, his mind already back in Mazar-i-Sharif, with Chris, and the aftermath of the failed peace negotiations. He'd advised General Nur to wait out the Taliban. They weren't going anywhere, and the Northern Alliance was strong enough to hold position for weeks while the enemy got hungrier. After a few more days, he'd gone one step further and suggested offering safe passage if the Taliban put down their weapons. After all, an act of mercy would bode well for the post-conflict reconciliations that were sure to come. He'd been surprised when Chris had supported him, more so when his colleague made a personal appeal to General Dostum. Surprisingly, the Uzbek warrior had gone for the plan and convinced General Nur.

At dawn the next day, the Taliban fighters walked out of the school. Al Kanadi, Chris, and the Afghan generals watched from a ridge that overlooked the valley. As the *muezzin* finished the morning call to prayer, hundreds of men began to mass in front of the school, their faces gaunt and caked in grime, their gazes downcast. Within twenty minutes, the enemy fighters began to work their way into the mouth of the valley gorge when there was a roar overhead. Al Kanadi looked up and saw a pair of F-18s scream through the air and then the bombs dropped, and explosions ripped through the Taliban. Bodies flew and Northern Alliance soldiers ran to the edge of the ridge and opened up with their guns.

"Cease fire!" al Kanadi had yelled. Frantic, he waved his arms in the air and reached for the radio to call off the jets.

Chris grabbed him. "Shut your goddamn mouth," he said. "You want to get us killed?"

"We need to call off the fighters," al Kanadi said.

"Don't worry, I'm sure that first one was just a mistake," Chris said, a grim smile on his face. Overhead, a second pair of F-18s rolled in and dropped more ordnance. Cut off from the school, the remnants of the Taliban fighters charged the gorge, into the kill zones of the Northern Alliance fighters.

Al Kanadi peered at Chris. "You did this."

"How do you think I got Dostum to agree to offer safe passage?"

"It's not right." Al Kanadi grabbed Chris's tactical vest, pulled him close. "They're not even armed."

"You think the Taliban give a shit about fairness?" Chris shoved al Kanadi and picked up the radio handset. "If you knew your Afghan culture, you'd know that letting them walk makes us look weak. We kill them, they'll get the message."

His cheeks burned with the accusation, but he stood fast. "We promised them safe passage."

"Good for you," Chris said. "And while you're worried about keeping promises to a bunch of terrorists, stay out of my way so I can win this war. Just don't forget you owe me."

Indeed. As al Kanadi watched Yahya drive off, it occurred to him that he might have a chance to repay his debt in full.

* * *

FRONTLINES, ERBIL, IRAQ
18 MAY 15 – 1620 LOCAL

Baked beneath a merciless sun, a flag fluttered from atop a cinderblock bunker. The bunker crowned a two-story makeshift fort that held a commanding view over the parched land to the west. No-man's land. As the flag snapped in the breeze – its small, yellow sun dancing amid a field of red, white, and green colors – reports of rifle fire came from within the bunker, the concussions accompanied by laughter that echoed over the barren ridge.

Erik stood beside Rafiq's SUV, parked inside the fort's courtyard, and stared up at the bunker.

"Come with me," Rafiq said. He told Walid, his driver, to stay with the SUV and then marched into the fort's entrance.

Erik followed Rafiq inside and up a set of stairs onto the roof of the first level. Another flight of stairs led to the roof of the second level, where a rickety ladder ascended to the bunker. Inside, two men hunched over a rifle, a third stood behind them.

"Come down here," Rafiq yelled at the bunker.

The man in the rear, a Kurdish soldier clad in American fatigues and a combat rig glanced down at Rafiq, then spoke to the other two men. Another shot rang out.

"I know you can hear me," Rafiq yelled again. "I brought your fresh meat." He turned to Erik. "With apologies."

A head swiveled, and shoulder-length black hair spilled out from under a baseball cap. Chris smiled down at Erik. "Hey, old-timer. You made it." He patted the man with the rifle on the back, then moved to the ladder and slid down. "Good to see you."

"This is a long way from Menagh," Erik said.

"Plan changed, Pops." Chris shrugged. "If it makes you feel better, come up top and take a few shots. You might have to wrestle Mark off the gun, but I'm sure he's up for that."

"Care to tell me what your plan is?" Rafiq said.

"Nope. All you need to know is that I'll be taking ten of your men for about a week," Chris said. "I'll brief Pops here after you leave."

"I'm in command of this sector –"

"But your uncle is the one who's contracting me." Chris drove a finger into Rafiq's chest. "Do I need to tell him you're making it difficult for me to perform my services?"

Rafiq's mouth formed a thin line. "I hope you're not lying to this man."

Chris smiled. "I wouldn't dream of it." He spun and climbed the ladder, paused half-way up. "Oh, and by the way, I'll need Walid to stay with us. He's gotta drive the vehicle for Pops."

"He's my driver – how will I get back to Erbil?"

"You're the battalion commander, figure something out." Chris disappeared back into the tower. "You comin', Pops?"

Rafiq spat and looked at Erik. "I hope you will reconsider my offer," he said. "I'll leave in the next hour. *Ma el-salama.*" Without a further word, he descended back into the fort, calling Walid's name.

Erik stood at the ladder, then moved aside as the Kurdish soldier descended from the tower. When the ladder was clear, he climbed up to find Mark hunched over a rifle and Chris beside him, a pair of binoculars to his face.

"Too quick on the trigger that time," Chris said. "The shithead made it to the hut."

Mark grunted. "He's got to come out sometime."

Erik peered over Mark's shoulder, out over a blasted landscape of scrub, sand, and rock. Around a mile away, a small cluster of buildings topped a ridge. "What are you shooting at?"

"Couple fighters in those buildings over there," Chris said. "Take a look." He handed Erik the binoculars. "Check out the doorway of the building on the right."

Erik studied the building through the binoculars, saw how the walls were pockmarked from bullet holes, but aside from that, nothing stood out. Then he glimpsed movement outside the building, a man crawling. "I see him," Erik said. "He's headed for the hut."

"He's been doing that for a while, but I never let him get there," Mark said. "He's bait for the guys inside the compound."

"What?" Erik lowered the binoculars. "You can't do that."

Chris took back the binoculars. "No laws out here. You want a shot?"

"No, I'm good," he said and turned to Chris. "You said you wanted to talk about the plan? Are we still heading to Sanliurfa?"

Amidst a roar of noise and dust, Mark's rifle kicked back. He reseated the gun against his shoulder and cursed under his breath.

Chris shook his head and raised the binoculars. "We've got something better lined up."

"Sanliurfa is where my daughter crossed the border," he said. "That's where we'll find her trail."

"Maybe," Chris said.

"More likely she's already in Raqqa," Mark said.

"Even more likely, she's with al Kanadi."

Erik frowned. "How do you figure?"

"We asked around," Chris said. "So now it's easy."

"I don't follow."

Chris smiled. "We get in touch with al Kanadi, and he tells us where she is."

Erik snorted. "That is the stupidest thing I've heard in a long time," he said. "Al Kanadi's in the top ten on the coalition's target list."

"Top five," Mark said.

"That doesn't make it any better," Erik said. "You think you're going to find him when all of Western intelligence is out to get him?"

"All we need to find him is someone with access to him," Chris said. "Someone with knowledge of his people smuggling operations."

Erik ran a hand over his face. "Rafiq was right," he said. "You're wasting my time."

"We've already got a meet lined up."

"When? With who?"

"In a few days," Chris said as if it was no big deal. "Some rebels close to al Kanadi who can get a message to him."

"What rebels?" Erik asked. "The rebels in Iraq are affiliated with the Caliphate. They're not going to betray one of their own. Plus, al Kanadi is Syrian based, I've never heard of him in Iraq."

"Nobody's selling anyone out. This is business, that's all," Chris said. "And if the local HUMINT can be believed, al Kanadi's working out of Mosul these days. Hell, that's only a couple of hours down the road."

"Who's your source?"

"Guy by the name of Abu Yusuf. He's al Kanadi's fixer in Mosul."

"And what makes you think he'll help?"

"Everyone has a price." Chris tapped Mark on the shoulder. "Someone's coming out."

"Got 'em," Mark said. Seconds later, the rifle roared. "Nailed him." The two men hooted.

"Did you see his John Wayne?" Chris chuckled, and then he clutched his chest and his face twisted in mock pain.

Erik fought the urge to rip Chris's binoculars from him. "What price? My daughter isn't a hostage."

Chris stopped laughing and stared at Erik. "You sure about that?" He was silent and then looked back out over the ridge. "Listen, don't worry about it. Mark and I have history with al Kanadi, and we've got something he won't be able to resist. He'll bite, trust me." He nodded at the rifle. "Sure you don't want a shot? Might be good to wipe off the rust."

"No thanks."

"Don't have the stomach for it?" Chris asked. "Maybe we were wrong about you."

"My stomach's fine," Erik said and began to climb down the ladder. "When do we leave?"

"That's the spirit," Chris said and laughed. "We're out tomorrow morning. Walid's your driver, and we'll give you more deets when things firm up."

Sure you will, Erik thought.

* * *

SAHARAN DESERT, NIGER
20 MAY 15 – 1610 LOCAL

Arielle had never experienced heat like the Saharan desert.

Two days out of Sirte, on a bearing more or less due south across endless dunes, the temperature had climbed to higher and higher extremes. Arielle drank as little as possible – there never seemed to be enough water and the stops were rare – but even with the Landcruiser's air conditioning on full, she sweltered inside her *niqab*. At least she'd gotten Reza to talk, or the endless hours in the back seat would have been unbearable.

"How much longer, brother?" It was perhaps the tenth time she'd asked, and she forced her tone to be warm so Reza would know it was a joke.

Reza's tight smile appeared in the rear-view mirror. "Another few days," he said, "but we're almost done for today."

"We're stopping early?"

"Soon there will be mountains," he pointed to the horizon, "and we will take a break."

Arielle peered out through the windshield, but only saw sand, dunes, and dust. "They must be small." Like near her uncle's farm on the prairies, the hills he'd joked were mountains. She smiled and settled back into her seat. Thoughts of her family, her friends, had been with her more and more, their presence a comfort. "Or else they're still far away."

"They are closer than you think," Reza said and his smile faded.

"Aren't you eager for this trip to be over?" she asked. "I am. It feels like we've been in the desert forever."

"The desert can be a rare beauty," Reza said. "Besides, what is coming is not always better than what has gone."

"You're in a grey mood today, brother."

His gaze met hers in the rearview mirror again. "In truth, I am scared."

"You?" she asked. "Were you not telling me of all your battles in Iraq, of how good you are in a fight? Were those all just stories?"

Reza did not bite at her attempt at humor. "Some things cannot be fought. There are very few men who scare me, but I remain scared nonetheless. It is not shameful."

She was thankful the *niqab* hid the surprise on her face. "Scared of what?"

He gazed at her a long time in the rearview mirror and then pointed out the window. "There are your mountains."

Outside, rocky, jagged, hills had emerged from the dunes, moonscape slopes that looked like they'd cut a person to pieces. They traveled in silence, and after a while, they entered the hills and the road narrowed to little more than a track. The vehicle began to pitch back and forth, and Arielle had to brace herself against the seat to her front, and the whole time the convoy wound deeper into the hilly terrain. She was no longer hot beneath her *niqab,* and despite what she'd told Reza, she no longer wanted the day's journey to end.

"Why are we stopping so early today?" she asked.

"Too many questions," Reza said, although his tone was not unfriendly. After a pause, he continued. "This is where we will wait for Mamdouh."

"And then?"

"Then we prepare for our final journey."

"Brother, what aren't you telling me? What will happen when we reach our destination?"

Reza glanced in the rearview mirror, and his eyes widened. "You must say nothing because that's what I have told you," he said in an urgent voice. "We all serve Allah and bring his message, and that is enough. No more talking." Then he looked back at the road and refused to answer any more questions.

The convoy slowed to a crawl as the drivers eased through the rocky terrain, where even a few feet off the trail could cripple a vehicle. Each jolt and bounce of the SUV caused Arielle to flinch, and she began to feel as if the vehicle was pressing in upon her.

She wanted answers.

When the convoy stopped, she waited for Reza to get out, stretch, and then let her out, which is what he'd done the previous nights. She'd be expected to collect firewood to boil water while some of the men pitched tents, and while she waited, she began to look around and noticed that the convoy had stopped in a line beside a few stone ruins in a semi-circle. Reza opened her door, and she hopped out, and saw Faisal appear out of the lead vehicle. In Mamdouh's absence, Faisal had commanded the convoy, gave out tasks, and set the schedule. If anybody knew what awaited at the final destination, it would be him. She strode toward him.

"What are you doing?" Reza grabbed for her shoulder.

She shrugged off Reza's hand and continued toward Faisal. "Hello," she called out and caught Faisal's gaze. "Yes, you. I need to talk to you. I want to know –"

Faisal walked up to her and then lashed out and slapped her in the head.

Arielle fell back. Struck the ground hard enough to force air from her lungs. She gasped for breath and then Reza had knelt beside her and had offered his hand.

"Out of the way, idiot," Faisal said in a snarl. He shoved Reza aside with his foot and then stooped down and grabbed Arielle by the throat and dragged her to her feet.

"We're not supposed to hurt her," Reza said.

"Shut up," Faisal said, and his gaze never left Arielle's face. "You were supposed to keep her in line." He tightened his grip and then he flung her to the ground.

Arielle clutched her throat and her vision narrowed as if she peered through a cardboard tube that somebody was pinching shut at the other end. Faisal's boots appeared by her face.

"Get up." His voice sounded far in the distance.

Coughs racked her body as she worked her way to her knees, then to her feet. Hunched over, she faced Faisal.

"So, you want to know something," he said without emotion. The stale reek of sweat emanated from him, and she stifled a gag, which set off a new round of coughs.

She forced herself to meet Faisal's gaze. "What will we do at the next camp?" She coughed, started again. "Reza said –"

Faisal's gaze shifted to Reza. "What have you been telling her, fool?"

"Nothing," Reza raised his hands in protection.

"He hasn't told me –"

A flash of darkness appeared in her peripheral vision and then she was on the ground again, her ears ringing. Faisal's face swam into view, his voice hard and cold.

"Whatever Reza told you, there is no going back," he said. "At the camp, we will prepare you to be Allah's messenger, that is all. You should be honored. As for you..."

She looked up from the ground to see Faisal drive Reza against one of the trucks. Two other men held him down, and Faisal began to talk. "You should have kept silent, brother," Faisal said. "But we'll find out what you told her." He lashed out and struck Reza in the gut and stood over him as Reza crumpled to the ground.

"No," she said. "He told me nothing."

Faisal walked closer. "Then you should have held your mouth," he said and drew back his foot to kick her in the head.

Arielle closed her eyes, and the sparks came again, and this time she dove after them into the blackness.

* * *

NEAR KISIK, IRAQ
21 MAY 15 – 1455 LOCAL

Erik clung to the pickup's holy-shit handle while the vehicle rocked along the battered highway. They'd been on the road for several hours, first backtracking through Erbil, then north through small towns like Bardarash and Hatarah. After Hatarah, they'd passed the Mosul Dam and adjusted the route to west-south-west. Erik still didn't have a good idea where they were going, and when he'd asked, Walid had grumbled that they were going to a border crossing, *Insha'Allah,* and it would have been quicker to go straight through Mosul, which was impossible since the city was in Caliphate hands.

A road sign with Arabic script blew by. "What did it say?" Erik asked.

Walid grunted. "We're almost at Kisik."

"Is that where we're going?"

Walid shook his head.

Erik checked his watch and decided it was late enough that people would be at work in Ottawa. He pulled out the cell-phone he'd picked up in

Erbil and dialed Stephanie's number. Seconds later, she answered.

"Erik?" Stephanie asked. "How are you? I've been worried."

"Hi, Stephanie," he said, warmth in his voice for what seemed like the first time in ages. "Sorry I haven't called. Things have been a bit fluid."

"Where are you?"

"Near the Mosul Dam, hoping it holds." The already shaky dam – labeled most dangerous in the world by the US Army Corps of Engineers – had been further weakened in battles with the Caliphate the previous year. If breached, a torrent of water would rage down the Tigris river valley to flood Mosul and Baghdad itself. "Other than that, all's good."

The bouncing truck settled down, and he peered out the window. They'd pulled onto a highway with stone walls paralleling both sides. Up ahead were several one-story mud and brick houses, the walls baked light brown, Stone Age holdovers except for the satellite dishes on the roofs. Walid muttered, and his fingers squeaked on the steering wheel as his grip tightened.

Erik held the phone to his chest and glanced at Walid. "Everything all right?"

"No people."

Erik scanned out the window. "Are we near the defensive lines?" If he remembered right, the FLOT was another twenty kilometers to the south.

Walid shook his head and then pointed through the windshield. "Checkpoint up ahead."

Erik followed the direction of Walid's finger. Two car lengths in front, Chris and Mark's truck had stopped, and a Kurdish soldier was at the driver's side window. Almost a block farther, two tan Toyota Hilux pickups flanked the street. Kurdish soldiers stood in the back of both trucks, the one on the right behind a large machine gun, the one on the left behind what looked like the cannon of a tank. Erik put the phone back to his ear.

"What's going on?" Stephanie asked.

"Going through a checkpoint," he said. "Everything's under control."

Having finished with Chris's vehicle, the Kurdish soldier approached Walid's truck. Walid rolled down his window and on request, handed over a set of papers. The soldier flipped through the documents and exchanged a few words in Arabic with Walid. After a minute, the soldier returned the papers and waved them on. Walid put the truck in gear and rolled through the checkpoint.

"He said some Caliphate fighters may be in the village," Walid said. "Peshmerga are going door to door to find them."

As if on cue, Kurdish soldiers appeared on the side of the road in twos and threes, their uniforms a mishmash of camouflage pattern and civilian clothes. At a T-intersection up ahead were three more vehicles, two with heavy machine guns mounted in the back, the third with a recoilless rifle pointed down a road that led to the south. The men in the trucks watched Walid and Erik drive past with hard eyes and their fingers on the triggers of their weapons.

"That road leads to Tal Afar and Sinjar," Walid said as they drove through the junction. "This territory was recently recaptured, and the caliphate may have left cells behind."

"Is everything okay?" Stephanie asked.

"Fine." Erik focused on the southern route, which led through an expanse of featureless desert with no obstacle in sight to stop Caliphate forces. "Just getting some ground truth."

"And? Are you finding what you're looking for?"

"I have a lead," he said. "I'm checking it out right now."

"What does that mean?"

He smiled. She'd transitioned from Stephanie his friend to Stephanie the analyst. "My colleagues think they can introduce me to someone who'll know where Arielle is," he said. "They believe this person is a key acquaintance of our mutual friend."

"Al Kanadi?"

"The one and only. Is there any way you can confirm or deny that information? I was pretty sure he never left Syria."

"Do you have a name?"

"Abu Yusuf. Supposedly he's a rebel leader based in Mosul."

"That's a common name."

"I know, I'm sorry."

"I'll see what I can do," she said. "There might be something there. I can't get into specifics, but there's reason to believe Kanadi has been in that part of the world as recent as the past few weeks."

"That's unusual."

"The general consensus is that an upcoming attack may have moved from the planning stage to preliminary movements."

Up ahead, there was another checkpoint, two more Hiluxes with machine guns mounted in the back. Walid eased to a stop a few feet back of Chris's truck, itself behind several other vehicles in line.

"He's never relocated to Iraq during previous attacks," Erik said.

"I know, but there's been increased communication between the

Caliphate and its affiliates in Africa, and a lot of that activity is in Mosul."

"Which affiliates?"

"Most of them. Al-Shabab, Ansar al-Sharia. Boko Haram declared fealty, too, you might have missed it."

"Boko Haram's desperate," he said. "They need a big win to remain relevant, and the Caliphate has momentum."

Walid drove up, close to the bumper of Chris's truck which was about two hundred feet from the checkpoint and behind two other vehicles that weren't part of their small convoy.

"Any rumored locations for the attack?" Erik asked.

"Europe is mentioned a lot," Stephanie said.

"It always is these days."

"Hard not to. The Caliphate's foothold in Libya gives them possible access."

"Across the Mediterranean?" Erik asked. The soldiers at the checkpoint called up the lead vehicle. "Aren't there easier –"

White light bloomed at the checkpoint and thrust Erik back into his seat. He shielded his face as the shock wave rode through him, unable to hear anything amid the noise. When he opened his eyes, a smoking crater almost ten feet wide blocked the road between the two Kurdish pickups. Both of the tan pickups were charred and bent out of shape, unrecognizable from moments before.

He reached for Walid. "You okay?"

Walid groaned, held a hand to his eyes, and nodded. He reached for the door handle and opened it, then tumbled out.

Erik patted himself all over, the motions disjointed amid muted sound, like his ears were stuffed with cotton. He seemed to be okay. He looked up and through the cracked windshield saw Mark step out of his truck with a rifle tucked into his shoulder. Erik leaned across the truck's cab and called after Walid. "Walid! Get in the truck!" He flinched as something hit his boot and glanced down and saw his cell. *Shit, Stephanie.* He stooped for the phone and covered his free ear as he tried to hear.

"– all right?" Stephanie was saying.

"It's me," he said. "I'm okay."

"Thank God," she said, relief in her voice. "What's going on?"

"I think a vehicle bomb just went off."

Mark's mouth opened in a yell, the tendons taut on his neck, but no sound reached Erik.

"What?" Stephanie said, her voice urgent even through his dulled hearing.

"We're good," he said and then stopped and considered that he was stuck in the middle of a highway, visible for miles. And since a huge bomb had just gone off, everyone in the area was no doubt watching. Ahead, Mark stalked about, rifle pointed in all directions.

"– get out of there," Stephanie said, and he knew she meant Iraq itself, but her words applied in this situation as well.

"I have to go," he said and hung up. He pushed open his door and almost fell out of the truck, and then recovered and went to check on Walid. The Kurd's eyes were vacant, and he stumbled as if drunk and Erik steered him into the passenger's seat.

Kurdish troops rolled up in several pickup trucks and disgorged soldiers onto the south side of the road. Several opened fire, lone pot shots that didn't draw return fire. From the back of one of the trucks, a Kurd yelled, and the firing stopped and then started again, accompanied by the shouts of the soldiers.

He got Walid into the truck, and then hands gripped him by the shoulders, and he whirled and found himself face-to-face with Mark.

"Get back in your fucking vehicle!" Mark yelled.

"What do you think I'm doing?" Erik yelled back. "Get back in your own truck!"

Mark's eyes widened, and he stepped back, made a circular motion in the air with a raised finger. "We're outta here."

Erik shook his head as Mark headed off, then raced to the driver's side. This was crazy and yet, Ziad had said he needed to have faith in something. Maybe this was what faith felt like, the belief he'd accomplish something when the best information showed no proof whatsoever. He crawled into the driver's side and kept up with the convoy as they drove through the ruined checkpoint.

CHAPTER THIRTEEN
THE SHIFTING SANDS

BORDER NEAR GUINEA AND MALI, AFRICA
22 MAY 15 – 1420 LOCAL

The camp appeared from nowhere.

The convoy had barely left the savannah for the treed hills when they came upon a chain link fence stretched across the road. The vehicles sped through an opened gate so fast that Arielle almost missed the two men with chest rigs and assault rifles. Then they were through, and the men had closed the gates. They parked outside a two-story prefabricated building, like two oversize sea containers placed on top of each other, and Arielle's new driver, Nassir, got out. Arielle used the opportunity to scan the camp, though her right eye was swollen shut and her neck was so stiff she had to twist her whole body to peer around.

Several smaller buildings occupied this area of the gravel lined compound. Deeper into the facility was another chain link fence that made a compound within a compound. Tied to this inner fence was a sign, a red triangle with three pincer-like semi-circles in black, layered on top of a smaller circle. It looked familiar, but before Arielle could examine the sign further, Nassir yanked open her door.

"Get out," Nassir said. When she didn't respond, he undid her seatbelt and pulled her from the vehicle.

She let herself be dragged up the corrugated steel stairs that led to the second floor of the prefab building. She took her time as she climbed and tried to see as much of the compound as she could, noticed how Nassir's gaze was also drawn to the fence inside the compound. Then Nassir pulled her and she tripped up the stairs.

"Stop looking around," Nassir said in a growl.

At the top of the stairs, she followed Nassir through a pair of double doors and into a hallway. Nassir shoved her through the first door they came to and into a small, white, room and then pulled the door shut. The room was empty except for a few folding chairs and a window and as she wondered what was going on, she moved to the window.

She peered out through a crack in the blinds and once again saw the inner fence. From this vantage point, several of the signs with the red, pincer-like circles were visible. They bothered her, like hazard signs, but why would they be posted inside the camp? And then the image came to her, so vivid she wondered how she could have forgotten.

Biohazard.

Before she'd left Canada, the Ebola outbreak in Africa had been all over the news. Even in Raqqa she'd heard reports of the worsening epidemic, and in most of the clips, the same pincer-like circles. Her hand trembled, and the blinds made a rattling sound as they shook. It wasn't possible. The Ebola outbreak had been in West Africa, and they'd landed in Libya, and then headed south. Or had it been south-west? It was so easy to get turned around in the desert and Reza had never answered what direction they were going.

Reza. He'd said he was scared, but not of anything human. And on the ship, he'd told her to be brave, when the men had said, '*marad*.' Disease.

"This has to be a mistake," she said. Her breath quickened, and she held the blinds aside to see more of the inner compound, but all that was visible was the corner of the fence and one small, shack-like building. "This has to be a mistake," she said again. "I'm taking a message to Canada."

Except that hadn't been quite what al Kanadi had said.

Steps passed in the hallway and she dropped the blind and stepped back from the window. The footsteps went past the door, and she held her hands to her head, still able to see the fence with its hazard signs outside. Still able to hear al Kanadi's voice and she repeated his words out loud. "He'd said I would be a great carrier of the message," she said and then she knew that she had to get away and that she wouldn't get another chance.

She walked to the door, paused, and then poked her head into the hallway. A few meters to her right were the doors she'd walked through onto the second floor. In the other direction, about ten yards down was another set of doors, and for the moment the hallway was empty. She rearranged her *niqab* and then entered the hallway and walked toward the doors she'd come in. When she reached the doors, she paused with her hand on the door handle.

What exactly was the plan?

She shook her head. It didn't matter, she'd have to improvise. She eased the door open and peeked out and at the bottom of the stairs were the vehicles. Then a man yelled from behind, and she looked back and locked gazes with Nassir at the other end of the hallway, his eyes wide. He raised his hand to point at her and opened his mouth and then she leapt onto the landing and hiked the hem of her *niqab* and raced down the steps toward the SUVs.

* * *

KISIK, IRAQ
22 MAY 15 – 1652 LOCAL

Erik looked through the binoculars and rotated the focusing knob and a one-story building came into view. The building lay on the far side of an empty village square strewn with bricks and refuse, and there were several trucks parked outside, a mixture of Toyota Hiluxes and Landcruisers.

"That's where we're meeting your contact," he said.

"Yup," Chris said from his side, both of them hunched over the hood of Walid's vehicle.

Erik lowered the binoculars, but kept the rubber eyepieces on his cheekbones. "It's safe?" Ever since the VBIED attack, he'd been unable to shake a feeling of impending dread.

"As safe as anywhere around here," Chris said. "Think you can remember what to do?"

"Tell me again who these guys are?" He raised the binoculars for another look.

"We've been over this before," Chris said.

"One more time."

Chris snorted. "Free Iraqi Army."

"They're fighting the Caliphate."

"Not really," Chris said. "They both want the same thing, but they've had differences over methods."

"And about who's calling the shots."

"Of course. Fucking country," Chris said. "Hell, two years ago all these shitheads were serving together in the Iraqi military."

"And you think they can find Arielle?" Erik asked.

"I know it, man," Chris said. "People smuggling is just a line of business for these guys, and they're well connected with al Kanadi's network. They'll either know where your daughter is or be able to find out. All you need to do is convince them to help."

"They're going to want money," he said. "Smugglers don't do anything for free."

"Cross that bridge when you get to it. The important thing here is to make contact," Chris said. He placed a hand on Erik's shoulder. "Walid will make the introductions. We'll be back here ready to ride to the rescue." He nodded at a building beside them, where Mark had disappeared a few minutes before. "Mark's your top cover, and we've got another ten guys who can handle anything up to a hundred Caliphate shit-heads. But it won't come to that."

Erik handed over the binoculars and joined Walid in the truck. In silence, the Kurd eased the truck across the square toward the building. Every bump jarred Erik, and the minute-long drive seemed to take an hour, and then Walid had parked.

"*Tawakkaltu Ala-Allah,*" Walid said. He put his hand on the door handle and looked at Erik. "Ready?"

Erik met Walid's gaze and nodded. "Ready." He exited the truck and trailed Walid to the door of the squat building. Walid pulled open the door and entered and Erik followed the Kurd into a dim room. His eyes were slow to adjust to the dark, and his hearing tried to compensate, but except for the scrapes of chair legs on tile, the room was silent. He stayed close to Walid as the Kurd walked across the room toward a table with two men. The men looked up and nodded, and then Walid sat down, and Erik sat beside him.

While Walid and the men exchanged words in Arabic, Erik scanned the room. There were several other tables in the large, open space of what he took to be a restaurant, despite the look of abandonment from the outside. A massive pillar dominated the center of the room, and several televisions hung from racks in the ceiling. Tucked in one corner was a set of double doors, one held open by the body of a man on his phone. Beyond the doors was the kitchen.

Walid tapped him and then nodded to the swarthier of the two men sitting at the table. "This is Abu Yusuf," Walid said. "He says he can help."

Abu Yusuf smiled, and his teeth were misshapen and yellow. "I have many contacts in Mosul," he said.

Erik frowned. "Don't you want to know what's involved first?" he asked. It was strange not to spend more time on pleasantries. He'd had more than his share of sketchy meets in the Middle East, and they almost always started with small talk. "Besides, my daughter's in Raqqa."

Abu Yusuf shrugged. "Mosul, Raqqa, it is of little consequence."

Light poured into the room, and Erik squinted at the door, where three additional men had entered the restaurant. Two of the men held AK-47's and their gazes searched the room and when they saw Walid and Abu Yusuf, they stopped looking around and began to walk forward.

Walid stiffened and began to stand up.

"What's going on?" Erik asked. A chair scraped on the floor behind him, and he looked over his shoulder, and Abu Yusuf smiled back through his thick beard and began to laugh. "What is this?" he asked.

"Business," Abu Yusuf said.

"We don't want trouble. I just want to find my daughter."

"And yet trouble is what you have found." Abu Yusuf's smile grew larger, and he pushed back from the table and stood. Then he placed his right hand over his heart and gave a slight bow to the three men as they neared the table. "*As-Salaam-Alaikum*, Khalid."

The newcomers stood with one man in front flanked by the two with rifles. The lead man was tall and gaunt, dressed in tan cargo pants and a tan long sleeved shirt and he wore a black skull cap pulled tight to his head. He nodded at Abu Yusuf. "*Wa-Alaikum-Salaam*," he said and then glared at Erik. "Get up."

"Easy." Erik held up his hands. "I think there's been a misunderstanding."

"No, there hasn't," the man said, and Erik took him to be Khalid. He spoke over his shoulder to the fighter on his left, a man with a wicked scar across his cheek. "Take him."

The other man nodded at Walid. "What about the Kurd?" he asked in perfect English.

Khalid's expression did not change. "Kill him."

The man cocked his rifle and the metallic clank of the bolt going back and forth echoed in the room. Erik glanced at Walid and then back to the fighters. He had time to wonder where Chris and Mark were, and then the fighter with the scar had reached for his neck.

Erik twisted out of the fighter's reach, and as the man paused to reorient, Erik grabbed his wrist and elbow and hyperextended his arm. Shock registered on the man's face, and then Erik stood and threw all his weight into the man's locked elbow. A loud snap pierced the room, and the fighter screamed, and his arm went limp in Erik's hands.

In the corner of his vision, Erik saw the other fighter swivel his weapon in his direction. He took a step in the fighter's direction and then Walid launched across the floor and grabbed the barrel of the rifle. The Kurd yelled and forced the rifle up and a loud shot filled the room.

Erik returned to his opponent. They might come out of this yet.

He held onto the fighter's mangled arm and rammed his knee into the man's thigh. The leg buckled and as the man collapsed, Erik smashed a fist into his throat and then kicked out the man's remaining leg. The man fell to the ground, and hit his head on the floor with a loud crack and did not move.

Erik glanced around. Walid and the third goon wrestled on the floor with the rifle between them. Khalid had begun backing up to the entrance of the restaurant, his hands held low and ready at his waist as if he was unsure how the tables had flipped on him. Erik darted forward and feinted at Khalid's head.

Khalid raised his hands and flinched back and then stumbled. Tottered on his heels and his arms began to windmill to recover his balance, and it was too good a chance to pass up.

Erik kicked low and fast, and the toe of his boot struck the inside of Khalid's ankle. Khalid grunted as his ankle went over and his arms went out. Erik punched him in his now uncovered abdomen, and when Khalid doubled over, he smashed his forehead into Khalid's face. The nose broke with a crunch and Khalid collapsed to the floor.

Erik took a moment to scan the room while Walid wrestled with the remaining fighter. Near the back of the room, Abu Yusuf and his companion stood by the kitchen doors, apparently intent on leaving. The rest of the room had emptied, and so Erik shuffled closer to Walid and waited for an opening to help. There it was. He tensed.

Light flowed into the room once again, and Erik whirled to face the door. More fighters entered the restaurant, four, six, all armed with rifles. One of the men stooped beside Khalid, thrust a hand under his arm and dragged him to his feet.

Erik looked for an escape, but the sole option was through the kitchen, at least fifteen feet off. More than enough time to be mowed down. He crouched and reached out to grab Walid's attacker.

"Enough," Khalid said in a nasal tone. He grabbed the rifle from the man who'd helped him up, leveled the barrel at Walid and his attacker and pulled the trigger. The rifle rocked in his hands, the heavy concussions of firing offset by the thuds of rounds striking flesh and bone. Within seconds, both men had stopped moving, their bullet-riddled bodies entwined.

Khalid pointed the AK-47 at Erik. "On your knees."

Erik met Khalid's gaze, read the hatred and loathing on the man's contorted face and hesitated.

Khalid came closer, eyes red over the mangled remains of his nose. "On your knees!"

If he let Khalid take him, he'd be tortured, and he was under no illusions how that would end. They'd break him sooner or later, and when they found out his background, he'd be in for a long, slow road to hell, never mind the information he might give up.

Khalid raised the rifle to his shoulder and pointed it at Erik's chest. "I won't tell you again," he said, "get on your knees."

Then again, if he died now, he'd never see Arielle again. At least alive, there was a chance, no matter how small. He whispered a silent apology to Stephanie, then dropped to one knee and interlaced his fingers behind his head.

Khalid stepped closer. "On your belly."

Erik eased onto his stomach and pressed his cheek to the gritty ceramic floor.

Khalid knelt beside him and then pulled a knife from his robes and held the jagged blade in front of Erik's face. "Take a good look," he said. "You may be tough now, but you'll scream when it happens. They –"

The front entrance of the restaurant erupted in an explosion of sound and light. Bricks and wood and dust cascaded into the room and Erik flung his arms over his head and curled into the fetal position and was covered by dirt and debris. He was aware of Khalid struggling to his feet and then a second concussion rocked the room and he saw Khalid ripped in half. Then the blast wave reached him and he hit his head and there was silence and darkness.

* * *

GUINEA, AFRICA
22 MAY 15 – 1523 LOCAL

Arielle fumbled the key into the Landcruiser's ignition. She'd been lucky to find the key ring in the cup holder, but her hand shook. Above, the second story door opened and Nassir strode onto the landing. Arielle concentrated on the key, ignored Nassir taking the stairs two steps at a time. She grasped the key with both hands and then it was in the ignition. She depressed the clutch, stood on the brake and turned the key. The engine roared to life and she said a silent prayer to her dad for hours spent learning to drive stick.

Her door jerked open and fingers clawed at her *niqab*. She slammed the SUV into reverse and stomped on the gas. Gravel sprayed from the Landcruiser's tires, and as the vehicle backed up, the open door hit Nassir with a thump. His fingers let go and then disappeared, dragged with the rest of his body under the vehicle. She spun the steering wheel so the Landcruiser faced the main gate and then ground the gear shift into first and stomped on the gas. The wheels spun, and the SUV sped off and fishtailed in the direction of the gate.

Up ahead, a guard poked his head out of the small shack beside the gate. He looked at the SUV and frowned, then stepped out of the shack, rifle slung from his shoulder. Arielle did not stop, now fifty yards from the gate, then twenty-five, close enough to see the thick padlock on the chain that held the gate shut.

At twenty yards, the guard raised his rifle, then thought better and threw himself backwards into the shack. Seconds later, the Landcruiser hit the gate dead in the middle. The gates flew open with a deafening bang and then she was through. Adrenaline surged through her body, and she yelled with joy. She drove on and then spared a glance in the rear-view mirror and was able to make out a group of figures near Nassir's body.

Then the Landcruiser lurched, and she flew up, hit her head on the roof, her pursuit momentarily forgotten. The SUV slowed, and she wrenched the wheel to bring herself back on the road. She glanced at the dashboard and saw she had three-quarters of a tank of gas. She was going to make it. The road straightened, and she floored the pedal, checked the mirror again. The camp had faded into the trees, but she knew that meant nothing.

The chase was on.

A loud bang to the front drew her gaze. The SUV's hood had come up and covered the windshield. She braked, and the hood slammed back into place. The front grill was bent in at the top, about where she'd hit the gate. Heart pounding, her foot returned to the accelerator as she stole glances in the rearview. Nothing yet, but they wouldn't be far behind. She'd have to nurse the vehicle and hope the hood stayed down.

Another corner and then she cleared the trees and broke onto the savannah. She applied more gas and then the hood flew up again, hit the vehicle's roof hard enough to send tiny spider-web cracks through the windshield. With a quiet moan, she tapped the brakes, and the hood dropped back down. "No, no, no," she said and pushed down the accelerator again. She stole another glance in the rearview and caught her first glimpse of pursuit, four vehicles at the edge of the tree line behind her. She focused on the road.

Ahead, a small clump of roofs appeared on the horizon. She sped up, but the hood lifted again. This time when she hit the brakes, the hood remained stuck to the windshield. She braked to a stop, flung open the door and leaned through the gap to push the hood down. It wouldn't budge.

"Come on!" She jumped out and reefed on the hood with both hands. With a stubborn screech, it fell into position. She leapt back into the Landcruiser, jammed it in gear and began to move and then her chasers crested a hill behind her, a few car lengths away.

Foot on the gas, she swung the Landcruiser from side to side, but the hills had leveled out, and her pursuers took advantage of the terrain. On the left, a brown Hilux bounced up and down as it drew even with her. On the right, another brown Hilux pulled ahead, swerved onto the road in front of her and then its tail lights lit up, and it slowed.

She kept the accelerator down and rammed the truck, sent it skidding off the road. Tendrils of smoke emerged from under the Landcruiser's hood, and the engine began to make a high-pitched whine, but she had no time to worry about that now. She glanced right, to another truck that had closed in on her and then she was blocked on all sides, the vehicles rubbing up against the Landcruiser as they pulled in tight.

She screamed and kept the accelerator on the floor, but the Landcruiser had begun to slow and then ground to a stop in a cloud of brown dust. She worked the pedals, jammed the gear shift into reverse. The engine roared, and the SUV rocked, and then another truck jammed in from behind and a man yelled at her.

There had to be something. There, in the leg space of the passenger side, she saw where Nassir had left his rifle. She clawed for the gun, her fingers on the greasy metal.

The driver's side door ripped open, and hands grasped her neck, yanked her out of the SUV. She kicked and flailed, and the rifle tumbled out of her grasp and back into the passenger's side of the vehicle as she was dragged over the hood of a truck and then slammed onto the ground. Her head hit the hard-packed track and stars filled her vision, bright lights followed by darkness and men's yells.

So close.

She was being dragged by her foot. She wriggled onto her back, and panic filled her as the open door of a Toyota Landcruiser filled her vision. She kicked with her free leg, screamed as two men jammed her into the backseat of the SUV. One of them followed her in, sat on her while the Landcruiser did a U-turn and then headed back to camp. She gasped for air beneath the crushing weight, fought harder and then the vehicle had passed through the smashed gate and into the camp.

When the vehicle stopped, the door nearest her head opened and hands reached in for her, dragged her to land in a heap on the gravel. She renewed her fight, almost broke free of her captor before he regained hold of her arm.

"Where did you think you would go?"

Even in her panic, Mamdouh's voice sent fresh ripples of desperation through her. She writhed and bit deep into the hand of the man who held her by the wrist. The taste of dust and grime made her gag, but she held on, and the man let go. She lashed out with all four limbs in a frenzy, took grim satisfaction each time a foot or hand connected.

And then she was free.

She braced herself on the ground, pushed to her knees and looked around. In front of her stood Mamdouh, flanked by three other men, all with rifles pointed at her.

Mamdouh glared at the men near her. "I said not to harm her," he said and then extended a hand to Arielle. "On your feet."

She raised her chin in defiance.

When she didn't move, he reached under her armpits and pulled up. "You must be tired after your little escapade," he said. "You should rest. You'll need it for the next stage of the journey." He gestured to the men behind him. "Take her."

Their faces fierce, the three men shouldered their weapons and approached, pinned her arms as she writhed. "Leave me alone," she said.

"You should be proud." Mamdouh hovered beside the group as they walked closer to the inner compound. "You shall give your life for Allah."

"Al Kanadi said I could go free," she said.

"And so you shall," Mamdouh said. "If you survive."

She spit at him, missed, and the whole time she was dragged forward.

"At the very least, you should accept your fate," he said. "We will not fail."

She screamed, strained at the hands that carried her through a chain-link door into the inner compound. She caught sight of one of the red hazard signs and began to cry.

Mamdouh called after her. "When we meet next, you shall be carrying our message to the West. And we will find ourselves one step closer to judgment."

Then the door closed.

* * *

KISIK, IRAQ
22 MAY 15 – 1744 LOCAL

Chris watched the ruined front of the building through his binoculars. The door and a portion of the front wall had caved in, but otherwise, the structure remained standing. Outside, one of the three Caliphate vehicles that had rolled up was a smoking shell, and the two Caliphate soldiers that had been posted by the main door lay prone on the ground, dead from the unnatural bent of their limbs. The drivers of the other two vehicles were alive, but not for long. For now, the biggest threat was whoever had survived inside the building.

"Think I should fire again?" Mark asked.

"Light up another vehicle, then we'll send up the Pesh," Chris said. "Karzan, get ready to move," he called over his shoulder to the Kurdish section commander. "Time to mop up."

"Not sure what I'll hit," Mark said. He loaded another warhead into the RPG-7 and raised the launcher to his shoulder. "This thing ain't real accurate at this range."

"Doesn't matter," Chris said. "Another round in the building is fine too. Just too bad we don't have more of those thermobaric rounds." He turned to the Kurdish commander. "Get your asses in gear, we've got you covered."

The Peshmerga loaded into their trucks and sped out from behind the building as Mark pulled the trigger. The warhead sped through the air in a cloud of smoke and heat to hit one of the remaining trucks. Smoke erupted from its engine compartment, followed by dust from the building beyond.

"You missed," Chris said.

"Like fuck I did," Mark said. "The round over-penetrated." He laid the RPG-7 down and then picked up his McMillan TAC-338 sniper rifle and settled the bipod on the edge of the roof. Seconds later, a shot rang out. "Another one down."

"Ease up, Pesh are almost on site," Chris said. On cue, the Kurdish vehicles roared up and stopped short of the Caliphate vehicles. Ten figures dismounted, followed by the tacca-tacca of machine guns opening up on the remaining driver. "Those fuckers are crazy. All they know how to do is frontal assault."

"You think our man inside the restaurant made it?" Mark asked.

"Don't care," Chris said. "Doesn't look like al Kanadi's here, so the best we'll walk away with is killing his men."

"Did you really think he was going to show?"

"I gave it 50/50," Chris said. "Better odds than what we're used to."

"He must hate you a lot," Mark said. His rifle swung to the side. "Hold on. Vehicles coming from the south."

"Where?" Chris scanned out another two hundred yards beyond the restaurant, where two dust balls had appeared over a hill. "Can't make them out. You got a bead on them?"

"Wait one," Mark said. "Shit – first one's a suicide car."

"You sure?"

"You shitting me? Truck covered in sheet metal? I'm sure." Mark squeezed off a round.

Chris raised a small hand-held radio. "Karzan? This is Chris, come in."

"Bad news, there's a second one." Mark threw down the rifle and grabbed the RPG-7.

"Karzan, this is Chris. You've got vehicle-born suicide bombs approaching from the south, over." Chris stood and waved his hands. "For fuck's sake, look behind you!"

The first vehicle rounded a corner into the town and sped toward the restaurant, where the Peshmerga were engaged with the remaining Caliphate fighter. At some point, the car bomb had been a truck before it had been covered in layers of welded steel plates, orange with rust. A metal cone protruded from the front of the box-like structure, a primitive ram, but effective considering the massive amount of explosives the truck no doubt carried.

The Kurds oriented on the newcomers. Some sprinted back to their vehicles, others scrambled for the building. Some brave, foolish few fired their rifles at the truck. Amid the staccato-like cracks of rifle shots, tiny pings reverberated off the vehicle, which didn't slow.

Mark drew a bead with the RPG-7.

"Down!" Chris grabbed Mark's shoulder and pulled him to the roof. Seconds later, a massive explosion came from the direction of the restaurant. With a clatter, pieces of metal landed in the square in front of the building. Chris stuck his mouth close to Mark's ear. "Time to get the fuck out of here!"

"What about Petersson?"

"Fuck him!"

Mark nodded and lurched to one knee, RPG-7 at his shoulder. He aimed at the second vehicle, less than 100 yards out and headed straight for his own position, and pulled the trigger. Amid a cloud of smoke, the warhead launched out and struck the hood of the suicide vehicle. Fire spewed from the vehicle as it exploded. Mark ducked and pulled Chris down beside him, and then pieces of shrapnel began to land all around them. They waited a few seconds, then snatched their weapons, sprang to their feet and ran in hunched over positions to the back of the building.

"You think that's it?" It was hard to hear Mark, even though he was shouting.

"No chance," Chris shook his head. "Suicide cars are always the lead assault. There're more troops on the way, I guarantee it. We've got to go."

At the edge of the roof, Chris hopped down to the ground, then caught the rifle and rocket launcher from Mark. Then it was Mark's turn. The men sprinted for the remaining vehicle, their own black SUV. The vehicle was maybe ten yards away, but it seemed like ten miles. Halfway there, bullets began to hit the vehicle, and tiny pockmarks appeared in the metal as if by magic. The rear window broke into a spider web of cracks, shattered.

"Five o'clock!" Chris yelled. He raised his rifle and engaged a pick-up truck flying a black flag with white Arabic letters that had appeared to their right. A second truck appeared beside it, a soldier behind a machine gun mounted in the bed. Light flashed from the gun's muzzle, joined by the steady tuk-tuk-tuk-tuk of large caliber bullets.

Beside him, the SUV disintegrated. Something struck Chris in the leg, and he collapsed, his rifle's barrel grinding into the dirt as he fell. Mark stood over him and returned fire, the single reports of the .338 deafening. Chris fired a burst from his rifle, wild and into the air.

"Get up!" Mark yelled. "Get off the X!"

A Caliphate soldier dropped, then another. A third vehicle rolled up and disgorged six additional fighters, who dashed into a line and then dropped to the ground. All of them took aim, and dust sprayed the street in front of Mark and Chris as bullets ricocheted.

"Back to the building," Chris yelled. "Covering!" He fired a burst.

"Moving!" Mark took a shot, then sprinted for the building they'd just vacated.

Chris sprayed another burst at the soldier with the heavy machine gun. A hollow thunk sound came from his rifle and the trigger turned to mush. On instinct he canted the weapon, although he already knew he was out of bullets. "Stoppage!" he roared, leapt to his feet, willed himself to ignore the pain in his leg. He twisted, froze.

Mark lay on the ground about ten feet from the building's entrance, red flecks on his chest. He struggled with the .338, tried to bring it around while bullets sprayed the ground nearby. Chris stumbled as his right leg gave out. Fire bloomed inside his other leg, and he collapsed on the ground to the muffled thud of a bullet striking flesh. He forced himself to half-crawl to Mark. "Don't let them take us alive."

Mark glanced at him, nodded.

Chris writhed onto his side and zeroed in on a group of four Caliphate soldiers. While two of the soldiers took aim at Chris and Mark, the other two dashed up three or four steps and then flopped to the ground and began to shoot. When the fire was steady, the first two men rose and sprinted closer. Chris tucked his rifle into his shoulder, lined up one of the men, now fifty feet away and the next time one of the men sprang to his feet, he squeezed the trigger and nothing happened. *Fuck*. He'd forgotten the stoppage.

Beside him, Mark dropped the .338, drew his pistol and fired. One soldier dropped, hands clutched to his abdomen, then the head of another exploded. "Stoppage!" Mark yelled. His hands were a blur as he reloaded.

Chris went for his own pistol, holstered at his waist. It stuck, pinched between the ground and his body. The remaining two men had closed to thirty feet away, and both were on their feet. Beside him, Mark grunted in pain. "Come on, come on, come on," Chris said. He twisted to free his pistol, got it, raised it, and looked up to see the butt of an AK-47. The lights went out.

* * *

GUINEA, AFRICA
23 MAY 15 – 0805 LOCAL

The isolation partition of the half-dome shelter was small, so small Arielle could have touched both walls by extending her arms. Except for the moment, her hands were pinned to her side, held by a man clad in a head-to-toe yellow plastic suit, his hands covered with blue rubber gloves and a mask on his face. He and Arielle stood in front of a transparent plastic door. Six feet behind them stood a similarly clad man, this one with an assault rifle. As small as the partition was, Arielle was in no rush to leave as the plastic barricade was all that separated her from the tent's main compartment, where four patients lay on four cots, all covered with thin, white blankets that stood in sharp contrast against their dark skin.

The guard who held her fiddled with a control panel on the partition wall, and the door opened. From within the main compartment, one of the bedridden men lifted his head, but the effort seemed too much. With a groan, the patient sank back onto the cot. The guard tugged on Arielle's arm.

"No." She shook her head. Unlike her escorts, she wore a tattered t-shirt and light pants. She pulled back, her bare skin slippery with sweat under the plastic touch of the guard's gloved hand. "I'm not going in there."

The guard tugged again, more forceful this time. She struggled, dug her feet into the plastic covered wood that was the floor of the shelter, but he was much bigger. He heaved and dragged her into the room. The guard with the rifle closed the door behind them.

The smell struck her first. At least one of the bed-ridden patients must have defecated where they lay and she crinkled her nose at the stink. But there was something else as well. Even with the hum of forced air fed through vents in the ceiling, there was a malevolent undertone that made her skin crawl and break out in goose bumps. Bile rose in her throat, and she covered her nose with a hand, tried her best to block out the reek.

The guard shoved her to a corner of the room, where she fell to her hands and knees. He pointed to a small table that held a metal bowl half filled with water. A filthy rag lay on the bowl's edge, dripping over the side. The guard said something, the words indecipherable through the gas mask and whatever language he spoke and then he pointed again, this time to one of the patients.

Arielle swallowed and avoided the guard's gaze. He put his foot on her shoulder and pushed her, pushed her again and then she was in front of the bowl. A tear fell from her eye. She wiped it, flinched as her fingers came in contact with her eye. She needed to be smarter than that.

Stupid. How long did she think she'd stave off infection? She got to her feet and picked up the bowl and carried it to the nearest person, a man. She set the bowl on the edge of the mattress and sat on a stool beside the cot and then got her first good look at the patient.

The man's eyes were closed, his arms on top of the thread-bare sheet that covered the rest of his body. Dark purplish sores discolored the skin from his elbows to his wrists and blisters bulged on the inside of his forearms, some of which had burst to stain the sheets deep red with blood. Arielle covered her mouth with a hand.

As if he sensed her presence, the man opened his eyes, the whites discolored to a deep red. He ran a blistered tongue over his swollen lips and tried to speak, but all that came out was a hoarse groan from deep in his throat, then a weak, hacking cough. The scent of disease grew more intense, like the man's breath itself contaminated the air.

Arielle stood and moved away from the cot with her hands over her face, backed into something solid and unyielding. The guard pushed her and she stumbled toward the cot and caught herself on the stool. She whirled, kept the stool between her and the patient, and the guard advanced on her, his outstretched hand pointed at the man, then at the bowl, then to herself. She shook her head, unable to see through moist eyes. "I won't."

The guard spoke louder, harsh commands accompanied by more pointing.

"No."

The guard waved for the man with the rifle to join him. The other guard opened the door and stepped in, then walked to the foot of the cot where Arielle stood and aimed the rifle at the patient. The first guard grabbed Arielle and forced her nearer the cot, held her elbows behind her back. He yelled into her ear, shoved her toward the man on the bed.

"No." Her body trembled all over.

The rifle fired, and the man's lower jaw disintegrated. Blood shot from the man's eyes and nose, tiny droplets that splattered Arielle's face. Beneath the remains of the man's head, the pillow stained deep red as blood dribbled down to reach the mattress. Yet somehow, the man managed to breathe, clung to life while air bubbled through the red soup at his throat.

Arielle's breath came in gasps, and the room spun. "Why are you doing this?" she cried. They'd won already, they didn't need to force her to care for these people or hurt them more than they were already suffering. In a daze, she felt herself dragged to another cot, the patient in this one a woman, her eyelids swollen into grotesque bulbous protrusions.

The metal bowl was jammed into her hands, and she took it, barely aware of the guards, unable to block out the horror that filled the room. She closed her eyes and relived the man's face exploding and then she blinked her eyes open and stared at the woman in the cot, focused on her wounds, her suffering, willed herself to feel nothing.

The guard with the rifle moved to the foot of the cot and pointed his rifle at the woman's chest. The other guard dragged over the stool and shoved it at Arielle's feet, then pointed to the metal bowl. When Arielle didn't move, the guards exchanged words, and the rifle's muzzle lowered to point at the woman's stomach.

"No more," she said, and sobbed. "No more."

She sat, picked up the bowl and set it beside the pillow, then dipped a hand in and felt for the rag, the water lukewarm against her numb skin. She'd gotten her chance to care for wounded after all. She wiped her nose with the back of a hand and took up the rag. Best to forget whatever dreams a stupid girl had once had, best to forget that girl had ever existed.

The woman moaned, struggled to open her eyes and failed. Her head rocked from side to side, and her bug eyes seemed to stare up at the ceiling as if she could see through the bloated horrors that obscured her sight.

The girl who had once been Arielle Petersson pulled the rag from the bowl, drained it, then lowered it onto the woman's forehead. Held the filthy cloth against the woman's feverish skin and wondered if the woman saw God in the ceiling, or Allah, or anything at all. Coughs racked the woman's body, deep hacks that sent red-flecked spittle onto her cheeks.

The girl looked away, eyes shut. When the coughs subsided, she faced the woman again, her eyes dry, never to shed tears again. The two guards forgotten, she rinsed the woman's face.

CHAPTER FOURTEEN
THE RECKONING

MOSUL, IRAQ
23 MAY 15 – 2010 LOCAL

It was cold. Erik shivered, scrunched up his face to fend off the light. The darkness had been warm, and now he was being dragged up and out, and he was cold, and his face was wet. A drop fell onto his forehead, and he flinched, twisted his head, and the droplet ran along his face into his ear.

Arielle.

He gasped and woke to the world. Harsh light seared his eyes, and he blinked, tried to move his head and could not. He tried to block out the light with a hand, but his arms were held fast beside him. He thrashed in the shackles and they made an empty rattle that echoed hollowly in the small, dark room that had formed in his vision.

"Hit him."

Erik didn't recognize the man's voice. He started to ask where he was and then fabric stretched over his face, damp cloth that molded to his features and bound his head to the hardness he lay upon. He shook, fought his unknown assailants, but the material pulled tighter. It occurred to him that he lay at a slant, his feet higher than his head.

Then the water came.

A dribble at first, followed by a gusher. Into his mouth and nostrils, filling his throat. He snorted and blew out through his nose, spat, anything to get the water out, but the cloth held tight. The water stayed in his mouth followed by even more. He gagged and flailed against his restraints until a ragged, gurgle sounded deep in his throat, and darkness began to overwhelm him once again.

"Enough."

The water stopped. Then the cloth came off his face and his body tilted up as if he lay on a rotating plank. Water trickled out of his mouth, and he coughed in deep, hacking barks.

"Look at me."

Erik struggled to open his eyes, had iron fingers dig into the flesh under his chin to force his head still. He looked up and a face with a light beard swam into view, and he recognized Abu Noor al Kanadi. Fatigue filled him, weighed down his limbs not with the expectation of what the hours and days to come would bring, but with the knowledge he'd failed Arielle.

"You know who I am?" al Kanadi asked.

Erik nodded. "Yes."

"Good," al Kanadi said. He was seated, one leg crossed, hands rested on his knees. A stainless-steel watch decorated his wrist, its large, polished case showing both digital and analog data.

"Where am I?" It hurt to talk.

Al Kanadi smiled. "Classified," he said. There was a concrete wall behind him, where electrical wires hung in haphazard fashion. "Your partners are here also, although not in as good condition as you. For the moment, anyways."

"What do you want?"

"Shut up." It was Chris's voice, hoarse and broken.

"One of your colleagues." Al Kanadi nodded to his side. "The first he's said in twelve hours. That's good, we're making progress."

"Fuck you," Chris said. A muffled thud came from his direction, followed by a hissed intake of breath.

Erik glanced over. Beside him, tied to two separate chairs, were Chris and Mark. Chris leaned against his restraints and glared at al Kanadi. Bandages stained in red were tied about Mark's shoulders and abdomen, and his head lolled onto his chest.

Al Kanadi rose, addressed Chris. "Consider that one a mistake," he said in a soft voice that died in the small room. "But don't worry, the other ones won't be."

"Leave them alone," Erik said. "These men are helping me find my daughter."

"Is that what they told you?" al Kanadi asked. He knelt by Chris's chair, just beyond arm's reach. "The lies never get old, do they?"

Chris raised his head to glare at al Kanadi.

"Why don't you tell him the truth?" al Kanadi said. "It gets easier the more you do it."

Chris spat. "It's like he said. We're helping him get his daughter back, and we know you have her, you fucking traitor."

Al Kanadi gazed over Chris's shoulder and then nodded. A dark-skinned fighter with a shemagh half-wrapped around his face came and stood behind Mark's chair. The man reached over and dug his fingertips into the top of Mark's eye sockets, used the leverage to wrench back the head. A serrated hunting knife appeared in the fighter's other hand and found its way to Mark's neck.

Chris glanced over and then struggled against his restraints. "Get away from him!"

Mark's eyes popped open, and he yelled, beat his fists against his legs. "Do it yourself you cowardly fuck!"

Al Kanadi nodded again, and the soldier started to saw. Mark screamed, and his cries rang in the tiny room until they were cut off with an empty gurgle that competed with the echoes of his yells. Chris looked away and al Kanadi wrestled his head back and forced him to watch as blood trickled down Mark's neck, a slow dribble at first and then spurts. The knife stuck, and the soldier wrenched it, paused, jerked the blade free. Mark's shoulders slumped, and as his body went limp, the soldier moved around the chair to hack and saw from a different angle. His shemagh slipped down off his face, and Erik sucked in a breath of air as he recognized Farah Roble Xarbi.

"The spine is always the worst," al Kanadi whispered into Chris's ear.

Erik watched as Mark's grimace of pain gave way and his eyes and lips drooped and sagged. Part of him howled, the part that smelled the warmth of the blood, the part that felt sick as the final resistance in Mark's neck gave way and the knife cleaved through the remaining flesh. The head teetered for a moment and then tumbled into Mark's lap, and Xarbi scrambled to snatch it up before it rolled onto the floor and then placed it on Chris's lap.

Chris screamed and strained against his restraints. "You sick fuck! I'll kill you!"

"Warm, isn't it?" al Kanadi said. "There's life there yet, for a few moments more. He may even be able to hear you if you have any last words."

"Fuck you!" Chris bucked his legs and Mark's head tumbled to the floor.

Xarbi stooped to pick up the head, but al Kanadi waved him off with a shake of his head. "Tell the truth," he said in a gravelly imitation of Mark. "What brought you to Iraq?"

"To kill you! To erase you and your betrayal!"

Al Kanadi glanced over Chris's head at Erik. "I thought you were helping your friend here find his daughter."

Chris snarled. "Fuck him and his whore of a daughter."

"You thought I owed you one, right? Thought you'd use that to draw me out?"

"I saved your life."

"That you did, and I shall save your life in return."

"You're sick." Chris sneered up at him.

Al Kanadi stood. "The Prophet, peace be upon him, said that, 'there is no disease that Allah has created, except that He also has created its treatment.' By my actions, I relieve you of your pain that you might see the beauty of Islam and save yourself from Hell." He pulled a pistol from his waistband and held the muzzle to Chris's temple.

"You owe me." Chris pressed his head into the pistol, the tendons on his neck taut.

"Which is why we're not recording this. I can give you that small dignity, even if it's more than you deserve," al Kanadi said. The pistol bucked, the concussion deafening in the small bunker. Chris's head jerked back, and tiny flecks of red appeared on the concrete wall behind him. "Besides, if I'd have made you a hostage, who would've cared?" Smoke drifted from the pistol's barrel as al Kanadi returned it to the holster at his waist and then sat down.

Erik swallowed, and he knew it would be his turn next.

"You keep poor company," Al Kanadi said.

Erik stared at the floor.

"Is it true you're looking for your daughter?"

He glanced up and met al Kanadi's gaze then nodded.

Al Kanadi sat forward and rested his elbows on his knees. "What's her name?"

"Arielle Petersson."

"I see," al Kanadi said. "And you would be?"

"Erik Petersson."

"Well, Erik Petersson, I admire you. Few would have attempted what you've done. What made you think I had anything to do with her?"

"Chris told me you were connected."

"And you believed him?"

Erik swallowed. "The police had mentioned you were involved. I don't know how they reached that conclusion."

Al Kanadi studied him, and the room grew silent, and then al Kanadi leaned back in his chair. "Mr. Petersson, I hope you appreciate how lucky you are."

"How do you figure?"

"Because although I suspect you're not telling me everything, I choose to believe you really were searching for your daughter and didn't know these two were trying to kill me," Al Kanadi said and then smiled. "And you shall be rewarded since I know a thing or two about your daughter."

"Like what?"

"For one, she isn't in Syria or Iraq."

"Where is she?" Erik studied al Kanadi's face, looked for a sign the man was lying. "When did she leave?"

Al Kanadi stood and began to pace. "Mr. Petersson, I'm not unsympathetic to your position. I myself struggle to protect my family, so I understand what you're going through."

"We are nothing alike."

Al Kanadi smiled. "You're skeptical, of course. But it's true." He stopped and faced Erik and clasped his hands behind his back. "Your daughter is beyond you. She serves Allah."

"Let me see her."

Al Kanadi shook his head. "I'm sorry, that's quite impossible. She's in Africa right now."

"Why?"

"Mr. Petersson, do you work for the Royal Canadian Mounted Police?"

Erik started and then dropped his gaze to the floor.

"What do you think will happen if you don't talk?" al Kanadi asked.

"You're going to kill me anyways," he said.

"Perhaps. Perhaps not," al Kanadi said. "I'm a father also. I love to watch my boys run. They're so free, free from the imperfections of this world. I like to think I'd do anything to protect them, so maybe we're more alike than you think."

Erik glanced up. "Like I said, we're nothing alike."

"Mr. Petersson, I may not know much about you, but I know enough. And believe me, I can find out more. We have soldiers in every country, including Canada. Ottawa. Montreal. Calgary. These cities are not beyond our reach."

Erik thought of Sahraoui and Reyad Slimani and even Nathan Martel and knew the threat to be true. He knew he could not talk and knew even more that in time, he would. "Why don't you just kill me now?"

"Because you have not answered my questions and until you do, your suffering will continue," al Kanadi said and his eyes sparkled. "But don't worry. It is written that, 'Allah does not tax any soul beyond that which it can bear,' and so I'll ask one more time, do you work for the RCMP?"

Erik wracked his brain, realized there was no way out and that he would need to preserve his strength for the real questions, the ones to which al Kanadi didn't already know the answers.

"Yes," he said and nodded. "I work for the RCMP."

Al Kanadi stared at him and then walked closer and put his hand on Erik's chin. Lifted his face and forced him to meet his gaze. "It would have gone bad for you had you lied," al Kanadi said and then released Erik and straightened. "You will tell me everything you know about the RCMP's investigations."

"Why would I do that?"

Al Kanadi smiled. "Because you will anyways. We both know that." He walked back to his chair. "Besides, as I said, we're both fathers. Should you cooperate, I may give you a chance to see your daughter."

Erik frowned. "You're lying."

"Think that if it helps," Al Kanadi said and then leaned closer. "But know that I speak the truth when I say that I can make both you and your daughter suffer like you cannot imagine."

Erik clenched his jaw and looked down.

"You need some time to think. Fair enough." Al Kanadi stood and walked past Erik and then stopped. "But don't take too long. Hit him again." His footsteps sounded on the floor as he left.

The platform on which Erik lay rotated back and down until his head was again lower than his chest. The damp cloth descended over his face once more, and then the water came, and he choked as it filled his nose and throat and then the blackness took him.

* * *

MOSUL, IRAQ
23 MAY 15 – 2120 LOCAL

Al Kanadi stood and watched Yahya supervise the bunker's clean-up. The Petersson man had been carted back to the improvised holding cell in the library above, along with one of al Kanadi's men as a guard. The set-up was not ideal, but then again, the Mosul facility was supposed to be a safe place to plan and stage attacks, not a prison to hold hostages.

Xarbi entered the bunker and began to remove Mark's body. Petersson had started when he'd seen Xarbi, as if he recognized him, which was a possibility. Xarbi was Canadian, and if Petersson worked with the RCMP as his daughter's information sheet had said, then it was possible he was aware of the Somali revert. Just another example of the information that might be in Petersson's head.

That is, if he used the resources to guard him, interrogate him, and all the other dog shit that came with prisoners. It would be far easier to call in the *Hisbah,* who had no small skill in interrogation, but that might erode the persona he'd crafted of self-sufficiency, not to mention raise questions of how he'd captured Petersson in the first place, questions he didn't want to answer. More than anything else though, the timing bothered him. Why had Petersson shown up now, in the final stages of attack planning?

His foot bumped against Mark's head, and he stopped mid-stride, then knelt. He rolled the head, so Mark's limp face stared up. "And you, what would you do?" he asked and then turned to Chris's corpse, still tied to its chair. "Or you? How do I turn this to my advantage?"

He knew the answer to that question. Chris would kill Petersson and have done with the whole thing. Still, al Kanadi was certain he could get Peterson to talk. Too bad the man wasn't better placed in the RCMP. Hafsa's questionnaire had indicated he was a forensic technician, but one had to play the cards that were dealt.

He moved aside to let Yahya remove Mark's head. The thing is, he would even consider letting Petersson speak with his daughter if he'd thought it would make her more compliant. Mamdouh's last report had said that his biggest concern was that the girl might harbor a trace of resistance. Mamdouh was so close to breaking her, but he needed something else, some additional leverage to erase any hint of free will.

He smiled. Leverage was of course what he now had.

He watched Yahya and Xarbi cart out Chris's body, the last thing to clean up. The men paused in the doorway of the bunker and looked back at him.

"Will there be anything else, emir?" Yahya asked.

"Yes," al Kanadi said. "Work on the prisoner for the next few days. Take lots of pictures, we'll need to send them to Mamdouh."

"As you will it, Emir," Yahya said and bowed his head and then turned to leave.

"One last thing, Yahya."

"Yes, Emir?"

"If he hasn't talked by then, kill him."

CHAPTER FIFTEEN
THE SUN AND THE MOON

OUTSIDE MOSUL, IRAQ
28 MAY 15 – 1741 LOCAL

The truck slowed to a stop, and Erik propped himself up and tried to peer through the tiny hole in the hood over his head. He had a rough idea how long he'd traveled since al Kanadi's men had thrown him in the back of the truck, maybe an hour, maybe less. Xarbi had been among the men, had made sure the ever-present knife at his belt was visible, but whether he meant to follow through on his threats to add another head to his collection was left unsaid.

A truck door creaked open, and gravel or sand crunched under boots. Erik tested the flex-cuffs that bound his hands together in front of his chest. The thin plastic dug into his wrists, and he wasn't sure he'd be able to break them, although he had a feeling he'd soon find out. At least his hands hadn't been tied behind his back.

The truck shook as a person jumped into the bed and then hands grabbed him under the armpits and dragged him to his feet. He stumbled toward the tailgate where the hood was ripped off. Bright sun blinded him, and he raised his hands to block the glare even as he struggled to get his bearings.

"Get out," a man said, and Erik recognized Xarbi's voice. He'd been a fixture at Erik's side these past days, taunted him with the threat of death during what he called the 'sessions,' prodded him with questions about the RCMP. So far, Erik had said nothing and over the past day or so he'd been left alone. He wasn't sure if that was good or bad.

He lowered his hands and squinted to block out the light, then eased himself to the ground. The truck had stopped on the crest of a small ridge, and there was another pickup in front of the one he'd been in, along with two soldiers who leaned against the grill, rifles held loose in their hands. Beyond them were the faint smudge of buildings on the horizon, a distant city. Mosul, perhaps. He let his gaze roam farther, tried to get his bearings and was yanked away from the truck by Xarbi.

"Walk." Xarbi, dressed in black shirt and pants, pointed to a worn trail that meandered down the ridge through knee-high scrub. Sweat glistened on his forehead beneath a black skull cap, and he carried a two-way radio at his belt and a pistol in a loose shoulder holster. On the other side of his belt was a knife, the blade at least a foot long. Xarbi's normal garb was fatigues and pilfered combat uniforms, but Erik had no problems recognizing the outfit he had on today. It was what he wore in the beheading videos. He shoved Erik down the path. "I said, walk."

Erik stumbled, glanced once at the other soldiers dressed in black, then picked his way down the path. A fighter with a camera fell in behind, the same fighter who'd taken pictures of him in his cell, where he'd been chained with his arms in the air, or when he'd hung from a hook in the ceiling and been beaten with electrical cables. He'd even gone through several staged executions, but always close to wherever he'd been held. Now he was in the middle of nowhere, and the thing this most reminded him of were the Caliphate execution videos, filmed against backgrounds of sand and brush without exception. The question before him was whether this was another staged execution, or the real thing. He tested the flex cuffs again and decided that all his options were bad.

"Far enough." Xarbi grabbed him by the scruff of the neck and drove him to his knees. The soldier with the camera walked farther, stopped about twenty paces farther out, then faced him. The other two soldiers had stayed by the trucks.

Xarbi's hands left him, and Erik glanced over his shoulder to watch Xarbi's skull cap turn into a black balaclava that he pulled down over his face. "Al Kanadi said he'd let me talk with my daughter."

Xarbi grabbed Erik's collar and pressed the blade of the knife against Erik's throat. "On condition that you talk. And what did you say? Nothing."

"I'm a technician. I don't know anything."

"Then your time has run out," Xarbi said. He grabbed Erik's head and forced him to look to the front and then pointed his knife at the soldier with the camera. "Start recording." Xarbi put his free hand under Erik's chin and pulled his face up to look into the camera. "You who –"

Erik thrust to his feet and drove his head up into Xarbi's chin. Xarbi stumbled, and a tiny amount of space opened up, and Erik twisted and yanked Xarbi's pistol free from its flimsy holster. Xarbi clawed for the gun, struggled and Erik kicked out his legs. While Xarbi fell, Erik aimed the pistol at the fighter with the camera and fired. Fired again and again and tiny red spots appeared on the fighter's chest, and then he dropped to the ground.

The sound of shots erupted from the ridge where the convoy had stopped. Bullets zinged off the rocks, and Erik spun and fired at the two fighters by the trucks. One of the men dropped, and the other sought cover behind the rear pickup. Erik fired again, and the pistol went empty, and then he glanced at Xarbi, who'd staggered to his knees. Erik clubbed him with the pistol and Xarbi fell to the ground, limp.

Erik located the body of the fighter who'd held the camera and scuttled to the man's body and more importantly, the pistol the man had carried. As he moved, the rear pickup roared to life and then backed up in a spray of sand and gravel. Gun in hand, Erik fired from his knees and then sprang to his feet and fired again. The passenger window shattered, and the truck began to turn in a half-circle. Erik ran headlong up the trail while the vehicle bounced in the rough ground beside the road and then came to a stop. Its rear wheels spun in the loose soil, but the pickup didn't move. Erik took a shooting stance, fired again. Tiny spider web cracks appeared in the windshield.

The driver's side door opened and the barrel of a rifle poked out, got hung up. While the fighter wrestled with the rifle, Erik took careful aim, then fired. The man fell back into the cab. Crouched low, Erik moved up, stopped to confirm the other fighter he'd shot was down, then crept closer to the rear vehicle. He led with the pistol around the driver's side door and found the fighter strewn across the front seat, struggling to raise the rifle. Erik fired again, and the man stopped moving.

Erik searched the man's body and recovered a knife and had almost freed the zip ties on his wrists when a bang came from the middle pickup. He sliced through the ties, then whirled and stalked toward the pickup, pistol at the ready. He circled the back of the vehicle, took aim at a pair of legs about to disappear into the passenger side door, fired. He missed, pulled the trigger again, but nothing happened. Stoppage. He was a few feet from the truck now, and he dashed the remaining distance and grabbed the man's foot and pulled. Xarbi kicked and screamed his way out of the truck, the handset to a vehicle-mounted walkie-talkie radio clutched in his hand. Erik heaved, and Xarbi tumbled onto the ground. Freed, the handset sprung back into the truck's cab.

Xarbi rolled onto his back, hands in front of his face. "Don't kill me!"

Erik aimed the pistol at Xarbi's face. He might be out of bullets, but Xarbi didn't know that. "Al Kanadi said my daughter was in Africa, where?"

"I don't know."

"I don't believe you." He put the pistol's barrel against Xarbi's forehead.

Xarbi scrunched his face up tight. "Please, no!"

A tinny voice came from the vehicle's radio. It spoke in Arabic, but Erik picked out Xarbi's name, repeated over and over. He glared at Xarbi, whose eyes rolled in his head. "One more chance. Where is she?"

"I don't know!" Xarbi said in a high-pitched squeal. "They went to Libya, but after that, I don't know."

"What's she doing there?"

"Planning an attack!"

"What?" He pressed harder with the pistol. "What attack? What's the target?"

"I don't know, I don't know! They don't tell me that stuff!" Xarbi tried to shield his face. "I just do what I'm told."

"When?"

"Huh?"

Erik shook him. "I said when! When is the attack?"

"Soon."

He ground the pistol into Xarbi's temple. "What does that mean?"

"I don't know! A week, two?" The voice from the vehicle changed, grew more urgent.

Erik nodded over his shoulder. "What's he saying?"

"They're asking me to repeat what I said."

"And what did you tell them?"

"That you got free." Xarbi lips tightened in a grim smile. "Reinforcements are on their way. They'll be here any minute."

"And where is here?"

Xarbi frowned. "Mosul, of course."

"Thanks," Erik said and smashed the butt of the pistol into Xarbi's head. Xarbi went limp, and Erik studied him, restrained the urge to hit him again, then started when the voice on the radio spoke again. Xarbi might have lied, but Erik didn't think so. Which meant he didn't have much time.

He frisked Xarbi, found nothing useful, then stopped to take a rifle and some ammunition from the other fighters. He looked up, saw that the sun had already started to set, but if he got moving, he might be able to reach the front lines before all light was gone. From there, he might be able to make contact with the Kurds and cross back over – if he was careful.

He hopped into the remaining truck and started it up. He glanced into the rear and smiled at the sight of his backpack. He snatched it up, dug through the pockets and found most of his things there, including the two GPS trackers Jordan had given him stored in one of the inner pouches. He put the truck in gear and then it occurred to him that however this worked out, there was a chance al Kanadi's men would recover the trucks he was leaving behind. He hopped out, activated the magnets on the GPS transmitters and attached them to the roll bars of both trucks. If nothing else, Jordan could at least find out if they worked. Then he returned to the truck he'd liberated and put it in gear.

Next stop, the front lines.

* * *

MOSUL, IRAQ
28 MAY 15 – 1815 LOCAL

Yahya clutched the now silent handset and spoke into it again. "Xarbi?"

Static was all he got back.

"Tell me again what he said," he said in a snarl to the man beside him, a young Syrian named Mohammed who was not even able to grow a beard.

"That the prisoner had been freed," Mohammed said. "He told me to tell you, that it was important."

"What did he mean? That he's dead?" Yahya asked. "Are you sure that's what he said?"

Mohammed cringed. "Maybe, I think so. It was in English. He sounded excited." Mohammed held up his hands. "I'm sorry."

"Idiot." Yahya shoved him. There was no reason for Xarbi to report that the execution was done, he could do it in person when he came back. The ICOM vehicle radios limited the ability of Western forces to intercept their transmissions, but the risk wasn't zero, so they'd been ordered not to use them unless they had no other choice. Even stranger was that having called in, Xarbi now wouldn't answer. "Xarbi?" he asked again to no avail.

He shouldn't be worried. No doubt, Xarbi would return in an hour or so. But something about this bothered him. The prisoner had been freed? It didn't make any sense. He scowled at Mohammed. "Did he say the prisoner had been freed, or that he got free?"

"I don't remember," Mohammed said.

"Think!" But his exhortations did no good and he threw Mohammed to the ground and stalked off toward the library's entrance. The easy answer would be to drive out and find Xarbi, but that would be admitting something had gone wrong.

"Everything all right?"

Yahya started, glanced up to meet al Kanadi's gaze. "Emir. I didn't hear you."

"You seem deep in thought," al Kanadi said. "Something going on?"

"It's fine." He gave a tight smile. He felt Mamdouh's absence, and he didn't want the Emir to worry he wasn't able to take hold of his nerves. "Just anxious to get back to Raqqa."

Al Kanadi clapped him on the shoulder. "A few loose ends to tie up, then we'll be off." He returned Yahya's smile then walked away.

Loose ends, no kidding. Yahya's thoughts went back to the prisoner's execution. If Xarbi hadn't returned in an hour, he'd go out after him. And that idiot Mohammed would be along for the ride.

* * *

NEAR KALAK, IRAQ
28 MAY 15 – 2025 LOCAL

A faint sliver of light clung to the western horizon, the sky a collage of orange and red. Erik searched for movement, lights, anything, but there had been nothing since he'd abandoned the truck. He could make it out a few miles back, stuck in the rocks where he'd tried to ford a stream. Bad luck, when everything had been going so well.

He'd stuck to back roads for about an hour and then came across a sign for Qaraqosh, which he recalled from the map in Rafiq's headquarters. Iraq's largest Christian town, at least at one point. If he remembered right, it was southeast of Mosul, about halfway between the Caliphate capital in Iraq and the forward defensive lines. He'd nursed the truck east along dirt paths, closer to friendly lines. When the sun had begun to set, he'd come across the stream and tried to cross, gotten stuck. After a few attempts to free the truck, he'd set out on foot, more or less due east.

By his calculations, he had to be close to the FLOT. He picked his way along a hard-scrabble ridge that would have a commanding view of the surroundings, especially to the east. From there, he might be able to see the Kurdish defensive line. He shifted the rifle in his hands and kept climbing.

At the top of the ridge, he paused, tried to see through the near darkness to the east. The ground dipped into a small valley, and on the other side, maybe a mile or mile-and-a-half away were several lights, as well as the sparkling glow of what might be a fire. A series of spotlights illuminated a road dotted with several large shapes that he took to be concrete barricades, and there was a building shrouded in darkness beyond the lights. That had to be a Kurdish checkpoint. He'd made it. He stepped down the ridge, then froze.

Staked into the ground was a small triangular sign bearing a white skull and crossbones and Arabic script on a dark background. Farther along the ridge was another sign, the same markings. A bitter laugh escaped him.

Minefield.

He considered his options. He could follow the signs and skirt the edge of the minefield, hoping to hit a road that led through, but even though he was close to the FLOT, he didn't have a good idea where he was, or how far a road might be. Or how long the minefield extended. Or if the road would be mined.

He should've been more careful fording the stream. He glanced back to the pickup, then dropped into a crouch. Lights of two other vehicles had appeared near where the truck was stuck. Cold sweat trickled down his back. One set of vehicle headlights disappeared, then reappeared moments later, moving in his direction close to the path he'd taken. The other vehicle followed. Much closer and they'd be able to see him, even in the twilight.

Erik edged farther down the far slope bordering the minefield, then hunkered low where he was able to observe the vehicles without exposing himself. About a half-mile out, they shifted to the north. As they turned, the lead vehicle came into the tail vehicle's headlights and he could see the distinctive roll bars and sandy colored paint, the same as the ones he'd left behind. Erik hugged the ground as the trucks creeped along, then stopped. Two men exited the lead truck and picked their way to the ridge. As they walked, the trail truck did a U-turn and headed south. Toward where Erik was.

He thought about hiding out where he was and dismissed the idea. The moon had risen low in the sky, but it was large and would provide a degree of light. If he stayed on the ridge he'd be found, and all he had for ammo was a few magazines, enough for a last stand but not a sustained fight. No, he needed to put distance between himself and these men. He pushed to his feet and stepped down the far side of the ridge, on the hostile side of the warning signs. His foot settled on a rock, rolled as the rock moved beneath his boot, then went firm. He let go of the breath he'd been holding, shifted his weight and scanned the ground. Nothing but more rocks and scrub.

The sound of a truck engine grew louder from the other side of the ridge.

No choice but to keep going. He took one more look, then sidestepped down the ridge and into the minefield.

* * *

NEAR KALAK, IRAQ
28 MAY 15 – 2112 LOCAL

"There." Yahya pointed out across the valley. "What's that?"

Beside him, Xarbi raised the binoculars, and Yahya prayed he'd make something out. The moon gave a faint glow, but it hadn't yet risen enough to help. While Xarbi scanned, Yahya stared at the horizon. Thirty miles to the east lay Erbil, tantalizingly close, although he had more pressing concerns. His gaze settled on the Kurdish check-point on the other side of the valley.

"What do you see?" Yahya asked. The two men crouched at the top of a ridge, mere feet from the edge of the minefield markers. Even this position was risky as the markers didn't always start where mines themselves had been laid. And of course, this close to the defensive lines, either the Kurds or coalition drones would discover them sooner or later.

"There's someone out there." Xarbi's tone did not inspire confidence.

"Let me see." Yahya snatched the binoculars and peered into the darkness.

"About a quarter of the way across," Xarbi said.

Yahya trained the binoculars at a spot about four hundred yards out, cursed, fixed on a darker spot among the rocks. It was small, but it could very well be a person. "Give me your rifle."

Xarbi handed over his AK-47 in silence.

Yahya raised the rifle and took up a sight picture. He cursed again, strained to see the target in the dark.

"Is it worth risking a shot?" Xarbi asked. "The Kurds will see us."

"We need to know if it's him," Yahya said. He resettled the rifle against his shoulder and tried to find the target.

"Then let me. I'm a better shot." Xarbi took the rifle and went prone on the ground. There was a moment of silence, and then a shot split the dark with a loud crack. Yahya flinched, but he'd seen enough. The shape had moved. Xarbi fired again and the shape merged into the ground.

"Is it him?" Xarbi asked.

"Who else would it be, idiot?" Yahya focused the binoculars on the

Kurdish checkpoint, where shadows had passed across the lights. The shots had been heard and time was ticking.

Xarbi shot again, and Yahya placed a hand on his shoulder. "That's enough."

"If he makes it much farther, there's no way we'll hit him."

The fool was right, and yet as it was, they'd need Allah's intervention. The Kurds would already be trying to locate them, and no doubt had night vision, which meant the longer he and Xarbi stayed on this ridge, the riskier it became. Coalition air support might already be on its way. "Once more," he said and then located the shape in the minefield, this time up and moving.

The rifle rang out again, and Yahya saw the person drop, but whether Xarbi had hit or not was anyone's guess. *Inshallah*, the troublesome infidel would be dead. "Let's go," he said and scuttled backward until the ridge sheltered him from the Kurdish checkpoint, then stood and scrambled for the trucks.

Xarbi followed. "Did I get him?"

"I think so," he said. "But if you didn't, either the minefield or the Kurds will finish him."

"You think so?"

"If you were a Kurd and came under fire at a checkpoint, then saw somebody in your protective minefield, would you think they were friendly?"

"No." Xarbi sounded sheepish.

"Neither will the Kurds. They'll shoot on sight."

From Xarbi's silence, he must have agreed. Either way, they needed to get out of this area, but when they were safe, he'd go up one side of Xarbi and down the other.

Then he'd try to figure out what to tell al Kanadi.

* * *

Near Kalak, Iraq
28 May 15 – 2231 Local

Erik eased himself to his feet. It had been almost half an hour since the last shot. To the east, the length of the valley stretched before him, the lights of the Kurdish outpost distant. To the west, the ridge where al Kanadi's men had shot at him was a darker shape in the night, although as the moon rose, they would have better light with which to see him. He didn't think they were still there, but he couldn't wait any longer. Besides, at this point, his greatest risk was that the Kurds would shoot him.

He squinted at the outpost. He should have thought of that before, but it had been a distant threat compared to his pursuers and the minefield. Now, with the possibility that he might make the Kurdish lines, he needed to not be seen as a threat. Slow and deliberate, he set the rifle down and then raised his hands to his shoulders. He shivered. The night air, which had been warm when he'd started, now chilled him and his damp shirt clung to his body. He went to take a step, but his foot remained riveted to the rocks.

He closed his eyes. Standing here wouldn't solve anything. There were two ways out, die in the minefield or keep walking. Whether he died by a mine, or a Caliphate bullet or even a Kurdish bullet made little difference. He called Arielle's face to mind and readied himself to take another step. Her hair, he couldn't remember her hair. It was brown, he knew that, but what did it look like?

A chill settled over his body. It hadn't even been two months, and he had already forgotten his daughter's face. Just like Audray. He thought of the old answering machine he'd kept, the one that held his wife's voice and her soft, French accent. He would listen to it and remember making love, the memory cold across the years, heard her whispering, *"oui, plus fort."* He forced his eyes open and before he could think any further, he took a step. Another. He scanned the ground, saw nothing, took another step.

Halfway across, at least.

Was it his imagination or had the sky grown lighter, a sliver of orange along the eastern horizon? What time would that be, three o'clock? Earlier, later? No matter. Take another step. The sweat had long since dried up. Now his mouth was caked as if the landscape's sand and dust had infiltrated his pores and come to roost on his tongue. Focus. Another step. Another.

Two-thirds of the way across, the valley began to rise in a gentle slope. Something brushed his foot, and he stumbled, looked down and saw a shoe. A lady's shoe, black, like a ballet flat except with an inch-tall heel. Out of place and yet he knew how it had come to be there. Another step.

And then he saw it. He didn't know how, but there it was, five tiny prongs standing up among the rocks to point at the sky. He crouched and stared at the mine, which was a little more than a yard from his lead foot. The prongs meant it was a bounding mine, a Bouncing Betty. It was a mine that killed, not just amputated. An OZM perhaps, from Russia, or maybe a PROM-1. When he stepped on it, it would launch into the air, waist high, and spray molten hot metal fragments. If he was lucky, the blast would shred him. Not so lucky and he would bleed out through the morning, less a limb or two.

It occurred to him that there might be others nearby, especially since the prongs were visible. Bounding mines were often protected by other mines, ones that weren't visible, like pressure-activated mines. He studied the ground around the mine and now he was sure the blacks and greys of the night had begun turning to browns and greens in the early morning light. But nothing showed.

He willed himself to relax and gave the mine as wide a berth as possible. Each step was an eternity, yet the sky was no brighter by the time he'd passed the mine, or even when he'd left it twenty feet behind. He stared up at the top of the slope, where the road dead-ended at a chicane of concrete barricades maybe two hundred yards away.

He'd almost reached the road when he heard men begin to yell. He glanced at the searchlights, and then five soldiers in combat uniforms appeared on the other side of the concrete barriers that formed the roadblock, maybe a hundred yards away. They aimed their rifles at him and shouted. One of them pointed at the ground.

Erik kept his hands raised. "Please," he said in a croak. He licked his lips, swallowed. "Help me," he said, louder.

Now the men yelled in English. "Come closer! Keep your hands up!"

The Kurdish soldiers cleared him closer then yelled at him to get on the ground. He lowered his backpack and lay spread-eagled on his stomach. Boots appeared beside him, and his body rocked as he was frisked, and despite all that, he felt like he could run a marathon. He'd made it.

"Sit up."

He moved into a cross-legged position, and two of the soldiers pointed rifles at him.

Another soldier appeared between the two with rifles. "Who are you?"

"My name is Erik Petersson."

"Caliphate deserter?" It was said with a sneer.

"No," he said and shook his head. "I'm Canadian."

"Do you think us stupid?" the soldier asked. "The Caliphate has Canadians as well."

"Of course, I'm sorry," he said.

"Where have you come from? What are you doing here?"

"Mosul, I think," Erik said. "I was captured. Maybe a week ago?" He scrunched up his face. Was it even that long? "Yesterday, I escaped."

The men spoke among themselves.

"Rafiq Talibani can vouch for me," he said.

"Be quiet," the soldier who spoke English said. He continued to confer with the other soldiers, then at last turned back to Erik. "Stay here. Don't move." He walked off through the chicane, and the remaining soldiers closed ranks behind him, their rifle barrels pointed at Erik.

* * *

MOSUL, IRAQ
29 MAY 15 – 0415 LOCAL

Abu Noor al Kanadi woke to shouts and was halfway into his boots and a chest rig when he caught the anger in the voices instead of urgency. He allowed himself to move slower, took a moment to be grateful that he hadn't woken up to a coalition attack, then entered the bunker's stairwell. It was nice to sleep underground, cool. He'd miss it when they returned to Raqqa. But return they would, and soon, *Inshallah*. At the top of the stairwell, he found Yahya and Xarbi. A vein throbbed at Yahya's temple as he yelled at Xarbi. "What's this?" he asked.

Xarbi's eyes widened, and Yahya's face grew even redder, if that were possible. "My apologies, Emir." Yahya bowed his head. "We did not mean to wake you."

"Then why did you?"

Yahya shut his mouth and glared at Xarbi, who'd broken out in a sweat. "It was a mistake, Emir," Xarbi said, and Yahya slapped him, and he became silent.

"The prisoner escaped," Yahya said.

Al Kanadi forced his face to remain a calm mask. "How?"

"He overpowered these idiots and fled in one of their trucks," Yahya said with a snarl. "The others are dead."

"And this one survived?"

"Regrettably."

"He's dead, though," Xarbi said. "We shot him in a minefield." Yahya slapped him again.

"Explain."

"We found him crossing a minefield toward Kurdish lines," Yahya said. "We –"

"I shot him!" Xarbi said.

"We think." Yahya glared at Xarbi, then faced al Kanadi. "By the time we found him, it was dark. We shot at him, but then the Kurds saw us, and we had to leave."

This was the risk of empowering subordinates, they sometimes failed. "Is he alive?"

"No, Emir," Xarbi said. "I hit him."

"Shut up." Yahya beat Xarbi around the ears, then met al Kanadi's gaze. "It's possible, Emir. I'm sorry."

Al Kanadi looked away. He had to assume the worst, that Petersson would make it to freedom. The Caliph didn't like failure, and the escape of a prisoner would devalue al Kanadi's stock. For that alone, Xarbi would have to pay.

And what of Petersson? The man couldn't know much, there'd been no opportunity for him to learn anything. He didn't know where he'd been held, or anything about his daughter. "I assume we got pictures of Petersson?"

"Of course, Emir," Xarbi said.

"I was talking to Yahya." Al Kanadi smiled at the dead man and then turned back to Yahya. "Send the photos to Mamdouh soonest. He must be ready to go."

"Should we tell him Petersson escaped?"

Al Kanadi considered the question and then shook his head. "No. Don't trouble him with that."

"Should we activate the cells in Erbil to see if they find him?"

"No. The man is no threat."

Yahya nodded. "I understand."

Al Kanadi paused. "One last thing."

"Yes, Emir?"

He nodded at Xarbi. "Get rid of this thing."

CHAPTER SIXTEEN
DARKNESS FALLS

GUINEA, AFRICA
02 JUNE 2015 – 1114 LOCAL

The woman squeezed the rag and drained its blood and sweat into the filthy water.

She'd lost count of the patients she'd tended. The tears had returned one time, when she'd wondered where the patients came from. Had they been like her at some point and were being punished? Or had they been made playthings in her torment? The idea pained her, and since concern for the patients increased her suffering, she pushed it deep down inside and tried to forget.

She took a breath and wiped sweat from the forehead of the man in front of her.

The door to the isolation shelter opened with a whoosh of air. Composed – the one thing left to her was how she faced death – she glanced over her shoulder.

"Hafsa." A guard beckoned, clad in the omnipresent yellow suit and blue gloves. She stood and followed him outside, eyes squinted against the sunlight. She tried to remember a time when she hadn't been Hafsa, but her mind played tricks on her. It was like hearing stories about when she'd been a kid, familiar, but not her. She'd always been Hafsa.

The guard steered her to another shelter, through a screening anteroom and into an isolation chamber that held a single wooden table and two flimsy folding chairs. A person sat at the table, a man from the size, although the yellow plastic suit made it difficult to tell. She thought of her father and then summoned what strength remained and pushed her father from her mind. She would not sully the memory of the last thing she held dear by associating him with this place.

The person at the table gestured at the empty chair. "Sit." Mamdouh's voice was unmistakable, even through the metallic tone of the gas mask's voice box.

She sat. Deep inside, another girl felt the urge to leap across the table and rip off Mamdouh's mask, spit in his face. But not Hafsa.

"I'm told you're infected."

She swooned for a moment and then met his glare. "No. Not yet," she said. "I don't have any symptoms."

"They haven't presented, but they will." He shrugged. "We'll be leaving soon."

"We?"

"I will accompany you," he said. "It is my duty."

"Where are we going?"

"Canada. As you were told."

"No." The room spun. "You're a monster." The words had slipped out, and Hafsa cowered into the chair, certain the blow would come. It always did.

"No different than our enemies," Mamdouh said. "Not a week goes by when the Syrian apostate doesn't use chemical weapons." He slapped the table and Hafsa jumped. "On his own people." Mamdouh stood. "The Iraqis used chemicals too, with Western assistance, tested them on other Iraqis. I experienced it firsthand. All told, they've killed millions with their bombs, their landmines, their weapons of mass destruction. Under the principle of reciprocity, it is, therefore, permissible to attack them with the same methods."

"But why? What will this accomplish?"

Mamdouh peeled off his gas mask. Uncovered, his eyes glowered beneath a sweaty brow. "They have no respect for us, and yet they preside over a society as diseased as the bodies of these pathetic people," he said. "Our culture has thousands of years of history, and they treat us like slaves. They are concerned with nothing but pleasure and money, and you ask me why? Their arrogance has made them ignorant of God and the prophet Mohammed, may peace be upon him. It dooms them as surely as their filthy drug addicts crave their next fix. They are weak, and they think they're untouchable, but they shall reap the rewards of their diseased ways. We will destroy them from the inside out. And you will help."

She struggled to breathe. "I will not."

He stared at her, then pushed a yellow manila folder across the table. "Look inside."

"No."

"Then I'll do it for you." He opened the folder and tossed the contents on the table.

She glanced at the documents and then reached out and picked up a photo of her father. "Where did you get these?" she asked.

"We captured him in Iraq."

"That can't be." She sifted through the pictures. In one, her dad's face was dirty and blood trickled from a cut over his eye. In another, a masked militant stood over her father's shoulder, knife pointed at the camera. She pushed the photos away. "You're lying."

"He went to Iraq to find you. Little did he know you'd already moved on."

Her heart beat in her throat. "What have you done with him?"

"Your weakness disgusts me." Mamdouh's face darkened. "He is the enemy. An infidel."

"He is my father."

Mamdouh's hand shot out, grabbed her under the chin. His fingers dug into her flesh as he lowered his face to her level. "He is not Hafsa's father."

She struggled, but was unable to free herself. She pictured her dad's head, severed and with its tongue protruding from his mouth as she'd seen in countless other executions. But what did it change? Was his life more important than those who'd suffer in the horror Mamdouh sought to unleash? She shuddered. *Forgive me, Dad.* "I can't do this."

Mamdouh held her and then shoved her backward. "So be it. Come." He crossed the room to the door, which swung open as he neared. He barked a sharp command in Arabic and then continued through the isolation area. Two guards burst into the shelter and prodded her along after him with the muzzles of their rifles.

She trekked behind him, out into the blazing sun and then back into the room from where she'd been summoned, the man she'd been treating in the same position where she'd left him. In the next cot over was a woman, and it was to this cot that she was steered.

She and Mamdouh stood in silence before the cot, unspeaking, and then the partition door opened again and another guard entered, a young boy before him. The boy wore dirty, white shorts and his ribs showed through his thin chest.

Mamdouh pointed at the bed. "There is your mother. Go to her."

"No." Arielle moved to block the boy's path.

Mamdouh's gloved hand flew up to her chest, held her back. "There are five more children waiting outside."

The boy stared at them, his face expressionless, and then ran to the cot.

He hopped up beside the woman, threw his arms around her, buried his face in the crook of her neck.

A sob rent Arielle's heart. She'd thought she was Hafsa now, that everything had been excised, that her last trace of empathy gone. She'd been wrong.

"There are villages full of children within an hour's drive from here," Mamdouh said. "I will spread this disease like the misery the West spread through my homeland if you do not cooperate."

It was too much. She clenched her eyes shut, held her hands to her ears as her whole body heaved, one racking sob after another.

Mamdouh grabbed her wrists, peeled her hands from her ears, yelled into her face. "You think these people will survive? The West could cure this in a week if they wanted. But they don't." He snarled, like an animal. "They're safe behind their democracies, their freedoms, unwilling to get their hands dirty. That leaves us to care for them, but that care comes with a price. Allah demands that we all serve."

"Enough." Snot and spittle dripped from her mouth.

"You will come, and you will cooperate, Hafsa," he said, the words like knives into her heart, "or I will bring your father here to help infect every child in the area."

Her heart snapped. "All right," she said through her tears. *I'm sorry, Dad.* She wasn't strong enough to do what had to be done, not like him. "I'll do what you want."

Mamdouh's grip on her wrists relaxed. "Good –"

She leaned into him, pressed her lips against his and forced her tongue into his mouth. Hands grabbed her shoulders, tore her off him and she bit down on his lip, held on, tasted the coppery tang of blood and then she was off, thrown to the floor. She glanced up, anxious to see his dismay or even anger. To her horror, he was smiling.

"Didn't I tell you the Iraqis experimented on their own people?" he asked. "I can't be infected twice. Why do you think I'm in charge of this operation? Why do you think I'm the one who will accompany you?"

She no longer felt the hands on her body. Numb, she looked to the bed and stared at the boy, who still hugged his mother.

"We leave in one hour, Hafsa," Mamdouh said. "Be ready." He walked out, leaving the guards to supervise her. A pair of robes dropped to the floor at her side.

She knelt for a moment, the ground hard on her knees and then felt a hand on her head. She flinched, glanced up to meet the gaze of the boy. He'd reached out to touch her, but now he pulled back. They stared at each other for a moment, then he went back to his mother, nestled into her wasted chest.

Hafsa looked down and then picked up the clothes and began to dress.

* * *

ERBIL, IRAQ
02 JUNE 15 – 1541 LOCAL

Rafiq's headquarters was more inviting than Erik remembered.

"Let's get you settled," Ray Parker said. He entered the main room with Erik's duffel bag over his shoulder. "Rafiq will come by a little later."

"I've got a lot to thank him for." Erik followed Ray into the room. The aches and pains from the past week had taken their toll. "I understand he and his dad helped get me out of custody." From the checkpoint on the FLOT, the Kurdish guards had transferred him to a detention facility for questioning. He'd dropped Rafiq's name every chance he got, but had still endured four days of interrogation until Rafiq's father had been able to secure his release.

Ray scratched his head. "Yeah, well Rafiq's old man is busting his balls over this whole thing. Don't get me wrong, Rafiq wanted to be clear of Chris and Mark, but not like this."

"Rafiq didn't have a choice, Chris made that pretty clear."

"You and I know that, but Rafiq's old man don't care," Ray said. "All he knows is he's down two cowboys who were delivering body count."

"I get it."

"Listen, I'm sure you want to call home." Ray gestured toward an adjoining door. "Why don't you use Rafiq's office?"

"Thanks, I'll take you up on that." Erik moved into the office and sat at a desk. Outwardly calm, the gears in his brain wouldn't stop, untouched by the weariness that had settled over him. He'd failed. He was no closer to finding Arielle. If al Kanadi and Xarbi were to be believed, she wasn't even in the Middle East anymore and he didn't know if he should stay here and try to dig up leads, or limp back home. Instead, he pulled out his phone.

Jordan answered on the fifth ring. "Holy shit, you're alive," Jordan said. "We were getting worried. How are you?"

"I've been better," he said.

"Buddy, there's so much to follow up on in that statement," Jordan said.

"Did you..."

"Find her?" he asked. "No. I don't even think she's in Syria anymore."

"Ah, shit. Sorry, man. Stephanie said things were getting pretty intense."

Right, the last time they'd talked had been during the suicide bomb attack. "You could say that."

"What now then?"

"I'm not sure," he said. If Arielle was no longer in Syria, he was practically back at square one. He didn't know if Rafiq's offer to work in the headquarters was still open, but even if it was, he wasn't sure there was much point. Whatever information he'd gather would likely be about Caliphate networks and who was working with al Kanadi as opposed to his daughter. Which reminded him. "By the way, Farah Xarbi is alive."

"No shit. How did you learn that?"

"He tried to cut my head off."

"Pardon?"

"It's a long story. I'll give you all the details when I get home."

"I can't wait. In fact, the whole team will want to sit in on your debrief," Jordan said and his smile could be heard through the phone. "And you thought the counter-rad team was a waste of time."

Erik smiled, remembered how he'd bitched about Xarbi, about his hockey player associate from Montreal. "Speaking of which, are we still keeping tabs on Nathan Martel?"

"Of course, although his wings have been clipped."

"What do you mean?"

"His passport was revoked."

"I see."

"He's still trying though. Apparently, he has a plan to go to the airport in a few days."

"Why?"

"He's supposed to be meeting a family member, but we'll have to take his word for it because his follow has been pulled. Wiggins decided it was a waste of resources to track a guy who can't leave the country anyways. Caused a big argument, but he didn't change his mind."

"He never does."

"Are you going to be able to handle coming back to a desk? Maybe you'll get the itch to be an operator again."

"Depends if I have a desk to come back to."

"Yeah, about that," Jordan said. "Stephanie keeps asking if I've heard from you."

Erik fidgeted. "I had a good reason for not calling." Not that she would like it.

"Hey man, forewarned is forearmed, right? When will you know if you're coming home?"

"Soon."

"Well, let me know your timings. Can't wait to get caught up."

"Me too." A brick formed in his gut. "I better give Stephanie a call."

"Good luck."

"Thanks," he said and then hung up. Part of him wanted to talk to Stephanie, to hear her voice, but another part dreaded it. At some point though, he'd have to take his lumps.

She answered on the first ring. "What took you so long?"

"Good to talk to you, too."

"I have a report saying the Caliphate executed two Americans who were trying to extract a girl who'd traveled to the Middle East," she said. "Know anything about that?"

He frowned. "Where did you hear that?"

"Not important. Were you involved?"

"Yes."

"What were you thinking?"

"The important thing is I'm okay," he said.

"Was there a period when you thought you might not be okay? Why didn't you call?" She drew a deep breath. "I'm sorry. I've been worried."

"It's all right, Stephanie." Warmth bloomed in his chest, the first in a while. "Thanks for being concerned."

"Don't feel too good about yourself," she said, "you've got lots of questions to answer. Did you find what you were looking for?"

He cleared his throat. "No. Not really."

"I'm sorry, Erik."

"I know, but I had to take the chance." He snorted. "I'm not even sure what to do next."

"Come home. We could use your help."

"What's going on?"

"It's busy. Sahraoui's study group has been a gold mine."

"What?" It had been the farthest thing from his mind.

"Reyad Slimani was connected through the study group to a man called Sayyid Mubarak. Mubarak is linked to drug dealers in the US, as well as Mexican cartels, which is where we think the drugs are coming from."

"Did you pick him up?"

"We're still building the case, but this is consuming the entire Task Force these days. The cartels have well-established smuggling routes and if they can get drugs into the country –"

"They can get other things in as well." He drew a deep breath. "What about Sahraoui?"

"Unconnected for now, but it's early. Either way, he'll probably sue. If I had to guess, I'd say that Mubarak and Slimani were using Sahraoui as cover because they knew his history would make it sensitive for us to investigate."

"Great work." A fragment of his conversation with Jordan tweaked him. "I don't suppose Nathan Martel is linked with any of this?"

"Not so far as we know. He went to Sahraoui's mosque several times, but he wasn't a regular, and his follow never observed him speaking with Sahraoui."

"I heard Wiggins pulled his team. Why?"

"I support that decision. His passport was pulled, and he's been added to every watch list there is, so it's impossible for him to leave the country. We have higher priorities."

"What if I told you a Caliphate associate of Martel's is working for al Kanadi?"

"Who?"

"Farah Xarbi. He's a Somali-Canadian who traveled to the Caliphate over a year ago. We thought he was dead, but he's not."

"Should I ask how you know this?"

"Probably not. But would it elevate Martel's importance for being followed? Jordan said Martel was planning on going to the airport to meet someone. Doesn't that seem strange?" He was missing something here, something important. Al Kanadi had said he had teams able to reach out anywhere, what had he meant by that?

"It does, yes, but Martel doesn't have any connections. His passport was pulled because of his social media activity and the fact he tried to buy a plane ticket, not because he's linked to any domestic group."

"But he does have connections," he said. "He used to talk to Xarbi, who's still alive."

"We have no proof they continue to talk." Stephanie sighed. "The truth is, we're strapped for resources. Putting a team on Martel means pulling from another suspect, all of which have more compelling reasons. If you have an idea of how to surveil him, I'd love to hear it."

"What about chatter? Any threat reporting?"

"I don't want to discuss that over the phone."

"Humor me."

She sighed. "There's a single source, ungraded report about an unspecified attack being planned out of Libya that could target several Canadian cities; Ottawa, Montreal, Calgary, Vancouver." She sounded tired. "I hate to say it, but this is boilerplate stuff, Erik. Libya is a Caliphate haven, so it's reasonable to expect that planning is going on, but the source has no reliability rating, and there's nothing to distinguish it from any other threat reporting."

"When is the attack planned for?"

"Erik –"

"Last question. I promise."

"It didn't say. Maybe tomorrow, maybe next year, you know how these go. This is why we need your help. When are you coming home?"

"Soon," he said and ran a hand over his unshaven face. "Listen, one last thing you might want to look into, or at least pass on. I forgot to tell Jordan, but do you remember those geo-locators you gave me?"

"Of course."

"I used a couple. Jordan should be able to download the tracks."

"I'm sure he'll be thrilled. Where did you put them?"

"On a couple of al Kanadi's trucks outside Mosul."

"Excuse me?"

"I'll explain when I'm back, okay? I promise."

"I'll hold you to that."

He hung up and leaned back in the chair. He needed to think. Al Kanadi had said Arielle wasn't in the Middle East, which might have been a lie, except Xarbi had also said she'd gone to Africa. *To Libya, as part of an attack.* He sat forward, wide awake now. Martel was linked to Xarbi, who worked for al Kanadi, so if al Kanadi was indeed planning an attack, it wasn't impossible that Martel was involved as well, even if he was a minor player as Wiggins thought. They needed to know what Martel was doing in the airport. Too bad all the surveillance teams were already tasked out.

Except for him.

He poked his head out of the office door. "Ray, how soon can I get a flight to Canada?"

"Gimme a minute." Ray turned to his computer and worked for a minute. "There's a flight tomorrow. Want me to book it?"

"Yes, please." He tucked back into the office and dialed Jordan's number. If Wiggins wouldn't take the chance on following Martel, he'd do it himself. But he'd need some help.

CHAPTER SEVENTEEN
THE CROOKED PATH

Mosul, Iraq
02 June 15 – 1841 Local

Abu Noor al Kanadi gazed up into the large, open space of the Mosul Library's main room. Light from the setting sun streamed in through thousands of holes in the roof and mingled with the shadows and the rubble to create an otherworldly scene. Footsteps crunched on the rubble behind him, disturbed his contemplation.

"Mamdouh sent word," Yahya said. "He's on the move."

Al Kanadi nodded. "Finally."

Yahya shifted from foot to foot.

Al Kanadi stooped to pick up a stone, felt Yahya's gaze. "Something else?"

"With respect, Emir," Yahya said, his tone deferential, "I think it's a mistake not to tell Mamdouh about Petersson's escape."

"If he survived." Yahya raised a good point, but breaking silence again risked the attention of the unblinking eye of western surveillance. It was one thing to communicate through a schedule, with purpose-built e-mail accounts discarded after each use, quite another to actively reach out to an operative in the field. He tossed the stone from hand to hand. "What would we gain?"

Yahya coughed. "He could interfere –"

"I can't see how," al Kanadi said. "He knows nothing of our plans."

"With respect, Emir, he knows his daughter went to Africa. He also knows about an attack."

A ripple of anger passed through him. "Who told you that?"

"Xarbi. He –"

"When?" Al Kanadi stalked toward Yahya.

Yahya raised his hands and backed up. "He was begging for his life."

"What else did he say?" Al Kanadi paused, realized he'd almost yelled.

"Libya. He told Petersson she'd gone through Libya and that we were planning an attack in Europe and then I killed him. That's it."

"And you didn't think to bring this to me sooner?"

"He was blabbering, and it seemed so vague."

Al Kanadi stopped, bit back another retort. Breathed deep and struggled to re-exert control. Think. What else could Xarbi have said? His brow knit together.

The fact of the matter was that Xarbi hadn't known much. The idiot had been kept out of the planning because he didn't need to know. He might have pieced together that an attack was being planned – *because that's what we do* – but he would've had no concrete details to pass on, which was obvious if he'd told Petersson it was in Europe. It would be a stretch for anyone to link the girl in Africa with an impending attack and what if Petersson did make that connection? He shook his head. "It has no bearing."

"But Mamdouh –"

"Knew the risks."

Yahya spread his hands as if to plead for patience. "Emir, the attack –"

Al Kanadi threw the stone into the dirt. "The girl will get into the country." He held his anger in check, enunciated each word. "That is the mission. What happens after that is opportunity."

"But I thought they were supposed to cross the border into America."

He nodded. "That's right, at Cornwall." Crossing the St. Lawrence into the United States would be easy near Cornwall Island, where the Akwesasne Mohawk reserve straddled both sides of the Canadian-American border and where the local Mohawks had a history of smuggling people, drugs and other contraband across the border. From there, it was a short hop to Syracuse, then New York City, the biggest city in America. Al Kanadi waved a hand. "But the sole aim of this attack is to sow fear. Getting her into Canada accomplishes that, and it will happen. It doesn't even matter if she infects anyone, we will have laid the western defenses bare for all to see. There will be panic." People thought the security crackdown after 9/11 was bad when transport-trailer trucks had lined up for twenty miles at border crossings. It would be nothing compared to this. He paused, took a deep breath. "Once we've perfected the virus, there will be more, and those will use the cartels for more discrete, guaranteed entry."

Yahya nodded, but his brow was furrowed in seeming confusion.

Al Kanadi grabbed Yahya's shoulders. "If we contact Mamdouh now, we risk drawing attention at the most vulnerable time of the operation." He smiled. "Besides, Mamdouh can handle whatever happens." And if not, then the problem of Mamdouh's ambition would be solved.

"As you say, Emir." Yahya glanced at the pick-up trucks parked outside the library. "Then are we ready to go?"

"We are."

"I'll get our things," Yahya said and then headed into the library.

Al Kanadi watched Yahya depart, then moved to the trucks. He stopped at the first pickup, rested his arms on the box and traced a finger in the dust that covered the roll bar. Things were going to turn out all right. He slapped the truck, then headed into the library after Yahya.

***

MOSUL, IRAQ
02 JUNE 2015 – 2314 LOCAL

The convoy left Mosul a couple of hours after night had fallen. There were two trucks, each with two people, and they drove west-north-west along Highway 1 until Qaryat al Ashiq, a trip of fifty kilometers in ninety minutes. At Qaryat al Ashiq, the trucks turned onto Highway 47 to head due west, through Tal Afar, through Wardiya. Another ninety minutes and ninety kilometers went by, quicker on this leg as the road was in better condition except for a stretch of highway near Sinjar, where Mount Sinjar loomed to the north, more felt than seen in the near pitch black.

The vehicles continued west across the imaginary border between Iraq and Syria, a line whose greatest impact on the travelers was to change the highway name to 715. The town of Ash Shaddadi was next, where they got onto Highway 7 and drove south, then south-west, to arrive in Deir al-Zour two and a half hours later.

The trucks made a short stop to refuel and let the occupants conduct their morning prayers, the *Fajr,* and then the drive continued. They left Deir al-Zour as the sun peeked over the eastern horizon and the reddish-orange light chased them down Route 4, parallel to the Euphrates River toward Raqqa. The drivers went slower now, and the occupants enjoyed the greenery of the Euphrates valley whether they would admit to it or not. The trip from Deir al-Zour took three hours, and they arrived at the outskirts of Raqqa around mid-morning.

The trucks wound their way through Raqqa's downtown, through twisting streets and rubble on an inexorable path into the suburbs. A few minutes after noon, the convoy stopped outside a compound, indistinguishable from many in the neighborhood. Two young boys played in the courtyard, and when the trucks stopped, their mother herded them inside. She stood at the entrance to the residence while a man got out of the lead truck and opened the compound gates to let the vehicle into the courtyard. The driver exited, clasped hands with the man who'd let them into the compound, and then cross-loaded into the remaining truck, which drove away. The man who'd stayed behind closed the gates, hugged the woman, then entered the house.

The truck stayed in the courtyard, the hisses and pops from the engine heard by no one and nothing as the metal and fluids cooled. And on the truck's roll-bar, indistinguishable from the layer of dust that had already grown thicker, a tiny GPS tracker continued to emit its signal.

CHAPTER EIGHTEEN
JUDGEMENT

MONTREAL, QUEBEC
04 JUNE 15 – 1444 LOCAL

Erik stared at the frosted glass doors of the international arrivals section in the Pierre Elliott Trudeau airport. It had been nine years, three months and six days since he'd said good-bye to Audray in almost this exact spot. He could still picture her on the far side of security screening, a forlorn, eleven-year-old Arielle held at her waist. He'd never once dreamed it would be the last time he saw her. He felt for the ring hanging from his neck. Still with him, after all this time.

"You okay, man?" Jordan asked.

Erik cleared his throat. "Just nervous."

"I'm supposed to be the nervous one, remember? The one with no field experience?" Jordan smiled, but it was fleeting. He nodded at the arrivals gate. "So, how do we handle this?"

Once again, Erik glanced at the overhead screens with flight information, tried to pick out ones that might be of interest. They'd searched all the flights arriving this afternoon, the time Martel had said he'd be at the airport, and found only a few flights from African destinations. Yet it was nearly impossible to determine how many had connected through Europe or the United States and likewise, a search of the passenger manifests had resulted in nothing.

He took a breath. "We watch for Martel. You take the entrances, and I'll stay close to the gate in case he slips by."

"Do you think he'll show?"

"All we can go by is what the surveillance tapes said." Erik's gaze locked onto the gate. "If nothing happens, all we've lost is our afternoon."

"I might be okay with that." Jordan's face was pale. "And what do I do if I see him?"

"Call me. Keep your distance and take pictures." Erik gave what he hoped was a reassuring smile. "Don't worry. Chances are, the worst thing that happens today is we get stuck in Montreal traffic on the way home."

"Either way, you'll owe me a few drinks when this is over," Jordan said and then headed for the nearest entrance.

Erik leaned against a cylindrical pillar and did his best impression of a bored man waiting to meet a traveler. It wasn't long before he stifled a real yawn. He'd hardly slept in the scramble of the past days, and he alternatively felt like he was about to have a heart attack or pass out. He hated all the loose ends, losing Arielle's trail, the possible attack, but he had to start somewhere. He shook his head and scanned the crowd for Martel.

His gaze settled on a man halfway to the nearest exit who would have fit into any *souk* in the Middle East. The man wore a traditional white *abaya* for men and towered almost a full head over the athletic, bald man who stood just behind him. The man in the *abaya*'s face seemed familiar, his olive skin and long, neat beard not unlike so many faces Erik had seen in Iraq.

Erik blinked, realized the man in the *abaya* was staring back, then faked a cough and looked away. Christ, he was getting paranoid. The frosted doors slid apart, and he peered through the crowd. A single male traveler in tracksuit pants and a cellphone stuck to his ear exited through the doors. Erik settled back into place, forced his hands into his pockets. Several other travelers exited, and the sequence repeated, and he went back to checking out the crowd. He studied the man in the *abaya* once again. The athletic, bald man had moved up to stand beside him, and for a second Erik felt he was missing something, and then the arrival doors opened, and he tore his gaze away.

And then she was there.

She walked like she'd aged a hundred years, slumped under a yellow silk *hijab* draped over her shoulders. Had she been looking in the opposite direction, he might not have recognized her, so different did she hold herself. Her face was gaunt, almost skeletal, and the slight upward tilt at the corners of her lips was gone, replaced by a dour set to her mouth, her thin lips pressed together. He almost dismissed her, and then, as she skirted the barrier that separated travelers from the crowd, she looked up and bit her lip like she had when she was a kid and looked straight at him. Her smoky blue eyes pierced him as she stared through him, past him, and he knew it was her. Arielle.

He approached her and when he could have reached out and touched her, he stopped. He opened his mouth, and all that came out was a hoarse croak. She was so close and yet so far away and then she'd moved past him and he cleared his throat and tried again.

"Arielle."

She stopped.

People flowed around him like white flecks of plastic in a snow globe, unable to break his concentration. She looked back, and their eyes met. Then a man was beside her, burly, with sunken, dark eyes. He pulled a suitcase with one hand and with his free hand, he took Arielle under the arm and dragged her toward the exit.

"Arielle?" Erik's heart leapt into his throat. "Arielle!"

She glanced over her shoulder, stumbled as she was tugged along. Her eyes were wide and deeply bloodshot.

"Arielle, wait!" he said and sprung after her.

The people closest to Arielle turned their heads, including the man who held her arm. He glanced at Erik, did a double take, then bent to whisper in Arielle's ear. The pair stopped and faced him. This close, her face seemed swollen, as if she'd been crying, but she was calm, the set of her mouth firm.

"I can't believe it's you." He raised his arms to embrace her, but the burly man stepped between and held up a hand.

"Please leave my wife alone," the man said in a deep growl.

Erik hesitated and frowned. "This is my daughter. Arielle." He turned to her. "Sweetie, it's me. Dad."

"You must be mistaken." The man's hand pressed into Erik's chest and pushed him back. "My wife's name is Hafsa."

"No, that's not right." Erik shook his head. "Arielle, talk to me."

"Tell him who you are," the man said to the woman, his tone full of anger.

The woman shied from the man, her eyes downcast.

He shook her. "Answer him."

"Hafsa," she said in a quiet voice. "My name is Hafsa."

The man glanced at Erik and held his chin high. "You see? You are mistaken."

Erik shook his head. "No, Arielle, I know it's you."

The woman glanced up and met Erik's gaze and drew back from him. "My name is Hafsa," she said, louder, and she clutched her arms close to her chest. "Please. Leave us alone."

A sneer came over the man's face. "Can't you see you're upsetting her?" He tightened his grip on her elbow and pulled her away. "There is nothing for you here. Let us go in peace."

Erik held out his hands and then dropped them to his side. Al Kanadi's words echoed in his mind. "Your daughter is beyond you. She serves Allah."

Arielle and her escort were halfway to the exit now, headed straight for the *abaya*-clad man. The athletic bald man was also still there, and as Arielle neared, the bald-man man stepped aside and gazed out over the airport concourse and as he did, Erik realized he recognized him. But from where? He sought out Jordan, saw him farther down the concourse. Too far to help.

"Wait," Erik called out. He walked past the man in the *abaya*, who'd moved off to greet a woman and two children, and then stopped. A young man stood near the exit, hands folded over the strap of a messenger bag strung from his shoulder. The man's thin, blond beard looked like it had been glued on and he wore a hockey jersey emblazoned with the logo of a torch with flame coming from the top, three interlocking rings beneath the torch.

Nathan Martel.

Erik turned. He found Jordan, pointed at Martel, then looked for a security guard or policeman, but there was none in sight. Arielle was almost at the exit now, and somehow he knew that if they went through those doors, he would lose her for good.

"Stop!" he said and pointed at Arielle and her escort. "Police!"

People around him froze, stumbled back from him as if they'd discovered he was contagious. He ignored them, shouldered his way through the crowd. "Out of the way!"

"Hey, buddy," a man said from behind him.

"Not now." A few feet more to go. He saw that Jordan was almost there and headed for the door and then Erik saw Martel's hand disappear into his messenger bag. Erik readied himself for a tackle and pulled up short as a hand tugged at his shoulder. He twisted. "I said –"

A fist slammed into his gut. He doubled over and gasped for breath, flailed and was hit again and then pulled into a bear hug. Before his face was crushed against a muscular chest, he caught a glimpse of the athletic bald man, the man from Sahraoui's study group.

"Forget you ever saw her," the man hissed and then threw him to the ground. "It's okay folks, this gentleman isn't feeling well."

Erik fell to his hands and knees. He gasped for breath and struggled to look up and saw that the man who'd escorted Arielle off the plane was once again leading her off, the bald man at his side. Martel stood aside to let them pass, and in the gap, Erik saw that Jordan blocked the exit.

* * *

MONTREAL, QUEBEC
04 JUNE 15 – 1502 LOCAL

Arielle winced as Mamdouh's grip tightened, a reminder she was still trapped, still Hafsa. Still weak. She hadn't even been strong enough to use her real name. She didn't deserve her father's love. And where had he come from? All she'd been able to think of was making sure her father didn't get hurt, or infected, and now he lay on the sand-colored tile of the airport floor. Several people knelt beside him, a woman in black yoga pants and an older man with a pony-tail who'd offered a hand.

She rubbed her temple. The pinpoint of pain that had grown in her head during the plane ride from Paris made everything hazy, and she felt like she was two seconds behind as things happened. She looked for her father, but the young man with the messenger bag, the one called Nathan, blocked her view. Mamdouh's hold on her arm grew stronger, and she found herself dragged along.

The bald man appeared at Mamdouh's side, and she realized she knew him, remembered his bald head and designer beard as if she'd met him an hour ago. His name was Sayyid, and he'd attended Dr. Sahraoui's study group a few times, always with Reyad.

Mamdouh's scowl deepened. "That was unnecessary."

"He was about to create a major scene," Sayyid said.

"No kidding. Didn't you hear him yell for the police?" Nathan said as he joined them.

"Hold up." A commanding voice came from behind. "What did you do to this guy?"

She struggled to glance over her shoulder. Her father was almost on his feet, supported by the woman in black yoga pants and the man with the pony-tail had left his side to come after Sayyid. The man was older, and stocky, like a football player twenty years past his prime.

"Where is the car?" Mamdouh asked.

"Short-term parking," Sayyid said. "Across the street and up one level."

"Idiot," Mamdouh snarled. "Why not right here?"

"The flight was delayed." Frustration radiated from Sayyid. "You can't park on the street all day."

The man with the ponytail reached their group, tapped Sayyid on the shoulder. "Hey, I'm talking to you."

Sayyid glared at the man. "Keep your hands off me."

"Stop talking," Mamdouh said. He snapped off some quick words to Sayyid in Arabic, then tugged on Arielle's arm and put her hand in Nathan's. "Take her to the car."

She twisted for a last glance over her shoulder and found herself staring into her father's eyes. She opened her mouth, then lurched to the side, yanked by Nathan.

He leaned close. "Do not say a fucking word. We're going," he said and dragged her toward the exit.

"Sorry, can't let you do that," a new voice said.

Nathan stopped to look at a tall, broad-shouldered man with reddish-blond hair who'd blocked the exit. "How about you get out of the fucking way?" he said, a forced smile on his face.

Arielle squinted at the man, and he smiled at her, although he did not look relaxed. Worry lines stood out on his face, and his lips were tight.

"Arielle, it's me, Jordan," he said. "I work with your dad."

She stiffened and Nathan dragged her to the side to bypass the man and then Jordan blocked the exit once again.

"Just relax, all right, Nathan?" Jordan said and raised his hands.

"Stop harassing me," Nathan snarled. "I haven't done anything."

"Your acquaintance assaulted my friend, and he's going to have to hang around to talk to security," Jordan said. "Plus, my friend's going to want to talk with his daughter." Jordan's gaze flickered to Arielle, and he tried to smile. "Welcome home, by the way."

"You've made a mistake," Nathan said, and he let go of Arielle and slipped his hand into his messenger bag. "We've done nothing wrong."

"I think we both know that's not true, Nathan," Jordan said. "The police will be here any minute."

Sweat trickled down Arielle's back and she stumbled as she walked as if she was back on the boat that had carried her to Libya. A man yelled from behind her, and she turned to see that the man with the ponytail had poked Mamdouh in the chest. Sayyid grabbed the pony-tail man's finger and wrenched it, and the man sank to his knees and screamed. Mamdouh left them and then he was beside Nathan, and she reeled.

"Wait," she said, the words so quiet that nobody heard. She staggered, looked up and saw Jordan's mouth move as he spoke to Nathan. "Wait," she repeated, and Nathan yanked on her arm, and she stumbled, almost tripped. The concourse wobbled in her vision, and her *hijab* stuck to her sweat-drenched face, and it was so hard to think. She needed to get away, to get help and she knew then that she must not be taken from the airport or she wouldn't have the strength to resist. Nathan tugged her again and this time she collapsed to her knees on the floor.

"Get up." Nathan yanked on her arm.

Pain shot through her shoulder and for a moment, as Nathan's voice pierced her delirium, she saw what she had to do. His hand moved to her shoulder, and his fingers dug into her flesh as he prepared to drag her to her feet.

"Get up you fucking bitch!"

"That's enough." Jordan grabbed Nathan by the shoulder, then was shoved by Mamdouh. Nathan bent over, his grip on Arielle tightening even more.

She smashed her elbow into Nathan's groin, and he collapsed in a heap beside her. She began to crawl away from the struggling men, deeper into the airport. She stumbled to her feet, her one thought to put space between her and the men and then she fell again, knocked onto her face. Stars spun in her vision and nausea gripped her, and she felt herself being flipped over and Mamdouh's angry face appeared in front of her.

Rage seared through her. She'd been so close. She pulled against him and his face contorted in a snarl and he raised his fist to strike her and then a hand grabbed his wrist.

"Keep your hands off her," her dad said, Mamdouh's wrist clenched in his hand.

"Stop! Police!" a man said. "Everybody down on the ground."

Arielle glanced at the airport's exits, where two police officers in blue now stood. Her father and Mamdouh looked as well, their bodies trembling as they strained against each other.

"Everybody get –"

A loud bang rang out in the concourse. One of the police officers rocked back, and blood sprayed from the side of his head. The other officer crouched, and his hand went for the gun at his side, and then something struck him in the shoulder, in the neck. He dropped his pistol and fell backward into the door. A red smear of blood stained the glass as he collapsed to the floor and his legs kicked once and his pistol went skittering across the tiles.

"Gun!"

Arielle glanced at Jordan, halfway off the ground, an intense gaze on his face. She followed his line of sight to where Nathan knelt beside the exit, a pistol in his hand that he aimed at the fallen officers. In slow motion, the pistol swung toward Jordan.

"Arielle!" a man called.

She wanted to close her eyes, but couldn't stop looking. Jordan had almost reached Nathan, but the pistol had come closer, and she raised a hand. "Watch out."

"Arielle!" a man said. "Give me your hand."

She turned and met her dad's gaze. He held out a hand, and she reached for him and then drew back. Would she infect him? Her father stretched forward and their fingers almost touched, and then Mamdouh's head slammed into her dad's face.

Arielle twisted onto her stomach, began to crawl. More shots rang out, thunderbolts of agony inside her head, and she focused on putting one hand in front of the other. Tears ran down her cheeks, and a hand closed on her ankle, and she screamed, howled her frustration and flipped onto her side and tried to claw Mamdouh's face. He batted her hands away and jammed his knee into her chest, and her chest heaved with her failure as she struggled for breath even as Mamdouh's hand closed around her throat.

"We've got to go." Sayyid appeared beside Mamdouh.

Mamdouh snarled and slapped Sayyid with the back of his hand.

Nathan ran up and crouched beside Mamdouh. "No time for that." He pulled a magazine out of his messenger bag and reloaded his pistol.

Mamdouh released Arielle, clenched his hands into claws in front of his face as if he would strangle Nathan. "Why do you have guns?"

"In case something like this happened." Nathan raised the pistol and fired two more shots, sent concrete from a pillar near the exit.

Arielle twisted under Mamdouh's knee and saw a body on the floor of the airport. The man was curled on the floor, hands clutched to his chest over a red stain growing under his fingers, his face scrunched in pain. Jordan.

Mamdouh stood, glared at where Nathan had fired. "I want him dead."

"He grabbed one of the cop's pistols," Nathan said.

"This is stupid. We have to go," Sayyid said, his words fuzzy. He held a hand out to Nathan. "You got another gun?"

"Of course." Nathan dug into the messenger bag and pulled out two more pistols, gave one each to Sayyid and Mamdouh. "What now?"

"Parking lot," Sayyid said. "We can make the car."

"No," Mamdouh said. His face was eerily composed, no trace of his anger from moments before. It made Arielle shiver. "We find a place in the airport where we can be secure for a couple of hours."

"Are you kidding?" Nathan asked. "We have to get out of here."

"The plan has changed," Mamdouh said. "That way." He pointed at the international arrivals area.

"Can't get through there from this side," Sayyid said.

"Then we'll go there," Mamdouh said and pointed at the domestic baggage claim. "Bring her." He pointed at Arielle with the pistol, waited for Sayyid to drag her to her feet, then strode off, following the signs toward domestic arrivals.

Arielle stumbled, fell again and hit her head and then felt herself lifted and slung over Sayyid's shoulder like a sandbag. She willed herself to stay conscious, but the darkness was too inviting.

* * *

Montreal, Quebec
04 June 15 – 1518 Local

Erik crouched behind the circular pillar and clutched the pistol tight to his chest. The gun had fallen where he'd dove for cover when Martel had started shooting, and he'd been able to snatch it up. But Arielle had been too close to Martel and the others to risk a shot. So he'd hid, and now he needed to risk a look, although the last time he'd peeked around the pillar, the bald man had nearly taken his head off.

He cursed under his breath. Jordan had taken a round to the chest and needed help. And he'd almost had Arielle, had felt her fingertips against his own and then she'd pulled away. His hands shook.

The sound of another gunshot came from farther into the airport. Time to get going. He led with the pistol and inched around the pillar. No sign of the group, or Arielle.

He scanned the concourse and then scrambled to Jordan's side. Jordan lay on his back, and his head was up, his gaze fixed on the widening stain of blood on his chest. Erik put his hand on Jordan's stomach. "How're you doing?"

Jordan coughed, and blood flecked his lips. "I've been better."

"I'm sorry I got you into this," Erik said and pulled out his phone.

"Don't be." Jordan's breath hissed between his lips. "It was my choice."

"You're going to be all right."

Jordan tried to smile. "Go after her."

"Just hold on." Erik dialed 911 and pressed the phone to his ear. "Yes, there's been a shooting at Pierre Elliott Trudeau Airport. The international arrivals section, main floor. Multiple wounded, all gunshots. Three active shooters." Erik lifted Jordan's shirt with his free hand and cringed at the large, circular hole below Jordan's left nipple. Bloody bubbles foamed from the hole, and Jordan's chest made a sucking sound in time with his ragged breathing. "Oh, shit," Erik said. He dropped the phone and scrambled to the body of one of the police officers.

"It's okay," Jordan said, and he sounded weaker.

Erik fumbled through the officer's tactical vest and found a tiny pouch on the side marked with a cross. He ripped it off and dumped the contents on the floor. A tourniquet, a trauma pad, several gauze dressings, and a roll of tape fell out. He snatched up the trauma pad and tape, hurried back to Jordan.

Jordan closed his eyes. "Go after her."

"Stay with me, big guy." Panic tinged his words, and it scared him. His world shrank to the two foot by three-foot workspace that was Jordan's chest. He tore open the trauma pad and cleaned off the blood around the wound. Spread the plastic wrapper over the hole and secured three of the sides with the tape. "You're going to make it," he said and looked up, saw Jordan's face, his relaxed features. "Jordan?" he said. He reached up and cradled the side of Jordan's face. "Jordan? Jordan, stay with me." He stuck his ear by Jordan's mouth, heard nothing and then placed his fingers at Jordan's neck, searched for a pulse, repositioned his fingers and searched again. Nothing.

"Is he all right?" a woman said from behind.

Erik grasped for the pistol and whirled around. Almost shot a woman in a white sundress, her face pale beneath bright red locks, her hands held in the air.

"I'm a nurse," she said.

"Please help me," he said and lowered the gun.

The woman knelt, picked up Jordan's wrist and searched for a pulse, then lowered the arm to the floor. She put her ear to his chest, near the opening of the bandage Erik had secured, then raised her head. "I'm sorry."

Another gunshot came from farther into the airport, and both Erik and the woman glanced up. She stared down the concourse and then looked to Erik and the gun in his hand. "Are you a cop?" she asked.

"Something like that."

"Do you think they'll come back?"

"No."

"I can stay here," she said. "You go after them."

Erik glanced at her and then at Jordan, his body unmoving and limp. He nodded and then stood. "Thank you," he said and press-checked the pistol. It was loaded and had a full magazine, and as he let the slide forward, more gunshots sounded from deep in the airport concourse. "More police are on the way," he said. "Hang tight, and you'll be all right."

She nodded. "Be safe."

"I'll try," he said and then headed for the sound of gunfire.

He walked up the concourse, past a man's body, a woman huddled beside him, sobbing. The body was draped in white, and Erik did a double-take when he recognized the man in the *abaya*. He paused, and the woman looked up. "Which way did they go?" he asked.

The woman wailed and looked at the domestic arrivals section.

He walked on, scanned the concourse ahead and saw people cowered behind sales booths, behind pillars, behind whatever cover was available. He wondered how many police officers and security guards worked in the airport itself, how many more people might die today and then he set his jaw and kept walking.

When he reached an escalator, he paused. If he remembered right, the departures level above had a skywalk to the parking lot. He poked his head around the escalator, saw another man twenty feet ahead crouched in the cover of an ATM.

The man saw him and cowered deeper behind the ATM. "Don't shoot!"

"I'm with the police," Erik said. "Where did they go?"

The man jerked a thumb over his shoulder in the direction of the baggage carousels.

Erik took another look up the escalator and then darted across the floor to kneel beside the man. "I need your hat," he said and grabbed the man's ball hat, jammed it onto his head. "And your shirt."

"Take it, take it," the man said and scrambled out of his hoodie.

Erik put on the hoodie and then peeked out from behind the ATM. Crept to the next pillar where he was able to see into the baggage claims area. At the far end of the concourse, a group of almost twenty people stood between several luggage carousels. Near one wall, he spied two of the three men he'd seen before, the man who'd been with Arielle when she'd exited the arrivals area, and Martel. He craned around the pillar and tried to spot the bald man, but he needed to be closer. He broke cover and crept to the nearest luggage carousel, then poked his head above.

The gunmen were forcing people through a door into the oversize baggage claim area. As Erik watched, Martel went through the door. The other man stayed outside. Arielle was nowhere in sight.

Erik ducked below the lip of the baggage carousel. He'd thought the men would flee the airport. Instead, it looked like they were taking hostages. That was bad. Sure, hostages would slow them down and tie them to a location, but it would also give the men a chance to regroup and collect their thoughts. Plus, they'd shown no hesitation to kill, so the likelihood of a mass casualty situation would go up. He needed to act, and he needed to do it now when they were desperate and before they'd settled in.

He scrambled past the carousel and moved to the next one, passed another body on the floor. Blood had pooled onto the sand colored tile, and he ignored it, risked another look and caught himself staring straight into the eyes of the bald man.

"You, by the luggage belt!" The bald man stood at the rear of the group of people and pointed his pistol in Erik's direction.

Erik ducked behind the luggage carousel.

"Come out from there," the man said.

A gunshot rang out, and Erik heard the whine of a ricochet near his head.

"I said come out."

Erik took a deep breath and then jammed the pistol into the waistband of his pants at the small of his back. He tugged the rim of the ball hat low over his eyes and then raised his hands up above the lip of the carousel. "Don't shoot."

"Stand up!"

He stood, kept his head down so the cap covered his eyes and part of his face.

"Come over here," the bald man said

Erik walked out from behind the carousel while he scanned the area from beneath the brim of his cap. To Erik's left, people were being directed through the kiosk for oversize baggage and into the handling area, where Martel was forcing them to lie on the floor. The third man waited beside a kiosk outside the entryway, and the bald man stood at the rear of the group, which had thinned out as people moved into the baggage handling area.

Erik walked slow, and as he did, he saw that with most of the hostages inside the oversized baggage area, he had an unblocked view of all three terrorists. A little closer and he might have one chance at a clean shot. At ten feet from the bald man, he took a deep breath and stopped.

Anger creased the man's face, and he strode closer. "Get over here." He grabbed Erik's shoulder, pulled him and shoved him toward the oversize luggage area.

Erik dropped to a knee and reached for the pistol at his back. The bald man hesitated and then raised his gun, and Erik shoved the pistol into the side of his ribcage and pulled the trigger twice. The man cried out and his body buckled and crumpled to the ground. Erik ignored him and scanned for the other two men. Drew a bead on Martel and fired. Sparks flew off metal paneling in the baggage area, and Martel ducked. Erik bore down on the sights, centered the front post on Martel's head and squeezed the trigger, and then a slug struck him in his right shoulder.

Erik half turned, and the pistol fell from his hands, slid along the floor. He twisted, saw the olive-skinned man taking aim, and dove to the side. Pieces of tile burst up as bullets ripped into the ground around him and he gasped in pain as his shoulder hit the ground, and then he scrambled along the ground behind the safety of the baggage carousel.

* * *

MONTREAL, QUEBEC
04 JUNE 15 – 1528 LOCAL

Mamdouh aimed at the sliver of red hat above the luggage carousel and fired. The bullet ricocheted off the carousel with a whine and the hat disappeared, and Mamdouh fired again and wished he had a more powerful weapon. He fired once more, and the pistol ran dry, and he cursed and then reloaded. Turned and yelled at the idiot Martel to get the hostages into the room and then crossed the floor to Sayyid's body.

Allah had indeed cursed him by saddling him with these fools.

The hardest part of the mission had been over. He'd gotten through customs, had even let himself think of the rewards on his return to Syria. He would be elevated to at least al Kanadi's stature, maybe even meet the Caliph. Perhaps his hubris had been his downfall and Allah had decided to teach him humility.

He knelt beside Sayyid, who wheezed and flopped on the ground. They were all so weak. He glanced at the man, and the yellowy paleness of his face told him all he needed to know. He'd seen many men die and was about to see one more, although this one would take a while.

Too bad he didn't have time to wait.

He leaned down and put his hand on Sayyid's throat and squeezed. Sayyid gagged and grabbed Mamdouh's wrist, and Mamdouh batted away his hand as if the man was a baby. "Unfortunate for you that I can't spare a bullet," he said in a low growl.

Sayyid's face went blue, and his struggles grew weaker and then stopped. Mamdouh kept his hand in place for another minute while his gaze remained locked on the luggage carousel. There was nowhere for Hafsa's father to go and it occurred to him to wonder how the man had come here. He decided it didn't matter. Unlike al Kanadi, he would make sure the man was dead. He realized he shouldn't be angry. After all, he'd accomplished the mission, and yet, these tiny pleasures were all that were left to him.

When he reached sixty, he left Sayyid's body and walked around the carousel with the pistol held at the ready. On the far side, he found Hafsa's father. He hadn't gone far, and he'd left a red slick on the ground as he'd tried to crawl away. Mamdouh aimed near the man's head and fired, and floor tiles exploded. The man flinched and covered his head with his uninjured arm.

"You've caused a lot of trouble, my friend," Mamdouh said. "But it will be over soon."

Petersson pushed off the ground and leaned his back against the carousel. "You've lost," he said and coughed. "Why don't you save us all the trouble and kill yourself now? We both know that's where this is headed."

Mamdouh pistol-whipped the man in the head and then held the gun to his temple. "Look at me," he said, and when the man's head remained bowed, he hit him again. "Look at me!"

A grimace contorted Petersson's face, and then he looked up and met Mamdouh's gaze.

"Your daughter will be joining you soon," he said. "In the end, it is you who have lost." Mamdouh's finger tightened on the trigger while he stared Petersson in the eyes and watched any hope die and then something hit him from behind. He stumbled, and the pistol fired, a wild shot that went into the carousel beside Petersson's head, and then he tumbled into the carousel itself while a weight pinned him down on his back.

Mamdouh roared and twisted as he began to be dragged on the conveyor. His attacker was small, and he heard a gasp as he slammed an elbow into their ribs and then he was free. He flipped the person over his shoulder and dug a hand under their chin and jammed the pistol into their side and then froze.

It was Hafsa.

Her *niqab* had come loose, and her eyes rolled in her head, and he snarled at her. No, this *sharmuta* didn't deserve the honor of an Islamic name. She would always be known by her filthy infidel name. Arielle.

"What's going on over there?" Nathan shouted from the oversize luggage area. He sounded panicked, and it was one more sign of the fool's incompetence he hadn't even noticed Arielle had slipped away.

Mamdouh's hand tightened on Arielle's throat, and he jammed the pistol under her jaw. In five seconds, he could be rid of both this insolent bitch and her troublesome father. He would kill Martel too, he should have known better than to trust a coward unwilling to become a *muharijah*. He shook the girl and yelled, and her hands gripped his wrist and her eyes closed.

The bitch wanted to die.

"*Ibn al khara!*" he said and flung her to one side. In the gap, he glimpsed movement and instinctively rolled to the side and so narrowly missed being struck by Arielle's father, who'd climbed up the carousel. Mamdouh snarled and rolled off the conveyor belt onto the floor and came up in a crouch to find Petersson covering his daughter with his body. The woman clutched her throat and tried to crawl out from under him, and for a moment he wanted to laugh. The infected bitch being protected by her father.

"Enough," he said and grabbed Petersson's foot. Yanked him off the carousel and kicked him in the ribs. The man went limp, and he turned to the woman, dragged her off the conveyor belt as well to lay beside her father. She collapsed to her knees and then rolled onto her back and glared up at him, defiance in her eyes as she stared into the barrel of the gun.

A gunshot came from the oversize luggage area, followed by yells from Martel. The idiot couldn't be left alone much longer. Mamdouh's finger tightened on the trigger, and then he stopped. No, he had one more thing to do to salvage this mission, and for that, he needed her.

And he needed her compliant.

He trained the pistol on her father, and the girl moaned and made as if to cover her dad's body with her own and he backhanded her across the face. "Shut up."

"I need help over here!" Martel yelled.

He slapped the girl again and then kicked her father in the ribs and aimed the pistol at the man's head. Stood over him and looked the girl in the eyes. "You cooperate, he lives," he said. "Otherwise he dies."

She stared at him with hate in her eyes and then nodded.

"Get up," he said.

She struggled to her feet, and then Mamdouh pointed with the pistol to the oversize baggage area. "Move." When she'd begun to walk, he grabbed one of Petersson's feet by the ankle and began to drag him. He kept the pistol trained on Arielle. "Do as I say unless you want to watch him die."

She kept walking, her head down, shoulders hunched, feet dragging. Her last gesture had taken all her effort and she was beaten now. He looked forward to killing her father in front of her.

He permitted himself a smile and continued to drag Petersson along.

* * *

MONTREAL, QUEBEC
04 JUN 2015 – 1849 LOCAL

Erik's head throbbed. A voice penetrated the darkness, and he swam to it, up to the surface. He floundered at the edge of consciousness, tried to piece himself together.

"This is the Royal Canadian Mounted Police."

Was someone calling him?

"You're surrounded."

He could barely hear them, whoever they were.

"We want to talk."

Arielle.

Erik's eyes popped open. He strained to sit up, and his shoulder screamed. The edge of his vision tried to go black on him and he grunted and sank back down.

"Welcome back, *kafir*."

Erik oriented on the voice. It was the man who'd shot him, the one at the center of everything. "You've caused me a lot of trouble," the man said.

"Then why am I still alive?" Erik clutched his shoulder and when he pulled his fingers off, they were stained red with blood.

"To watch." The man lashed out with a kick that caught Erik in the ribs.

Erik sucked air between his teeth to bottle up a cry and the act of breathing intensified the pain in his chest. He focused on the man's feet as they disappeared behind a metal counter, forced himself to fight off the numbness and tingling in his fingers and toes. He drew another breath, shifted his gaze to a clump of black and yellow rags at the base of the metal counter while he fought to stay conscious.

After several breaths, the blackness began to recede. The rags came into focus, not rags but a robe, the hemline draped over black ballet flats. A person. He glanced up and saw he was face to face with Arielle.

Her face was down, and she rubbed each temple with a finger. A vivid red mark flared on her right cheek, and he remembered she'd been slapped.

Anger surged through him, enough to help him make it into a sitting position, his lip curled at the stab of pain that came when he moved. "Arielle," he said in a croak.

"You don't seem to learn," another man said from beside him.

Erik snapped his mouth shut. Shoes squeaked on the floor, and then Martel stood in front of him, a pistol in his hand. A black headband with white Arabic script covered Martel's forehead, and combined with his unkempt hair and scraggly beard, he looked feverish.

Martel bared his teeth in a smile and pointed the gun in Erik's face. "*Allahu Akbar.*" He drew the thumb of his free hand across his throat, gestured with the pistol. "Hands on your head."

Erik moved into a cross-legged position, braced his back against a wall and brought his hands up. Martel grabbed him by the shoulders, twisted him to face the wall, then mashed his hands together on top of his head, fingers interlaced.

"Like this. Stay." Martel shoved Erik's hands again, then stood back. He stood for a moment and then walked off, his footsteps crossing to the other side of the room.

Erik peeked sideways at Arielle, who hadn't moved, then tried to check out his surroundings. The room was small, a bit larger than an average hotel room, with a grey concrete floor and white, cinder-block walls. A metal counter stood in the middle of the room and beyond that was an alcove where the end of a conveyor belt was visible. There were perhaps another fifteen or so people sat on the floor like him, facing the wall, hands up. Some wore blindfolds. If a person's hands dropped from their head, or they slouched, Martel would walk over, brace his knee against their spine and pull back on their elbows.

"Get a blindfold on him."

Erik glanced to the other man, who stood at the counter in the middle of the room. The man's dark, shark-like gaze stared straight at Erik. While Martel grabbed a piece of clothing from a suitcase, the man reached into a messenger bag on the counter and pulled out a tablet.

Martel knelt at Erik's back and bound the cloth over his eyes. Erik scrunched up his face while Martel struggled to tie a knot in the too-small piece of clothing. When the blindfold was on, Martel grabbed Erik's wrists and repositioned his hands on top of his head, and Erik grunted as pain shot through his shoulder.

"Don't drop those hands," Martel said into his ear and with a final shove, he moved away.

"Take this," the other man said. "Access the internet."

Erik worked his nose and eyes and felt the blindfold shift a little and found a tiny gap through which he could see. He faced the wall at right angles to where Martel and the other man stood at the counter, and if he risked it, he could make out what they were doing.

"Okay, we're on," Martel said.

"Stream a video of me," the other man said.

"Give me a minute."

Erik's breath was loud in his ears.

"And...we're...on," Martel said.

The man stood straight. "In the name of Allah, the merciful, I bring the people of the Crusader West a message from the Caliphate, which has been re-established through Allah's will," the man said. "I am Mamdouh al Qassam, and I swear before Allah, the just, that your reckoning is at hand. Your armies desecrate and defile the holy lands of *al-Sham*, but instead of defeating us, we grow stronger. Ignorance of the murders your armies commit can continue no longer. Against all your designs, the soldiers of God have brought *jihad* to your shores. It is time you discovered what it is like to be under attack."

Mamdouh al Qassam? Erik wracked his brain to remember the name while he canted his head farther to get a better look. Martel stood by the metal counter, the tablet held out like a camera.

"Any attempt to prevent this attack will result in the death of these people, none of whom are innocent," Mamdouh said. "You are all complicit in the global atrocities of your infidel governments."

A woman gasped, and Erik twisted to see Mamdouh with the muzzle of his pistol against a woman's head. She shivered, and her shoulders trembled as Mamdouh dragged her upward by the hair.

"If you want to avert this attack, you will let me speak to the Canadian Prime Minister. Failure to do so will result in the execution of these infidels," Mamdouh said. "You have one hour." He flung the woman to the ground and looked back to Martel.

"Got it," Martel panted, as if out of breath.

"Spread these *kafir* out," Mamdouh said. "Place some near the rear doors."

Martel set the tablet on the counter, then grabbed a man by the scruff of his neck. "Get up." The man stood, and Martel marched him deeper into the room. As Martel worked, Mamdouh returned to the counter and picked up the iPad.

Erik glanced at Arielle, tucked at the base of the metal counter. She remained seated, fingers at her temples. He coughed, and she glanced up, stared at him, her face pale, eyes bloodshot and red.

"It'll be okay." He mouthed the words. "I love you."

Her bottom lip quivered, then she clutched her arms tight to her chest, clenched her eyes shut and leaned back into the corner of the wall and the counter.

Erik faced the wall and considered what he knew. They'd been moved into the oversized baggage area, and from the sounds of things, the police already had a cordon up, which meant nobody was going anywhere for the time being.

Riding things out wasn't an option. He didn't know Mamdouh's current plan, but he'd bet a year's salary it didn't involve the safe release of the hostages. At a certain point – like when the first hostage was executed – the police would be forced to enter the room, and there would be a blood bath. And the longer Mamdouh was left alone, the more time he'd have to prepare that outcome.

That left precious little for Erik to do, except try to keep Mamdouh off balance and maybe force him to make a mistake. A poor option, but now that Erik had been reunited with Arielle, he had to try.

He spoke over his shoulder. "Excuse me," he said, and the words came out as a croak. He cleared his throat and tried again. "Excuse me. Can we talk? It doesn't have to be like this."

"Go on," Mamdouh said without emotion.

"We don't have to die here."

"We all must die. Some sooner than others."

"The police cordon is already in place. They can't let you walk out of here. They'll negotiate for a bit, but once they have a good option, they're going to take you down." He willed the man to see common sense. "Why not talk to them? Whatever reason you're doing this, you can't speak to that if you're dead."

"Be quiet," said a woman from the other side of the room. "You'll get us all killed."

"He will answer." Mamdouh's footsteps moved from the center of the room toward the speaker, followed by the muffled thunk of metal striking something soft. "Talk."

Erik said a silent apology to whoever had been struck, then kept going. "I work with the police," he said. "I've seen these situations play out before. I'm sure you have, too."

"Not like this, you haven't."

"Mamdouh al Qassam?" a mechanical voice said from outside the room, the main concourse if Erik had his bearings straight. "This is Staff Sergeant Andrew Johnson from the Royal Canadian Mounted Police. I'd like to talk."

Footsteps approached Erik, stopped behind him. "Let me tell you something," Mamdouh said, his voice calm as if he hadn't just been hailed by the police in the middle of an armed standoff. "Everything happening here today, including your death, is as Allah wills it. You can do nothing to change that." Mamdouh's footsteps headed back to the center of the room.

Erik risked another peek through his blindfold and saw Mamdouh bent over the blonde woman he'd threatened before. Pistol in one hand, he wrapped his other hand in her hair and dragged her to her feet. "You've done well," he said and pushed her to stand in front of the door that leads to the concourse. "Now do so again."

"Don't hurt me." Snot hung from the woman's lips, and tears streamed down her face.

Mamdouh jammed the pistol into the small of her back. "Open the door."

There was a silence, broken by the woman's sobs, and then a creaking sound as the door opened. Erik twisted to the other side, spied the main baggage area through the tiny crack in the door and then Mamdouh jammed the woman into the crack.

"Have you met my demands?" Mamdouh called out.

"This is Staff Sergeant Andrew Johnson of the Royal Canadian Mounted Police," a man replied. "Are you Mamdouh al Qassam?"

Mamdouh jammed the muzzle of the pistol into the back of the woman's head, his own head tight behind hers and yelled through the door. "Unless the Prime Minister is out there, you're wasting your time," he said. "I want media coverage. You have thirty more minutes. Then I start killing people."

"We need more time," Johnson said in return, but Mamdouh had already leaned into the door with his shoulder. It slammed shut, and he shoved the woman back to her place on the ground and went back to the counter.

Erik kept watch through the corner of his eye as Martel appeared.

"What was the point of that?" Martel asked.

"I want their attention." Mamdouh bowed over the tablet.

"Then what?"

"Check on the *kafir*."

"But –"

"I said check on the *kafir*."

There was a pause, then Martel's footsteps wandered off. Grunts came from deeper in the room, along with the sound of Martel swearing.

The silence grated and Erik's shoulder continued to throb. He waited in silence and the seconds became minutes, and his skin began to crawl from waiting.

"How long do you think you can hold this position?" Erik spoke to the center of the room, got silence in return. "What is it you really want?"

Footsteps stalked in his direction, stopped over top of him. Lightning shot through the top of his head and stars sparkled in his darkened vision. Fingers dug into the flesh beneath his jaw, dragged his head upward.

"Do I have your attention?" Mamdouh's breath was hot on Erik's face.

Erik nodded, struggled not to pass out.

"Do not talk again." Mamdouh drove Erik to the ground, then stomped on the bullet wound in his shoulder. Erik's head lifted off the ground as he yelled and Mamdouh kicked him back down. His footsteps led away as Erik dangled at the edge of awareness.

He forced himself back to a sitting position, made it. The wound in his shoulder throbbed and his shirt clung to him, sticky with fresh blood. He didn't know how much he'd bled out, but if he didn't stop the bleeding soon, he wouldn't be conscious much longer.

"It's time." Mamdouh's voice pierced the fog in Erik's head.

"For what?" Martel asked.

"Every media outlet is now covering this event. Now we tell the rest of our story."

"But the police haven't come back yet."

"Nor will they. Hold this."

Erik risked a glance at the center of the room and saw that Martel had again pointed the iPad at Mamdouh.

"In the name of Allah, the most just, I bring a message to the people of the West," Mamdouh said.

Both men were focused on the video and Erik realized this might be his chance. He inhaled, willed the room to come back into focus, and got ready to move.

"You think we are weak, that we have only rifles and bombs to strike you," Mamdouh said, "but you are wrong. Your traditions talk of four horsemen, and yet you're unaware that these forces are moving even now to unseat your morally corrupt nations."

Keep talking. Erik slowly moved from a seated position to his knees. He just needed Mamdouh to talk for a few more seconds.

"We in the Caliphate have proven adept at using the instruments of war against you. Despite Western aid, we overthrew the apostate regimes in *al Sham* and recreated the Caliphate," Mamdouh continued. "You, yourself have sown the seeds of your destruction through the oppression and evils of capitalism. So it is fitting that we help you fulfill your destiny. I bring you Pestilence." Mamdouh reached down and dragged Arielle to her feet beside him.

Erik froze.

"This woman carries a new, airborne strain of the Ebola virus," Mamdouh said. "She was infected a week ago."

In the room, the other hostages scrambled to tuck themselves as far from Arielle as possible, voices raised in panic. Erik hardly noticed. Mamdouh talked – at least his mouth moved – but the words were soundless against the blood rushing through his ears. He stared at Arielle, met her gaze, the abyss in her eyes and the fact she did not flinch or move.

No.

Sounds crept back into his awareness as time fought to resume its normal flow.

No, not her. He would not let this happen.

"– are more." Mamdouh sounded strong, triumphant. "Even now, other *shahid* enter your countries via every flight imaginable."

He had to save her.

There wasn't much time. The police were no doubt monitoring this feed, and if not, soon would be. They could not let the broadcast continue. The panic that had already gripped the small room was a foreshadow of what would take the entire country. His head was clear now, and every detail in the room stood out in painful detail, Martel's slack-jaw mouth open in a perfect circle, the other hostages crawling over each other to get away, even Mamdouh's monotonous drone. In seconds, he knew, a SWAT team would blow into the room. They would kill Arielle. He had to stop it.

The room's obvious entry point was the metal door where Mamdouh had spoken to the police. The entry team would use explosives to breach the door – there was no time for stealth – which would be bad news for anyone in front of it, whether they were hostages or terrorists. If there was a door in the rear of the room, an entry team would be en route there as well. He might have forty-five seconds.

Mamdouh nodded to Arielle. "Take off your *hijab*, sister. Show the world."

Arielle raised her arms, a pinched look frozen on her face. Her movement was jerky, like a time-lapse video.

Erik tensed. He'd have one shot.

Eyes closed, Arielle began to unwrap her *hijab* and then there was a muffled thunk from the door that led to the main concourse. Both Mamdouh and Martel's heads turned.

Erik sprang to his feet and launched himself at Mamdouh. Arielle fell to one side as Erik knocked the larger man back into the counter. Martel stood rooted to the floor and followed the battle through the tablet. Erik fell to the concrete on top of Mamdouh and they wrestled on the floor, wormed their way toward the door. Mamdouh rolled on top and grabbed the collar of Erik's shirt, then smashed his forehead down into Erik's nose. Blood spattered, and red filled Erik's vision, but he held on, a death grip around Mamdouh's torso. The terrorist reached for the pistol tucked into the waistband of his pants, struggled to free himself and bring the weapon to bear.

How much time had passed? With one eye to the door, Erik felt the muzzle of the pistol work its way into his ribs. He released his bear-hug on Mamdouh to push the gun away, then felt Mamdouh's knee in his gut. The knee dug in, drove Erik to the ground, broke his hold. Erik gasped for breath, even as he fell to the floor and watched Mamdouh regain his feet.

"Look at me!" Mamdouh yelled.

Erik glanced up.

Mamdouh stood in front of the door and smiled, the pistol pointed square in Erik's face. "See you in –"

With a deafening roar of white light and smoke, the top of the door exploded inward. Still connected to the frame by the lowest hinge, the door rotated, crushed into the right side of Mamdouh's head. The man crumpled under the blow.

Fatigue washed over Erik, and he fought the urge to stay on the floor. The entry team would be right behind. He rolled to his knees and found Arielle near the counter. Flecks of red covered her face. Beside her, Martel held one hand to his ears and was reaching for his pistol with the other, the iPad in mid-air as it tumbled for the ground.

Move! Erik stumbled to his feet and lurched at Arielle. Martel's attention shifted from Erik to the door, but Erik ignored it. He had one thing left to do.

Arielle backed away from him, her head shaking, one hand on the metal counter to hold herself up. She met his gaze, silently spoke to him. "*No.*"

But he had no choice.

He threw himself toward her, his arms spread to envelop her, to cover every inch of her. Behind him came the sounds of gunfire and stabs of pain lit up his shoulder and his back. He clung to Arielle and fell with her to the floor. Used the last of his energy to spread himself on top of her, his legs on hers, his arms clutching her arms under his chest. Blackness crowded his vision, and he looked in her eyes, the eyes of his daughter, Audray's eyes. The same eyes of the little girl who'd asked him to tell stories as they walked to the bus stop, or in the bath, stories that had to have a fairy, a mermaid, and an elf or some other combination she'd dreamed up. Too often he'd been in a rush. Too often he'd said he didn't have a story and then one day, she'd stopped asking. How he wished those stories had never ended, how he'd taken more time. He tried to get his mouth to work. *I'm sorry.*

He closed his eyes, felt lips brush his ear. "I love you, Dad."

He smiled and sank into the darkness.

CHAPTER NINETEEN
THE CLEAR PATH

OTTAWA GENERAL HOSPITAL, OTTAWA, ONTARIO
05 JUNE 2015 – 1023 LOCAL

"Where am…"

"Shh."

"What's…" Two figures took shape, both clad head to toe in white. "Am I dead?"

One of the figures reached out for him. "You are not." Its voice was metallic, toneless.

"My daughter…" he said from across a chasm. "Arielle…"

"She's resting." The figure reached for a knob above Erik's head. "You should rest, too."

"Can I see her?" The figures faded into tiny specks of light. He tried to rise from where he lay, but the more he struggled, the more he sank. The voices grew faint and the words muffled.

He fought to hold on and the specks of light shrunk to pinpricks and then disappeared.

* * *

OTTAWA GENERAL HOSPITAL, OTTAWA, ONTARIO
08 JUNE 2015 – 0910 LOCAL

Light pierced Erik's eyes. He squinted at the painful intrusion like a newborn, unready to face the world.

"Welcome back."

He blinked and then focused on the voice. He tried to speak, made a dry croak instead.

"Drink this."

Something smooth and cold pressed against his bottom lip and liquid poured into his mouth, a trickle that tasted as if it had come straight from a mineral spring. He strained forward, tried to get more and a gentle weight pushed back on his forehead.

"Careful. A little at a time."

He eased back, took another sip, then licked his lips. Opened his eyes and focused on the man who'd spoken. The man's light-brown face was protected by a transparent shield, part of a plastic helmet that encased his head. The rest of the man's body was covered in a white plastic suit, except blue gloves that covered his hands. The man withdrew the water and set it on a table beside the bed. Erik cleared his throat, then tested his voice. "Who are you?"

"Dr. Chirag Valsangkar," the man said. "You're in the Ottawa General Hospital."

"Why are you dressed like that?"

"Because you're quarantined. You were exposed to a derivative of the Ebola virus."

Mamdouh's words echoed in Erik's head. *This woman carries a new, airborne strain of the Ebola virus.* "Arielle..."

"She's here."

"Can I see her?"

Dr. Valsangkar had dark circles beneath his eyes. "I'm sorry, but that won't be possible. For one, you're both quarantined. Second, you need to rest. I'm a bit surprised you're even awake."

"Is she all right?"

"Is she all right." Dr. Valsangkar reached up as if to adjust his glasses, stopped with his hand in mid-air, then awkwardly dropped it to his lap. "Your daughter is quite sick."

Erik strained to sit up and came up short, restrained by a strap across his arms and chest. He leveled a glare at the doctor.

"You were thrashing around quite extensively." Dr. Valsangkar looked apologetic behind the mask's plastic shield. "We didn't want the chest tube to come out."

Erik frowned. "The what?"

"Mr. Petersson –"

"Erik."

"Erik. Where should I start? Your own injuries or your daughter's condition? Let me start with you." The doctor referred to a plastic-laminated sheet of paper near the foot of Erik's bed. "Four days ago, you were subjected to several gunshot wounds, one of which penetrated your upper torso and two which penetrated your right shoulder."

"I got shot again?"

"Yes, by the police SWAT team." Dr. Valsangkar glanced up, seemed about to say more, then looked down. "The bullets did quite a bit of damage. The ones in your shoulder perforated the tissue without disintegrating too much, although there will be some extensive recovery time."

Erik glanced down, flinched from the mass of white bandages that covered his chest.

"It looks bad, but it easily could have been worse," Dr. Valsangkar said. "Had all the bullets struck the center of mass as they had been intended, we would not be having this conversation."

"And the one in my chest?"

"Technically, that bullet also entered near your shoulder, however, we believe it struck your collar bone and disintegrated. Most of the matter exited up and out of your body, however, at least a portion of the fragments went into your chest cavity and punctured your lung."

"What?"

"At the time of injury you were having difficulty breathing, so the paramedics inserted an endotracheal tube as a precaution. We were able to take that out after twenty-four hours."

He closed his eyes and sank his head into the pillow. "What day is it?"

"Saturday. Four days since your exposure."

"Exposure?" He cracked open his eyes. *Arielle, of course.* "Where's my daughter?"

Dr. Valsangkar returned the paper to the foot of the bed and crossed his arms. "In isolation. As are you."

"Is it…?"

"Yes. She has Ebola."

"Can you cure her?"

"Mr. Petersson – Erik – Ebola is notoriously difficult to treat." The doctor's voice grew soft. "We have what might be the best treatment facility in the country – the infectious disease center is next door – but there are many unknowns."

"And is it…" He swallowed, not wanting to say al Qassam's name. The sooner the memory of that man faded, the better. "He said it was a new strain, airborne."

Dr. Valsangkar stood, swayed for a moment and then steadied himself on a bed rail. "At this point, we can't confirm. We're culturing samples, but it takes time, so until the tests come back, we're treating it as such."

Erik pictured how crowded Montreal's international airport had been and of the other airports Arielle had travelled through. And Mamdouh had said there were more. He felt numb. "Have there been any other cases?"

Dr. Valsangkar shook his head. "Thankfully, no, although I suppose that sentiment will be misplaced if there are indeed other infected out there. Even still, it's been a nightmare, as I'm sure you can imagine." Dr. Valsangkar's voice broke, and he coughed. The next time he spoke, his voice was steady. "For my part, I'm optimistic the virus is not airborne. It would take significant manipulation to evolve to that point."

"I need to see my daughter," he said.

"I'm sorry, but that's not possible," Dr. Valsangkar said with a sad smile. "You're in isolation as a precaution and for the moment, you aren't showing any symptoms. She, however..." He shook his head. "For the moment she's in no condition to accept visitors."

Erik raised his head, strained against the strap. "Do you know what I've gone through to see her?" An ache ratcheted through his shoulder, and he cringed.

"I do, actually," Dr. Valsangkar said. "Your friend, Stephanie, told me all about it. I know that the police bullets that hit you were intended for your daughter, so in all likelihood, you've given her a fighting chance. We're going to do everything possible to help your daughter get better, believe me." He reached across to fiddle with an IV bag beside the bed. "For now, you need your rest."

"I need to see her before she...she..." He couldn't say it, could not acknowledge the possibility.

"We'll talk later, Erik," Dr. Valsangkar said and then walked out of the room.

"Let me see her." He strained to hold on. The room blurred. "Arielle..."

* * *

OTTAWA GENERAL HOSPITAL, OTTAWA, ONTARIO
13 JUNE 2015 – 1312 LOCAL

"Ready to go?"

Erik nodded from within the plastic bubble that covered his wheelchair. "It would be easier if I walked."

"Absolutely not," Dr. Valsangkar said. "You are under my positive control the entire time. Don't make me regret bending the rules."

"In that case, I'm ready." Erik's throat was tight. "I appreciate this."

"These are special circumstances," Dr. Valsangkar said.

The doctor didn't explain himself as he eased the wheelchair into the corridor. Nor did he need to, since Erik already knew. This was his chance to say good-bye.

"There are some rules to review," Dr. Valsangkar said. "You stay in the wheelchair. If you need anything, the bathroom, water, anything, you tell me, and we go back to your room. Under no circumstance will you be allowed to enter her room."

"I understand," Erik said. Hospital staff in protective suits bustled through the hallway. When they caught sight of Dr. Valsangkar and the wheelchair, many stood still along the walls and watched as Erik wheeled past. He felt like a lab experiment. "Why are they staring? Do they not approve?"

Dr. Valsangkar cleared his throat. "There isn't a single person on staff here who doesn't know your story, Erik. It's been nine days, and you have no symptoms. Over the past few days, we've been doing patient transfers often, thankfully, so although it's not routine to allow one patient to visit another, we all feel we can make an exception in this case."

"Thank you." Earlier, Dr. Valsangkar had explained that the tests of the Ebola samples had showed negative for airborne transmission. In fact, from what Erik had been able to follow, the strain seemed similar to that of the last African outbreak. None of the people who'd been quarantined had been discharged yet – they'd undergo observation for a full thirty days – but had instead been spread out among a number of facilities able to handle routine Ebola cases, if there was such a thing. It was a glimmer of good news, although it had already receded to a distant thought for Erik. As he got closer to Arielle's room, the dull pain in his shoulder throbbed in time to the beating of his heart. "What can I expect?"

"Unfortunately, we don't know how long your daughter was infected prior to receiving her," Dr. Valsangkar said. "She had symptoms, though from what we could tell, they were relatively minor. As best she could recall, she was infected six days prior to arriving in Montreal."

He glanced up. "You spoke with her?"

"Briefly."

"Will I be able to talk to her?"

"I'm sorry, but that won't be possible."

"Isn't there a way to communicate from outside her room?"

"At present, she's rarely conscious."

They came around a corner and approached two glass windows that stretched from floor to ceiling. One of the windows had a small red sign at eye level with the warning, Do Not Enter. Farther along the wall was an elevated chair and desk where a nurse was seated.

"Here we are," Dr. Valsangkar said. He rolled the wheelchair to one of the windows and parked it beneath the Do Not Enter sign.

The room didn't look much different from Erik's room, perhaps a little more sterile and a bit bigger, but still with the standard monitor hung from the ceiling, treatment equipment along the wall and of course, a single, Spartan bed. On the bed lay his daughter.

Air hissed through Erik's teeth, loud in his isolation bubble.

Angry red spots began just above Arielle's wrists and climbed her forearms to disappear beneath the pale blue sleeves of her hospital gown. The spots extended up her neck as well like she'd been severely burned. Her face was swollen, eyes puffed shut, and an IV was stuck into her left arm, the tube connected to a bag suspended by the bed.

"How..." The words stuck in his throat.

"The redness on her arms is a rash, a symptom that develops in about half the cases." Dr. Valsangkar's voice took on a clinical tone. "The intravenous is to help with rehydration, as well as to manage the pain." He took a deep breath. "We're doing all we can, which in all honesty is not much."

"What do you mean?"

The doctor's fists clenched. "With Ebola, the patient is the primary fighter. Treatment is oriented on being supportive, keeping them hydrated, addressing secondary symptoms. Your daughter was undernourished, so we've been trying to help her with that, but it has been difficult as her body was already fighting the infection when she came to us. I'm thankful it wasn't worse."

"How could it be any worse?" Erik could scarce believe that the frail, pitiful body belonged to Arielle.

"She has no signs of internal or external bleeding, which is fortunate."

"I see," he said. After everything they'd been through, this is how it ended.

"As I told you before, you almost certainly saved her life," Dr. Valsangkar said. "If even one of those bullets had hit their target, her body would not have been able to handle the extra stress."

"For all the good it did."

Dr. Valsangkar knelt beside Erik and looked at him. "You have given her the chance she needs."

Erik blinked his moist eyes and did not meet the doctor's gaze. "And now?"

"We wait."

"Is that all?"

"I'm sorry."

Erik felt as cold as the metal wheelchair he sat in.

"I'll leave you alone." Dr. Valsangkar stood and moved to talk to the nurse at the desk.

It hardly seemed real that the person on the other side of the glass was his daughter. Arielle's eyes had been full of life, her smile brightened every room. The woman in the other room looked like a corpse.

The coldness spread through his body. Dr. Valsangkar had said she'd been undernourished and that was true. She'd been undernourished for a long time. He'd wanted to protect her, to nurture her, to be there for her. But if he'd made the world such a good place, how had this happened?

His breath came fast now, and the devastation of her body seemed to sear his eyes. This was the result of his protection. He'd sworn to Audray he would protect her and he'd failed except he hadn't failed six months ago, he'd failed a year ago, three years ago, when he'd started at the High-Risk Traveler Task Force.

High-pitched, repetitive beeps sounded in the hallway. Erik looked around, tried to spy the source of the sound, glanced into Arielle's room. Vomit bubbled from her mouth and dribbled down her cheeks to stain the pillow. Her head did not turn, and her body began to convulse as she gagged.

"Nurse." Erik glanced to the aid station, saw it was vacant. "Nurse!" A side door into Arielle's room burst open, and two people clad in protective suits entered. They beelined for Arielle's bed and rolled her onto her side, a pot held under her mouth as they helped clear the vomit with their gloved fingers.

"Time to go," Dr. Valsangkar reappeared at Erik's side.

"No," Erik said. "I need to stay." He pushed on the arms of the wheelchair as if he would stand, strained at the restraint that buckled him to his seat. The chair whirled, and he found himself face to face with Dr. Valsangkar.

"There's nothing you can do, Erik," he said. "This is her fight, now."

Time ticked by as he stared into the doctor's eyes. He would stay, he would witness this. He owed it to her. He owed it to Audray.

The doctor's face softened. "I need to be in that room to help, and I can't spare the staff to be with you here –"

"I won't do anything." Erik's hands gripped the sides of the wheelchair, his knuckles white.

"No. That's not what we agreed. Now, do you want to let me go into that room, or do you want to keep me in the hallway so we can argue some more?"

Erik's gaze dipped, and he sank back into the chair.

"This won't be the last time you see her, I promise." Dr. Valsangkar stood and beckoned for a nurse to take Erik back to his room. As Erik rolled down the corridor, the doctor called after him. "We'll bring you back when it's less busy."

"When will that be?" Erik called over his shoulder. He hadn't said good-bye.

His answer was the continued beeps from the aid station.

***

OTTAWA GENERAL HOSPITAL, OTTAWA, ONTARIO
15 JUNE 2015 – 1424 LOCAL

Erik sat outside Arielle's room, protective bubble in place on his wheelchair. Although he was walking now, Dr. Valsangkar insisted the wheelchair was for everyone's protection since Erik remained in isolation, symptoms or not. Erik had been so glad for the chance to see Arielle, he hadn't pushed the issue and so he sat and watched his daughter fight a battle with an enemy that ate her from the inside out.

She did not seem to be winning.

The redness on her arms had grown vivid, almost uniform from the backs of her hands to her cheeks. Blisters speckled her wrists and forearms, and she no longer coughed. When she threw up – deep heaves that wracked her entire body – little came out. As quick as fluids were forced into her, they were ejected, most often as diarrhea. For the moment, Arielle lay motionless while a nurse mopped her brow.

Footsteps approached in the corridor, stopped beside him. "How is she?"

His gaze flickered to the newcomer in the protective suit, then returned to his daughter. "Hello, Ziad." His tone was empty. "I didn't think visitors were allowed."

"Your colleague may have pulled some strings for me."

"Oh?" A hint of curiosity tinted his words. "Who was that?"

"Stephanie. She contacted me a few days ago and asked me to come in, said she would clear it with the hospital. Like everyone else, I've followed the story on the news and wanted to help, if I could."

"I'm starting to think I should be concerned at how often the hospital breaks the rules."

"They follow the most important ones," Ziad said. "The first one being to care for the patients, one of which is you." He gestured to his plastic suit. "And, I still had to get dressed up."

"I'd forgotten I'd mentioned you to Stephanie," Erik said. "Did you know she's the one who suggested I talk to an Imam?"

"I did not."

"She's good people."

"I'm sure she would say the same thing about you."

"I wouldn't know."

"Something tells me that's not true, but I understand." Ziad's tone held a mild rebuke, tempered by a smile. "How long have you been here?"

"Almost an hour," he said. The nurse finished mopping Arielle's brow, began to gather the bowl of water and her cloths.

"I'm sorry."

Erik let the silence remain for a minute or two and then spoke. "I was gone a lot when her mom was alive." He wondered why this story had come up, of all things, but he continued. "The times I was home, I never let work go, nor my hobbies. I'd get up early and go to the basement to train martial arts, shadow boxing, that sort of thing."

Ziad remained silent.

"I would get up before everyone was awake, but Arielle was an early riser too, and when she was four or so, she started wanting to come downstairs with me."

He would tip-toe through the upstairs hall, careful to avoid creaks in the floor. At the top of the stairs, he'd installed a retractable gate to stop Arielle from sleepwalking her way into breaking her neck, and in the dark, he would climb over it, and sometimes he'd kick it and the noise would wake her.

"She'd always hear me, and she'd say, 'Dad, don't forget me.'" He licked his lips. "She never wanted to go to sleep at night and then she'd be up as early as possible in the morning. She was always scared she'd miss something."

"And so you took her?"

He nodded. "She'd ask me to carry her, and to bring whatever stuffie was her favorite at the time." She'd called them her 'guys.' "And her blankie, of course. Blankie always had to come." Eyes moist, he turned back to the window, on the other side of which his four-year-old daughter still lay, hidden somewhere in her tortured adult body.

"We had a television in the basement, and she'd watch cartoons while I trained," he said.

"I imagine that she enjoyed it."

"It was our thing. Our special thing we did that was just the two of us. How stupid is that?"

"Not at all."

He saw it in his mind as if it had happened that morning. Arielle's teddy bears, dogs, and unicorns lined up on the edge of the couch, watching cartoons beside her. Every now and then he'd ask her a question about her show, and she'd answer.

"When did it stop?" Ziad asked.

"I don't remember." Erik shook his head. "I went away one time, and when I came back, she was doing something else. When her mom..." He went to wipe his eyes, paused, then sighed. "It was a bad time."

"But you got through it."

"Arielle got me through it," he said. "One Saturday morning I woke up and she was in my room, sitting on the foot of the bed. She asked me to go to the basement and watch morning cartoons like we used to, me training and her watching television. She even brought her blankie. She was twelve." He sat with his elbows balanced on his knees, head hung. "I thought she did it for me, to help me get back on my feet." She'd seemed so strong, always the one he'd turn to, more like an equal than father and daughter.

Ziad crossed his hands in front of his waist and waited in silence.

"When I got out of the military, things got better." Erik straightened. "Then the world seemed to get worse and worse. I started working longer hours. All I wanted to do was make the world a better place."

"I understand," Ziad said. "Your intent was to help."

"Yes," he said. "I was scared something would happen to her."

"Ah," Ziad said, "fear. A powerful motivator."

"I only wanted what was best for her."

"And are you still scared?"

"Of course. How could I not be?"

"Who are you scared for?"

"For her."

"But you said you were scared something would happen to her. Does that not mean you were scared for yourself?" When Erik said nothing, Ziad sighed. "Do you remember we talked about how actions are by intentions?"

Erik nodded. "Yes."

"Well, it is said that a small action is made great by a great intention, whereas a great action is made small by a small intention. Fear is a low emotion. It causes us to be selfish and think about ourselves. Fear almost always undermines great actions."

"I'm not sure I need to hear this right now," he said in a quiet voice.

"Erik, what's the most important thing in the world to you?"

A tear ran down his cheek. "Her."

"Then love her. Live for her, not just for her safety."

"How?" The word caught in his throat. The whole time he'd thought he had been.

"I wish I knew," Ziad said. "All I know is that love is like a plant. To survive, plants cannot be neglected. They don't need constant attention, but nor can they be ignored. They have to be nurtured. And plants can sense fear, it will cause them to wither."

"What if it's too far gone?"

"Love will bring it back."

Everything sounded so good, to hear Ziad say it, but he was still scared. When it came down to it, he'd been scared for so long. "I don't want to lose her."

"*Inshallah*, you won't. Have faith."

He wiped his eyes and stared toward where Arielle lay, oblivious. "Oh, hell." A soft chuckle escaped his lips. "Never thought I'd see the day an Imam talked to me about love."

"Is it so strange?" Ziad asked. "Most religions aren't so different. They ask us to live a good life, treat people with respect, and above all, they're founded by love."

"Then how did we get to this point?"

"Fear."

Erik glanced up. "Just like that?"

"Were you expecting more? We all fear the unknown, or change, and when that fear controls our intentions, our actions are affected accordingly." A small smile touched Ziad's face. "And as a great man once said, when questions are complicated, the answers are simple."

"And which distinguished religious scholar said that?"

Ziad's smile grew bigger. "Dr. Suess."

Erik snorted, and in spite of himself, he returned Ziad's smile. Very well, if that's what it would take, he would be scared no longer.

***

Ottawa General Hospital, Ottawa, Ontario
25 June 2015 – 1130 Local

To an observer, Arielle knew she appeared to be on the way to recovery. A week earlier, she'd been told that blood had flowed like tears from her eyes. Both a priest and an imam had been on standby, and then, her fever had broken. Now, the red lesions were almost all gone, as were the blisters, and she'd even begun to gain weight. The doctors had informed her it had been at least twenty-one days since the onset of her symptoms and they were confident she would survive. And yet for all that, Arielle wasn't sure she was ready to face getting better.

Two people stood in the doorway to her room. The first was a nurse, a gaunt woman with a warm face who Arielle didn't recognize, which didn't mean a lot. So much of the past few weeks, almost the past few months, seemed more like a dream than reality. The nurse entered with a tray of food, then busied herself about the room. Arielle's gaze shifted to the other person, a man with short, cropped hair and rich, dark-brown skin whom she did recognize.

"How are you feeling today?" Dr. Valsangkar asked. He remained in the doorway, blocking the entrance.

"Fine." Arielle glanced from the doctor to the nurse, then back. "My stomach feels a little upset."

Dr. Valsangkar adjusted his glasses. "Would you like to postpone? At this stage, more rest is a good thing."

The nurse closed a cabinet door, then exited past Dr. Valsangkar, who'd stepped aside. In the gap, Arielle caught a glimpse of a third person in the hallway, partially hidden behind the corner. She met Dr. Valsangkar's gaze and shook her head. "No. I'm ready."

"You're sure?"

She nodded.

Dr. Valsangkar leaned into the hallway and then entered the room and stood to one side of the door. Then the person who'd waited outside came in.

Her dad.

He hesitated in the doorway, his awkwardness palpable, and she glanced at him and then studied the tips of her toes underneath the white sheet on her bed.

Her dad took a step backward, and Dr. Valsangkar reached out and placed a hand on the small of his back. "Go ahead, Erik," Dr. Valsangkar said. Her dad took two slow steps into the room, then paused. "I'll give you both some time." Dr. Valsangkar backed into the hallway and pulled the door shut.

Arielle flinched as the door closed, continued to look anywhere except at her dad, even as the chair beside her bed crunched with the sound of him sitting down. She clenched her eyes shut, could not stop a tear from escaping. What could she say? That she'd been stupid? That she was sorry? The anger she'd bottled up inside? Maybe he would talk first.

Except he didn't. Instead, he sat in silence, less the rhythmic ins and outs of his breath.

"I guess you want to know why I did it," she said and risked a look at him. Wondered who this man was that sat beside her, the well-worn lines on his face, the hollowed cheeks and stern lips, the two soft blue eyes that looked moist as if doing his best not to cry.

He cleared his throat. "Not if you don't want to talk about it," he said.

She stared at his face a few seconds longer, the deep eyes that threatened to pull her in with their sadness, with their love. He looked like he'd been through as rough a trip as her. She looked away and then his hand found hers. She flinched, tried to pull her hand from his, but he held on. "I could still be contagious," she said.

"You're not." His voice was firm and unflinching, unlike his hand, which trembled. "And even if you were, I wouldn't care."

She did not move, and when the tightness of his grip relaxed, she left her hand where it was, soft against his touch. How was it possible for him to care for her now? After everything. "I'm sorry, Dad."

"Don't be."

They sat in silence for a minute and then her dad drew a breath. "When you were three, you asked me if it was okay for good people to do bad things to bad people," he said. "Do you remember?"

She nodded.

"You were such a serious kid, so smart. I should have paid more attention," he said. "I always believed in being honest with you, and so I said that sometimes, it was okay for good people to do bad things. Like if someone was trying to hurt you, the only way to stop them might be to hurt them back, hurt them so bad they'd leave you alone. It's still a bad thing, but sometimes we have to do what's required to protect what's important to us."

All the emotions she'd suppressed over the past months hammered and beat at the walls she'd erected to protect herself, a dam about to burst. She pulled back her hand and drew her knees to her chest and wrapped her arms around her legs. "You said that when we hurt others, we also hurt ourselves, no matter how much good comes from the act," she whispered. "That's what you said."

"Yes, I did," he said. "When we hurt others, we also hurt ourselves."

Her whole body shook. "And at what point do we all just become bad people? Hurting each other because someone hurt us in the past? Or because we're scared?"

"I don't know Arielle," he said.

"Dad, there's so much hate. When does it stop? When the world goes dark? When we destroy ourselves?" She took his hand now, didn't flinch as he sat on the bed beside her and wrapped an arm around her shoulder.

"I hope it doesn't come to that," he said. "I'd like to think we'd pull ourselves back from the brink before that happens, but it's so easy to get caught up in the day to day battles. To lose our way in the dark. I know I lost mine for a time."

She let her head sink onto his chest and now the tears came, hot and burning. He held her and said nothing, and she thought of al Kanadi. Did al Kanadi think of himself as a bad person? Was he worse than the boy who'd raped her? Worse than her dad?

"I don't have many answers, Arielle," he said. "All I seem to know anymore with certainty is that we have to do whatever we can to keep the darkness at bay."

"Only light can drive out darkness, Dad."

"So I've been told," he said and his hand stroked her hair. "But I don't think I understood what that meant until recently. I never realized I was so scared of losing everything that made life worth living, that I inadvertently pushed it all away. And I don't want to do that anymore."

Her bottom lip trembled, and she leaned into him, wrapped her arms around him and gripped him every bit as strong as he held her.

"Arielle, I know now that the opposite of love isn't hate, it's fear. So what I want to offer you is my love. I know that's no guarantee against being hurt, but I have faith it'll get us through the darkness. You're my favorite person in this whole wide world, and I love you."

She buried her face in his chest, and lost herself in his smell, the smell that had been on his pillow where she'd sometimes slept with her mom when he was gone for work, the smell that had gotten her through the long nights that followed her mother's death. It spoke to her, of strength, of sadness, of joy, of disappointment, of nights roasting marshmallows and of being stranded after school, waiting for a ride. Most of all, underneath, it spoke of hope. It spoke of a difficult road ahead and she didn't know if she had the strength, but she knew she had to go on.

"I forgive you, Dad," she said into his shoulder, damp with her tears. "And you're my favorite person, too. On earth, and in space."

He smiled. "And in space."

CHAPTER TWENTY
THE TRIUMPH

OTTAWA, ONTARIO

29 JUNE 2015 – 1015 LOCAL

"You ready?"

"Yes," Erik said.

Stephanie put her hand on his shoulder and squeezed. "You sure? You don't sound convinced."

He met her gaze, gave her a tight smile. "I'm just thinking of Jordan." And Arielle, and how he wasn't sure he'd be strong enough to withstand the lure of the Task Force. But he knew this debrief needed to happen. "Let's get it over."

"Hang in there." She rubbed his shoulder and then swiped her pass card through the electronic key reader. A green light appeared and the reinforced door opened, and she walked into the Task Force's operations center.

Erik took a deep breath and then followed.

The room was how he remembered it, except for the people. The operations center held twenty workstations and on a normal day, ran with around ten people to a shift. Today though, a person sat at every work station and all the floor space was filled. The room quietened as he entered, those who were seated stood, all staring at him.

He stopped, his mouth dry, and whispered to Stephanie. "There was only supposed to be a few people."

"The whole team came out." Wiggins's voice boomed from the back tier of desks. "Nobody wanted to miss the show."

"Less one," Erik said.

Stephanie's hand found its way to Erik's back, and they exchanged a glance while Wiggins pointed to a screen at the front of the room that showed the black-and-white image of a small, walled compound.

"Not every day we get a ring-side seat of a live operation," Wiggins said.

Erik peered at the screens, noticed the pickup truck in the compound's courtyard, the most noteworthy difference from the adjoining compounds. Another screen displayed three people walking along a deserted street. White hash marks and data scrolled along the top and sides of both screens, altitude, bearing, and GPS coordinates. "What are we watching?" he asked and joined Wiggins on the top tier.

"What do you think?" Wiggins clapped him on the back.

Erik winced at the twinge in his shoulder. "If I didn't know better, I'd say it was a drone feed," he said. Although the operations center had the capability to receive video downlinks, in all Erik's time on the Task Force, they'd never been authorized to join a feed. It was outside their mandate.

"It is, and you're in for a treat." Wiggins guided Erik to a large chair positioned in the center of the tier. It was the director's chair of the operations center, with the best view.

Erik sat amid the uncomfortable impression of being subject to a sales pitch for a used car and stared at the screens.

Wiggins rested a hand on Erik's shoulder and gestured to the screenshot of the compound. "This is Abu Noor al Kanadi's residence," he said. "He's about to have a very bad day."

Erik looked at Stephanie. "I thought this was just a debrief."

"The debrief can wait," Wiggins said in a proud tone. "This all just came together, and it did so because you made it happen. Recognize that truck in the compound?"

Erik squinted at the pickup on the screen, tried to push his annoyance at Wiggins into the background. Wiggins would do well once promoted. Like a true bureaucrat, he hated risk, but loved success and had a knack for taking credit. And what the hell made this truck any different? There were thousands of pickups in Iraq and Syria – if that's even where al Kanadi was – never mind trucks with roll bars. He paused. "The tracker..."

"Good work, good work," Wiggins said. "Although we don't know for sure if it's the same one. The GPS stopped working weeks ago, but not before it showed up at this compound."

Erik closed his eyes and thought of Jordan. Jordan was responsible for this and would never see what he had accomplished. Would never feel the electricity of an operation about to succeed. He opened his eyes. "Where is that?" he asked.

Wiggins sat in the chair beside him. "Stephanie? This is your work too, why don't you do the honors?"

"Sure thing, Chief." Stephanie stood at Erik's other side. "We picked up the GPS's signal in Mosul and were able to track the vehicle as it drove to this compound in the suburbs of Raqqa. We assumed the compound housed a high-value target and called in some favors to get assets on station to corroborate our suspicion. Even still, we were all surprised to find out we'd found al Kanadi's residence, or at least one of them. From there, one thing led to another, which leads us to the right screen, where we have al Kanadi himself, on his way home."

"A dead man walking," Wiggins said and leaned back and put his hands behind his head. "And one more piece will come off the chess board, thanks to you."

To be replaced by whom? Erik thought, and his skin crawled at al Kanadi's name. "How did we get the feed?"

"Let's just say the collective intelligence community was very happy to find this guy. And once people found out about your personal involvement, it was easy." Wiggins's smile grew broader. "More importantly, the seniors are already talking about this being a possible new direction for us. Consider this a trial run."

Hard to believe that barely two months earlier, Wiggins had suspended him. Erik focused on the screens, this time the one with what was supposedly al Kanadi. Three dark heat spots walked along what looked like a sidewalk, one big and two small, the occasional car passing in the street. "Who are the others with him?"

"His kids."

"Many Caliphate commanders use that tactic these days," Stephanie said. "They keep their families or civilians with them most of the time to increase the collateral damage consideration for coalition airstrikes."

"Although in al Kanadi's case, two is well within the range of acceptable collateral," Wiggins said.

Erik's heart beat a strong rhythm against his chest. "So the kids will die?"

Stephanie shook her head. "We haven't had time to establish a robust pattern of life, but he sometimes sends the kids ahead when they get near the house. For a moment, he'll be outside by himself, so if nobody else is around, there'll be a short window."

"And if there's not?"

Wiggins shrugged. "We wait for another opportunity. But the coalition can't wait forever. Al Kanadi's too valuable a target."

Erik followed al Kanadi's movement on the screen. This should make him feel better, to know that the man who'd orchestrated so much pain would soon be reduced to a smoking crater in the ground.

"They're nearing the compound," a man called from the front of the room.

"Here we go." Wiggins rubbed his hands together.

Sweat beaded on Erik's forehead and he wiped it off while his gaze shifted between the two screens. He'd worked toward this moment for two years since al Kanadi first rose to prominence. This was war. The target had tortured Erik and forced his daughter to become a biological suicide bomb. Left unchecked, al Kanadi would continue to plan attacks, horrific ones. If anybody deserved to die, it was al Kanadi.

The images on the two screens began to converge until they both showed different angles of the same picture, three forms stood in front of the compound. The larger of the three figures on screen seemed to place its arms around the two smaller ones, and the heat spots merged into one.

"Come on," Wiggins said and leaned forward in his chair.

"What's he doing?" Erik asked.

"Who cares?" Wiggins said.

Erik stared at the screen, felt the anticipation build in his chest. It had been years, a lifetime, since he'd seen a target struck in real-time. Now he'd watch his greatest accomplishment play out in real time, the death of Abu Noor al Kanadi.

"Talking to his kids about something," Stephanie said. "But we don't know why he sends them ahead. They're fast, once they go."

"Probably getting them all worked up about how one day they can aspire to be martyrs," Wiggins said, then snorted and shook his head.

"He likes to watch them run," Erik said under his breath and leaned on the desktop. This was an important thing to do, he believed that. Yet he felt the lure, the pull of operations, the surge of adrenaline. He wanted to look, to watch revenge exacted, justice delivered. And yet when would it all end? He twirled the black bracelet on his wrist that he'd worn out of habit, rotated it until the white letters came up on top. Arielle Rose Peterson.

He stood. "Good luck," he said. "I hope it turns out." He ignored Wiggins's frown and hopped down from the desks, then headed for the exit.

"Where are you going?" Wiggins called. "Don't you want to see this?"

He paused, then looked back over his shoulder. "Not anymore," he said and then walked out.

* * *

Erik walked out the main entrance of the High-Risk Traveler headquarters and into the sunshine. He closed his eyes and soaked in the warmth of the rays, waited for the bitter pang in his stomach that would tell him he'd made a mistake. For the moment, all he felt was lightness. He put on his sunglasses, descended the concrete stairs and headed for a bench near the trailhead of a bike path.

Inside the operations center, his teammates would be ecstatic. Al Kanadi had been a high-value target for years, and his military background, personal discipline, and mastery of tradecraft had helped him defy the combined weight of western military and intelligence might with near impunity. The fact the Task Force had provided the key to al Kanadi's location – even, or perhaps especially, through unsanctioned methods – meant the organization had arrived on the global stage. Even now, he wanted to go back, to learn how the strike ended.

But he knew where that path led.

He stopped short of the plain bench, leaned on its wooden back. Two riders biked past, a man on a hardtail cross-country bike, a woman on a cruiser, wicker basket on the front. It was the kind of bike Arielle had joked she would ride on campus. He glanced down, realized he'd gripped the bench so hard that his knuckles had gone white. With an effort, he let go and reached up to readjust his sunglasses.

No, he wouldn't be going back in. Not today. As for the future, well, time would tell.

He watched the bikers ride off, then sat down on the bench. The wood had grown warm in the sun, and its hardness comforted him, a solid base from which to draw support. He rested his hands in his lap, stared to the front and tried to empty his mind.

He wondered how he'd missed this little oasis, nestled within old growth forest less than two hundred yards from the three-story glass-walled building. In the past three years, he must have walked past this trailhead almost every day, and yet all his memories of the task force involved sitting in the operations center or poring over data in a planning room. It reminded him how he'd promised to take Arielle hiking on the West Coast Trail, but had never managed to organize himself enough to book the reservations. There'd always been an emergency. The year before she'd graduated high school, they'd made it to Vancouver Island with a plan to hike off the standby list, but had been forced to take the Juan de Fuca trail instead when there'd been no unused reservation spaces. What was the excuse that time? Another high-risk traveler heading to the Middle East or maybe al Kanadi himself. It didn't matter.

He inhaled, drank in the sharp tang of newly mown grass. Had Arielle smelled anything like this when she'd been in Syria? When she'd been infected? His hands clenched into fists.

"You all right?" It was Stephanie, just behind him.

"Sure," he said.

She stopped at the far end of the bench. "May I?"

He gestured to the open space. "Please do."

She sat, crossed her legs, her arm on the back of the bench.

"How did it turn out?" he asked. On the bike trail, a single crow landed and hopped into a patch of direct sunlight. Mouth open, the crow stretched out its wings.

"Do you really want to know?"

Did he? The crow cocked its head, one eye attuned to the pair on the bench, the other on the trail. "I guess it can wait," he said.

They sat in silence and his pulse began to ease back to normal. It always seemed to do that around Stephanie.

"You never told me what happened with Sahraoui," he said after a minute.

"Drugs and Organized Crime are tearing that network apart," Stephanie said, referring to two branches of the RCMP. "It runs deep, though. As for Sahraoui himself, he's under investigation, but I honestly don't think he knew what was going on."

Erik glanced over. "He's that stupid?"

Stephanie smiled. "More like willfully blind."

He returned her smile. "You did good." A bike rode by, and the crow jumped to the side of the path. Erik watched the rider head down the trail and then stared at the crow, who'd begun to forage for food. "You know, I'm thankful to have been part of this team, and a lot of that is because of you."

"There's a place on that team for you," she said. "Whenever you're ready."

"Thanks," he said. He didn't know if he'd ever be ready.

"There's already talk that Wiggins will get promoted, maybe even an assistant deputy minister position –"

"Do you think we're at war?" he asked.

"War?" she asked and drew back. "Who, us?"

"No, the country, the government, our agency." He waved around him. "Are we at war, and if so, are we in it to win it?"

"I guess I never thought about it."

"You never thought about it?" He raised his eyebrows. "You help stop people who want to attack our country and never considered whether we're at war?"

Her face reddened. "You mean the Global War on Terror –"

"The G-WOT," he said and emphasized the two syllables. "It's called the G-WOT."

"Right, the G-WOT." Tiny dimples appeared in her cheeks. "I thought that was more like a metaphor, like the War on Drugs, or Graffiti."

"The War on Graffiti? Who's at war with graffiti?"

"Toronto, of course." Her dimples became a full-fledged smile.

"Really?"

"Does that surprise you?"

"I'm surprised Toronto's interesting enough to have graffiti, never mind a war on it."

"Smartass," she said, "But that's my point. How can you be at war on graffiti? Same thing with terror. It's not a country or an army, so how can we be at war on it?"

"With it."

"Pardon?"

"Technically you go to war with something, not on something."

She shook her head, but her smile stayed. "Maybe I should go back inside."

"Please don't." He met her gaze, his face serious. "It's nice having you here." He blinked, then looked away. "Sorry if I offended."

"You didn't," she said. "I just didn't expect you to be joking around."

"I don't know what else to do." God knew it was true. His body didn't seem to know if it should laugh or cry these days.

"What do you think?" she said.

"About what?"

"About war," she said and slapped his knee. "That's it, I'm going inside." She tensed as if to rise.

"No, wait." He took her hand, pulled her back. As she sat, he went back to staring at the path, met the gaze of the crow. "I've been telling myself I was at war for the past fifteen years. It's how I rationalized my sacrifices," he said. "I guess I assumed everyone else was at war too."

"Why is it so important to you?"

He shook his head. "You know how it is, make the world a better place, be part of the struggle of our time." He snorted, then looked at her. "It never occurred to me that war might be the easy button."

"The threats are still out there," she said. "None of that's changed."

"I've changed," he said. "I've changed."

She reached out with her hand, and he took it, felt the warmness of her touch.

"All those years, I told myself I was fighting for our way of life," he said. "I never stopped to wonder what winning looked like." He hung his head. "If we lose the things most important to us, winning looks a whole lot like losing."

"Very deep," she said.

"Yeah, well, I'm a little slow on the uptake, but dangerous when I get going."

"What will you do?"

"Get to know my daughter, for one," he said. "After that? Who knows. Maybe go live in the woods, practice martial arts and seek enlightenment."

"I'd miss you."

He smiled and stared at her, the careful set to her face, the way her lip trembled as if having put her emotions out for him to see, what she expected most was for those feelings to come hurling back at her. Instead, he squeezed her hand. "I'd miss you, too."

Silence descended upon them, and he looked away, her hand cupped in his own. After several minutes, she stirred. "I should get back," she said. "Will you be all right?"

"Sure," he said and released her. "I'm going to enjoy the fresh air for a while."

She stood and smoothed her dress along the front of her legs. When she looked up, he met her gaze and her face reddened. "I'll talk to you later." She smiled and headed back toward the building.

Jordan's voice spoke to him. *Don't let her go.* He sprang to his feet. "Stephanie."

She turned, a question on her face.

His mouth wouldn't work. "Would you want to hang out sometime?" he asked, the words awkward. God, it had been so long. What would Jordan have told him to say? "Maybe play Warcraft or something?" *Nice going,* he thought and cringed.

She smiled, walked back to him. "Did you just invite me out to play video games?"

"I didn't mean that." He didn't seem able to string two words together. "It just popped into my head. It's been…it's been a while."

She continued to stare at him, then leaned into him and kissed his cheek. "I'd like that," she said and then her smile grew wider. "But don't get jealous when you see my avatar."

"What?"

"I may have played once or twice," she said, then walked away. "I'll call you later."

"I'll be damned," he said, engrossed in the swish of her skirt as she climbed the stairs to the building's entrance. When she was out of sight, he sat back down and once more stared up the path. The crow was still there, fixated on him, its head cocked to one side.

He reached for the ring hanging from his neck and with a sharp tug, broke the leather cord and unthreaded it until the ring lay in his palm. He put the cord in his pocket, then held Audray's wedding band pinched between his thumb and forefinger. The simple ring sparkled in the sun as tiny beams of light refracted here and there, and he twisted it, studied it from all angles. He'd sacrificed so much, and almost gotten it all wrong.

He glanced at the stairs, where Stephanie had gone, and smiled. He still had time though, and like he'd said, he might be slow, but he was dangerous once he got going.

He held the ring to his lips and kissed it, then slipped it into his pocket. Maybe Arielle would like to have it, and if not…well he'd cross that bridge when he got there. Either way, he wouldn't need it anymore.

He stood and stretched, then headed down the path. The crow stood its ground until he was nearly on top of it, then it flew off with an angry caw. He watched it go, then carried on.

For the first time Erik Petersson could remember, he was done with war.

Now, he was ready to live.

ACKNOWLEDGEMENTS

If I've taken one thing from writing *Jihadi Bride*, it's that I have a lot to learn. And since that's no small task, I'm so very thankful to those who had the patience and willingness to help me along the way, and who in turn helped make this novel a reality.

Ashley Little mentored me in the Humber College Creative Writing program while I wrote this book, and her insight and feedback were always on point and helped me tighten up all aspects of my writing. She also challenged me to better understand my characters, and while I have a long way to go as a writer, I'm much farther ahead having had the opportunity to learn from Ashley.

I had a number of early beta readers who volunteered their time and energy to give feedback, including Margaret Smith, Tiffany Smith-Fraser, Barbara Clarke-Nolan, and of course, Laura Kennedy. I also turned to a much larger second round of beta readers near the novel's conclusion, and their feedback helped me learn to trust my instincts. I'd make special mention of my mom (although she prefers to be called Mum), who continues to be my biggest fan.

I would also like to thank my agent, Linda Langton, and my publisher, Reagan Rothe. This novel wouldn't have happened without either of them, and along the way they've taught me about the business of publishing, an area where I know I can improve.

My family, of course, also deserves recognition. They teach me something about myself almost every day, if I'm perceptive enough to notice. My wife Tabatha gave me the time to write, and pushed me to keep going on my off days, or when it seemed I'd forgotten how to string a sentence together. From her, I've learned how to support someone else's dream, and I hope I can do the same for her. My daughters gave me the inspiration for this story, and from them, I've learned how to stop taking myself so seriously, and how to be passionate about storytelling.

Lastly, I'd like to thank you, Dear Reader. The more I write, the more I learn what an awesome commitment it is to give of one's time to read a book. There are so many other ways to spend your time, and so thank you for choosing to spend that limited resource with me. I hope you enjoyed the experience, and that you'll consider spending more time with me again in the future.

NOTE FROM THE AUTHOR

Word-of-mouth is crucial for any author to succeed. If you enjoyed the book, please leave a review online—anywhere you are able. Even if it's just a sentence or two. It would make all the difference and would be very much appreciated.

Thanks!
Alastair

ABOUT THE AUTHOR

Alastair Luft writes out of Ottawa, Ontario, Canada, where he lives with his wife and two daughters. Alastair's first book, *The Battle Within*, was published in 2017. A graduate of the Royal Military College of Canada, and a 20-year veteran of the Canadian Armed Forces, Alastair is also an accomplished speaker who has presented on how violence begets violence and the importance of discovering one's passion.